The Glassmaker

The
Glassmaker

TRACY CHEVALIER

Viking

VIKING
An imprint of Penguin Random House LLC
penguinrandomhouse.com

Copyright © 2024 by Tracy Chevalier
Penguin Random House supports copyright. Copyright fuels creativity,
encourages diverse voices, promotes free speech, and creates a vibrant
culture. Thank you for buying an authorized edition of this book and for
complying with copyright laws by not reproducing, scanning, or
distributing any part of it in any form without permission. You
are supporting writers and allowing Penguin Random House
to continue to publish books for every reader.

LIBRARY OF CONGRESS CATALOGING-IN-PUBLICATION DATA
Names: Chevalier, Tracy, author.
Title: The glassmaker / Tracy Chevalier.
Description: New York : Viking, 2024.
Identifiers: LCCN 2023034985 (print) | LCCN 2023034986 (ebook) |
ISBN 9780525558279 (hardcover) | ISBN 9780525558286 (ebook)
Subjects: LCSH: Women—Fiction. | LCGFT: Novels.
Classification: LCC PS3553.H4367 B43 2024 (print) |
LCC PS3553.H4367 (ebook) | DDC 813/.54—dc23/eng/20230825
LC record available at https://lccn.loc.gov/2023034985
LC ebook record available at https://lccn.loc.gov/2023034986

Printed in the United States of America
1st Printing

Designed by Amanda Little

For Ronna

A BRIEF EXPLANATION OF TIME

alla Veneziana

THE CITY OF WATER RUNS by its own clock. Venice and its neighboring islands have always felt frozen in time—and perhaps they are. It is a city built on wooden piles over a lagoon, veined with canals, and its aesthetic and much of its exquisite architecture have remained unchanged for hundreds of years. The boats may have engines now, but time still seems to run at a different speed from the outside world.

One of Venice's glittering treasures has for centuries been the glass on its attendant island, Murano. Glass is a peculiar substance, the sand it's manufactured from magically turning translucent or even transparent when melted. There is some debate about whether glass is a solid or a liquid. Science teachers have mistakenly taught that, long after it cools, glass continues to flow—albeit at its own glacial pace—citing the example that very old window panes are sometimes thicker at the bottom than at the top. The truth is that the glass is not flowing down, imperceptibly slowly, to pool at the bottom of the pane; the thickness is a result of the way glass panes were once made. But perhaps the myth is perpetuated because we want to believe that glass, like the island where it is produced, abides by its own natural laws. Like Venice and Murano, it has its own pace.

People who make things also have an ambiguous relationship with time. Painters, writers, wood-carvers, knitters, weavers and, yes, glassmakers: creators often enter an absorbed state that psychologists call flow, in which hours pass without their noticing.

Readers, too.

It's surprisingly hard to gauge the rate at which time passes—whether it moves faster for others than it does for you. How would you know if all the clocks in one place moved at a different speed from elsewhere? Or if the artisans of the City of Water and the Island of Glass seem to be aging more slowly than the world beyond?

Part I

GOBLETS,
BEADS
and
DOLPHINS

1

IF YOU SKIM A FLAT STONE skillfully across water, it will touch down many times, in long or short intervals as it lands.

With that image in mind, now replace *water* with *time*.

Start at the northern edge of Venice, stone in hand, facing the glass island of Murano, half an hour by gondola across the lagoon. Don't throw the stone yet. It is 1486, the height of the Renaissance, and Venice is reveling in its position as the trade center of Europe and much of the rest of the world. It seems the City of Water will always be rich and powerful.

Orsola Rosso is nine years old. She lives on Murano, but has not yet worked with glass . . .

✧

THE CANAL WASN'T as deep as Orsola thought. When she fell in, the water's coldness jolted her and she flailed about, sinking until her foot touched the muddy bottom. At that moment what had seemed so deep and powerful suddenly lost its mystery. She heard her mother cry out, but her brother Marco was laughing as Orsola came up spluttering, the water only to her shoulders.

"You pushed me!" she cried. "*Cretino!*"

"Orsola, *basta!*" Laura Rosso scolded. "People are listening."

They were. Muranese residents were standing in the doorways of the glass workshops that lined the fondamenta, laughing at the Rosso girl in the canal.

"I didn't push you," Marco retorted. "You're so clumsy, you went and fell in, *bauca!* What a stupid sister I have!"

Orsola and her mother and brothers had been returning from a visit to her aunt and grandmother on the other side of the island. Her nonna was poorly and insisted on seeing them, convinced she was dying, though she was well enough to get up and hand Orsola a little sack of pine nuts she had recently bought at the market, because she didn't want them to go to waste if she did die. Zia Giovanna rolled her eyes at the thought, but Orsola carefully took the sack from her grandmother and promised to give it to Maddalena, their servant. The Rossos had been walking back beside the Rio dei Vetrai—the Canal of the Glassmakers, which cut through the part of Murano where many of the glass workshops were located—when Marco bumped her hard and she went reeling into the water. She did have the presence of mind to throw the sack of nuts behind her as she fell. That was what the family pointed out whenever they later retold the story: that young Orsola had had the sense not to waste precious pine nuts.

Giacomo, always the kinder brother, and never as interesting as a result, picked his way down nearby steps covered in algae. Kneeling in the muck, he reached over and pulled Orsola up the slimy stairs. She fell onto the fondamenta, gasping and spitting out water, then lay there for a moment, mortified. Only drunkards fell into canals, or people out at night who had lost their bearings in the dark.

Laura Rosso helped her daughter to her feet and began to dry her with her shawl. "Cold you are, and dirty," she muttered. Glancing around to check that people had lost interest, she nodded at a door close by. "You should go into the Baroviers' and warm up by their furnace."

"She can't do that," Giacomo interjected. "They'll never let her in."

"They won't let a girl catch her death, even a rival's daughter." Laura glanced through the door's iron filigree window, her face a set of calculations, then pulled it open and beckoned to her daughter. "Quiet, now. Keep your eyes open, and report back what you see."

Orsola hesitated, but her mother was not someone you argued with. And she was cold and wet, and the nearby furnace was tempting; she could hear its muffled roar. She scuttled in, her mother pulling the door to and shutting her off from her family. Looking back through the small window, she noted Marco's smirk, Giacomo's worried face, Laura's shooing gesture.

Orsola headed down a passage that opened out into a yard, empty of people but cluttered with crates and barrows full of broken glass and stacked wood and long glass canes in many colors leaning against the wall. The ground glittered with fragments of glass, like multicolored frost. There seemed to be little order to the yard. Surrounding it were small buildings: a storeroom for more glass and the ash and sand and lime to make it; a room with its door ajar, where she observed shelves stacked with plates and bowls and platters, vases lined up of different shapes and sizes and colors, rows and rows of glasses, chandeliers like octopuses tangled together—all waiting to be packed and eventually shipped to Amsterdam or Lisbon or London or Hamburg or Constantinople, cities Orsola sometimes heard her father speak of. To one side was a small shop where visitors could buy a variety of finished products.

The Barovier arrangement was similar to the workshop of Orsola's own family, though the Rossos' was smaller and Lorenzo Rosso was meticulous about order and cleanliness. His apprentices complained of spending their first months laying out tools and wheeling barrows back and forth, and never handling hot glass. Each workshop had a different style, dictated by the maestro's character. It seemed Maestro Giovanni Barovier was the messy sort.

Despite this, the Baroviers were the stars of the glass world. From disorder, Giovanni's father, Angelo Barovier, had conjured up countless inventions, including cristallo veneziano—clear glass that transformed the work on Murano once other maestros were allowed to copy it—and calcedonio, a glass that looked like chalcedony stone. The Baroviers had also pioneered the practice of drawing glass into long canes, which all glassmakers now used in making the decorative elements of goblets and chandeliers and plates. Angelo had died years ago but Giovanni was carrying forward the traditions in carefully guarded methods. All glass families had their own secret recipes they held close. They would not want intruders coming in to see what they were up to.

Orsola hesitated by the door leading to the workshop. She could hear the furnace, and men calling out to one another as they worked. Why was she here? Surely she would be discovered and tossed out like a broken bowl. But her mother had been firm, and so she opened the door a crack and slid in, her stomach tight.

The workshop was full of men, pulling punties—long iron rods— in and out of the furnace with molten globes of glass on the ends, twirling them, rolling them on a marver—a flat iron sheet—squeezing them into molds of various shapes, placing finished pieces in the annealer to cool down slowly. Boys fed the fire and swept and carried buckets of water back and forth. All were moving around the maestro seated at his workbench. Orsola recognized this particular buzzing energy, though the Baroviers' workshop was bigger and louder than Lorenzo Rosso's, with more whistling and shouting. She knew to keep out of the way, and crept closer to the fire. Her movement caught the eye of one of the garzonetti—young boys who helped out around fur-naces with an expectation of becoming a garzone—an apprentice training to work in glass. He was sweeping the floor, and froze when he saw her. Orsola held a finger to her lips. Don't shout, she silently pleaded. Don't give me away.

Then she spied someone standing among all the moving men who made her forget the garzonetto: a woman, slightly to one side, hands on hips. Everything about her was square: her broad shoulders, her forehead, even the pinned bun of her gray hair. In contrast to the ac-tivity around her, she remained very still.

This was Maria Barovier, daughter of Angelo, sister of Maestro Giovanni. Orsola knew of this woman, had seen her from a distance, stumping along the riva or across Campo Santo Stefano or sitting at Mass, her eyes closed as if she were asleep, her jaw set sharp like a spade. Maria Barovier, a rare woman glassmaker, who let fools feel her keen tongue. She was known as Marietta, but Orsola thought the diminutive did not suit such a formidable woman.

She was frowning at a thick glass cane held out to her by one of the garzoni—a narrow-faced youth a year or two older than Orsola's brother Marco. "No. The red should be more prominent, for the bal-ance, otherwise the bead will be swamped by the white and blue. Do you never listen?" Her voice was deep and annoyed. "Where's the mold? I'll have to show you again, and I'm bored of doing that."

The lad wore the fearful expression of most new garzoni when they weren't sure of their position. As he looked away from his em-ployer, his eyes fell on Orsola. They were very dark, almost black, and Orsola felt pinned to the spot.

Maria Barovier followed his gaze. Her frown did not change, not even when she noted the canal slime down the front of Orsola's dress. "Out, Rosso," she barked. "*Spia.*"

Orsola fled, scrabbling at the door in her haste to get away.

Absorbed in their glass, the men didn't even turn; this was a drama for women and apprentices. She crunched quickly across the crystals in the yard to the outer door and stepped back out onto the Fondamenta dei Vetrai. Though she'd only been away for a few minutes, it felt like hours, as if she'd gone into a new world and come back. Her family had disappeared. They would be waiting back at home, her mother expecting a full report, even though Orsola had seen very little. Glass families were not unfriendly, but they didn't share their spaces, their work, their secrets. Occasionally the maestros drank together and played cards, complained about tariffs or Rialto merchants across the lagoon trying to gouge them or the fickle Venetian Council of Ten issuing new directives that limited what they could or could not produce. But they never talked about the glass they made. It was the Muranese way to be supportive of the island and the industry in general, but to criticize others' work behind their backs: techniques not refined enough, work derivative or dull. Their own was always better.

Orsola had been by the warmth of the Barovier furnace barely a minute and was still wet and cold. She ran along the fondamenta and over the Ponte di Mezzo toward home. Bruno, a burly young boatman familiar to every Muranese, was rowing along the canal and about to duck under the bridge. He pointed with his oar at the slime streaked down the front of her dress. "Mucky pup!" he called. "Your brother told me you jumped in the canal. Practicing to be a mermaid, are you, or a dolphin?"

"I didn't jump! He pushed me."

Bruno chuckled. "Which Rosso should I believe?"

She scowled and ran on, ignoring other remarks made by neighbors about how dirty and clumsy she was. Reaching the Rosso compound, she pushed at the iron door that opened onto the glass yard, with storerooms on one side and on the other a courtyard leading to the family house. At the back of the yard was the workshop, with its furnace burning all day and night. It was never allowed to go out except during August, when it was too hot to work and the glassmakers took a summer break. A passage down the side of the workshop led out to a small dock on the lagoon from where boats could take glass pieces going to merchants in Venice, or drop off the sand needed to make glass or wood for the furnace—constant loads of wood from barges that came from terraferma, the mainland, where there were many more trees than on the islands.

Orsola wanted to go to the workshop furnace to dry herself in its bright, intense heat, but her mother would expect her to show her face immediately. She turned instead to pass through the courtyard to the kitchen, which had a different kind of warmth—a smaller fire for cooking that didn't have to be as hot for boiling water as for melting glass. Sometimes when she needed very hot or very low heat, Maddalena would slip dishes into the various parts of the workshop furnace, though Lorenzo Rosso always looked uncomfortable when she trespassed in his workspace.

In the kitchen Marco was sitting at the long table where the family took its meals when it wasn't warm enough to eat outside in the courtyard. He was steadily making his way through his grandmother's pine nuts while Laura Rosso chopped onions and Maddalena fried sardines for sarde in saor, the sweet and sour dish they often ate.

"Your dress!" Maddalena cried. "What have you been doing? Take it off this instant!"

Laura glanced up from her onions. "You didn't last long. What did you see?"

Her eagerness, coupled with Marco's nonchalance—he was now tossing pine nuts in the air and catching them in his mouth—made

Orsola wonder if it had been planned, her brother deliberately bumping her so that she fell into the canal next to the Barovier workshop and had to go inside.

"It was busy there, lots of men," she began.

"What were they making?"

"I don't know." She had been absorbed by watching Maria Barovier rather than the maestro. "Goblets, I think." Most glassmakers made wineglasses, so it was a safe guess.

"You didn't even notice what they were making!" Marco jeered. "*Bauca!* You should have let me go instead."

So she *had* been sent. A small part of her was pleased she had been chosen instead of her brother.

Maddalena snatched the sack from him. "Stop eating so many or there won't be enough for the saor!"

"Maria Barovier was there," Orsola continued.

"Marietta?" Laura Rosso set down her knife to concentrate on her daughter's words. "What was she doing?"

"She was talking to a garzone. Scolding him about cane."

"Cane, eh? Did you see it?"

Orsola nodded.

"How thick?"

"Like Papà's thumb."

"What color was it?"

"Red, white and blue."

"Strange colors to put together."

"She said the red was important. For the balance." Orsola stopped. "*Rosso*," she repeated. Her family's name. It suddenly occurred to her that Maria Barovier had known she was a Rosso—knew who she was. But she didn't tell her mother that the glassmaker had called her a spy. "It was for a bead. She mentioned a mold."

"Beads! Red, white and blue beads. And not just pulled cane, but molded too." Her mother looked thoughtful. "*Per favore*, put that dirty dress and shift in the pile and find something dry to wear. Not a word to anyone about this bead. I must tell your father."

Orsola stripped off her damp clothes and dropped them in the dreaded pile of laundry, which never seemed to lessen. The men and boys in the workshop sweated so much from the heat of the furnace that they changed their clothes daily, and she and her mother were constantly heating water and stirring laundry in a vat full of stinging lye or hanging out shirts and breeches and underclothes to dry by the fire, or laying out wet sheets in the bleaching fields behind the convent at Santa Maria degli Angeli. Laura Rosso hated doing laundry, and Orsola sensed that when she was old enough to handle it on her own, her mother would turn the task over completely to her daughter to hate.

That night Orsola perched in a corner of the kitchen with Giacomo, rolling back and forth between them a marble their father's assistant Paolo had made for them. Marco was poking at the fire. Lorenzo was drinking wine while Laura patched one of his shirtsleeves, which had been burned by a piece of hot glass.

"Marietta Barovier is making something new," Laura said to her husband. "I heard rumors from some of the maestros' wives. Now I know. She's making beads."

"Beads, eh?" Lorenzo Rosso remarked. "That's nothing to be concerned about."

"It sounds like special beads. Fancy beads that may sell well."

"But we don't make beads, so there's no competition there."

"Perhaps we should."

"Should what?"

"Make beads." Laura sounded irritated, as if she wanted to tell her husband to *keep up*.

He shook his head. "We do well enough with glasses and pitchers and bowls. We would have to pull cane if we wanted to profit. My men don't know how." To make cane—whether the kind for producing beads or that for other glasswork—men had to pull a piece of heated glass between them, thinner and thinner, into a cylinder. It required a long alley, as well as skills that others had already perfected. The Rossos bought cane from other glassmakers rather than pulling their own. Lorenzo also limited what the workshop made to glasses and pitchers and bowls, reasoning that it was better to make a few things well—things that people would always need, rather than elaborate chandeliers and candlesticks. It was a conservative workshop, with a steady business that would always have orders and never grow rich.

"Will you make the calculations?" his wife persisted. "Divide the cost of buying a length of cane by the number of beads you can make from it to sell? Work out the profit?"

Lorenzo Rosso gave her a brief look that Orsola knew meant: No more questions.

✧

A MONTH LATER the Baroviers introduced to the world the rosetta, a barrel-shaped bead the size of the first joint of a man's thumb. It was made of layers of red, white and blue cane that had been placed in star-shaped molds rolled to form a long cylinder. The cane was then cut up into individual beads, which were beveled so that twelve points of white stars emerged through the blue. It looked like a scalloped shell, unique and ingenious. The first time she held one, Laura Rosso declared that they were exceptionally ugly and who would want to wear them? But Orsola loved them—they were so surprising, like nothing anyone on Murano had made before. Slowly rosette began to be sold—not many at first, as they were oddities and needed time to catch on and become the pride of African chiefs. The Doge of Venice even granted Maria Barovier permission to set up her own small furnace and produce the special bead she had created. A woman tending her own furnace: this was something new. It was unlikely to happen again unless the world changed substantially.

Orsola sometimes passed Maria on the Fondamenta dei Vetrai or in the market in Campo Santo Stefano, where she was haggling over sardines as if every soldo were a ducato, even though the Baroviers were wealthy enough not to need to care about the price of fish. Or occasionally Orsola would see her strolling alone around the edge of Campo San Bernardo during the evening passeggiata, when Muranese came out to socialize. Maria Barovier never acknowledged the girl, but sometimes she glanced at her sideways. You are Orsola Rosso and I know you are there, the look seemed to suggest.

✧

ORSOLA'S LIFE REVOLVED around the endless pile of laundry, as well as gardening and cleaning, but when she could she found ways to go into the workshop, delivering messages or bringing the workers biscotti Maddalena had made. Then she would linger to watch them make vases or glasses or, once, ornate goblets for one of the palazzos Venetians owned on Murano's Grand Canal. Murano was only half an hour by boat from Venice, but wealthy Venetians used the island as a break from the crowded sophistication they normally lived in. They did not mix much with the glassmakers and fishermen; they didn't drink in the tavernas, they held their own parties, they brought their own servants, they used their own gondoliers. But they liked to see what the glassmen were making. Most Muranese glasswork was sent abroad, but a few pieces were always kept back to sell to Venetians and other visitors.

When they came to look in the small Rosso shop, Orsola watched her mother pull off her apron, run her fingers through her hair, smooth her perfect arched eyebrows and hurry to show them what

Maestro Lorenzo Rosso had recently made. Often the wealthy Venetians simply looked and left with nothing. But sometimes they bought pieces by the maestro, or they surprised everyone and bought a pitcher or goblet Paolo had made. Bald, with a barrel chest and strong arms, silent Paolo was Lorenzo's servente—his main assistant, just below maestro—and handled glass skillfully. Whenever one of his pieces sold in the shop, Laura Rosso liked to tell him, and he would go red and turn back to the furnace with a small smile while the others teased him. He was a gentle teacher, never shouting or scolding, but simply adjusting a hand to reshape a piece, or handing over a different tool, or nodding at the furnace for the glass to be reheated.

The Rosso workshop employed garzonetti to keep the furnace fed and the floors swept, to put away tools and fetch water to quench the workers' constant thirst. If they stayed on for five years they became garzoni, serving a six-year apprenticeship to learn from Lorenzo and Paolo. Orsola loved watching the garzoni swirl around her father in a kind of dance, kneeling to blow through the punty to inflate the molten glass while he turned it, taking the rod from him to reheat in the furnace, handing him wooden and metal tools—paddles or pincers or tongs or scissors—when he needed them, laying out gold leaf, bringing smaller pieces of glass heated to the right temperature to add to what he was working on, breaking the piece from the punty and carrying it between pads to the annealer to cool. The maestro was in the center of a dance, the conductor orchestrating everything going on around him. There was a smooth rhythm to it; there had to be, or the piece would not turn out right. He seldom spoke other than the odd short command. In some workshops the men sang and told jokes or stories about women or boats, but Lorenzo Rosso preferred to work in silence. His workers went along with it; if they didn't like it, they moved on to noisier workshops.

Marco and Giacomo had started out as garzonetti, for their father refused to treat his sons differently; they had to put in their time running and fetching before they could move up to garzoni, learning the trade from the bottom. Giacomo was steady like his father, doing what he was told and studying each process intently. He shadowed Paolo and was always the one to dart in and sweep up shattered glass or find the missing paddle or carefully pick up with tweezers gold leaf swept from a worktop by his brother's careless sleeve. Even when his work was done Giacomo would stay on, turning out endless goti— everyday glasses apprentices made to practice their technique.

Marco was different—lazier, and more sure of himself. He was skilled, more so than Giacomo, possibly even more than his father, if he would settle down and practice. But he never made goti. He would get excited about a new technique or color or design, and work nonstop on it, pushing aside everything else he was meant to do. If he couldn't master the technique, though, or found the design too complicated to carry out, he grew frustrated, breaking pieces unnecessarily and storming out. "Whoever becomes his wife will have her hands full," Laura Rosso commented after one of his tantrums, but she and her husband didn't chide him as they did Orsola when she got angry. Paolo also said nothing; he knew Marco would be his boss one day. Giacomo tried to stand up to him, with the bruises to show for it, for he was not hard like his brother.

Marco did make one exceptionally beautiful piece: an ornate goblet of clear filigree, with handles shaped like the winged lions that decorated every flag in Venice, and a bowl so shallow it was almost a plate. He spent weeks drawing it and practicing all the different parts before making a final version. He was immensely proud of the result and decided not to sell it to a Venetian as he'd first intended. Instead of displaying it in the shop, he built a little shelf for it in the workshop. One day when no one was around, Orsola tried to fill it with water, but the shallow bowl held scarcely any liquid, and the moment she moved it what little water there was spilled down her dress.

✧

BY THE TIME Orsola was seventeen she looked much like her mother, with matching dark hair and eyes, arched eyebrows and an air of impatience, as if waiting for something to happen.

Something did happen.

One day she was bringing a pot of stewed eels to keep warm in the bottom of the annealer and paused in the doorway of the workshop to watch the men at work. Her father was at the bench, where the maestro always sat, his servente and garzoni moving around him with their punties and their tongs. They were working on a long filigreed tube, possibly the arm of a pitcher. Paolo pulled the punty it was attached to out of the furnace and brought it to Lorenzo Rosso, who used tongs to gently pull at the curve of the hot orange tube, then measured it with a compass and nodded. *"Perfetto"* was his last word. A garzone approached with a forked rod to hook around the curved tube. Orsola's father gently tapped the glass to break it off the punty, and the garzone lifted it to carry it off to the annealer to cool overnight. But he had hooked the rod carelessly, and swung it a little too casually, and the curved glass arm fell from the hook onto the bench and shattered, sending shards of glass all over the workshop, one even landing at Orsola's feet. The one with Lorenzo Rosso as its target flew like a hot dart straight into his neck.

The apprentice froze with the forked rod held aloft like a weapon. Lorenzo reached up to his neck, felt the glass, grasped it and pulled it out. It was like a cork unstopped: a bright gush of red sprayed across the floor. He stared at the shard of glass in his hand, puzzled. As the blood poured down his neck, his face went gray, and he toppled from the bench.

Orsola dropped the pot of eels at the same moment as the garzone dropped his rod, and the clatter seemed to unfreeze her brothers. Marco and Giacomo scrambled to their father's side. The apprentice ran. "Go and fetch the doctor!" Marco called after him. "Get our mother!" he shouted at Orsola. "Get linen!"

She was glad to have something concrete to do. Running to the kitchen, she grabbed her mother's arm and pulled at her, hardly able to speak. "Padre. Accident. Linen."

Laura Rosso studied her daughter's face as if reading the words there. Then she gathered herself. "Maddalena, fetch the stack of sheets from the cupboard," she commanded as she hurried to the workshop, Orsola following.

Maddalena began to scream when she arrived with the sheets and saw the mess of eels and the broken pot meeting the red pool that had spread across the floor; the eels seemed to be swimming in the blood. Laura was kneeling in the pool next to her husband, using her skirt to try to stem the flow. Orsola stared at her mother's exposed ankles, slippery with blood.

"*Basta*, Maddalena!" Laura cried. "Throw me a sheet."

Maddalena stood frozen in the doorway, and Orsola had to snatch the tower of sheets from her and hand one to her mother to press against Lorenzo Rosso's neck. The sheet immediately turned red; the deep color in contrast to the stark white was almost obscene. "Another," Laura called. Orsola handed her another sheet that she had spent much time washing and bleaching in the sun. Now all her work was being ruined in a flash. She felt guilty thinking so.

Giacomo was kneeling at his father's other side, squeezing his hand. Paolo stood with his arms around the garzonetti, one wide-eyed, the other with his face buried in the assistant's side. Meanwhile

Marco raged around the studio. "Where's that little *canagia* of a garzone?" he cried. "I'm going to slice him open and show his guts to his mother! Where's the doctor? I bet he didn't even go for him."

In fact, the apprentice didn't go for the doctor, but stole a boat and took it to terraferma. He was not seen again. If anyone ever mentioned his name, the Rossos spat on the ground and cursed him.

"Madre, should we—should we go for the priest?" Giacomo whispered.

Without a word Paolo stepped away from the garzonetti and disappeared to find one. Even if he ran to the closest church—San Pietro Martire, where the Rio dei Vetrai met Murano's Grand Canal—and the priest ran back with him, it would take several minutes. Orsola looked at the size of the puddle of blood, and at her father's face. His eyes were closed, his skin white as a mushroom. She knew it was too late to give him the last rites.

Laura Rosso had made the same calculation. She felt for her husband's pulse, then sat back on her heels, dropping the bloody sheet from Lorenzo Rosso's neck. *"Che Dio abia pietà della so anema, e de la nostra,"* she said, and crossed herself.

✧

MARIA BAROVIER CAME to Lorenzo Rosso's funeral, as did all the Murano glassmakers and even the Venetian merchant Gottfried Klingenberg, with whom he had done most of his business. Orsola's father had been a popular man, not for a big personality—he was quiet and focused on family and business—but because he was honest and fair and his work was simple and solid. He had not specialized in chandeliers or other ornate pieces, so he didn't step too far into others' territories. His workshop was clean, and the men who worked with him were well behaved, apart from Marco—but you couldn't choose your sons. His sudden death shocked glassmakers who'd never given Lorenzo Rosso much thought. And so they came, packing the Basilica of Santi Maria e Donato for the funeral Mass, accompanying his body to the Rossos' boat, a flat-bottomed sandolo that would take him the short distance along the canal to the cemetery at the northeastern edge of Murano, with Marco and Giacomo rowing and the rest of the family following alongside on the fondamenta. Maria Barovier was among the hundreds, and this time she did look at Orsola, a long, cool gaze, dispassionate but not unfriendly.

Several weeks later Orsola was crossing Campo San Donato, leaving the basilica after saying prayers for her father, when she passed Maria sitting on a bench. "Help me up, Orsola Rosso," she commanded. "With the gout it's not so easy."

Orsola took her elbow and helped her to her feet. It was the first and last time she ever saw weakness in the older woman.

"Been praying for your father?" Maria indicated Santi Maria e Donato, with its beautiful brickwork and its double rows of colonnaded arches. Inside were stunning centuries-old mosaic floors that Orsola liked to study during Mass. It was not the church nearest to the Rosso home, but it was the finest on the island.

She nodded, fighting tears. She did not want to cry in front of this woman.

Another woman would have crossed herself, but Maria did not. "No one deserved what happened to him." She looked her up and down. "You've grown, Orsola Rosso. Almost a woman. You need a new dress."

This was true. Orsola's bust had swelled and her dresses were tight there and around the arms. She hadn't said anything to her mother; Laura Rosso had been suddenly thrust into the business of running a glass workshop and was either staring at ledgers or measuring the woodpile or counting canes or goblets, working out with Marco how it was all done. Orsola knew a new dress was not a priority.

"I suggest brown with a drop of red in it," Maria Barovier continued. "The red would work well with your coloring and hair. Needs to stand up to it."

Orsola flushed to think the glassmaker had noticed the color of her olive skin, her dark mouth and hair. She nodded low to Maria, almost a bow, and hurried away.

A week later a boy brought to the door a package of folded fabric—fine linen, brown but with something in it of red. No note. "Quality." Laura Rosso smoothed the fabric. "Maybe someone is paying one of their bills this way. But we need money, not linen. Once they confess, I'll make them pay."

Orsola cleared her throat. "It's for me."

"Who's it from?" her mother demanded, suspicious in the way any mother of an unmarried daughter receiving gifts would be.

Orsola hesitated. It would be easier to say the cloth was from a man. That would surprise no one. Her mother would laugh and have the dress made and bar the man from their door. But—

"It's from Maria Barovier. A gift."

Laura snorted. "Why? What has Marietta got to do with you, or you with her?"

"Nothing. She told me I needed a dress, that's all."

She expected her mother to take the fabric and throw it back in Maria's face. But Laura fingered the fine cloth, looked her daughter up and down and said, "I'll make it tomorrow. You'll wear it when you go to see her and ask for her help."

Orsola's mouth went dry, as if she had eaten a slice of lemon. "What do you mean? What help?"

Laura gave her a long look. "*Andiamo*," she said, and led the way across the courtyard to the workshop. "Look." She pushed open the door.

Orsola had avoided the workshop since her father's death. It wasn't that she feared seeing the bloodstain on the floor—she and her mother and Maddalena had scrubbed it as clean as they could, Maddalena weeping the whole time, Laura and Orsola with their mouths set. The garzonetti had then rearranged the space so that a pile of wood now covered it—a pile that would never run out and expose the faint outline of their maestro's blood. But Lorenzo Rosso had been the principal in the dance he and his workers had participated in every day, and Orsola couldn't bear to see the gap he left, or the faltering movements of the other men trying to navigate around that gap. Marco had stepped in, but he had only just taken his prova—the exam that made him a servente. He was nowhere near experienced enough to lead the workshop as maestro. And yet he must. When a maestro died, the business went to his eldest son. Sometimes Orsola glimpsed Marco looking completely overwhelmed, a man drowning in responsibility. Then she felt for him, and wanted to say something comforting, but knew that acknowledging his weakness would only make him angry.

Now she gazed over the workshop floor. Marco and Paolo were not there. Two garzoni and a garzonetto were playing spigoli, slapping down the cards, and another garzonetto was asleep—things they would never have done in front of Lorenzo Rosso. Only Giacomo seemed to be working, sorting pieces of glass into piles—a task usually done by garzonetti. He glanced up at them, apologetic and defensive. Normally he would be making new glass, mixing together sand and ash and lime, using the Rosso formulas taught to him by his father to create the needed colors. But it seemed the workshop didn't need new glass, for it was producing nothing.

"You see?" Laura Rosso said. "We're in trouble, and I need Marietta Barovier to tell us what to do." She picked up a chunk of clear glass that should not have been left on the floor and tossed it into a barrow of remnants.

Orsola leaned in the doorway, studying her mother. Since her father had died, her mother had physically changed. It wasn't that she had aged—though she had a bit, with gray hair more prominent and a marked gauntness from not eating, for food no longer interested her. The transformation was more than those things. Laura had always been a model maestro's wife. She did not parade along the canals during the evening's passeggiata to show off her maestro wife's fur as did some of the wives; nor did she have servants do all the work. She looked after the household, and had taken an interest in the workshop and discussed the business with her husband, though she never made the decisions. She could read and work with numbers a little, enough to help keep the books. She didn't scold or carp, but was firm with Orsola, with Maddalena, with the assistants, with the butcher and fishermen and vegetable sellers she bought from. She kept a clean house. She did not drink too much wine. Her only weaknesses were biscotti and dried fruit.

In the first days she had remained frozen, not crying at the Mass said for her husband, nor when following his boat to the cemetery, nor at his graveside. Orsola knew that her mother was not emotionless, but her eyes seemed to be focused on the distant mountains on terraferma that were visible when the day was clear.

Their mother privately complained to Orsola and Giacomo that Marco was far from having the cool head needed to run a glass business in a competitive place like Murano, where many workshops fought for the same customers—the English and French and Germans and Dutch and Turks buying through Venetian middlemen. Marco could blow and adorn a goblet, but he didn't know how to lead the men around him to make dozens of them, all exactly alike—or near enough that only a sharp eye could spot the differences. He hadn't had dealings with the sophisticated merchants by the Rialto Bridge, who could strip you clean of your wares without your even noticing as you sat mesmerized by their fine black velvet robes and their beautifully trimmed beards and their way of making you feel clever and funny as they smiled and poured you more wine. Lorenzo Rosso had managed to negotiate decent terms through dogged persistence and a refusal to drink the wine or be seduced by smiles. But Marco loved the wine and the seduction. He would ruin the family business unless someone went along to curb his enthusiasm for the drink and the jokes and the false admiration. Someone was needed in the room who never smiled. Orsola knew her mother could do that.

A few weeks before, Laura Rosso and Marco had taken a traghetto—one of the regular gondolas ferrying passengers between Murano and Venice—over to see Gottfried Klingenberg at the Fondaco dei Tedeschi, where the German merchants lived and worked. On their return Orsola's mother had said little about the meeting except that they'd promised to fill the latest order already placed for goblets and bowls. And they had, with Paolo quietly working to fix as many of Marco's mistakes as he could. But Klingenberg had not ordered more. And so the workshop ground to a halt.

"Ask Marietta Barovier what to do," Laura repeated now.

Orsola nodded.

"There is another thing to contend with," her mother added. "It will soon become obvious to all." She pulled her dress against her belly and Orsola started: it seemed to be the one part of her mother that had grown while the rest of her shrank from grief. She did not pat her stomach as other women might have done when relaying this news. Laura Rosso wasn't obvious like that.

"Then you must eat more, Madre, so you don't lose this one like the others," Orsola said, focusing on the practical to hide her shock. Her mother was old to have another baby, and without a husband to support it.

"Tell Marietta about the baby," Laura said, "though no one else. It may soften her a bit."

Before Orsola went to see Maria Barovier, her mother made the dress with the fabric the glassmaker had given her. Orsola was to wear it for many years, even as fashions changed, and it got compliments for its timeless cut and fine fabric and the color people could not quite place: the everyday of the brown, the nobility of the red.

The second time Orsola went inside the Barovier workshop, now a young woman in a crisp new dress rather than a girl in mucky clothes, the yard was as chaotic as she remembered. If anything, there was even more broken glass scattered on the ground. The Rosso yard might well look like this soon. This time she knocked on the door of the workshop rather than creeping in. The young man who answered was the same one who had been scolded by Maria Barovier over the rosetta cane. He was no longer a half-grown garzone, though he was still slim, but had the strong arms of a servente; his eyes were so black you couldn't see the pupils.

"*Sì?*"

"I want to see Signora Maria. Tell her it's Orsola Rosso."

"She doesn't see anyone." The assistant made to close the door, but she grabbed the jamb to stop him. He looked at her hand.

"Tell her it's Orsola Rosso," she repeated. "If you don't tell her and she finds out afterward you've turned me away, she'll have you making goti for the rest of your days."

The assistant stared, then went to find Maria. Orsola didn't follow him, but remained in the yard. She was tempted to note the different colors of stacked cane, peer through the window of the shop to see what they were selling, poke through the discarded shards of pieces that had broken. But she wasn't here as a spy this time, so she stood still, arms wrapped around herself.

Maria Barovier didn't make her wait: there was no game playing or assertion of hierarchy. She was confident enough of her place that she didn't have to resort to such tricks. She came out immediately from the furnace, the assistant trailing behind until she waved him away without looking. "Stefano, go back and keep an eye on the blue."

He nodded and, with a last glance at Orsola, slipped back inside.

"Here." Maria led her out of the yard and into a courtyard much like the Rossos', with a stone wellhead in the center, carved with urns on four sides. Chickens scratched around it, clucking indignantly as their mistress kicked them out of the way so that she could lean against the wellhead. The courtyard smelled of the basil growing in pots in the sun. For all the Baroviers' success, they were not ostentatious.

Maria Barovier folded her arms. "What do you need?"

Orsola explained as clearly as she could, knowing that the older woman wanted the simple facts. Maria listened carefully, only raising her eyebrows when she heard that Laura Rosso was pregnant.

"Gottfried Klingenberg is your Rialto merchant, am I right?" she said. "I saw him at your father's funeral. It was an honor that he came. What exactly did he say when he didn't place more orders?"

"He said he was grateful that we had managed to complete the orders on time, and that he would see how these pieces fared with the usual customers."

"'These pieces'? Is that what he said?"

"*Sì.*"

"That means they're different from previous work. He's comparing them to your father's, and they're not as good. Klingenberg knows his glass. All the glass in the world passes through Venice, and he has seen most of it. I'll talk to him, find out what the flaws are. I've known him a long time. He may not tell your mother or brother, but he'll enjoy telling me. Once you know, you can decide if the faults can be corrected. Come back in three days." The older woman pushed herself away from the well, their meeting clearly over. She walked her through the yard to the door leading onto the calle. Opening it, she looked Orsola up and down and gave a small nod, her only indication that she noted and approved of the new dress.

Three days later Stefano opened the workshop door to Orsola and stood aside, his eyes following her; she could feel his gaze on her back like a stick poking her.

"The goblets don't match," Maria Barovier announced as they stood by the well. A cat was curled up in the sun by the basil pots. "The bases are too thick. The bowls don't lie steady, and there are bubbles in them. Your brother and his workers have lost control of the glass. Out of respect for your father Klingenberg took the work, but he's had to sell them at a loss. He won't make that sentimental mistake again."

Orsola was silent, taking this in. It was what she had expected, but it was still painful to hear. "What do we do?" she said at last.

"Make a greater variety of things," Maria suggested. "Your father concentrated mainly on glasses and pitchers and bowls, is that right?"

Orsola nodded.

"What about more kinds of glasses? Not just goblets, but more everyday glasses? Pretty goti that garzoni can make. Plates. Serving platters. Simple things, not too adorned. It may be that one of these things is something Marco is better at. Or Giacomo is good at but hasn't had the chance to show what he can do. They must take the time to work out what they can make well, rather than follow what your father made. Each glassmaker is different, just as each singer sounds different, or every woman's pasta is different. Your father's servente Paolo makes excellent work. He'll show them, though in the end he won't lead them, for he's not a Rosso. But they must work it out quickly, before they lose Klingenberg's goodwill. He will fill his orders with others' work before long."

It was sensible advice, but it was what anyone might have told them, what Laura Rosso and even Marco would have worked out eventually.

"Another thing: beads."

"Beads?" The Rossos had never made beads. They were cheap and unflashy and earned glassmakers little; they were something workers produced between more prestigious fare. Only the Barovier rosetta had become a bead of any value.

"Beads that *you* can make."

"Me?" Orsola had never touched hot glass. She did the laundry and helped Maddalena with cooking and cleaning; she gardened and looked after cousins. Occasionally she helped pack glass pieces for shipping. She didn't even help in the shop but left that to her mother. Maria Barovier was the only woman she knew of who was a glassmaker, and she wasn't sure how that had happened. Maria had never married: Was that because she worked with glass, or did she work with glass because she hadn't married?

"Beads fill the spaces between things," Maria explained. "They don't get in the way. They are inconsequential, and women can make them because of that. No man will be threatened by you making beads. But they're in demand now. Beads are taken on voyages and used in trade. The King of Spain ordered beads for his ships going west from there."

"West?" Orsola was used to hearing of ships going east, to Constantinople and Alexandria and Acre, or west as far as Spain. There was nothing west of Spain.

"They're looking for a new route to Asia that way. My rosette accompanied them." Maria looked mildly satisfied at this triumph.

"Are you going to teach me to make rosette?"

"No, child. If you were my daughter I would. But Barovier work remains with Baroviers. However, you can learn to make other beads.

Plainer ones. There are plenty of sales to be had from simple beads. They're not the only answer to your family's problem. But they are one answer."

"My brother will never allow it. A girl in the workshop. No one does that." Orsola blushed, for of course the Baroviers had done just that.

Maria chuckled. "Make them in the kitchen, not the workshop. Marco needn't know until you're good at it. If you're skilled enough, he'll understand the value. Have you seen lampworked beads?"

Orsola shook her head.

"There are two ways you can make beads: with drawn canes chopped up and polished, or over a lamp. You melt a piece of glass in a flame and wind it around a small metal rod, then you roll it or work it with tools into the shape you want. I'm not good at it, but I have a cousin who could teach you. Go to Elena Barovier tomorrow evening, behind San Pietro Martire, and ask her to show you how. She has an extra lamp. I'll tell her to lend it to you until you make one of your own."

How could a few beads make a dent in the debt Orsola's family might soon incur? "*Grazie*, Signora Maria," she said anyway. "I will take your advice."

Maria Barovier grunted. "I always wanted a daughter, to slice through all the men."

✧

ELENA BAROVIER WAS ONE OF dozens of Baroviers on Murano, and lived in a family house filled with glassmakers and their wives and children. Elena was at least twenty years older than Orsola, with an echo of Maria Barovier's square forehead, sharp jaw and abrupt manner. She too had not married but tagged onto one of her brothers rather than enter a convent, absorbed into the household so that she was almost indistinguishable from the wives and mothers. She wasn't particularly friendly when Orsola appeared at her door, but she had clearly been forewarned by Maria, and was enough in awe of her cousin not to disobey her. She had set up her lamp at the corner of the table where the family had not long finished eating. Women and children passing by gave Orsola brief looks but didn't question what a Rosso was doing at a Barovier table. They too must have been spoken to by Maria.

"You've never made anything with glass, is that right?" Elena sounded both curious and condescending.

Orsola shook her head.

"Nothing fancy to start with, then. You need to learn how to make a simple bead, one color, no decoration. First, we set up the lamp." She picked up a pear-shaped metal box the size of her forearm and opened the hinged lid on the top. "We pop in some tallow—get some from your butcher—and melt it." She held the lamp briefly over the fire until the lump began to swim in a puddle of animal fat. Orsola wrinkled her nose and tried not to gag at the stench of rancid meat. "You'll get used to that," Elena remarked. "Lampwork is smelly."

With the tallow melted, she floated a metal cylinder in it with a rag stuffed through so that one end was in the tallow and the other poked out at the top and through a lip of the lamp. She set it on the table and lit the rag, then sat in front of it with her arms on either side. Holding a small, skewer-like iron rod in one hand, she picked up a piece of green cane in her other. "I put this in the flame, but nothing happens—it's not hot enough. *Allora*, I do this." She gestured under the table, where there was a large bellows with a tube attached, the spout at one end poking up through the table and pointing at the flame. Elena began to pump the bellows with her foot, and as air flowed through the spout it fed the flame, which brightened and strengthened. "The extra air makes the fire hot enough to melt cane. Now when I put the glass in it—there." The tip of the green cane turned orange and began to soften and wilt like a dying flower.

She took the glass out of the flame and wound a small bit around the thin metal rod, which she began twirling back and forth between her fingers. "Turn it one and a half times one way, then the same the other way, and back and forth," she explained, "to evenly distribute the glass so that it's symmetrical. Symmetry is crucial with beads, as with most things made with glass. As you Rossos must know."

Orsola nodded, her eyes on the turning bead forming so effortlessly on Elena's tiny rod. The beadmaker put it back in the flame to heat it more, then picked up a small metal paddle and began running it along the moving glass, making it barrel-shaped, then oval, then back to round. "Canella, ulivetta, paternostro," she intoned with each transformation.

She's showing off, Orsola thought. Nonetheless she was impressed by her teacher's easy skill at making different shapes.

Elena spent a long time studying the round paternostro, such as was used for rosaries, turning and turning it. Satisfied at last, she stuck the rod, bead down, in a metal box full of ash, burying it deeply so the glass was well covered. "We leave it overnight to cool. Now"—she stood—"your turn."

Eager as she was to learn, Orsola sat with reluctance in front of the lamp. She had not had to learn something completely new for a long time—and certainly not with someone like Elena Barovier watching over her.

"Choose a color." Elena indicated the bundle of canes on the table.

Orsola picked up a blood-red one. *Rosso* for a Rosso.

Elena shook her head. "Too difficult for a beginner. Red glass hates heat; it burns too easily."

Orsola set down the red and picked up a green cane.

"No, not opaque. It cools down quicker so you have to work fast.

Here, use this." She handed over the dullest cane—a transparent white. "More forgiving."

For the next hour Orsola struggled with the white glass, burning it and herself, dropping it, making one lumpy bead after another, bulging in the wrong places, ugly and misshapen. She found it impossible to turn the metal rod continuously and evenly, and to do so while managing something completely different with a paddle in her other hand, all the while pumping the bellows with her foot. It was like juggling three objects of different shapes and weights.

"*Mariavergine*," Elena grumbled, several beads in. "Why on earth does Maria think you can do this?"

Orsola turned as red as the cane she had first chosen. It didn't help that Elena was not accustomed to teaching. She didn't explain important things, she assumed knowledge, she quickly grew impatient. When you already know how to do something, it can be hard to put yourself in the shoes of someone who doesn't. It reminded Orsola of Maddalena, who had rolled her eyes and taken the knife back when young Orsola had been slow to learn how to string beans, or had put her hands over hers to agitate the paddle more quickly in the soaking laundry.

As they worked—Orsola struggling, Elena criticizing, occasionally grabbing the rod to fix a disaster—members of the Barovier family came in and out, fetching water, lemons, bread, olives, chasing balls and each other. Some didn't even glance at them; others peered over Orsola's shoulder to see what she was making. One child heard Orsola swear under her breath as she lost the perfect shape she had coaxed the glass into, and ran laughing into the courtyard. "*Maledizione!* The Rosso girl said *maledizione!*"

At last Orsola managed to make one reasonable ulivetta spoletta, the oval shape being more forgiving of asymmetrical bulges than the round paternostro. Elena nodded. "That will do." As Orsola stuck it in the ash box next to the one her teacher had made as a demonstration—the only one worth saving—a weary pride settled over her. She sat back and sighed, stretching her aching back.

Elena blew out the lamp, then set a glass of wine down in front of her—the first real kindness she had shown, though demonstrating to a rival family's daughter how to make beads was itself a generous act, even if one was commanded to do so by someone else.

"You have to practice so much before you master beads," her teacher remarked after swigging her wine. Orsola had only ever seen Marco drink wine like that. She thought wine was meant to be sipped.

"It's having to do three different things at once that's so hard," Orsola complained. "Turning the glass and shaping it and pumping the bellows."

"Wait till you start with a second or third color, for decorating. Then you'll know what hard is!"

Orsola had been so focused on mastering her sole dull white bead that she'd forgotten there were many more techniques lying ahead to learn.

"And each color—and whether it's transparent or translucent or opaque—responds differently to heat," Elena continued, "and you have to learn how to work with two responses at once. Then when you add a third or fourth color, you need to know how to add it without ruining what you've already got, because each time you heat it in the flame, it changes. And all the colors look orange when they're hot, so you must remember what is what. But you won't be doing anything complicated for a long time. First you must learn to control molten glass on the rod. Do you have any honey at home? Transparent and runny, not opaque."

Orsola nodded.

"It's a bit like melted glass. Get a dollop of that on a stick and twirl it round and transfer it from one stick to another. That way you can practice."

Orsola tried to imagine playing with honey and sticks in front of her mother and brothers. Giacomo might approve, but Marco would sneer and Laura Rosso would shake her head and tell her to get on with the laundry.

"Don't despair," Elena said suddenly. "You'll learn. Because you must, or so Maria told me."

"I'm doing this to help my family."

"Well, I do lampwork so that I don't have to enter the convent."

Orsola nodded. She too had no intention of entering a convent, as so many spare women did. She had no intention of being spare.

✧

"WHAT ARE YOU DOING?"

Marco was staring at his sister as she turned honey on a stick, shaping it with a second one. She'd got it all over the kitchen table and had to move outside to the courtyard, where the honey flamed gold in the sun. Orsola had thought she would be alone, and hadn't expected any of the men to come out of the workshop. Their mother was with him.

"I'm . . . playing."

Marco tutted. "Why have I been cursed with such a lazy sister?"

Orsola turned red. Her brother's opinion of her was already so low, yet it was Marco she wanted to impress; needed to impress. It seemed an impossible mountain to climb.

He wasn't a curious man; his one question and its weak answer sufficed. He was clearly busy with other things, for he was carrying his goblet with the lion handles.

"I should go with you," Laura Rosso said to him.

"I don't need my mother tagging along trying to do my business for me." Marco pulled open the door and strode into the calle.

"Where's he going?" Orsola asked.

"He's showing his goblet to Klingenberg. Apparently the German wants to see it. Marco thinks the design is so good it will bring the Rossos business."

As Laura hurried after her son, Orsola called out, *"Che San Nicolò te tegna 'na man sul cao!"* Though she wasn't sure a blessing was what he needed.

She began again with a blob of honey, rolling the stick back and forth between thumb and forefinger, trying to train her hand to move it smoothly and control the honey rather than the honey controlling her. There were moments when she felt she was in charge, the honey obeying her; then like a naughty child it sped up and managed to slide off the stick onto the plate she had set out to catch drips. By the end of an hour she was no nearer to mastering the honey than she had been at the start.

"What are you doing?" she heard again. It was Giacomo asking this time, his voice gentler than Marco's.

Orsola set the sticks down on the plate, where the honey puddled. "I'm trying to work with glass."

"Glass?" Giacomo scooped up some of the honey on a finger. "Funny, it doesn't taste like glass."

"I'm practicing with honey."

Her brother smiled.

"Don't laugh. I—I was going to learn to make beads. Wound beads, with a lamp. Have you seen them made that way?"

"A few. It's not very efficient. You can make many more at once by chopping up drawn cane."

"These would be fancier. Decorated." She explained what Maria Barovier had suggested about beads, and how Elena Barovier had begun to teach her lampwork, and about the honey. Giacomo didn't interrupt, or look skeptical, or chide her. When she finished, he didn't speak for a moment.

"Orsola, beads are not going to save us," he said at last. "Our debts are too great." He paused. "You know Marco has gone to Venice with his goblet to meet Klingenberg. He thinks that goblet will save us."

"I saw him taking it away. Do you know, I drank from it once in secret, and the water went everywhere."

"I did too!"

They laughed.

"Klingenberg is no fool; that will be the first thing he notices," Giacomo said. "He'll turn down Marco's offer to make them exclusively for him, and our brother will come back in a rage."

"All the more reason for me to make beads, then. It won't compete with the workshop, but it will bring in a little. Enough to buy things at the market, perhaps, or for the baby."

They were silent for a moment, thinking about their brother or sister to come. Giacomo nodded at the honey. "How are you getting on, then?"

"Terrible! I can't control it at all."

"How often did Elena Barovier say you should practice?"

"Every day for three weeks."

"And what day is this?"

She smiled. "The first day."

"Listen to Elena and keep practicing. Do you know how long I was stuck making goti? Six months! You need to be patient. Paolo taught me that."

"And you need to build me some bellows."

✧

MARCO DID NOT COME BACK from Venice that night. Normally the family wouldn't be concerned, for there were friends on La Serenissima he sometimes visited when he was over. But he'd had his important meeting with Gottfried Klingenberg. Orsola knew that if it had gone well, he would have come straight back and told them, celebrating with his Muranese family rather than with Venetian friends. Venice was where you found an anonymous taverna and drank to forget bad news. As it grew later, she and Giacomo and their mother sat around the table in the courtyard, saying little, waiting. Orsola was trying to mend shirts by candlelight but had to keep unpicking her stitches. Giacomo was making sketches on paper, while Laura Rosso just sat.

"I should have gone with him," she kept repeating, smoothing her skirt over her bump. "Klingenberg knows me; he listens to me. But Marco said no, he's the maestro, and it's his job to present to the merchant and negotiate. Even though he doesn't know how."

Giacomo paused with his charcoal. "Madre, you know his goblet holds hardly any liquid. And it spills everywhere when you try to drink."

"Of course I know. I tried it once."

Orsola caught her brother's eye and smiled at the thought of all three of them secretly testing the goblet.

"Couldn't he change it a bit?" she suggested. "Enough so that it can be used?"

"He won't listen," Giacomo said. "He's so proud that he'll be too ashamed to change it, whoever asks—Klingenberg or any of us."

How have we come to be ruled by a young tyrant? Orsola thought. But she knew: her parents had not reined in Marco but let him have his way and believe he was right in all things. Perhaps they'd thought he would mature in time, settle down and discover the value of humility. But Lorenzo Rosso had died too early, and Marco was expected to take charge without having learned that important lesson. Now Klingenberg would have embarrassed him at the meeting, and he would take it out on the rest of them.

When he wasn't back by the next afternoon, Giacomo asked Paolo to take charge of the workshop and hired Bruno, the Muranese boat-man who ran a traghetto gondola between Murano and Venice, to take him over to look for his brother. Although the Rossos had a boat, they used it mainly around Murano and on the lagoon to get to some of the smaller islands; rarely to Venice. Giacomo was not keen to ma-neuver it on the busy Venetian canals, in particular on the Grand Canal.

"Take me too," Orsola begged. "It's big. You'll need help searching."

Giacomo hesitated, then nodded. She tried not to look pleased, but she was thrilled to be going to Venice. Despite its being so close, she had been only a handful of times, her father complaining that a girl was unnecessary weight to be rowed across the lagoon.

Bruno was delighted to charge to row two passengers over, mak-ing lewd comments about Orsola until Giacomo said he wouldn't pay the rest of the fare unless he shut up. "Then I'll leave you on La Serenissima and you can swim back," Bruno retorted, chortling. But he stopped complimenting Orsola's curves and focused on his rowing as the gondola entered choppier water in the middle of the lagoon. Each time they passed a church, he crossed himself and announced it, his voice like a deep horn. "San Michele. San Cristoforo. Santa Maria Assunta."

The latter was the first church they reached as they arrived on the northern riva of Venice, with its tall campanile, common on many churches. Orsola's stomach churned as she stared at the crowded buildings lining the riva and along the canals. Murano had similar buildings, but there she knew each one and every person inside. Ven-ice's houses were one or two stories higher than those on Murano, and had tall chimneys jutting up, their tops conical. As they entered the canal that led toward the Grand Canal, the wide light of the la-goon narrowing into shadows, she felt the buildings close in on her. Everywhere there was laundry hanging like banners from poles stuck out from the windows, white shirts pegged along the middles of their backs and the sleeves dangling. Women leaned out of the long windows, beating rugs, dumping water into the canal, shaking out linen. They were doing things Orsola did every day, yet here their actions seemed exotic and fascinating.

Once in among other boats in the canal, Bruno turned into a different man. There was far more traffic here than around Murano, and he had to show off his skill with his oar, making tiny adjustments to avoid collisions. He became even cockier, whistling crude ditties and swearing far more than he did on the waters around Murano, where his curses would have been reported back to his mother. "*Oe, becco fotuo!*" he called out as a gondola veered into their path.

The gondolier grimaced. "*Puttana di Dio!*" he called back. "*Ta morti cani!*"

"*In mona a to mare!*"

"*Eh, cazzetto, ocio, mona!*" another called, for Bruno was paying more attention to his swearing than his rowing. "*Ti xe imatonìo?*" Then it seemed every boatman on the canal was gleefully swearing and even singing insults: "*Buzaròn!*" "*Mona!*" "*Magnamerda!*" "*Visdecasso!*"

"Cover your ears, Orsola!" Giacomo cried, but she was laughing at the vulgarity and at Bruno's seamless transformation into a swearing Venetian gondolier.

They passed Campo San Canciano, where Muranese normally disembarked from traghetti to continue on foot into the heart of the city, and headed along the canal until it brought them out into the Grand Canal. Suddenly there were boats everywhere, seeming to be heading in all directions with little organization. The water was choppy with them, and the Rossos had to grab on to the sides of the hull to keep from tipping into the canal. There were sandoli like the one the Rossos owned: simple flat-bottomed boats with one oarsman carrying one or two people or cargo. Larger peate that cruised up and down with two oarsmen carrying mainly freight. Graceful caorline with crescent-shaped stems at bow and stern. And many gondolas, long and narrow, flat-bottomed, with a felze in the middle—a little cabin frame with detachable black panels that protected passengers from sun and rain. They were maneuvered by one or two gondoliers, who wore blue, black or red tunics with white shirts pushing through slits in the sleeves, tight hose in red or patterned in red and white or black stripes, and red caps trimmed with white plumes. They made striking figures and they knew it. Orsola tried not to stare at their muscly legs and bottoms, but it was too tempting.

Equally striking were their passengers: noblemen mostly, in black robes and caps, and ladies wearing pearls and blue velvet gowns over white-sleeved chemises. One held a little white dog in her lap. They didn't seem to be heading toward particular destinations, but were being rowed around so that they could look at one another. Sometimes two gondolas would merge, the occupants chatting together while the gondoliers rowed in unison and cheerfully mocked each other and gossiped.

Orsola gazed at them in wonder and envy. Her own reddish-brown dress that had seemed so elegant and flattering on Murano was shabby by comparison. She would never wear pearls; though some maestros' wives did, Laura Rosso never had. Now Orsola wished Bruno's simpler gondola had a felze that she could sit under so she wouldn't turn brown in the sun.

It was equally lively on the fondamentas lining the canal, with Venetians strolling along or gathered in crowds, talking, arguing, buying from stalls. They were mostly men in red or black robes, though the odd woman accompanied by servants could be seen, as well as servants on their own, rushing from one errand to another. It was only half an hour's strong rowing from Murano, but the Grand Canal seemed like a foreign country.

And there were plenty of foreigners. Giacomo and Orsola's destination, the Fondaco dei Tedeschi, next to the Rialto Bridge, was a huge, square, four-story warehouse with offices and living quarters above, built entirely for German merchants. Orsola had heard about it from her father but had never visited. It was plainer than the buildings around it, the only ornamentation the five large arches of the portico entrance.

They approached from the Grand Canal, Bruno joining a long line of boats gliding toward the portico. Though he had done this before, he was silent and sweating while maneuvering them in without bumping into the boat ahead, piled high with carpets. Others around them carried silk, timber, barrels of wine and spices; there was even a boat filled entirely with lemons. As they waited their turn to disembark, Orsola saw a peata carrying Muranese wood crates like those the Rossos used heading past them down the Grand Canal. They were marked with letters, but she could not read.

"Moretti," Giacomo remarked, noticing her attention. "Their merchant will have inspected the glassware here and made an inventory, and it's now going down past San Marco, where the crates will be transferred onto ships going south and then east or west. The same happens to ours."

Orsola had never given much thought to the trip the glass made once it left Murano, though occasionally she tried to imagine where it ended up: on a table laid in London, for instance, with Rosso goblets at every place. In her mind, it resembled a Muranese table laid for a feast, for she had no idea what London was like—it was simply a name. She had never met any English to be able to imagine them. She could only think they were like her, though paler.

At last they pulled up alongside the portico where goods were unloaded, and Giacomo jumped out to help his sister up the slippery steps to safer footing. After arranging with Bruno to meet by the

Rialto Bridge a few hours later, Giacomo led the way through one of the five wide arches and into the damp courtyard, which had been flooded by a minor acqua alta a few hours before. Most Venetian and Muranese buildings were designed to accommodate high tides with an androne—a ground-level area that was often awash with canal or lagoon water. In the center of the Fondaco dei Tedeschi courtyard was a large stone wellhead, decorated with carved rosettes. The four walls surrounding it were made up of round stone arches: large ones at ground level and smaller on the upper three levels.

Orsola was so overwhelmed by the spectacle of this bank of arches that she stopped and put her hand on the lip of the well to steady herself as she looked up. If she had been with Marco, he would have hurried her along, telling her to stop gawping. But Giacomo understood and waited. Around them men were crisscrossing the mezzanine and heading upstairs to the merchants' offices, or carrying between them crates or large bundles of wrapped merchandise. It was as busy inside the Fondaco dei Tedeschi as on the Grand Canal.

"*Andiamo*," Giacomo said at last. "Let's find out what's happened to Marco."

They climbed the wide stone stairs up to the first level, where Gottfried Klingenberg had his offices. Lorenzo Rosso and his father and his grandfather before had all used the Klingenbergs as their main export merchants. As one generation passed the baton on to the next, they transferred smoothly from one set of relationships to another, merchant and maestro side by side, whatever the vagaries of time. Lorenzo's premature death had thrown this efficient understanding into disarray.

Gottfried Klingenberg looked up from his ledger and greeted Giacomo and Orsola with only the slightest hint of a frown, which he quickly erased. A tall man in a black robe, with thick hair and a salt-and-pepper beard, he was a widower with one daughter, and about the same age as the late Lorenzo Rosso. Orsola had met him a few times, for he occasionally visited the Rosso workshop to watch them make glassware. Her father had always appreciated Klingenberg's continued interest in glassmaking when so many merchants viewed it simply as goods to be sold and shipped.

"*Buongiorno*, Giacomo," he said, rising to his feet. "And Orsola, all grown up. You look so like your mother."

Orsola blushed, at the same time trying not to laugh. His Venetian was word-perfect, but the musicality of the language was flattened by his German accent, for he would have spent his formative years in Germany and learned Venetian later. Listening to him was like trying to walk through the ruins of a building, with uneven ground and potential holes and hidden rocks that might trip you up.

Klingenberg gestured to two chairs of polished mahogany, the knobs carved into roaring lions with luxurious manes, the seats covered by cushions made from Turkish kilims. "My clerk is down at the docks, or I would have him fetch some cicchetti," he said, "but I can at least offer wine."

Orsola was too nervous to eat anything or try the wine he poured. Instead she studied the thick Persian carpet on the floor with its swirling patterns in red and blue and gold.

"What can I do for you?" the merchant asked when he was seated back behind his desk, also mahogany, covered with papers squared in even piles.

"We've come about our brother," Giacomo explained in a low voice, as if embarrassed to have to bring up Marco. "He had a meeting with you yesterday but he hasn't returned home."

Klingenberg fingered his wineglass—not one made by the Rossos, Orsola noted. "That is a pity. Marco was somewhat . . . upset when he left. We had a disagreement."

He did not offer more detail, and Giacomo didn't ask. Orsola couldn't

42

bear the silence. "Was it about the goblet?" she said. "Because we know it doesn't hold liquid well. But it is beautiful, and the lion handles are clever, copying the Venice lion. He's very skilled; you can see that. We thought we could get Marco to modify it—keep it beautiful and unique but make sure it holds wine. Paolo could help him with that." She was gabbling, and Giacomo and Klingenberg stared at her in astonishment. A young woman was not meant to speak so openly.

Klingenberg barked with sudden laughter. "You are indeed like your mother, and not just in looks. Laura Rosso speaks her mind too. But I'm afraid I'm a step ahead of you, signorina. I already suggested exactly that to Marco, for one must be able to drink from a goblet, at the very least. He did not take it well. Indeed, he used some choice language that I had not heard before. It seems Venetian gondoliers are not the only ones to swear creatively. I shall have to spend more time on Murano, or ask my gondolier to teach me. At any rate, I now know what Muranese say when they fire their merchant."

Orsola gasped, and Giacomo tried to speak. "Don't worry," Klingenberg interrupted him, chuckling. "I didn't take him seriously—for the moment, anyway. He will cool down his hot head and see sense. You will cool him down. I expect that is why you are here?"

"Do you know where he went?" Giacomo was trying not to sound desperate.

"He didn't say, but some of the warehousemen may know. Come, I will ask for you. I must go down anyway for an inspection." He stood, and Orsola noticed that his velvet robe was trimmed with fur, even though it was a warm day. Tucking a ledger under his arm, he led them out—Giacomo gulping down the last of his wine before following—and back down the stairs to the courtyard. All along the way other merchants and warehousemen stepped back and nodded or bowed, depending on their rank. Klingenberg was clearly highly respected. Orsola hadn't realized; to her he had always been just a name and a distant figure viewed now and then. A necessary evil, Lorenzo Rosso might have said—the middleman who didn't actually make anything, but connected buyers and sellers. He was the oil that kept the wheels of business running smoothly. Despite this, she found herself admiring him, not just because of the mahogany and the Persian carpet and the fur and the expensive wine, but because he was clear-sighted and frank about commerce and his role, yet still curious and admiring of glass. The goblets he had served them the wine in, for example, were of excellent quality—better, she had to admit, than the Rossos'.

"*Perdonate*, signore," she began as they entered the courtyard. "Who made the glasses in your office?"

Klingenberg glanced at her. "Maestro Seguso. I do not represent him, though. I never use my clients' wares, lest they think I favor one over the others."

Clever, she thought.

He led them to a corner of the courtyard where two men had pried open several chests. Orsola peered in. They were full of sacks that had been tied shut. Klingenberg pulled out a small knife from a pocket in his robe and cut open one to reveal tawny brown sticks similar in color to her dress. The merchant ran his hand through them and nodded. "Dry. That is most important when shipping spices. Here, have one." He handed her a stick. "Cinnamon, from Alexandria, and before that, farther south in Africa. Scratch it with your nail."

Orsola scratched it, then held it up to her nose. It was dry bark, curled in on itself, and smelled sharp and sweet, and of somewhere hot and dry. She had no idea what to do with it, but knew it was expensive and precious, and so she thanked Klingenberg and put it carefully in her pocket, to sniff at until eventually it lost its scent.

He spoke to the men and they hurried off to ask about Marco. While they waited, Klingenberg inquired after their mother, and what Giacomo was working on. He did not mention the mismatched goblets or the wobbly bowls, or the fact that he was placing no orders with the Rossos. His manner was smooth, professional, slightly distant.

Orsola fiddled with the cinnamon in her pocket, scratching at it again to release its spicy aroma. When there was a pause in conversation, she cleared her throat. "Do you trade in beads, signore?"

Klingenberg gazed at her, not so surprised this time that she was speaking. "Sometimes. They are a curiosity in countries where glass is not made. That can make them quite valuable."

"Maria Barovier suggested I learn lampwork, to help out the family. Her cousin is teaching me."

Klingenberg's businesslike face softened. "Maria Barovier." He repeated her name as if reciting a poem. A German poem. "Of course. She asked me about the Rosso business." He looked at Orsola with renewed respect. "She is a good one to have on your side. *Allora*, Signorina Rosso, when you have learned to make beads to Maria Barovier's satisfaction, bring them to me and we will talk. It may take some time, but I am a patient man."

She nodded, casting a sideways glance at her brother. If it had been Marco, he would have been furious, but Giacomo simply shook his head with a puzzled smile.

The warehousemen returned and spoke to Klingenberg, who turned to the Rossos. "You are lucky. Venice is a crowded city, and there are many places your brother could have gone. If he went toward the Arsenale, for instance, you would never find him. But one of the men saw him last night in San Polo near the Frari. He may no longer be there, of course, but you could start with the tavernas in that area."

Giacomo looked blank.

"You are on foot?" Klingenberg's manner was still smooth, but tinged with the impatience of a merchant who had important things to do.

Orsola and Giacomo nodded. They had not hired Bruno to go farther than the Rialto.

"Go over the Rialto Bridge and up the side of the market. Then turn left and, keeping the Grand Canal on your left, head more or less straight ahead—as much as one can on foot in this city. Aim for the tallest campanile you can see. That is the Frari."

"*Grazie*, signore," Giacomo said.

"When you have found your brother and he has recovered from his Venetian revelries, tell him to put away his fancy goblet and focus on making better the things the Rosso workshop knows how to make. Pitchers, bowls and simpler goblets. What your father made. His assistant Paolo will know how to make them well, for he is almost as skilled as your father was. Marco needs to let Paolo lead for a time, to steady the boat before he begins making new things. I told him this, but he needs to hear it again, from you and from your mother."

Giacomo nodded and thanked the merchant again. Klingenberg bowed his head and turned toward the chests of spices, his mind already on his business. Then he pivoted back to Orsola. "Give my regards to Signora Barovier," he said with a gleam in his eye. "I have great respect for her."

✧

THE PONTE DI RIALTO was the only bridge crossing the Grand Canal at this time, and it was always crowded. Two wooden ramps led up from either fondamenta, with a central section that could be removed if a tall boat passed through. It was lined with stalls on both sides, so besides people crossing it between San Marco and San Polo, it was also filled with shoppers. The bridge creaked and groaned and swayed like a ship with many passengers, and Orsola was nervous going over it. She'd heard that it had collapsed once under the weight of too many people. She would have taken Giacomo's arm if she could, but they were forced to walk single file in among the many men traipsing up and down. She could feel eyes on her, and hands on her, and had to jab a sharp elbow behind her to stop the unwanted attention.

"If we get separated, meet me back at the Fondaco dei Tedeschi," Giacomo called over the noise of the crowd.

But she would not lose him—the thought was terrifying.

They got over the bridge and headed along the side of the market, which if anything was even more crowded. Orsola was used to the markets on Murano—sedate affairs compared to the Rialto's. Here young men were pushing through the crowds with bolts of silk, baskets of dyes, candlesticks, carved stacks of chairs, rolled-up Persian carpets, parrots squawking in cages. She was tempted to step to one side and watch the spectacle, but Giacomo was plowing ahead and she had to keep up.

At the end of the market they turned left into a wide calle lined with buildings that quickly narrowed and darkened. On Murano the passages were wider, the houses only two stories. Here they were often four or five stories, towering overhead and blocking out the sun. There were still people hurrying along, and Orsola felt she and her brother couldn't stop or they would be seen for what they were: Muranese out of their depth.

They emerged into a campo where it was light again. Laundry hung from the windows above, and women were calling out to each other and to their children playing below in a sibilant accent Orsola found both jarring and seductive, like charred meat.

Giacomo paused. There were four passages to choose from, none directly across from them. Few passages ran straight for long. Venice was a chaotic knot of canals and calles and campos; it was much easier to get around by water than on foot. Orsola's brother chose a passage at random, but it led to a dead end that smelled of piss, and they had to retrace their steps. They took another and it led them back to the Grand Canal. Finally they asked a priest crossing the campo, who pointed to a passage they hadn't noticed.

At the next campo they looked in vain for the tall campanile Klingenberg had mentioned, but the buildings blocked views ahead, so they chose the calle most people were using. The buildings pressed in on them in the narrow passageways, and they were jostled by Venetians pushing past who knew where they were going. Orsola had lost all sense of direction, with no idea of how to get back to the Rialto and the Fondaco dei Tedeschi, where Klingenberg at least would help if they needed it. She felt as if she and her brother were being drawn deeper and deeper into a labyrinth they might never escape from.

They reached a vast campo, bigger than any space on Murano, and Orsola assumed the church in it was the Frari, but in the distance there was a larger campanile, and when Giacomo got up the courage to ask, they found they were only in Campo San Polo. Plunging again into the labyrinth, but this time with glimpses of the tall campanile to guide them, they emerged at last over a humped stone bridge into the modest campo in front of the Frari, where the church was berthed like a vast brick ship. It had a few tall, arched windows and the campanile at one end with a hexagonal tower at the top, but otherwise it was plain. The Basilica of Santi Maria e Donato on Murano was much more striking, she thought. Perhaps the Frari was more interesting inside.

But they were not here to visit churches. "Where do we go?" she asked.

Giacomo's face was tight with worry. They had reached the end of Klingenberg's instructions, and he clearly didn't know what to do. As she studied him, Orsola understood why Marco should be maestro, and not just because he was the older brother; and also why she craved his approval rather than Giacomo's. The latter was already a fine glassmaker, but he didn't have the strength of character to make the decisions that needed to be made. Orsola loved Giacomo because he was kind and gentle and undemanding. But that meant little could be demanded of him either.

"Look, the rio runs up alongside the Frari," she said. "There will be tavernas along it. Let's start with those."

He followed her to the first taverna, crowded with fishermen, who whistled as they approached. Orsola stopped. "You go in."

Giacomo looked at her fearfully. "What do I say?"

"Tell them you're looking for your brother, who looks a bit like you, but older and shorter. Say he's a Murano glassmaker. There won't be many of them around here, so they may remember him."

She practically pushed him inside. As she waited, Orsola had to ignore the attention from the fishermen gathered outside to drink.

No one remembered Marco at the first taverna, nor at the next, nor at any along that canal. Each hosted a different profession: one was all butchers, another vegetable sellers, another sailors. On Murano the glassmakers and fishermen also drank separately.

They started up another rio, weaving in and out of the paths that sometimes lined it, sometimes ended at the water. It would have been better to go by boat, though Orsola doubted Bruno would have been familiar with these small canals. All the while they kept the Frari campanile in sight, towering over the houses. As they circled it, she began to wonder at the futility of what they were doing. Marco could be anywhere in this maze of canals and passages. And what would they do if they found him? Would he even allow them to bring him home?

At last they came to a quiet taverna with only a few men sitting outside, the owner lounging with the drinkers. When Giacomo repeated his script, the man grunted. "He was here last night. Talked a lot of nonsense about the 'flow' of glass. Can't say he made any sense." He said this proudly, as if he didn't want to know.

Giacomo and Orsola exchanged glances. Only when he was very drunk did Marco become sentimental about how glass was transformed when it was heated and that he had to master its flow.

"Do you know where he went, signore?" she asked.

The barman shrugged. "If I had to follow every customer, I'd be out of business fast, wouldn't I? Though I wouldn't mind following you down a calle," he added, his eyes on her chest.

Orsola opened her mouth to berate him, but Giacomo spoke over her. "Even what direction he went in? Or maybe your customers talked to him?"

"*I* talked to him. Or listened to him, mainly." The young man who spoke was sitting on the white steps running down into the canal adjacent to the bar. He had a mess of long dark-blond curls framing wide cheeks, a heavy brow, dark blue-green eyes and a concentrated expression, as if the essence of him had been condensed into this one look. "You must be Giacomo," he added. "And you, Orsola."

Orsola tried to ignore the thrum that vibrated through her when he said her name. "Marco must have been very drunk to mention us," she retorted. "He never would have otherwise."

The young man chuckled. "He was."

"Do you know where he went after you spoke?" Giacomo asked.

"He was headed to Campo Santa Margherita." The man glanced at Orsola. "He said he was going to the brothels there."

"Is it far?"

"No." The young man began to point, then clearly made the same calculation as Klingenberg: here were two lost Muranese. "*Andiamo*, I'll show you."

He jumped up and crossed over a bridge away from the Frari,

Giacomo falling into step with him. Orsola hung back for a moment to assess him. He had a strong, stocky body, with round limbs and a broad chest. He wore brown breeches tight as a gondolier's, and she could not take her eyes off the movement of his generous, muscled backside.

It was much easier walking through Venice with someone leading them. The man went right, then left, then past another large church and through a campo, over a bridge and finally into a long campo shaped like the curved prow of a boat. A church sat at either end. There was a busy vegetable market stretching down the center with produce brought from fields on Giudecca, the island south across the lagoon from Venice. It was much bigger than the markets on Murano. Orsola gazed at baskets heaped with bright carrots. "I'm sure those don't taste any better than what we have at home," she remarked to her brother, keen to put Venice in its place.

The young man gave her an amused sideways glance. "Murano is famous for its carrots, is it?"

"You'll have to taste and see, *bufòn*."

"Orsola!" Giacomo turned to the man. "I'm sorry for my sister's rudeness. She's upset about her brother, otherwise she wouldn't speak like that."

The man grinned. "I'll have to sample your island's carrots. Maybe some other things too: peaches, melons . . ."

Orsola felt her cheeks heat up.

"How do we— Where do we—" Giacomo seemed at a loss to say it.

"Find your brother? If experience is anything to go by—not mine, *ovviamente*, but what I've seen of others"—he winked at Orsola—"he'll have been to a brothel last night and will be sleeping it off down one of the little passages between here and the Rio de Santa Margherita. Here." He led them down one that ended in a canal, then turned back to the campo, then went down another, and another.

Partway down one they found Marco, curled up behind a pile of rotting vegetables—rejects from the market. He smelled of drink and worse, and it took Giacomo some time to shake him awake. When at last he opened his eyes and looked up, he seemed unsurprised to see his brother and sister leaning over him. Pushing himself up to sitting, he nodded at the man. "Ah, I see you've met Antonio," he said. "I've been telling him about glass, and he wants to come and work on Murano, leave behind his Venetian life." Marco brushed a slimy lettuce leaf from his sleeve.

"He does?" Giacomo turned to the man. "You didn't tell us you worked with glass. But you're not allowed to over here." Two hundred years before, the Doge had sent glassmakers to work solely on Murano, to isolate the fiery furnaces from the dense city and to keep track of the artisans so they wouldn't run away to the mainland with Muranese glass secrets.

"I don't," Antonio replied. "I fish with my father and uncle. But I have four brothers and they don't need me."

"Why glass, then?" Orsola demanded. "You could build boats instead, or make ropes."

"I would rather work with beauty. I've seen what maestros make."

"Glass is the best thing there is," Marco declared as he hauled himself up against the wall, staggering a little and almost falling into the vegetables. "Every color, every shape. Fragile and robust. You can make anything you want with it. Do what you want with it. Like a woman."

Orsola rolled her eyes. "*Mamaluco.*"

Antonio laughed. "Apparently I have the body for glass, your brother says. Strong up top. My father says I'm too big for the boat. He prefers us small and wiry."

Marco was looking around, suddenly less jovial. "Where is it? *Where is it?*" He began grabbing at the vegetable heap.

Orsola knew what he was looking for. "How should we know? We weren't here. Good riddance to that useless piece," she added under her breath.

"The goblet, you mean?" Antonio asked. "With the lion handles?"

"*Sì, sì!* Where is it?"

"You had it when you left the bar. You said you were going to sell it at the brothel."

Marco straightened up. "*Mimorti!*" He hurried up the passage, and they followed him out into Campo Santa Margherita. Shielding his eyes from the sun, he looked around, and suddenly he was a less cocky Marco, lost in a busy Venetian campo. He turned to Antonio. "Where did I go?"

The fisherman regarded him with eyes the color of the lagoon. "I'll find it for you, but in return you must take me on as your apprentice."

"He can't do that!" Orsola cried. "We don't take Venetians. And garzoni start out first as garzonetti, tending the furnace and sweeping the floor. Boys aged ten. They do that for five years before they even touch glass."

Antonio shrugged and smiled. "That is the Venetian price for finding mislaid goblets."

"*Va bene,*" Marco said. "Go and find it."

"I need money to buy it back."

Marco searched his pockets. "I have none. The whores must have robbed me."

Antonio shook his head and hurried off.

"Marco, are you crazy?" Orsola cried. "You can't take him on! We don't need another garzone. Klingenberg told you what you need to do for the business, and it's not taking on an apprentice, or making that goblet. What will Madre say?" Yet even as she argued against it, the thought of this Venetian in the workshop, in the courtyard, at their table, with his hair and his eyes and his tight haunches, thrilled her.

"I need that goblet."

She turned to Giacomo, who shrugged but didn't dispute his brother.

By the time Antonio returned, the church bells were ringing for evening Mass and the market was packing up. He handed Marco a sack. "A bit of one of the lions has broken off, but I expect you can fix it."

Marco pulled out the goblet and studied it. "Yes, I can fix it."

Antonio was also gazing at it, not with the fanatic obsession of a lover, as Marco was, but with the look of someone who cannot read but is trying to puzzle out the words. Orsola was tempted to snatch the goblet and throw it in the nearest canal, for the trouble it had brought them.

"How much did they want for it?" Marco demanded.

Antonio smiled with one corner of his mouth. "You sold it for a fuck. They sell it back for the price of two fucks."

"It's worth a hundred fucks!"

"Not if you can't actually drink from it, which is what they discovered. *Comunque*, you owe me ten soldi."

"I don't have any money."

Antonio glanced at Giacomo, who sighed and handed over a coin he could not afford to give. The fisherman pocketed it, then led them back to the Rialto, without being asked to, for it must have been clear that they couldn't find their way back on their own.

Orsola let him and her brothers walk ahead so that she could watch him. Antonio's confidence both annoyed and attracted her—how he made his way through the crowded passages without bumping into anyone, how he nodded and smiled at so many people, how he held himself so gracefully. She wanted to walk so straight-backed through Venice. At least she knew her way around Murano and could greet as many people as he was now. You come to Murano and see how you manage, she thought. Except she already knew he *would* manage: he would charm everyone.

Bruno was at the traghetto station closest to the Fondaco dei Tedeschi, where boatmen gathered to wait for the families they worked for or for fares to come along wanting to be taken to Dorsoduro, or San Marco, or all the way to the Arsenale. As they lounged along the fondamenta they sang and made fun of the Muranese boatman, who tried to keep up with the singing and the swearing. As they approached, he was singing a lewd song about a Murano nun and her lovers.

When he finished, one of the gondoliers clapped him on the back. "You know the saying '*Muranesi maganzesi*'? Well, you're proving us all wrong. Nothing dour about you, *puteletto de Muran!*"

Bruno beamed, unaffected by the condescension.

Orsola was still slightly behind the men, and the gondoliers began to stir. "*Oe, che bea cocheta!*" they called, and made kissing noises. They would have become more explicit, but she stepped up to join Marco and Giacomo and Antonio, and the comments cut off as if hands had been clamped over their mouths.

Only one mouth did not need clamping. Sitting among the others was a young African gondolier, tall and lean, with close-cropped hair and wide black eyes. He wore a handsome red tunic and a cap with a white feather, and his hose were of a fancy diamond pattern like something from the mosaic floor of Santi Maria e Donato. Orsola tried not to stare for fear of revealing yet again how unworldly a Muranese girl could be. In the few other trips to Venice she had made she had seen Turks in their turbans and Jews in their skullcaps, but she had never seen an African with his deep dark skin.

To her surprise, Antonio saluted him with a *"Buongiorno,* Domenego," and the African held up his hand in return.

"How do you know him?" she asked, trying to sound casual to mask her curiosity.

"We hunt ducks together in the lagoon sometimes, when my father can spare me and his family doesn't need him."

"His family is here?"

"The family he has to work for," Antonio corrected her. "His own family must be back in Africa."

She nodded and studied Domenego out of the corner of her eye while pretending to look elsewhere. He didn't laugh and joke like the other gondoliers, but kept still and quiet and careful. He caught her giving him the side-eye and looked straight at her. Orsola dropped her gaze, embarrassed to be caught out.

"Bruno, *basta,*" Marco barked, as always breaking the spell. Bruno peeled himself from his Venetian comrades with reluctance and led the way to his gondola. His nickname now appeared to be *Puteletto de Muran,* which was shouted after him with much enthusiasm.

"When shall I come to Murano so you can keep your promise?" Antonio asked Marco.

Orsola's brother looked pained. The drink was beginning to wear off, and the knowledge sinking in that he had agreed to take on an apprentice who had no experience with glass. "In October, after the summer break," he said finally. "The furnace is off in August, so no point coming till after that."

Giacomo and Orsola glanced at each other. It seemed they were to have a new employee.

"Va bene. Arrivederci!" Antonio called.

As Bruno maneuvered away from the fondamenta, she couldn't help herself and glanced over. Both Antonio and Domenego were smiling at her.

✧

MARCO DIDN'T GET properly angry until the next day. In Venice he was still drunk enough not to think about how his family had come over to fetch him. All the way back to Murano Marco regaled Bruno with descriptions of what he had done with the Santa Margherita whores, until Orsola had to stop her ears and look back toward the campaniles skewering the sky above Venice. Somewhere in those cramped buildings and stinking canals and lively campos was a Venetian fisherman with a Rosso coin in his pocket.

Once Marco had washed and eaten and slept, he emerged sober and sore, holding his goblet by the handle that was still intact. Orsola, Giacomo and Laura Rosso were eating in the kitchen. Marco set the goblet carefully on the table and glared at his brother and sister. "How dare you come looking for me in Venice," he began in a low voice that rapidly grew louder, "as if I were a child who needed shepherding. You embarrassed the family name and ruined our relationship with our merchant. If the Rosso business goes under, it will be your fault!"

"Don't be an idiot," Orsola was quick to retort. "You're the one who tried to fire Klingenberg. Luckily he's smart enough to ignore you."

"Who thinks she can speak for the family? Shut your face. Your place is in the kitchen or on your back."

"Marco!" Laura stood, her face flooded with anger. "Don't ever speak to your sister like that, or any of your family. Family comes first, always!"

Marco tried to speak, but she continued over him. "You should be grateful your brother and sister went to find you, otherwise God only knows where you might have ended up. Dead in a canal, probably." She crossed herself. "You should thank them. *Allora*, thank them!" She folded her arms and glared at him.

"What? No!" Marco folded his arms and glared back at his mother, who seemed to grow taller. Orsola watched, fascinated. Her mother was at last standing up to her son. And now that she was, it was clear who would win.

At last Marco dropped his eyes and his arms.

"Thank them," Laura commanded.

"*Grazie*," he muttered.

"Louder. Say 'Thank you, Orsola and Giacomo.'"

"*Grazie, Orsola e Giacomo.*"

"A brother protects his sister, always. He never says such things to her or about her. Tell her you're sorry."

Marco turned to Orsola, head bowed. "*Mi dispiace*, sorella."

She nodded, but she wasn't reassured. A humiliated Marco could be more dangerous than an angry one. Anger burned out, but humiliation could run long and deep, wrecking any chance of his ever valuing her and her work.

"*Ecco*, Madre, what are we going to do?" Giacomo was deliberate in asking their mother rather than Marco. "Klingenberg says we must improve what we're making. If we do that, he may take us back. But it has to be quick or the customers won't wait." He didn't add that Marco had foolishly promised to take on another garzone.

Laura Rosso sat back down and rubbed her lower back. The baby wasn't due for some months, but her bump was already prominent. *Mio Dio*, don't let it be twins, Orsola thought. Soon we may not be able to feed them.

Her mother was examining her fingernails. "There is another solution."

Her children watched her as she picked at dirt under a nail.

"Roberto Testa has offered to marry me. He would take on the debt, and would even accept this one"—she laid a hand on her belly—"as his own."

"Testa?" Marco cried. "What's that old dog doing sniffing around here?"

Orsola understood more quickly than her brothers. Roberto Testa was a widower, with no children and a small workshop. He would either be subsumed by one of his brothers or merge with another workshop. Eat or be eaten. The Rosso workshop was clearly in trouble, so the offer made sense.

Whether because he was hungover, tired or slow, Marco didn't catch on. "Why would you leave us for him?"

"I wouldn't be leaving you. The two families would join."

Marco narrowed his eyes. "But—two maestros?"

"First of all, you are not yet a maestro. You still must pass that prova. Second, you don't understand. Testa would be the maestro. You would remain the servente. He would only marry me if he could take over the Rosso workshop and rename it Testa."

"But I inherited the Rosso glassworks! It's not yours to give!"

"True. But we're one family. And that is Testa's offer."

"Never. Padre would be horrified that you even considered it for a moment!"

"Your father would be horrified that you make bowls that wobble."

Marco winced.

"*Comunque*, I haven't said yes, I haven't said no. I'm just telling you that it's an option. A way to clear the debt and put food on the table."

"But what would happen to me? To us?" Marco gestured at Giacomo.

"You would still work, doing the same thing, but without running the business."

"You mean we would work for him, as his assistants?" Giacomo said. "What about Paolo?"

"Paolo would fit in with what we decide. As I said, I haven't given him an answer yet."

"Do you want to marry him?" Orsola demanded.

"It would be good for this one to have a father, and some security." Laura Rosso tapped her belly.

Orsola nodded. A mother would be looking for security. But she couldn't imagine Laura marrying again, only a few months after she was widowed. However, her mother had always been practical.

"But *we* can give the baby security," Marco insisted. "Rosso security."

Laura turned her dark eyes on her eldest son. "If you want to give this baby security, you're going to have to set the workshop to rights. Do as Klingenberg said and fix your wobbly bowls and glasses with their thick bases."

"Let Paolo take over for a time," Giacomo suggested. "He was well trained by Padre and he has the experience."

Marco was pacing back and forth.

"For the sake of the family," Laura added, "leave that fancy goblet alone."

Marco strode out to the courtyard, swearing. They waited, watching as he went back and forth. The third time he came back in, he made straight for his masterpiece and swept it off the table. It crashed to the floor, splinters of glass scattering everywhere. Then he stumbled out, calling over his shoulder, "*Andiamo*, Giacomo—glass awaits us."

Giacomo bit his lip and followed.

Orsola fetched a broom and began to sweep up the mess. Her mother normally kept herself busy, but now she sat and watched.

"Are you all right, Madre?" Orsola asked.

"Baby's kicking hard. He's celebrating a victory." Laura smiled grimly. "We got the right result, didn't we? I'm glad to see that thing smashed." She nodded at the pieces of goblet her daughter had swept into a pile.

However annoying Marco was, it upset Orsola to see his goblet in pieces: his dream gone, set aside for pragmatic business. She considered saying something, but Laura Rosso was holding a hand up to her cheek as if in pain. Indeed, she seemed to be crying, until she snorted and Orsola realized she was trying to stifle laughter. "Madre?" she probed, puzzled.

Her mother began to laugh so hard she lowered her head onto the table. Her laughter made Orsola smile, though she didn't know what she was smiling about.

Finally Laura's snorts diminished. Raising her head, she wiped her eyes with the back of her hand. "To think you all believed Roberto Testa asked me to marry him! You really will believe anything."

Orsola leaned the broom against the wall. "You lied to us!"

"For a good cause. It made Marco go back to the studio with a little more sense between his ears."

⬥

MARCO THREW HIMSELF so vigorously into saving the Rosso workshop that he was hardly in the house apart from a snatched meal here and there, even taking on some of the night shifts, for the furnace burned day and night. Normally at night the apprentices used it for practice, but now it was Marco who practiced. He forced Paolo to go over and over the making of bowls until he was able to produce ones that sat on a table without wobbling. Then they moved on to matching goblets, and finally to pitchers, with the complications of making a lip that poured well and a handle the right size and in the right place. He hadn't paid enough attention while his father was teaching him, but now with the studio in trouble, he took on the role of the son saving the family business and played it as if to an audience of thousands. Soon Orsola was glad when he didn't appear at meals, for if he did, he spoke soberly and self-righteously about glass and its fickleness and the need for maestros to master it and show it who was in charge; about wood suppliers and how he would haggle with them; about competitors and how he would outdo them. Normally she might find some of this interesting, but Marco was performing a monologue, not a dialogue, and the rest of the family couldn't add anything without him talking over them or chiding them for being so ignorant. It was boring and exhausting to listen to.

She was amazed at how patient her mother remained, listening to her son pontificate and not rolling her eyes or teasing him or shouting, *"Basta!"* She was trying to be supportive, Orsola knew, getting Marco through the training process he needed to become a maestro who could make consistently reliable products.

Next our mother will be wanting him to marry, Orsola thought one day as she sat through another tedious dinner. It was hard to imagine who would put up with her brother. Others called him handsome, though she couldn't see it herself; his sharp jaw signaled sarcasm and cruelty. But some woman would be happy to put up with his caustic remarks if it meant wearing the maestro wife's fur. Indeed, by August he had married Nicoletta, a delicate girl with huge eyes from a glass family the Rossos had known all their lives, who would keep quiet and wear the fur like protection. She was a terrible cook and didn't have the muscle for laundry, but once married, she wedged herself into the Rosso household by giving Marco the absolute devotion that buoyed and softened him, knocking off some of his harder edges.

For the next few months Orsola focused on beads, bent over a lamp at a small table in the corner of the kitchen. By the time Laura Rosso gave birth to Stella in September, shortly after Marco and Nicoletta wed, Orsola had mastered simple, symmetrical beads of one color and size. She made many red beads because of the Rosso name, but her preferred color was that of the lagoon: dark green with a hint of the sky reflected in it.

Once baby Stella arrived, however, suddenly there was no time for lampwork. Laura Rosso was old to be a mother, and the birth left her weak and unable to nurse. Orsola had to find a wet nurse, and did much of the looking after of her new sister while their mother recovered. She was astonished to discover how demanding babies were. Feeding, changing, rocking, settling. She was constantly running from the Rosso house and over the Ponte Longo, which crossed the Grand Canal, to a woman in a fishing family who had her own baby to look after. With Laura out of action and Nicoletta trying to find her feet in a new household, it was also left to Orsola to do all the laundry—expanding now with the endless baby cloths Stella soiled. Orsola loved her sister but all the work her arrival created took her away from beads. Without constant practice, she feared that all she had learned during the last few months would be lost and she would have to start all over again, playing with honey between sticks.

✦

ONE AFTERNOON in October Orsola was bringing Stella back from the wet nurse and took the long way around so that she could walk along Murano's Grand Canal. It was quiet compared to the Venetian Grand Canal she'd had a brief taste of, but there were a few palazzos to admire and wealthy Venetians holidaying in them to spy on. The baby was in a post-feed daze and Orsola was in no hurry to get back to the stinking laundry and the grubby house Nicoletta was so hopeless at cleaning. She paused by the water, ever moving, glistening in the autumn sun, and took out a bead she'd made before Stella's birth and now carried in her pocket. It was a translucent green—like the canal, where you couldn't see the bottom. There were three types of glass she worked with: transparent, opaque and translucent, the last of which was neither clear nor opaque—you saw partway through it and got only hints of what lay beyond. Orsola was discovering she rather liked this third way, which was more subtle than the others.

She held up the bead to compare its color to the water.

"Admiring your own work, are you, Orsola Rosso?" Maria Barovier had come to stand beside her.

Orsola dropped her hand, embarrassed. "I—I haven't had the chance to make much."

The beadmaker nodded at Stella, asleep on her sister's shoulder. "They take up all your time, don't they? Show me." She held out her hand. Orsola reluctantly dropped the green bead into her palm and held her breath as the older woman inspected it.

"Not yet," she said, handing it back. "The shape and color are good together, but the symmetry is not quite there."

Orsola sighed. "Glass is so hard to control."

"That's what I like about it. It's an unpredictable mistress; it has its own laws. You have to practice more before you show your beads to Signor Klingenberg. He needs to have no reason to turn you down. There are no women in the glass business, because our work must be perfect to be accepted by men, and with glass there's no such thing as perfection."

"*You* are in the business, though."

Maria Barovier shrugged. "I am an anomaly. The exception to the rule. But I suspect it will take a very long time for women to be accepted into the glass world. Hundreds of years." She gazed at her protégée. "Are you sure you want to spend your whole life knocking on the door to the workshop?"

"Maybe."

"Imagine yourself in the future, then, trying to make a living. Making beads for gentlemen, for countesses and even empresses. Imagine they reject you. Because of a whim, changing tastes, wars and plagues and poverty. Things outside of your control. Can you imagine all that, and still do lampwork?"

Orsola looked out across the shifting, glittering water, contemplating the shifting, glittering, unpredictable path ahead of her. "Yes," she replied at last. "I can." Because already she was as attached to her lamp as if it were a child.

Maria nodded. "Take this, then. A gift to keep you going." She reached in her pocket, pulled out a bright new rosetta and handed it to Orsola, then turned away without even a goodbye.

Orsola studied the bead, beveled so its layers of red, white and blue glass shone through in a scalloped pattern, and smiled. "*Grazie, Signora Maria!*" she called after the beadmaker. Maria Barovier waved a hand in the air without looking back.

Orsola added the rosetta to the green bead and put them in her pocket. She was shifting Stella to her other shoulder when a sharp whistle made her look up. A gondola was skimming toward her, with two oarsmen—one tall African, one stocky Venetian with gold curls. When they pulled up alongside her, Antonio was staring at the baby in her arms; Orsola was gratified to see his face fall. "*Buongiorno,* Signorina Rosso," he said, more polite than she expected him to be.

"What are you doing here?" She would not be polite, nor explain Stella, yet.

"Come to see your brother about his promise."

"He'll have forgotten that," she declared, but her heart stuttered.

"Oh, I've helped him to remember." Antonio paused. "I see you've been busy." He nodded at Stella. "I didn't realize when you came over to Venice that you were . . . though I don't recall your dress being loose. The opposite, in fact."

Orsola raised the bundle slightly. "My sister."

Antonio visibly relaxed. "Ah, *me ralegro! Allora,* will you take me to your brother?"

"He was drunk when he made that promise to you, so it doesn't count. Go back to your fish." Orsola began to walk along the fondamenta, conscious that he would be inspecting every part of her.

"Never mind, we'll ask everyone we see where the brother of the saucy Rosso girl is. They'll know who we're talking about."

She didn't stop but called over her shoulder, "We're near the mouth of the Grand Canal, on the right not long after it opens into the lagoon. I'll wait for you on the dock." Before he could answer she turned and ran up and over the Ponte Longo, the one bridge over the Grand Canal. Once she was out of sight of their gondola, she slowed down as she headed toward home, to compose herself.

Orsola had suspected—hoped—that Antonio would eventually come to Murano. After the afternoon months ago when she'd met him, she had indulged herself in recalling every detail of that afternoon with him in Venice: what he had said, what she had said, how he had looked at her. For a time, going over it in her mind reignited the thrumming in her body. Eventually, though, such raking over made the few memories of Antonio and that day stale from overuse, the juice squeezed from them. And then Nicoletta arrived, and Stella arrived, and Orsola was too busy looking after them and her mother and all the stinking laundry to spend any time thinking of him. Until now. One glimpse of him and the buzzing began again.

She could not think much, though. Stella had been jogged awake by her running and begun to whimper. She didn't want to meet him again with a wailing baby, so she had to stop in the passage that led to the Rosso house and soothe her sister, rocking her until Stella calmed down. By the time Orsola got home and slipped through the courtyard and out the back of the workshop to the water, Domenego and Antonio were in sight and pulling hard on their oars.

When they glided in, Antonio swung a belted roll of clothes onto the dock, then handed the gondolier a coin. "*Grazie*, Menego," he said as he clambered from the boat. "Come over when the Klingenbergs give you a free day and we'll try hunting ducks on this part of the lagoon."

"You work for the Klingenbergs?" Orsola demanded.

Domenego nodded as he pulled away from the dock.

Orsola hadn't seen the African gondolier bring Gottfried Klingenberg to her father's funeral; but then, she hadn't been looking for him, for her mind had been on other things. She was so surprised that it was a minute before she took in that Domenego had left Antonio behind. "You really are here? To stay?"

Antonio smiled. "*De certo, bella*. I sent a message to your brother. He's expecting me."

"But you know nothing about glass."

"I'll learn."

"It's not like fishing."

"That suits me."

"And garzoni get no days off to go duck hunting."

"This is a fine welcome. Anyone hearing you would think you don't want me here. Am I that offensive to you?"

"No, I—" Orsola didn't know why she was being so churlish, but she couldn't help herself. "Marco won't be an easy master to work for."

"My father was not an easy man to work for." Antonio nodded at her. "What were you looking at when Domenego and I saw you on the Grand Canal?"

"I wasn't looking at anything."

"Yes, you were. You were looking at something. Show me."

Orsola pulled the green bead from her pocket and handed it to him, their hands brushing.

Antonio held it up to the light. "*Meravigliosa!* Who made it?"

"I did."

"You?"

Orsola nodded. "When they're good enough I'm going to take them direct to Klingenberg to sell."

A neighbor passing in a sandolo looked Antonio up and down, then raised an eyebrow at Orsola. The first of many such looks, she thought. She adjusted Stella on her shoulder. "You'd best come in, then." She turned and headed toward the glass yard.

Antonio picked up his roll. "Are you sure that baby isn't yours?" he said as he followed. "Because she looks just like you. She's scowling."

"She smiles at people she likes." Orsola smiled to herself.

"That's better."

"Hmph—you can't even see my face."

"I can see your cheeks move."

"Stop looking, then."

"Are you going to be arguing with me for the rest of our lives?"

"I won't waste my breath."

But privately she thought: *Sì.*

2

NOW: TIME TO SKIP AHEAD IN TIME. You can do that with time *alla Veneziana*.

We are back with the flat skimming stone, standing on the Venice riva that faces Murano. Hold it with your index finger curved around its edge, and flick it hard and low across the lagoon so that it heads toward the Island of Glass, touching lightly on the water's surface. Murano is physically too far away for the stone ever to reach it, but we are playing by different rules here. In one jump it leaps forward eighty years.

At a table in the corner of the kitchen, Orsola Rosso is turning back and forth in the flame a translucent green bead. She looks up and it is no longer 1494, but 1574. Yet not much has changed for Orsola. In this magical place where time passes differently, she and those who are important to her have not grown any older. She is eighteen years old.

That sudden passage of time: What does it matter, one century or another, as long as Orsola is accompanied by those she loves and those she needs and even those she hates? If they sail through the years with her, she can skip alongside the stone to the important moments, without worrying about who and what has been left behind.

(However, people do age and die, caught out eventually, even by time *alla Veneziana*. A moment of silence, please, for Maria Barovier, who has died of old age.)

Venetians and Muranese alike skate over what has happened in the rest of the world. During those eighty years, there have been new nations forged, new wars fought, old diseases succumbed to. New trade routes bypass Venice, thanks to Vasco da Gama and other explorers. Newly discovered continents are beginning to be traveled to and exploited. A new kind of Christianity makes Catholics roll their eyes. An English queen has been on the throne for sixteen years, with another twenty-nine to go. Artists flourish: Leonardo, Michelangelo, Carpaccio, Raphael, Giorgione, Titian.

Glass too is flourishing . . .

✧

ORSOLA COULD BE FORGIVEN for thinking that something between her and the fisherman-turned-glassman from Venice would immediately ignite. That there would be secret meetings in calles where they pressed themselves against each other; stolen bottles of wine shared in hidden corners of Murano; early-morning boat trips into the lagoon with only fishermen and a newly risen sun to see them. These fantasies occurred only in Orsola's head: dreams she played over and over as she did laundry or soothed her baby sister or weeded the garden. Instead, a formality set in from the start, both parties stepping back from the flame that had almost caught between them. Perhaps it was the X marked on the contract Marco presented to Antonio on his first day, formalizing the apprenticeship—an X that signed away the right to flirt with his master's sister.

Antonio was given a room off the workshop to share with another garzone, and he took his meals with the family, so Orsola saw him every day. At first it was excruciating, brushing his shoulder as she leaned over to serve him, catching his eye across the table, blushing when she did, feeling exposed in front of so many people.

To her surprise, no one teased her about the delectable young man with the dark-gold hair so tantalizingly close, nor warned her off him. Not her mother, less vocal now since Stella's birth; nor her sister-in-law, Nicoletta, with a timid suggestion. Not even Maddalena, pretty and robust, who clearly fancied Antonio herself and elbowed Orsola out of the way so that she could heap his plate with liver or sarde in saor or bigoli al nero di seppia, the squid ink turning his lips a mesmerizing black.

Antonio obediently flirted with Maddalena, though he never seemed to do so seriously. Nor did she: Orsola knew Maddalena had her eye on a particular servant who came over regularly from Venice with a noble family to their palazzo on Murano. Antonio wove this into his teasing. "I can teach you what Venetian men like," he offered.

"And you, what Muranese women expect from a man," Maddalena retorted. "Not your fancy Venetian ways!"

With Orsola Antonio kept a respectful distance. She found herself in the humiliating position of wanting to chase after him. After a period of awkwardness, she was relieved when he took up first with a fisherman's daughter, then a rope maker's daughter, and finally for longer with the daughter of the family's butcher. Orsola was angry, of course. Occasionally she caught Antonio's eyes on her, regretful, and wanted to slap him hard. And she hated with a passion the daughters of the fisherman, the rope maker, the butcher. Orsola might smile to the butcher girl's face, but she gave her the evil eye to her back.

Eventually what she felt about Antonio subsided into a hard knot under the surface that she could mostly ignore but occasionally press to feel the pleasurable pain.

She had enough to keep her busy anyway, mainly soothing Stella—a crier from the start—keeping an eye on her weakened mother, working side by side with Maddalena to keep everyone fed and washed and clean, trying to teach Nicoletta how to keep house, and then looking after her as her small frame struggled to carry the weight of her first pregnancy. It felt as if she was taking care of everyone and everything.

What she was waiting for: For Stella to be asleep. For her soiled cloths to be soaking in a bucket in the courtyard. For the pots to have been scrubbed and the floors swept. For the laundry to be dry and smoothed and folded and put away. For the chickens to be shut in their coop. For the men to have gone to the taverna or back to the workshop. For Nicoletta and Laura Rosso to be in comfortable chairs with their feet up. For all these things to have happened so that, if she still had the energy, she could get out her lamp and make beads in the corner of the kitchen at a table equipped with bellows Giacomo had fashioned for her. It was a distraction from Antonio, and its own passion, one that was far more satisfying than a man, for there was something concrete and beautiful at the end of it, something you could hold and turn and study and run your thumb over, something with a symmetrical shape and colors that blended or clashed. You could string them like a rosary, to count and pray by. Or make them into a necklace to wear on festival days, for all to see around your neck. Or keep one in a pocket, to be worried at like a talisman. Sometimes Orsola gave the imperfect ones to children in the calle, who played games with them and bartered with them as if they were coins. She was quietly proud that children who did not hold back from openly judging something ugly or boring or worthless seemed to value the beads. It was a start.

Occasionally she had a lesson with Elena Barovier when they could find the time for lampwork. They worked together, heads bent over their flames, losing track of the hours. Elena taught her how to make different shapes, and for a long time Orsola concentrated on making only plain-colored beads, practicing getting the shape right and maintaining symmetry. Only when she at last mastered that, able to turn out bead after bead of the same color, size and shape, did Elena introduce her to decoration, adding colors in drips and dots and lines and curlicues. She taught her how to gauge the temperature needed to melt different colors and opacities, each of which responded to heat differently; how to keep her hand steady when decorating; which colors went together best.

At first Orsola decorated every surface of a bead with dots and attempts at flowers and lines wriggling between them so that it was hard to see the underlying color. Elena tutted when she showed her one of these fanciful creations: a black bead with red five-petaled flowers surrounded by orange and white circles and interspersed with blue dots. "You young people always overdo things," she remarked. "You need to learn the value of simplicity. Two colors on the surface, not five. Dots or flowers, not both. And let the color of the bead itself show through. You've made it, so why cover it over with so much more? It's as if you're embarrassed by your work, so you try to hide it."

"Maria Barovier's rosetta isn't simple."

They both paused at the memory of Maria. Orsola patted her pocket, which still carried the rosetta her mentor had given her.

"It *is* simple, really," Elena explained. "Just three colors, a pleasing shape, an even pattern. Complicated to make, yes, but not complicated to the eye. Practice your shapes. Practice your techniques. The artistry will come later. *Allora*, start again."

The Rossos responded in different ways to Orsola's lampwork. Her mother said nothing; after all, she had encouraged her daughter to approach Maria Barovier for help in the first place, and this was the result. Giacomo was supportive but bemused that his sister would want to work with glass. Nicoletta sometimes stood beside her sister-in-law and watched open-mouthed, clearly in awe. When Orsola offered to show her how to make beads, though, she squeaked and jumped back, her huge brown eyes even bigger. "I couldn't do such a thing! So dangerous, I would burn myself. And—it's men's work, no? To work with glass?"

Nicoletta was obsessed with who did what, even though she herself did so little, perhaps *because* she did so little. She was constantly listing Orsola's and Maddalena's chores, counting them on her slender fingers like a child, as if to get straight in her head the responsibilities of each family member. Similarly, she was preoccupied with her husband's status. Marco did not yet have official maestro recognition— he would take his prova eventually—but Nicoletta always referred to him as *il maestro*, and made sure to wear her maestro wife's fur to the passeggiata as soon as it was conceivably chilly enough to do so— even in October, far earlier than the other maestros' wives wore theirs. She was so short that the fur dragged along the ground.

It was how Marco would respond to her lampwork that concerned Orsola the most. She suspected he would be angry at her intrusion into his territory, even though she was making something he would never bother with himself. He might consider it a criticism, that his sister was daring to contribute to the Rosso glass output because he wasn't able to keep the family business afloat on what he and his assistants made in the workshop. Since the crisis after his father's death, he had just about managed to keep the family out of debt, but the Rossos were not thriving, even during what many were calling a golden period for Murano glassmakers.

Orsola should have guessed how Marco would react to her beads, because it was so typical of him: he barely noticed. His sister was his blind spot, her normal activities merely background noise; making beads fell into the category of unimportant things he needn't bother about. He never looked at what she made, or asked her how she had learned to make them or what she was going to do with them. The only thing he did admire was Giacomo's ingenious foot bellows. Otherwise he merely complained of the smell of the tallow she burned. Orsola thought of Maria Barovier's assertion that men would not take seriously women working with glass and knew—as much as it irritated her—that it was Marco she most wanted to please. Until her brother rated her, she felt she did not really exist as a beadmaker. Perhaps she was asking too much of him, though; in his attitude toward women her brother was no different from most Murano men.

Occasionally Orsola sensed Antonio looking over her shoulder as she was making beads, if he came into the house to fetch a clean cloth or a few candles. She tried to ignore him, holding her hands steady and concentrating on paddling the glass into the most even shape or adding flawless decorative dots. Once, she made two perfectly round red beads in a row as he watched; Antonio caught her quick side glance and nodded. It was the first time in weeks that they had communicated.

Not long after, she passed him at the well in the courtyard, shirtless and pouring water over his head, cooling himself after the intense heat of the furnace, washing off the sweat. It was a rare moment when they were alone. Orsola stopped next to him, setting down the bucket of soaking cloths that threatened to take over her life, for Nicoletta would have her baby soon and double the load. "When is Domenego coming to hunt ducks with you?" she asked as he raised his dripping head, trying not to stare at his bare chest. She wanted to press her hand against the curves of his muscles.

"Next Sunday, after Mass. Why?"

"I have something for him to take to Klingenberg."

"Beads?"

Orsola nodded. Antonio smiled—not the flirtatious smile he used with women in the market, nor the condescending one of a maestro to an assistant, but an honest, delighted smile: the acknowledgment of one maker to another.

"Not a word to Marco," she added.

"*Naturàl.*" Antonio reached for his shirt and used it to dry his face before pulling it back on.

"Antonio . . ."

"*Sì?*" He looked at her, and for a moment she wanted to say something, about him, about them.

Then Maddalena appeared in the courtyard from the kitchen and the moment was lost. Orsola shook her head and laughed. "Watch you don't fall down the well from admiring your reflection in it." She sauntered off before he could respond.

On Sunday, her beads were at last ready. Earlier in the week she had been to see Elena Barovier, who had checked over the work and approved. The older beadmaker counseled her not simply to put the beads for Klingenberg in a cloth bag, but to string them by size and color and design and pin them to a bit of marbled card she gave her—special Venetian paper Orsola did not have the money for—so that they were presented in the best possible way for the merchant to consider. Elena even gave her a bit of silk to tie shut the linen bag Orsola had sewn to put the card in. She was skeptical of these niceties. "Doesn't he just care about the quality of the beads?"

"Of course, but you can make his first impression a pleasant one. Even an experienced merchant like Klingenberg responds to a bit of presentation. Doesn't food taste better when it's presented well? String the beads carefully, sew the bag well—in cream linen rather than this white, which is too stark—and make a ribbon from the silk."

Orsola did as she suggested. When, during Mass at Santi Maria e Donato, Antonio gestured for her to meet him afterward, she patted the parcel in her pocket, and during the Liturgy of the Eucharist rehearsed in her head what she would say to Domenego: "Stow this carefully so that it doesn't get wet. Give it to Klingenberg immediately. Hand it to him with both hands and a bow. Say, 'This is from Signorina Rosso, as promised, *con complimenti.*' And if you accidentally drop it in the lagoon while you're hunting, I will kill you dead with my own hands. Both of you."

Orsola said all these things to the gondolier when she and Antonio found him at a mooring north of the church, away from the gossiping post-Mass crowd. Domenego listened without expression, while Antonio grinned beside him. When she had finished, he took the package from her with both hands and bowed, saying, "*De certo*, Signorina Rosso." Orsola narrowed her eyes, suspecting with his solemnity he was making fun of her, but she could not accuse him, for she needed him.

At the end of the day, when Antonio deposited three ducks in the courtyard for the family, she quizzed him on the beads. Where had Domenego put them? Had he checked on them while they were out hunting? Was he going straight back to Klingenberg?

Antonio chuckled. "It's surprising, *bella*, but we didn't talk about your beads at all. We were actually paying more attention to the birds we were catching for your cooking pot."

"*Bastardo*," Orsola muttered.

During the next week she watched for a messenger bringing word that Klingenberg wanted to see her, wanted to buy hundreds—thousands—of beads. She dreamed about opening her own workshop and teaching cousins, Giacomo, even Nicoletta and her mother, how to make them. It is easy to dream when you hear nothing.

But as the days passed with no word from the merchant, she began to make excuses to herself as to why Klingenberg hadn't responded. Now she hated the silk ribbon and marbled card she had used for the package, and wished she had never asked Elena Barovier's advice.

Someone from a rival family was bound to have sabotaged her, however helpful Elena had appeared. Maybe Klingenberg was laughing now with his fellow merchants at the fancy package, their laughter echoing through the courtyard of the Fondaco dei Tedeschi. Or he was ill. Or Domenego had not passed on the beads but sold them.

Orsola fretted so much that she began lashing out at everyone. Stella cried in her arms, Nicoletta avoided her, Laura Rosso shouted at her, Maddalena teased her for having her *mar rosso*. Giacomo watched her, puzzled. One day Antonio murmured to her as he got up from a meal, "Patience, Orsola."

She felt the words as a touch and managed a small smile of gratitude.

After ten days she was sure Klingenberg thought her work shoddy—flawed symmetry, a mismatch between shape and color, or simply dull. Others might be doing the same thing better, so why should he take a chance on a new beadmaker? That evening, with unexpected time on her hands, Orsola did not sit down at her lamp, but strolled with her family during the passeggiata and found a young garzone from another glass family to spend a brief moment with in an empty passage, their hands exploring each other. It was a temporary distraction.

A few days later she was pegging out sheets in the bleaching fields behind the convent at Santa Maria degli Angeli when a neighbor's child appeared, out of breath. "The merchant's here, with his *moro* gondolier!" he cried. Message delivered, he raced off before even getting his breath back.

Orsola looked down at the basket of damp sheets. If she didn't lay them out now, they might not dry in time and she would have to rewash them—a tedious task she hated almost as much as washing Stella's cloths. But if she didn't go now . . .

She ran all the way home.

In the workshop, her mother stood in a corner while Paolo, Giacomo, Antonio and the garzonetti were lined up as if greeting the Doge. Klingenberg in his black robe was standing with Marco by the furnace. The family had clearly dropped everything to tend to him. Marco would take him to the glass shop and the storeroom, and even the woodpile and the chamber pots if that was what he wanted to inspect.

The merchant barely glanced at Orsola when she slid in to stand next to her mother. "Those blue candlesticks you sent me last month with the dolphins wound around the base—they have been well received in Prague. Do you have one here?"

Marco nodded at Antonio, who went to the storeroom and brought one back, handing it to the merchant with a bow. "Ah, yes." Klingenberg took it from the apprentice, held it up and turned it round and round, checking its evenness. He ran his thumb over the two entwined dolphins. Normally Venetian dolphins—in glass or stone or metal—were represented as fat and bulbous and childlike. These were long and sleek, more like what dolphins really looked like.

"Beautifully done," he declared. "And an unusual combination of fire and water. Candles and dolphins. Who thought of that?"

There was a pause in the workshop. Antonio looked at his feet with a small smile. Marco was struggling not to scowl.

"It was the garzone's idea." Laura Rosso stepped forward to handle the awkward moment. "Antonio Scaramal." She nodded at him, and he bowed to Klingenberg. He did not seem shy or embarrassed as others might. Orsola admired that.

"How long have you been apprenticed to the Rossos, Antonio?" Klingenberg asked.

"Nine months, signore."

Klingenberg raised his tufted eyebrows. "Very impressive. You have an eye, young man."

It was true that Antonio had a way with glass wholly unexpected in a fisherman's son. Most garzoni took years to begin to blow glass or design anything beyond a simple goto. Orsola had overheard Marco and Paolo discussing Antonio's surprising skill, incredulous that someone who had not grown up around Murano glass could do so well so quickly. He was even teaching himself to read and to use numbers. "He may be good, but there's no Murano blood in him," Marco had asserted, "so what's to keep him loyal to the Rossos?" This was a perpetual concern among maestros about their apprentices, even when they regularly poached good ones from one another. Antonio was only unusual in being Venetian. Orsola was secretly proud of him for his quick learning and good eye and steady hand. Of course she would never tell him that.

"It helps that you have a good teacher as well." Klingenberg nodded at Marco, neatly extracting the waspy sting his praise of Antonio must have caused her brother. Marco did not offer up the fact that it was mainly Paolo and Giacomo teaching Antonio.

"I will order fifty more pairs of those candlesticks," the merchant continued. "I intend to sell them in Vienna, in Paris, in Lisbon. Make them in different colors—blue, yes, but also a deep red, a filigreed white, perhaps one with gold leaf. But the dolphins should always be blue or green. Of course, I would not dream of telling you exactly what to make, but you understand my suggestions, *sì?*"

Nicoletta appeared then from the courtyard, carrying with shaky hands a tray full of glasses and a carafe of wine. She would have insisted on this honor rather than Maddalena, even though she was growing heavy with the baby, and wore her fur, though it was still too long for her, and it was not the season for it. Orsola rolled her eyes, only Antonio noticing and smiling at her. Then she had to jump forward to rescue the tray as Nicoletta's heel caught the fur, gliding the tray in to land on the marver.

Since Nicoletta might make a mess of it, Orsola poured the wine and handed a glass to Klingenberg, making sure it was one of the Rossos' best: clear glass beautifully balanced between cup and base, its stem filigreed, its base decorated with tiny baubles. He nodded at her and smiled. "*Grazie*, Signorina Rosso." He held her eye for a moment longer than usual, but not long enough for anyone else to notice. He had at last noticed her, was signaling to her. She would have to work out a way to see him alone.

She handed wine to everyone except Antonio—no one would expect a garzone to take part. Indeed, once Klingenberg had made his point about Antonio's candlestick, he ignored him and focused on Marco—for business—and Laura Rosso—for nostalgia. Orsola's mother looked pleased with the attention; it must have reminded her of the years when her husband was running the workshop and she was the maestro's wife. Klingenberg even paid his respects to Nicoletta, sweating in her ridiculous fur with her enormous bump peeping out. While they were all occupied, Orsola was able to slip out back to the water to find Domenego and tell him where to take the merchant so she could meet him.

When she returned, Paolo, Giacomo and Antonio had gone back to work, but Marco was plying Klingenberg with more wine, despite his firm refusal. The merchant was clearly not a drinker, though he admired the wineglass; likely he was keeping a cool head for business, and would expect a maestro to do so as well. Leaving his glass full, the merchant stood. "I would like to see what you're making," he announced, and turned to the men busy at the workbench. Paolo was attaching a gold handle to a clear pitcher, with Giacomo and Antonio assisting, handing him the tools he needed, taking the handle back to the furnace to reheat. Only when Paolo was completely satisfied with the pitcher did Giacomo place it in the annealer to cool.

Marco offered to send the pitcher over to Klingenberg in a few days. "A present," he added, smiling. His teeth were stained red from the wine.

"No need," the merchant replied, gathering his robes around him, nodding to the women and moving toward the dock where Domenego waited with the gondola. "Just make the candlesticks as quick as you can."

⟡

ORSOLA RAN ACROSS THE Ponte di Mezzo and down alongside the Fondamenta dei Vetrai to the southernmost tip of Murano, where a handful of Muranese and Venetian boatmen clustered on the riva to wait for fares to and from Venice. The Venetian gondoliers were better behaved over here, knowing they were in foreign territory; it was Bruno who dominated the group with his songs and his stories. Orsola tried to pass by unnoticed, but he spotted her. "*Oe*, I hear you're giving it out now. When are you going to give some to me?"

"The day you carry the Doge across the Grand Canal, *cretino*," she retorted.

Just then Stefano, the Baroviers' assistant with the staring black eyes, appeared on the riva. Orsola nodded at him. He went red, as he did whenever they ran into each other, then turned to Bruno.

"*Andiamo*, Bruno, our boat is leaking and we need you to take a crate to the Rialto."

"*D'accordo*." Bruno quickly untied his gondola and turned it around to row up the Rio dei Vetrai. The Baroviers were not a family you kept waiting.

Orsola was able to move past the traghetti to a point farther west along the riva, away from the spying eyes who might report back to Marco that his sister had been seen talking to Klingenberg alone.

Shortly after, Domenego appeared in the distance, standing with his feet apart on the stern, rowing in that manner unique to gondoliers: pushing the handle of his oar hard and fast away from him, then giving it half a turn and bringing it slowly back toward his chest, the oar seeming hardly to dip into the water before skimming back along the surface. It looked a bit like stirring soup, but done unevenly. You would not think such rowing would propel a boat forward, yet he moved fast and with confidence.

Klingenberg was sitting under the felze to escape the summer sun. He was paler than he had seemed at the Rossos', and sweating. Though his expression was almost as neutral as his gondolier's, layered behind it was an uneasiness that Orsola recognized as seasickness. She could scarcely believe it: Who could afford to be seasick in a city built on water? To get anywhere, you had to go by boat; it was part of Venetian life.

She held up her hand. "*Grazie*, signore, for coming to Murano to see us."

Klingenberg winced as the gondola was rocked by the wake of another boat. "I wanted to have a look at that garzone. Antonio Scaramal. Marco did well there to choose him."

Orsola did not reveal that Marco had taken on Antonio to repay a debt. "You received my beads?" she said instead.

"I did, indeed." Klingenberg paused, long enough for her stomach to drop. He doesn't like them, she thought. He likes Antonio's dolphin candlestick.

Then he surprised her. "*Molto belle*, Orsola. Your father would be proud."

"Oh! *Grazie.*" She looked down, flushed, wishing her father or Marco were there to hear the praise.

"The shapes are good, the matching sizes good, the symmetry excellent. They are simple, of course, but there is no shame in simplicity.

Eventually you will add more complicated decoration. But these will sell. I will place an order of one hundred beads a month, for the next three months, at half a soldo per bead. In red, green, blue and white."

Orsola kept her expression neutral. It was not as high a price as she'd hoped.

Domenego stamped a foot lightly and the gondola rocked. He gave her a little nod. Klingenberg patted his brow and upper lip with a handkerchief. Orsola was mesmerized by its whiteness, for she knew how much laundering and bleaching it took to get a handkerchief so white.

When she judged he was feeling sick enough, she made her counteroffer: "Two soldi per bead."

Klingenberg closed his eyes briefly. Orsola wanted to advise him not to, as that made the sickness worse; any Venetian would know that, though perhaps not a German originally from terraferma. But he was a proud man, and she didn't dare reveal that she had spotted his weakness.

"One soldo per bead," the merchant declared.

"All right," Orsola agreed, pleased, for it was the price she had been aiming for. Domenego casually shifted his stance and the gondola steadied. "*Grazie*, signore, for making this opportunity for me." She paused.

Klingenberg watched her, shrewder now that the boat was no longer rocking. "What is it, Signorina Orsola?"

"Is it necessary for Marco to know about our arrangement?"

"You want your own business, do you, separate from your brother's? Sensible. Maria Barovier would have approved. However, it is hard to keep secrets on Murano or indeed in Venice. I will say nothing to Marco, but he is likely to find out, and when he does, any differences you must sort out between yourselves."

Orsola nodded. He was supporting her by ordering beads, but he would not go further than that. He would side with wherever the most money was, and that would be with Marco's glasswork.

Klingenberg looked at her. "Be gentle with your brother, signorina. It is not easy for him, running a glass business when he is so young. You judge him harshly, perhaps." Before she could respond he added, "Would you like me to keep your money for you as well? Otherwise, what will you do with it—hide it under your mattress? I can keep it secure for you."

"*Grazie*, signore."

"I look forward to more beads next month. Domenego? Home now."

Orsola couldn't resist calling out as they pulled away, "Keep your eyes on the horizon, Signor Klingenberg! And next time chew mint leaves." Now that the deal was done, she didn't mind him knowing she'd spotted his weakness.

Klingenberg sighed. "You don't need to tell me, Orsola Rosso. Mint, ginger, eyes on the horizon, copper around my wrist: I have heard all the cures over the years from Venetians and Muranese alike. You all enjoy telling this land-loving German what to do. Nothing helps."

✧

IT FELT DIFFERENT TO ORSOLA, making beads that were to be sold. Before it had been as if she were just playing with glass, like a girl making cakes from mud rather than real ones that could be eaten. She became much more critical of her work. She would shape what seemed to be a perfectly formed red bead; then she would imagine it as part of a necklace of beads worn by a noblewoman in a Parisian palace, which in her mind looked just like Palazzo da Mula along Murano's Grand Canal. With the thought of releasing the bead into the world for someone else to buy and wear, she began to see that one part was minutely bulging, or flattened, or there was a bubble in it, and she would have to melt it down and start again. The ease went out of her lampwork; she felt stiff and awkward and self-conscious. For several days she couldn't get anything right.

Then Nicoletta gave birth, to a small, perfectly formed son they named Marco, and called Marcolin, and suddenly Orsola's days and nights were full of looking after her sister-in-law and the baby. She cursed herself for having wasted precious days making poor beads when now there was no time to work on them. She began to wonder if she would be able to fulfill Klingenberg's order at all. However, having less time seemed to spur her on to use what moments she could to work, mainly at night when the babies and Nicoletta were asleep. Finally during these late nights Orsola began producing beads she was not ashamed to sell.

✧

WHEN THE FIRST ORDER was at last ready, Orsola didn't send it to Klingenberg with one of the messenger boatmen who moved back and forth between the islands, but went over to Venice herself, alone, sneaking away when everyone was occupied. She didn't hire Bruno, who would tell her family he had taken her, and would probably pester her all the way there and back. Instead, she got a lift with a family from the neighboring island of Burano heading to Venice in their sandolo to sell lace in the markets there. They made their way to Piazza San Marco via small rios rather than along the Grand Canal, and she sat and looked at the passing churches and houses, with boats pulling into porticos to deliver barrels of wine, loads of wood, bundles of cloth, sacks of flour. Everything felt more normal and less like a pageant.

Until they got to San Marco. There the pageantry was overwhelming, and Orsola felt the danger of being a young Muranese woman alone in a crowded city. With reluctance she left the Buranese lace family, first arranging to meet them a few hours later. She leaned against one of the dozens of pillars opposite the Doge's Palace, briefly closing her eyes to the dazzle of pink and white brick set in geometric patterns, and rows and rows of arches stacked upon one another. Men in red and black robes could be seen hurrying along the arched colonnades, full of self-importance, with their messages to or from the Doge. As she often did since making beads more regularly, Orsola looked for inspiration in the colors and shapes of the building, but could fix on nothing she wanted to copy in bead form. The palace was spectacular but too boxy to be replicated in glass.

As was Piazza San Marco itself: a huge rectangle made up of more stacks of colonnaded arches, grounded with a campanile at one end, filled with a massive market the lace family was swallowed into. It was too big and busy for her; instead Orsola headed toward San Marco's church, next to the Doge's Palace. Here was a building that inspired her. It was more rounded than the palace, with a main dome flanked by two smaller ones and the main facade full of round arches and half arches, with elaborate carvings, and touched here and there with marble and gold-leaf mosaic. Needle-like spires and statues poked into the sky. Though large and heavy, the building seemed to be floating on clouds, reminding Orsola of a bowl of yellow and white glass baubles. She stared for a long time, wondering if there was a way to capture this confection in a bead.

She felt a gentle tug at her side, like the nibbling of a mouse, and clamped her hand onto a smaller hand that had made its way into the leather satchel she had slung over one shoulder. The beads were inside, wrapped in linen.

"*Ehi! Ti! Ladronetto!*" Orsola cried, and twisted the hand belonging to a boy who barely reached her chin. The would-be thief jerked free and wandered off into the market, Orsola shouting after him, annoyed that he didn't even bother to run.

She clutched the satchel to her as she began to wade through this city full of movement, of people, goods and water. You couldn't remain still here or people would rob you. Her heart sped that little bit faster. She made her way along a passage roughly in the direction of the Rialto, chiding herself for being so careless as to almost lose more than a month's work. It made her reluctant to ask anyone if she was going the right way. But from the steady stream of people all heading along the same calle, turning confidently here and there, it soon became apparent that she was. Orsola floated along in the crowd like a stick heading inexorably downstream, moving from the political and religious center of the city to the commercial quarter.

As she walked, she looked, eyes wide. A monkey perched on a merchant's shoulder. A woman wearing a tiara of seed pearls suspended like stars over her elaborate coiffure. A man in a dusky-orange turban and white robes unsullied by Venetian dust. A fisherman carrying a crate of langoustines. A man with a mahogany chair upholstered in silk strapped to his back. And the smells. An intense attar of rose wafting from a woman's cape. The delicate intensity of saffron buns on a tray held high. The stench of the canals she crossed, full of rotten vegetables and the contents of chamber pots. And the sounds. Plenty of Venetian, but also a babel of languages she didn't know. Turkish? Greek? Arabic? German? English? French? She could be hearing all of them, or none. This Venice was thrilling, and Orsola wanted to be where she was, in the center of it all; but part of her wished she were at home, safe from all this strangeness.

The stream of people spat her out in front of the Fondaco dei Tedeschi, and it was a relief to land somewhere familiar. She crossed the outer courtyard with more confidence and climbed the wide stairs up to Klingenberg's chambers, reveling in the cool stone after the intense summer heat outside. But the merchant was not there. Sitting at his desk was a young man with a beard cut close to his jaw, who gazed at her over his quill and ledger with steady hazel eyes and informed her in his stilted German accent that Herr Klingenberg was away, and if she didn't have an appointment she shouldn't have come. He managed to be clear and polite and at the same time dismissive. Orsola resisted growing sharp with him; she had her beads, and she needed to get them to Klingenberg. She said her name and mentioned the order of one hundred beads, pulling out the cloth parcel and beginning to undo the twine to show him, but he stopped her. "You're late."

"Only by a week."

"Ten days."

"I had trouble getting cane, and my sister-in-law had a baby, and . . ." She could see that none of this made any difference to him. Orsola doubted he had ever held a baby.

"Leave it there." He indicated a corner of his desk. "Herr Klingenberg will inspect it on his return."

"When will that be?" she asked, thinking that if she waited for the merchant to return from his errand, she might get to watch Klingenberg unwrap each bead, hold it to the light and admire it.

"In several weeks," the clerk said, and pointedly turned back to his ledger.

"Weeks?" Orsola cried. "But what about my pay?"

"If Herr Klingenberg is satisfied with the work, he will hold the money for you, as was arranged. Now, I am very busy. *Addio*."

"But—do I work on another order, or wait?"

The young man set down his quill, pulled her bundle toward him and began to unpick the twine. "Wait in the antechamber."

She could see a bench through the doorway. She didn't move.

The man stopped picking at the knots.

"I'm not sitting out there," she said. "You may have questions. Or you may try to steal a few."

The man pursed his lips. "They are *beads*, signorina, not pearls. Not gold. Not peppercorns."

It was clear he was not going to continue until she obeyed him, so she gave in and went to sit out on the bench, heart pounding, angry at herself for giving in to such a *sprotin*.

A few minutes later he called her back. He had wrapped up the beads and was writing again. He did not look up. "The same order for next month."

Klingenberg must have left behind instructions about her. "I need some of my pay now so that I can buy more cane."

He sighed, but he gave her twenty soldi, and Orsola gripped the coins with satisfaction. Money she had earned.

Outside she headed for the Ponte di Rialto, with time to spare and a soldo to spend. She crossed the bridge, jostled by the crowds, trying to ignore the groaning of the wood, and found her way to the fish market. She was suddenly starving and bought a handful of fried sardines in a twist of paper, burning her tongue as she ate them, sitting against a wall on the fondamenta and watching the action on the canal. There were boats everywhere, carrying passengers or cargo, or empty apart from oarsmen standing on the stern and in the body and steering their way through. It looked chaotic, but Orsola knew there was order to it all, that the gondoliers' curses were interspersed with directions, warnings, greetings: "*Oe!*" "*A premando!*" "*A stagando!*" "*De longo!*"

Domenego would always stand out from the other Venetian boatmen. Wearing his black-and-white hose and red fitted tunic, he was rowing toward Cannaregio with two young women in his gondola, one clearly a servant to the other. The latter had a broad face with sharp cheekbones and large eyes set a little too wide apart. She was wearing a blue dress awkwardly gathered in to try to emphasize her nascent bust. Her hair was more of a success: a tower of bright-blond curls topped with an ivory comb.

Despite the commotion on the water and the endless stream of people passing, Domenego seemed to have no problem spotting Orsola on the fondamenta. Though he didn't call out, he nodded at her and indicated with a quick bat of his hand that she should remain where she was. Although he was discreet, the girls in the gondola turned and stared at her as they passed.

Orsola sat back and smiled, the sun on her face. She knew someone in this city. It wasn't like being on Murano, where she knew everyone. Here, she could appreciate the foreignness as long as she could spot one familiar face.

He came back half an hour later, and she went to join him as he pulled up alongside the fondamenta. "What are you doing in Venice, signorina?" he asked, standing steady on the stern even with the canal water choppy from other boats.

"Brought my beads to Klingenberg," Orsola answered proudly, allowing herself to feel smug.

"He's away. Augsburg. His mother is ill."

"*Che Dio la tegna.*" Orsola crossed herself. She did not know anyone who went to terraferma for long. "Who was that you were rowing?"

"His daughter, Klara."

"She has beautiful hair." She restrained herself from running her fingers through her own dark, unwashed hair, which she had only quickly combed before coming to Venice.

Domenego did not reply to her remark—he was not likely to say anything about his master's family. Instead he focused on business. "Did you leave the beads there?"

"Yes, with his clerk. He's put in another order. And he paid me a bit."

"Did Jonas write you a receipt?"

She opened her mouth, then shut it.

Domenego's face shifted. Now that she knew him a little better, she could spot the disapproval under his neutral expression. "Go back and get a receipt. Do not leave until you get one."

"But—"

"If he refuses, tell him you will inform Klingenberg he forgot to give you a receipt. Get in, I'll take you across."

This was a far fancier boat than she had ever been in before. The gondola's felze was black like the painted body of the boat; its panels were up, so she could see and be seen. Its interior was lined in blue and yellow silk, and the cushions were made of Turkish kilims, like those she had seen at Klingenberg's office. Domenego was a smoother oarsman than Bruno; perhaps he had to be, to counter Klingenberg's seasickness. And quick—he got her to the entrance of the Fondaco dei Tedeschi far sooner than she would have liked.

"*Grazie*, Domenego," she said as he helped her out.

"Don't tell Jonas I sent you back for the receipt," he replied. "He can make trouble for me."

She nodded, gazing longingly at the gondola.

Domenego's face softened. "How are you getting back to Murano?"

"I'm meeting people at San Marco later."

"I'm not busy now. I can take you to San Marco."

"Oh! *Grazie*." Orsola smiled at him, and when Domenego allowed himself to smile back, his face was transformed.

She returned clutching the receipt that Klingenberg's clerk had grudgingly written out for her, and that she couldn't read herself. Domenego was waiting for her at the traghetto station where Bruno had collected Orsola and her brothers the year before. The other boatmen fell silent as the African handed her into his gondola, then whisked them to the center of the Grand Canal.

Orsola had never been along the Grand Canal for more than a few minutes. As they passed under the Rialto Bridge, there was so much to look at from this new vantage point that she didn't know what to focus on—a feeling that was becoming familiar in Venice. The wide expanse of water ahead of her, heaving with boats. The palazzos lining it with their brightly colored facades and their rows of arched windows and their balconies, where ornately dressed members of Venice's noble families looked down on the busy water and drank wine and spread the latest gossip or plotted the next marriage or discussed how to gain the ear of the Doge or the Council of Ten.

But she was most intrigued by the boats around her, carrying more of the nobility, mostly men but a few women, in ones or twos, chatting to each other or sitting alone, usually with the felze open, but occasionally—intriguingly—with it shut. The passengers weren't looking around openly the way she was, the visitor among the natives. Perhaps they were just more discreet. They seemed posed, knowing they were being noticed. As they glanced sideways at her, she felt her shabbiness—her unadorned hair, the plain dress Maria Barovier had given her, the lack of jewelry. It was offset somewhat by Domenego's grace and the luxuriousness of the Klingenberg gondola—its black paint fresh, its forcola of highly polished wood that held the oar, the hints of silk inside the felze. Only the passenger was lacking. Orsola sat up straighter, twisted her shoulders, placed her hands in her lap and held her head up as if she were sitting for a portrait.

The passengers were relatively quiet. It was the gondoliers who made the most noise, shouting to one another, steering nimbly between other boats, lively and amused. With Domenego they were less easy: a pause before passing by, a deliberate nonchalance. Your skin may be different from ours, they implied, but we're not going to notice that. Venetians reveled in their worldliness. On Murano canals he would have been openly stared at.

"Do you like working as a gondolier?" Orsola asked.

Domenego shrugged, and she winced at her crass question. Was it even possible to like something you were forced to do?

She blundered on, unable to stop herself. "How did you come to Venice?"

The gondolier's eyes were fixed on a point in the distance, his face not just impassive, but rigid. Orsola thought he might not answer, but eventually he said, "Brought on a ship. Many days. I lost the time."

"Do you remember home?"

He glanced at her. "Of course."

Orsola turned red and ducked her head. She would keep quiet.

But then he said, "No one ever asks me about that."

What was the right thing to ask? "You are so skilled with the gondola," she said. "Did you have them in Africa?"

Domenego's still face broke up and he began to laugh—so hard that he stopped rowing and they drifted into the paths of other boats. The boatmen cried "Oe!" and swore in earnest rather than in fun, scrambling to get out of their way.

"Domenego, ocio!" Orsola cried.

Domenego took up his oar and with tiny movements got them back in line. "Scusème, scusème," he called to the boatmen. To her he said, "You Venetians are so funny. You assume everywhere is like here."

"I'm not Venetian, I'm Muranese."

"Yes, well . . . I grew up in a village by the sea, but the boats there were different. We used sails and the wind, not oars and rowing. I had to learn how to do this." He gestured with his oar. "Canals and lagoons are not like the sea."

"Would you go back if you could?"

"To buy my freedom will take me a long time. And things would have changed so much. I try not to think about it."

Clearly he did think about it.

They had rounded a wide bend and were heading toward the place where the Grand Canal met the Giudecca Canal. Now there were much larger boats to contend with: ships from the East and the West, dropping off and picking up the goods that made Venetian trade so famous. Compared to these huge vessels with their sails bigger than all the Rosso sheets sewn together and their myriad ropes and their tough sailors scrambling about, Venetian gondolas looked like toys. Domenego rowed hard, concentrating on keeping his boat steady.

When he pulled up to the riva near the Piazza San Marco, the water was unsteady from the waves of the ships, and Orsola grasped his outstretched hand to let him guide her safely ashore.

"*Grazie*, Domenego," she said.

He nodded. "Where will you go now?"

"I'll have a look around the market." She was feeling a little more confident now about navigating the streets and the crowds.

Domenego pointed east along the riva. "Do not go that way."

"Why not?"

"They say there is illness in a convent on the Riva degli Schiavoni, near the Arsenale. Do not go farther than San Zaccaria."

"What kind of illness?"

Domenego hesitated, then said, "*La peste.*"

✧

THE PLAGUE DIDN'T ARRIVE like a wave crashing on the shore. Instead it was like one of those summer storms out at sea that you could see and hear but that never came closer. There were rumors of deaths in certain sestieri in Venice; then all went quiet; then came more deaths.

All that autumn, the rumble of the plague in the distance was low and constant. The Rossos heard about it, but it didn't affect them, apart from a decrease in traffic between the two islands. Fewer traghetti went back and forth, though glassmakers still sent their goods to be inspected and shipped out. Toward winter the news of deaths died down; as Orsola's nonna told her—for she had been through this before with earlier plagues—*la peste* did not survive in the cold. It seemed Murano—and Venice—had been reprieved of anything worse.

Each month Orsola wrapped up her beads and sent the package to the Fondaco dei Tedeschi with a trusted messenger—one of the young men who rowed back and forth between Murano and La Serenissima, carrying messages and cargo. Once he was back from Augsburg, Klingenberg sent a receipt each month and enough soldi for cane, gradually adding orders for more and new types of beads: "Twenty white filigree," he would write, or "Fifty gold leaf, variety of colors." Orsola had to show the receipt to Elena Barovier to decipher and learn the techniques from her if she couldn't puzzle them out herself. She was so busy and absorbed that she stopped thinking about Antonio and his butcher girl or worrying about Marco discovering that she was selling beads.

When she had saved a little, she decided to hire someone to help with the laundry, to free up more of her time so that she wasn't constantly washing dirty baby cloths. She mentioned this to her mother one day when they were in the kitchen stacking wood that had been delivered from terraferma. Hearing this, Maddalena drew in a sharp breath and tutted as she stood over a pan, frying dough for fritole, for it was the season of Carnevale, when the fried dough balls were popular. But Laura Rosso paused, a log in each hand, and thought. "Sensible," she said, and threw the logs on top of the pile.

"Strangers in the house doing your work." Maddalena tutted again.

Maddalena may have disapproved, but she said nothing to Marco. Nor did Laura, nor—surprisingly—did Nicoletta, who could so easily have let slip to her husband that her sister-in-law was making beads to sell. But the women seemed a little in awe of what Orsola was doing, and so they didn't complain when she didn't do all her housework, when they had to take up the slack, when she brought in a girl to do the laundry and began making beads during the day as well as at night. Orsola got into a pleasing flow of work, and it seemed Klingenberg was pleased as well, for he began placing larger orders. She took that to mean he was satisfied with her work.

After the quiet of winter, as it grew warmer, the plague began rumbling again in Venice. Orsola first got word of it where she picked up most news: in the market, this time at Bruno's mother's vegetable stall. She was handling artichokes, judging their weight—she wanted dense but not too big—when a woman leaned in toward Bruno's mother and whisper-shouted so that everyone nearby could hear, "Two deaths in Dorsoduro!"

"What from?" Bruno's mother demanded.

"You know! *La peste!*"

Everyone who heard her crossed themselves.

A week later there had been five deaths, then five more in Castello, a sestiere not even adjacent to Dorsoduro. And then the plague properly took hold of the city. The Venetian provveditori alla sanità swung into action, delegating citizens in each sestiere to monitor the cases in their area, keeping count of infections and deaths, boarding up houses where plague victims lived, working out whom they had been in contact with and confining them to their houses. Whole streets and sections of the city were closed off, with no trade or travel allowed. Curfews were set, food markets restricted.

Churches closed as well—though priests feared God was punishing them all for lax worship, so they held processions whenever they could to make up for the lack of Masses.

It was hard for the authorities and the population alike to respond fast enough. Always there was the feeling of disbelief that things were going to be as bad as they then became. What could a cluster of deaths in a distant sestiere have to do with the rest of the city? How could that possibly affect everyone else? People died all the time. Whole families died from illness, starvation, fires. Why was this different?

But it was. Victims suffered from high fevers, loosened bowels, delirium, their bodies dotted with pus-filled buboes, and there was little anyone could do for them. Seven out of ten infected with the plague died. And it spread easily.

Orsola regarded the water that separated Murano from Venice as a blessing, protecting the Muranese and allowing them to go about their business. Furnaces still ran, goblets and mirrors and chandeliers and vases were still made. Gardens were weeded, laundry bleached, fish caught, boats retarred. Children played in the campos and women made soup. Maids swept. Men drank. Babies were made and were born. Orsola heard about all that was going on in Venice but didn't think they would have to do those things as well: quarantine, board up houses, shut down streets, burn clothes, be counted by officials. Murano was safe from all of that.

East of Murano was the island of Sant'Erasmo, where fruit and vegetables were grown, and just to its north Lazzaretto Nuovo, with its warehouses full of cargo from Damascus and Constantinople and Cairo and Marseille, waiting out their quarantines. More ships were anchored each day in the lagoon around Sant'Erasmo, as well as smaller boats along its shores. They were for families of plague victims. Orsola's grandmother explained that if someone got sick, they were taken to Lazzaretto Vecchio, a different island off the Lido where a plague hospital had been set up. At the same time the victim's family went to live on Lazzaretto Nuovo for forty days in their own quarantine, to see if they got sick, often bringing their boat and living in it.

"The sick ones go to Lazzaretto Vecchio alone?" Orsola asked her nonna, horrified.

"If they care about their family, they don't want anyone to come with them, because it would kill them too," her nonna replied. "And by then they're so sick they don't even notice what's happening." She was shelling peas, and her hands didn't stop throughout this grim explanation. Later Orsola would remember her old thumbs splitting open the pods, the fingers stripping out the peas as she talked so matter-of-factly about death.

✧

THERE WAS A PLACE Orsola liked to walk to sometimes, to get away from family and laundry and beads—a northeastern point on Murano, reached by crossing the bridge at Santi Maria e Donato and heading alongside the Rio di San Matteo to its end where it emptied into the lagoon. It meant passing l'Omo Salvadego, a raucous taverna where Marco sometimes drank, but past it she could sit on the deserted riva and look north toward the mountains on the mainland. Even in summer they sometimes had snow on their tips, and Orsola wondered about them. She did not want to live on terraferma, but she was curious what it would be like so high up, surrounded by so much land.

One day as she sat on the riva, Orsola heard footsteps behind her and turned to see Antonio come to a halt, clearly surprised to find her there. She snorted. "Following me, are you?"

He smiled, but it was dimmer than usual. "I come here sometimes, to look out. At the mountains, and elsewhere." His eyes were drawn to Lazzaretto Nuovo, just about visible.

Orsola nodded toward the island. "There are more boats there every day. Poor souls."

Antonio flinched, and then she understood what he was looking for, and wished she could stuff her words back in her mouth. She didn't apologize—that would make it worse—but softened what she said next. "Have you heard from your family?"

Antonio kept his eyes on the tiny boats moored around Lazzaretto Nuovo. He must be looking for his father's. "Not for a few weeks. Menego saw them then and told me. They were all right so far. But he probably won't row over here now."

"Where do they live?"

"San Polo, not far from the Frari. Where we first met."

Orsola blushed. So he remembered that meeting. He had never mentioned it before.

She didn't know what to say about his family that would be comforting, so she crossed herself and looked toward the mountains. "Have you ever been there? To terraferma?"

Antonio sat down beside her, dangling his legs, as she was, over the side of the riva, the water a few feet below. "Once. I went hunting boar. I had never done such a thing."

"In the mountains?"

"No. In woods near the sea."

"What was it like?"

He smiled, happier now while remembering. "Strange when you're out of sight of the sea. I kept looking around for water."

"What were the people like?"

"Not so different from us."

"From you, you mean."

Antonio laughed. "How long must I live on Murano before I'm Muranese?"

"You'll never be Muranese."

"I thank God for that every day."

Orsola swatted his arm.

"The people on terraferma are . . . faster," he said. "We—Venetians and Muranese—are cut off from the rest of the world. Things move more slowly for us."

"Yes. Well, I like it here. I don't want to change."

"Do you never wonder about the places the glass goes to? Amsterdam. Paris. Seville. London. What those cities are like? I imagine the glasses we make gracing a table in Paris, under a Muranese chandelier. Are the people admiring the glass they're drinking from and wondering who made it?"

Orsola was startled that they had similar visions of the glass they made being used or worn. "More likely they're just getting drunk." She paused. "I've imagined such tables too," she confided. "And ladies sitting around them, wearing my beads."

Antonio kept his eyes on the mountains, but he was smiling. "What kind? Those with gold leaf inside?"

"How do you know about those?"

"I watched you making them one day. You were so intent, you didn't notice me."

"What color were they?"

"A deep blue green, like the lagoon, then gold leaf, then clear glass."

That had been good work. She would not have wanted him to watch her when she was tired and couldn't control the glass.

"You're doing well, Orsola. Menego overheard Klingenberg say so. And I can see it myself."

She flushed a hot red that felt like being close to a furnace. It was as hard to take a compliment from him as it would have been to hear criticism. She tried to think of something clever or cutting to say, but nothing came to mind. "How is your butcher girl?" was the best she could manage.

"She'll do. For now."

Orsola jumped up. "I can't sit here all day." She turned to go, wondering if he might follow, but he remained where he was, looking across the water toward terraferma. "You know you can't go there," she said. "Apart from time moving faster, there are laws. Murano glassmakers have to stay here, to guard our ways of working. They send people after you if you try. To kill you."

"So I hear." But he kept his eyes on the mountains.

Don't you dare, she thought. I will kill you myself.

✧

As had been the case the previous summer, it seemed the plague would remain in Venice and leave them alone. Its presence was like a fly trapped in a curtain and making a muffled buzz but never emerging into the open. Marco directed the workshop as usual, but Klingenberg suspended business, as everything was delayed—shipping and payments and new orders. There was still plenty of food, from the Rosso garden and for sale in the market from Sant'Erasmo. There was less wine, less olive oil, fish only from the lagoon rather than the sea. But they managed. Orsola made her beads for Klingenberg and stockpiled them for when things got better. Time passed in its unpredictable way.

Then the fly trapped in the curtain found its way out into the room.

One of the messengers got it first, a boy who assumed he was immortal and wanted the large fee promised for taking a note from a Muranese man to his mistress in the City of Water, despite boats now being prohibited from going back and forth between the islands. By the time he fell ill, his mother had already been to the market and infected Bruno's mother. She succumbed so quickly there wasn't even time to take her to the plague hospital on Lazzaretto Vecchio. Two health magistrates had been appointed for Murano, and they sent Bruno and the rest of his family to Lazzaretto Nuovo. That evening Orsola went to Riva di San Matteo to see if she could spy Bruno's gondola. His flirting and swearing were annoying but also a part of her life, and she couldn't bear to think of him stuck there. But the boats all looked like specks from where she was standing.

Almost overnight tavernas were shut, and markets limited to essentials. The market in Campo Santo Stefano was subdued by Bruno's mother's death, and the subsequent deaths of a few of her customers, so that people didn't stay to chat, but tucked away their purchases and hurried back home.

The Rosso furnace remained on, though Marco sent the garzonetti home. The men continued to work, but the family cut back on seeing other people. Orsola and her mother no longer took the children to Campo San Bernardo to play but kept them in the Rosso courtyard. Little Stella wasn't happy about being locked in and found multiple occasions to escape, racing through calles almost as fast as Orsola could run. "She'll be a nightmare when she's older, that one," Laura Rosso grumbled as Orsola brought back her unruly sister once more, tucked under her arm and kicking.

They told Maddalena to go out only for food, though she insisted on visiting her mother as well. Paolo stopped going home to his parents and began to sleep in a room off the workshop. Antonio and the other garzoni were also told to stay close, though it was hard to keep young men at home when there were boats to be rowed and young women to be found.

Nicoletta was pregnant again, with the baby due at the end of the summer, and remained mostly at home, nursing her swollen ankles and the creases where her thighs met her groin, painful now that her belly was big. Orsola tried to be patient, but one day when Laura Rosso had taken Stella with her to work in their garden, she asked Nicoletta to look after Marcolin so that she could make beads. Her sister-in-law was lying across a bench in the courtyard, fanning herself with a handkerchief, and gazed at her with big eyes. "Oh, I don't think I can," she replied, waving the cloth back and forth around her flushed face. "I'm just so hot and tired, and I can't run after Marcolin."

"Why are you having another if you can't even manage to look after the one you have?"

Then she regretted saying it, for Nicoletta flinched as if the words were a raised fist. "I—I will try." She held out her arms. "Marcolin, come to Mamma."

Marcolin did not come to his mother, but ran over to a corner of the courtyard, where a cat was chasing down a moth.

"Marcolin, no!" Orsola cried, but too late, for he had already grabbed the cat's tail. It swiped him across the face, and he ran screaming to his aunt, burying his scratches in her skirt while Nicoletta looked on helplessly.

"I'll wash his poor little face!" she cried as Orsola picked him up and carried him over to the well to do just that.

She did not make beads that day.

⋄

THEN THE FLY that had been circling the room landed in full sight on the Rosso table. The plague had arrived.

Antonio had borrowed the boat and gone out on the lagoon, bringing back two buckets of sardines for the family. Now that Venetian fishermen were no longer supplying Murano, fish were in shorter supply. The Rossos loved sardines, especially the way Maddalena managed to fry them so crispy. When she deposited a big platter on the table in the courtyard that afternoon, they all reached greedily for the tiny fishes and burned their fingers, having a long, lazy dinner for the first time in what seemed like months, ignoring for one afternoon that fly in the room. Afterward, the platter demolished, they sat at ease around the table with full bellies.

"*Grazie*, Antonio," Laura Rosso remarked, licking her fingers. "Those were delicious. So tiny the bones melt, the way they should."

She was not one to pay much attention to Antonio; Orsola suspected she felt he had wormed his way into the Rosso workshop when they were at a weak point. Perhaps this was true, though Marco and Giacomo didn't seem to hold that against him, since his work was so good. As he sat among them while they ate his fish, being praised by the matriarch, Antonio seemed to belong at last, with a place at the table rather than as an outsider perched on the edge. It was a feeling that made Orsola look at him for a moment longer when he caught her eye. They smiled at each other.

That butcher's daughter's time has come to an end, she thought.

Because she was distracted, she was slower than her mother to notice when Nicoletta slumped against her husband. "Marco, catch her!" Laura Rosso's sharp words cut through the chatter. Nicoletta was lolling back and would have toppled off the bench if Marco hadn't grabbed her. Laura was at her side in a moment. "*Cara*, is it the baby?" she demanded. "Are you having pains?"

Nicoletta came to and shook her head, looking frightened and ashamed. The two bright-red spots on her cheeks reminded Orsola of her fluttering handkerchief the day before, and fear spiked her heart.

Laura held a palm to Nicoletta's forehead. "Burning."

It felt then as if the whole table were underwater, the people around it indistinct, their movements slow and uncertain, time dragging to a halt. Marco was holding his wife gingerly, as if he wanted to pull his hands away but knew he mustn't. From one moment to the next he had gone from loving to repelled husband. Giacomo and Paolo sat very still, leaning against each other, Paolo with his bald head bowed as if praying, Giacomo hugging himself, arms crossed over his chest. Antonio was gazing at Nicoletta with pity. Maddalena stood frozen, holding the empty fish platter, its weight making the line of muscle along her forearms bulge. Orsola hooked her hands around the back of her neck like a yoke and pressed her elbows together. At least the children were, mercifully, asleep, exhausted by the meal and the heat.

Her mother took a deep breath and straightened her shoulders, seeming to physically take on the burden of organizer. "Orsola and I will put Nicoletta to bed and tend to her. No one is to come near the room. Marco, you will sleep in with Giacomo. Tomorrow you work as normal. All the clothes we're wearing now, burn in the furnace. And we'll burn herbs and tar—Giacomo, get some from the boat—in the house and workshop to chase away the plague. Neighbors are doing so anyway, so we won't stand out. For *no one must know.*" She looked at each of them in turn, as if daring anyone to challenge her. "You will not say a word. If you do, they'll take Nicoletta away and maybe the rest of us too." Nicoletta gave a little moan. "We must act as normal as we can, but keep to ourselves. No passeggiata in the evening. *Avete capito bene?*"

Everyone understood.

Laura Rosso turned to Maddalena. "You can go back to your mother if you want."

Maddalena's face flashed with hope and confusion. She set the platter down. "Signora, I cannot—" She stopped, unsure of what she could not do.

Laura appraised her with a look, then decided for her. "Go home to your mother. But not a word as to why. Make up something."

Maddalena nodded, then burst into tears.

Next Orsola's mother addressed Antonio. "I have a job for you—a risky one. Can you get to Venice to buy some Venetian Treacle? It will be hard to find, as it's in great demand. You may have to go all over the city to find any." Venetian Treacle was a potion for warding off the plague, made of many ingredients, chief among them desiccated viper. Apothecarists made batches every year, and it was meant to sit for six years before it could be used. It was likely all that was left now were newer batches that would be less effective. But they had to try whatever remedies they could.

Like Maddalena, Antonio's face ran through a range of emotions: pride, bewilderment, fear, hope. For Orsola it was plain fear she felt for him, especially when he answered, "I'll leave now, if I can take the sandolo."

Orsola felt her heart beat faster. Don't leave me, she thought.

Her mother looked to Marco. At last, a decision that as head of the family he could make. He gestured with the hand not holding up Nicoletta. "Take it."

Orsola tried to catch Antonio's eye, but his thoughts were already on more important things than her—out on the lagoon, heading to La Serenissima to find the impossible.

✧

THE NEXT WEEK Orsola was so busy she barely had time to think or eat or sleep. With Maddalena gone and Nicoletta needing constant care, it fell to her and her mother to share between them nursing, cooking, cleaning and looking after the children. Orsola preferred the household work to the nursing, which involved trying to get Nicoletta to eat and drink, pressing damp cloths to her brow, washing her when she lost control of her bowels and calming her when she became agitated, which grew worse as the illness sank deeper into her.

In health Nicoletta had been delicate, but now at times she grew so excited she thrashed about and hit whoever was with her, as if trying to fight off the plague. This went on day and night.

There was so much work to do and no one to help that Orsola began snapping at the children and falling asleep over the soup. She found Stella particularly trying, for her tiny sister liked to run up and down the calle and rebelled against being shut up inside the courtyard. One day Orsola lost her temper and slapped Stella after she pulled all the leaves off the basil plants and mashed them into a fragrant ball. Giacomo witnessed the slap and stepped across to his squalling sister and his baffled nephew—for Marcolin was trying to decide whether to join in the crying—picked them up, gave Orsola a look and took them to stay at Nonna and Zia Giovanna's. Orsola felt terrible, especially when she told Laura Rosso and Nicoletta that the children were gone. The two mothers looked at Orsola, then at each other and then down at their hands. They had not had the chance to say goodbye to their children, whom they might not see again. Then Laura sighed. "It's better for them," she declared. "Safer. They won't get sick there."

Orsola was also relieved, for now it was easier to look after the house and Nicoletta. Children were such a huge demand on time and energy, especially when there was no one else to hand them on to when you were busy or tired. For the first time she understood why Maria Barovier might not have had them. As Elena Barovier once told her, the beads they made became their children, spread around the world.

She still went out to the market, to the garden, to Mass—for Murano churches were not yet closed—and it was a relief to escape the confinement of the house. She kept her interactions brief, while also trying to act as if nothing was wrong, so as not to arouse the suspicion of the authorities watching out for the plague.

As the days passed and Antonio didn't return and Nicoletta grew worse—with blackening buboes appearing on her arms and neck—Orsola became despondent. Without the Venetian garzone and the children and Maddalena, the house was too quiet. Marco, Giacomo and Paolo went about their work, though with grim faces and little chat or singing or whistling.

Marco visited his wife once a day, remaining in the doorway. Nicoletta's breath was foul now, and despite the tar and wool being constantly burned, the room stank of shit and festering sores. Orsola and Laura Rosso were getting used to it, but Marco turned pale and breathed through his mouth.

Nicoletta continued feverish and agitated, but whenever Marco appeared, she made an effort to brighten for him. "*Mi dispiace tanto, amore mio,*" she whispered, holding out her hands to her husband as she apologized. He looked awkward and embarrassed, and did not step forward to take them.

"What news of Marcolin?" she persisted, letting her hands drop back on the bed but evidently trying to forge a link between them over their shared love of their son.

"*Bene, bene,* he's fine. I must get back to work." Marco left abruptly—angry either at his wife for being ill, at God for allowing it to happen or at himself for being weak and scared.

One night it took both women to hold Nicoletta down as she thrashed about, fighting the fever. At last she had exhausted herself and fell into a light sleep, occasionally moaning. It was hot in the room, but they kept a candle burning so that they could see her. Orsola watched her sister-in-law's shallow panting, which barely moved the great pudding belly of baby that rose from her ravaged body.

"She's not going to survive, is she?" she whispered to her mother, though it was unlikely that in her fevered state Nicoletta would take in the words.

Laura Rosso frowned. "Don't say that. People recover from the plague. I've heard that some in Venice have, and we're much stronger than Venetians. We must make her as comfortable as we can. She's carrying your nephew, after all."

"It might be a girl."

"It will be a boy. *Allora*, where's Antonio? He's been gone four days. We need that Venetian Treacle."

"It's probably hard to find, as you said," Orsola answered, defending him. "Perhaps he's gone to see his family." She did not voice her fear that he had fallen ill himself.

"He owes his attention to us who are teaching him his trade, not to his family." Laura wouldn't normally have spoken so bitterly, but she was clearly exhausted.

"Go and sleep for a bit, Madre," Orsola said. "Nicoletta's asleep herself. I'll sit with her."

Her mother nodded, and lay down on a pallet in the corner that they took turns using. She dropped off immediately.

Orsola sat in the dim light, listening to the two women breathing, one long and deep, the other short and shallow. There were many things she could be doing: scrubbing pots, washing soiled sheets, picking over beans and soaking them. Not making beads, though. She was far from that. Instead she closed her eyes and willed Antonio to come home.

✧

THE BANGING AT the courtyard door was not a surprise, for Marco was expecting a load of wood to be delivered from terraferma. Orsola turned from the sheets she was stirring in a cauldron and ran to the workshop. "Wood's here!" she shouted, then hurried back to open the door onto the street.

She hesitated, however, for their wood supplier usually brought his peata full of logs to the dock at the back of the workshop and called out as he arrived—though the plague had turned everything upside down. Was she imagining a heavy silence behind the door? She had no choice but to open it.

Perhaps she should have been more prepared for what she saw, but Orsola hadn't allowed herself to think ahead too much. She took a step back and hugged herself. A plague doctor stood in the calle.

She had heard about them but not actually seen one. He wore a long leather robe and gloves, a flat leather hat and a beaked mask stuffed with herbs to protect him. No part of him was uncovered. He looked like a walking bird man, with little left that was human. He was the embodiment of childhood nightmares, and Orsola was glad Stella and Marcolin weren't there to see him or they would have woken up screaming in their beds for months. She pointlessly wondered which maestro had made the glass domes that covered his eyes.

Beside him was the butcher whose daughter Antonio had been seeing; he had been appointed the health magistrate for Murano, charged with keeping track of the spread of the plague on the island. Next to him a man was already painting a red cross on their door, while another dumped a pile of boards by the windows and pulled a handful of nails from his tunic pocket, ready to board them up.

"*Mariavergine*," Orsola breathed, stepping back and crossing herself several times, as if the more she repeated the gesture, the more power it would have to protect her family from this visitation.

"Signorina Rosso, may we come in?" the butcher said gently enough, though it was clearly not a question.

Orsola could barely look at him, for she couldn't take her eyes off the plague doctor.

She stood frozen for a moment. Behind her someone drew in a sharp breath. She glanced back: Marco, Giacomo and Paolo had come out of the workshop and were hovering in the yard, staring at the plague doctor. Over their shoulders she spied Antonio hurrying through the workshop from the back dock, looking pleased with himself. When he saw the figures of the butcher and the plague doctor, though, he stopped dead, as if a ghost had crossed in front of him, and his satisfaction turned to horror. Orsola jerked her head at him to get out of sight before she let the men in.

"Stand aside, signorina," the butcher said.

Orsola stepped back as Marco came forward. Even her brother looked intimidated. She didn't wait to listen to what the butcher would say; she already knew. Instead she ran back to the storage room with its shelves of glassware, where Antonio was waiting. "Don't come out!" she hissed. "If the butcher sees you, he'll make you go to Lazzaretto Nuovo with us."

"Here." Antonio handed her a package. "I had to sneak to terraferma for it, hiding out. That's why it took so long."

"*Grazie*. But now you must go. Save yourself." Orsola was trying not to cry. "Go out the back, take the boat. And find my grandmother and aunt, tell them what has happened. Tell them to keep the children."

Antonio hesitated, then nodded. "*Mi dispiace*, Orsola. I'll do all I can for you." He backed up, as if he couldn't bear to turn away from her. But in the end he did turn away, and slipped through the workshop out to the sandolo. She watched him go, her throat tight.

Marco was arguing with the butcher in the courtyard. "She's ill from the pregnancy, that's all! She'll be fine soon. No need for you to go scaring her with this." He waved his hand at the plague doctor's costume.

"Bring her out."

"She's too tired. I won't do that to my wife."

"Bring her out," the butcher repeated. "We won't go inside where the miasma is worse."

They continued to argue while Giacomo and Paolo and the plague doctor stood silent. For all his bluster, Marco knew he was going to lose; he was simply putting off the inevitable for a few moments longer.

"Who told you Nicoletta is ill?" he demanded. "Whoever it was, they don't know what they're talking about."

"Your servant, Maddalena, died this morning," the butcher said.

Orsola gasped.

"Her mother is ill now," the butcher added. "She told us who gave it to her daughter. I need to speak to Nicoletta to trace where she's been, so we can isolate those people."

"She hasn't been anywhere," Orsola interjected. "Her ankles are swollen, so she's been here for weeks. Maybe Maddalena gave it to her rather than the other way round."

"Bring her down so we can examine her." The butcher looked tired. Orsola suspected that in a month he too would be dead, a casualty of this unwanted job.

She looked at Marco. He was grimacing as if he had a pain in his gut. When at last he gave a tiny nod, she went upstairs to the bedroom.

Nicoletta was, mercifully, asleep. Laura Rosso was stuffing sheets into a sack. "Get some candles, some herbs, some pitch," she ordered. "I must think what food to take—not that she's eating much anyway. But I'll need it."

Orsola froze. "Madre? No!"

Her mother's eyes pierced like two nails. "You think I'm going to let them take her in this condition without me? Who will look after her? Who will look after my grandson when he's born?"

"But—no one comes back from there," Orsola whispered, in case Nicoletta was actually awake.

"They do! They do," Laura repeated more quietly. "*We* will come back from there."

"But we need you. What about Stella? She needs her mother."

113

"You'll be fine. And Stella has you." Laura sat on the bed and gently shook Nicoletta awake. "*Mia cara*, it's time. We have to go, you and I, like I told you we would."

Nicoletta opened her eyes and gazed at her mother-in-law. "Do we?"

"*Sì*. But don't worry, I'll be with you."

Laura pulled Nicoletta into a sitting position. The women had changed her into a clean nightdress earlier, almost as if they had known she would be making a public appearance and needed to be presentable. Orsola's mother helped her swing her feet over the side of the bed. "Wait," Orsola said, and grabbed a comb to run it through Nicoletta's greasy, matted hair. It didn't make much difference, but she felt she had to do something.

"*Grazie*, Orsola," Nicoletta whispered. "You have always been good to me."

I haven't, Orsola thought. She had been dismissive of her sister-in-law, finding her frailty irritating. Now, though, Nicoletta was strangely dignified, getting to her feet and with the women's support slowly but steadily walking across the room. It made Orsola let out a sob, which she stifled when her mother gave her a look.

With difficulty they got her down the stairs and into the courtyard. There Nicoletta's courage failed when she saw the plague doctor, and she shrieked and tried to stagger away. Orsola and her mother got her to a bench, where Laura Rosso managed to calm her. Marco didn't go to his wife, but stood off to one side.

When Nicoletta stopped screaming, the doctor stepped up to her and took her wrist in his gloved hand to check her pulse. He used a long stick he carried to poke at her nightdress, pulling it back to reveal the blackened lesions he had been looking for on her neck and arms. He nodded at the butcher and stepped back.

"Signora Rosso, I need to know where you've been and who you've seen," the butcher explained, sitting down at the table and pulling out quill and ink and paper. "Who have you bought things from? Who have you chatted to in the campo during the passeggiata? Whose babies have you kissed? Who sat with you at Mass?"

Nicoletta gazed at him in bewilderment, each question confusing her more. Orsola wondered if she even understood what he was asking. But after a moment she answered him, slowly and with long pauses in between phrases to catch her breath, but clearly enough. "I've been here . . . for weeks . . . My ankles . . . No passeggiata. No Mass. I've only been with . . . them." She waved at the courtyard in general, but when she looked around, she seemed to be calculating. "Everyone here, and . . ."

"Who else?"

No, Orsola thought. Don't say his name.

"Maddalena," Nicoletta said.

Orsola let out the breath she had been holding.

"She will tell you," Nicoletta added. "Lovely Maddalena . . . She made sardines . . . Where is she?"

No one looked at her. "Anyone else?" the butcher prompted.

Nicoletta's sunken cheeks were flushed, her eyes beginning to glaze, and she was shivering. "Where is Maddalena?" she cried. "Where are the children?"

"Yes, the children," the butcher agreed. "Where are they?"

"Leave them be," Laura Rosso intervened. "They're safe with my mother."

"They may have to quarantine. As for this family, you must go—"

"Let's discuss that," Marco interrupted.

Nicoletta was shaking so much her teeth rattled. "So cold," she whispered. "I want my fur."

Laura hesitated, for the fur had been hers and was precious to the family. Then: "Go and get it," she said to her daughter. "They'll just insist on burning it anyway if we don't take it."

Orsola ran into the house to get the fur from the cedar chest it was stored in, worrying that if she stayed away too long Nicoletta would mention Antonio to the butcher.

Indeed, as she hurried back into the courtyard, Nicoletta was nodding at the different places around the table where they had eaten the sardine meal. When she reached Antonio's place she stopped, puzzling over whom she was forgetting. Then her face lit up with the memory.

"Nicoletta, your fur!" Orsola threw it around her sister-in-law's shoulders.

"Oh!" Nicoletta reached out and stroked the fur, then buried her face in it.

The butcher waited expectantly, but Nicoletta had attention only for this one luxury that could bring her comfort.

Marco beckoned the butcher over. As they talked, Laura Rosso told Orsola what else to pack: bread, handfuls of lentils, pancetta, flour, a small pot, a knife, a bit of lye for washing. "You may need those things for you too, if they send you to Lazzaretto Nuovo," she added. "That's what your brother is negotiating—trying to keep you here. It's far better to be locked up here than go to that island. If you do, though, stay with your brothers—I've heard stories of the bored sailors there looking for entertainment to take their minds off the forty days."

It seemed Marco was successful with his negotiation. When he came back, he nodded briefly to his mother. She took his face in her hands and kissed his cheeks. "Look after the business," she said. "Make the family name one to be proud of." When she kissed Giacomo she said, "Look after your sisters." Orsola threw her arms around her mother and held on to her as if that would keep her at home. "Look after the children," Laura said, prying her daughter's hands off her.

Orsola took a shaky breath, then remembered, and handed her the Venetian Treacle. "Antonio got it," she whispered.

Laura nodded and added it to the sack. Then she went over to Nicoletta, who was sitting in a feverish daze. "*Andiamo, cara.* We must go now."

She helped her to her feet. Nicoletta pulled her fur around herself, and although Laura had to support her, she managed to walk across the courtyard with more elegance than Orsola had ever witnessed in her. It seemed she had forgotten all about Marco, but when she reached the door to the street, she turned around and bowed to him. "*Addio*, Marco." Then she walked out of his life.

Orsola watched her mother and sister-in-law head down the calle, following the butcher and the plague doctor toward the Rio dei Vetrai, where a boat would be waiting to take them to Lazzaretto Vecchio. Nicoletta was leaning heavily on Laura Rosso as the little procession passed the neighbors who had come to stand in their doorways and watch. People had quickly shifted from friendly to suspicious, from a step forward to a step back, from arms extended to arms crossed.

The man with the boards and nails slammed Orsola's own door in her face. There came sounds of banging, then banging from the dock out back, where another man had come in a boat to board up that door. Then there was silence, and they were barred inside. Orsola and her brothers and Paolo looked at one another. A week ago the household had been full of people; now there were just four.

"How do we get anything?" she demanded. "We don't have enough food for forty days!"

"They've boarded up all the windows but one on the upper floor," Marco explained. "The butcher said we can use a rope and basket. Nonna will send us things."

"What about the furnace?" Giacomo asked. "Can we work?"

Marco shook his head. "We have to let it burn out, which we were going to do soon anyway, for the summer break. And we're meant to stay inside." He lowered his voice. "I paid extra for him to turn a blind eye and let us use the courtyard, but we have to keep quiet." He turned to Giacomo and Paolo. "We must prepare to shut down." As they headed back to the workshop, he called over his shoulder, "Orsola, bring the things that need to be burned before the furnace goes out."

On her own, she stood still in the courtyard for a moment, looking up at the pale-blue sky and listening to the sounds outside. It was quieter because of the plague, but she could still hear children crying, women calling to each other, boatmen whistling, and in the distance at the Ponte di Mezzo, the town crier shouting—probably already announcing the quarantine of the Rossos.

✧

ORSOLA MADE A MEAL she could not touch, but the men gulped it down as if their appetites weren't affected by what had happened. As she watched them eat, she wondered where her mother and Nicoletta were now. Lazzaretto Vecchio was a long way from Murano, around the eastern end of Venice and down next to the Lido. It would take two hours of rowing to get there. She wondered if Nicoletta would even survive the journey.

The men's talk was all of business: of the work they had not completed, of what cold glasswork they could do without the furnace on. Orsola sank inside herself, willing herself not to cry.

There were occasional thuds against the door as people threw rocks at the house, and shouts in the street of *"Demoni!"* and *"Buzaroni!"* The news of the Rosso quarantine had spread. The men seemed able to ignore it, but at last Orsola could stand it no more. "Stop it!" she shouted, racing to the door leading to the calle and pounding her fists on it. "*Bastardi!*" She heard the squeals of children as they ran away, laughing, not understanding that the next day they too might be quarantined.

Giacomo hushed her as he pulled her away. "It won't help."

"How dare they say such things, these people who were our friends yesterday. They act as if we brought the plague here deliberately! And it was Maddalena, not us!" Orsola began to cry, long, gasping sobs, tears and snot pouring down her face and dribbling off her chin.

Giacomo put an arm around her, and Paolo a hand on her shoulder, holding her until her crying subsided.

"Poor Maddalena," Orsola murmured when she got her breath back.

"Poor Maddalena was hanging about with a servant at one of the Venetian palazzos," Marco countered, gulping the last of his wine and setting his glass down near the carafe for his sister to pour more. "The *bauca* brought the plague here and poisoned my wife."

"You sound like them outside." Orsola jerked her head at the street beyond the door. "And leave the wine; we don't have much."

Marco grabbed the carafe and poured for himself. "We can get more. The problem is how to pay for it. Do you have any money?"

She stared at him. Did he know about the beads she sold to Klingenberg? "What do you mean? Of course I have no money."

"It cost us to stay here and not get sent to Lazzaretto Nuovo. That *bastardo* of a butcher gouged me. Between that and the business we'll lose from this quarantine and the plague in general, the workshop is in trouble."

Orsola thought about the money that had slowly accumulated for her over in Venice and wondered how she could get it. She couldn't send a message to Klingenberg, as no boats were allowed between the islands. They had food for only a few days, and they needed more wood, more candles and more bedding—they'd been ordered to burn the straw mattresses and any linen they'd been using; anything that might harbor the plague.

The men stayed up late in the courtyard, drinking and playing cards. Orsola slept in the room where her mother and Nicoletta had been until just a few hours before. Wrapping herself in a sheet, she lay on the hard floor and stared up at the ceiling, thinking of her father's death and how quickly their lives had changed. This plague was like that, but there was no end in sight. They had lost Maddalena, Nicoletta, Laura Rosso. Any of the rest of them could get sick too, including the children at Nonna's—and Nonna and Zia Giovanna too. Ever since Nicoletta had fallen ill, Orsola had paid close attention to her body for symptoms. Was she feverish? Were her bowels loose? Did her limbs ache? Just thinking of these things had made her feel ill. Now she lay in the room wondering if she had a fever or if it was simply the heat of a summer night.

During the next few days every headache, every tired muscle, every stomach pain, every flushed cheek made her nervous; she found herself treating her body as if it were a vase made of the thinnest glass, likely to break if jarred. The enforced idleness was equally hard. She couldn't go to the market or look after the children or bleach laundry in the fields or care for Nicoletta. There were only four to cook for, and little food to choose from. Orsola made a pot of stew from the fresh vegetables she had and hoped it would last. For the next two days she cleaned the house thoroughly with vinegar to combat the plague, and washed the clothes and bedding they hadn't burned. Once that was dealt with there was little to do. The men felt the same: after letting the furnace burn out and setting the workshop in order, they were without work except a bit of polishing and engraving, which they soon finished. Giacomo sketched some ideas for work, with Paolo watching over his shoulder, making suggestions. Otherwise they played cards or dice in the courtyard, gambling with bits of glass instead of with money.

The Rossos' lifeline to the outside world was the basket and rope dangling from the upstairs window. From that window Orsola watched what went on in the calle, keeping to the side so that no one would see her and shout abuse. Occasionally people glanced at the boarded-up house with its red cross on the courtyard door, but within a few days it was ignored, no longer a novelty.

Now that she wasn't allowed to go out, she found the calle endlessly varied and fascinating: the men going back and forth with loads of firewood and sand and ash for making glass, the fishermen delivering their catches or hauling nets and ropes and sails, women carrying bread from the baker or vegetables from their gardens or flour from the miller or meat from the butcher, children chasing one another or running errands or playing marbles or kicking a ball back and forth. The presence of the plague—specifically in their calle, but also on the island in general—made it less lively than it normally was, but people were still going about their lives and seeing one another. It made her jealous. She was grateful for the presence of Paolo and her brothers, but already she felt she needed fresh contact, the way a pond needs the flow of fresh water to keep it from stagnating.

When Zia Giovanna came on the third day of the quarantine, leading Stella and carrying Marcolin, Orsola stood fully in the window and called down to them. Stella cried out and held up her arms, as if her sister could reach down and pull her up into the house. Marcolin was less bothered, intent on a fish skeleton he'd found in the calle, squatting to inspect it. Orsola's aunt looked fearful, glancing around as if expecting neighbors to say something. She didn't stay long, but she brought bread, and promised to come back with candles, wine and vinegar. Then she dragged the children away, Stella screaming for her sister, Marcolin shouting for the fish bones Zia Giovanna made him drop. After they were gone, Orsola cried more hot tears.

That evening when they had eaten and the men were again playing cards, Orsola stood in the window, watching the sky darken and wondering what her mother and Nicoletta were doing. Were they still alive? Orsola knew Nicoletta was likely to die, but her mother was strong. She had not caught the plague while nursing Nicoletta; maybe she wouldn't on Lazaretto Vecchio.

"*Buonasera, bella,*" she heard. As she peered along the calle, Antonio stepped from the shadows. Orsola was so glad to see him that she didn't make a smart remark or pretend not to care. She called his name and leaned over the ledge to stretch out her hand, the way Stella had done with her. She couldn't reach him, but wanted to get as close to him as she could.

Antonio smiled up at her. "I heard they didn't take you away. I've brought you some things." He held up a sack. "From your aunt, what you asked for, and other things. Fish, oil, honey, some strawberries."

Orsola thanked him and lowered the basket.

"What else do you need?" he asked, packing the provisions into it.

"Sheets and straw. We had to burn them."

Antonio nodded. "Tomorrow."

Relief flooded her that he might visit every day. If he did, she could possibly get through the forty days.

"Is anyone else sick?"

He waggled his head. "Here and there. It hasn't taken over. Not like in Venice. Not yet."

His last words made her pause. "When you went looking for the Venetian Treacle, did you—your family—did they—"

He cut her off. "One brother has survived. And a niece."

"*Mi dispiace tanto,* Antonio." Orsola crossed herself.

He nodded. They were silent, looking at each other. There was so much loss in the world now. Orsola could not imagine losing her whole family.

"How are you in there?" he asked at last. "Your brothers? Paolo?"

"All right. They're playing a lot of cards. Soon they'll forget how to make glass."

"Orsola, is there any money? Your aunt has said she can't pay for the things you need."

She shook her head. "Marco has none. You know there have been fewer orders this past year with the plague, and Klingenberg has been slow to pay as well."

"Do *you* have any money?"

"You know I do. But it's with Klingenberg. I can't get to it."

Antonio chewed his lip, thinking. "Are there any works that can be traded? Any glasses or jugs?"

"I'll ask Marco, but I think they were making large vases. No one would want to trade flour or ham for something like that."

"I should go." Antonio had noticed that neighbors were poking their heads out from their windows and doors and staring.

But he didn't leave. "Where are you staying?" she whispered.

"In a shed behind your grandmother's. Staying out of sight as much as I can. But I can get around if I'm careful."

"It's awful being stuck here. I would give every bead I make to be able to go to Riva di San Matteo and look at the mountains."

Antonio gave her a funny look. "Do you have any beads?"

"About fifty, for an order. Why?"

"People might be willing to trade for them."

Orsola leaned against the sill, thinking. She had considered only getting money for the beads, not trading them for things. That was what coins were for: two soldi for a loaf of bread, five soldi for a bucket of squid, twenty soldi for a length of linen.

More neighbors were leaning out of their windows. "One soldo per bead," she said.

Antonio nodded. "*Addio*, Orsola. *A domani.*"

She watched him stride along the passage, the neighbor women turning to follow his fine legs with their eyes. Like the tide, he came close and then slid away.

The next evening he brought bedding, and she put in the basket ten white translucent beads in barrel shapes with a light-blue thread wound around them. They should pay for what he had brought so far. Antonio jiggled them in his hand. "These are beautiful." He looked up at her. "But I need ten more. People know your aunt and I are buying for the Rossos, so they're charging more."

"What? How can people take advantage of our misfortune!" Orsola was so angry she shouted it so that the neighbors would hear how she felt about being cheated by them, the butcher and the miller and the weaver and the wine seller.

"Orsola, they're terrified," Antonio said in a low voice.

"Why? They're not going to catch it by selling things to us!"

"Everyone is afraid: of catching it, or their parents or children or brothers or sisters dying." He swallowed, and she softened, remembering his family. "And of losing business. Everyone is trying to make whatever they can, to save against even harder times."

"But you're not afraid."

"How can I be afraid of you? And I'm grateful to your brother for taking me on and teaching me. I owe him that much at least."

Orsola put ten more beads in the basket. "These won't last long," she said as she lowered the rope.

"Can you make more? Do you have the glass and the tallow you need?"

Orsola hesitated. It would mean making beads in front of Marco—an activity she preferred he see little of until she was good enough at it that he would have to acknowledge her skill. So far she had managed to make her lampwork look like a hobby to him. But it seemed now there was no choice. At least it would keep her busy. She nodded.

They spoke for a little longer, Antonio catching her up on the island's news. Maddalena's mother had now died as well. Orsola's grandmother and aunt and the children were all right, though Stella was always trying to escape, and constantly asked about her mother and sister.

"Who are you talking to?" she heard behind her. Marco stepped up to the window and looked out—the first time he had done so in the four days they had been under quarantine. "Antonio! *Dime!*" He filled the window, pushing his sister to one side. Orsola didn't stay to listen to his questions about other glassworkers, the number of ships on Lazzaretto Nuovo, cases of plague in Venice and the other islands. Instead she went to see what glass she had left.

✧

THE NEXT MORNING she got out the cane, the lamp, the tallow, and set to work. The men were still asleep, since there was little else to do, but as the animal fat heated and released its rancid odor, Giacomo appeared, rubbing his face and wrinkling his nose. "How do you stand it?"

Orsola shrugged.

He cut himself a slice of bread, then stood and watched as she pumped the bellows with her foot to get the flame hot and stuck the end of a cane of white glass into it to melt it. She glanced up. Giacomo looked envious—after five days of idleness he was clearly longing to handle glass again. For a moment she considered teaching him to make beads, but there was only one lamp and set of bellows, and barely enough cane to keep her occupied—and she wanted to be occupied. And what if Giacomo turned out to make better beads than hers, since he knew glass so well? She was the beadmaker in the family; she didn't want competition.

He watched her twirl and paddle the bead into a barrel shape, then melt a thin cane of light-blue glass to wind around the barrel, replicating the beads she had given Antonio. She was not yet sure what to make to trade for goods. To start with, at least, she would walk the path she knew.

She had pushed the finished bead into a box of ash to cool and begun another when Marco thumped down the stairs. "*Mio Dio*, that smell! Stop it now! What do you think you're doing, trying to stink us out of the house with your"—he glanced at the bead forming—"trinkets?" Unlike his brother, Marco didn't look enviously at the lampwork. For him it was a complicated goblet or heavy vase or elaborate pitcher, or nothing. He would rather sleep and play cards than make a simple bead.

"It gives me something to do," Orsola answered mildly, turning the iron rod one and a half times, then back the other way, as Elena Barovier had taught her.

"Waste of glass," Marco muttered as he tore a piece of bread from the loaf and bit into it.

"Antonio needs money for the things he and our aunt bought, or he won't be able to buy more."

"Greedy *canagia*," Marco retorted, his mouth full. "He knows we have none."

She stopped turning the rod, and the bead melted off, dropping to the table. "What do you expect him to do? We're lucky he's helping us!"

Marco gave her a long look, still chewing. "Got your eye on him, *sorella*? Think again."

Orsola opened her mouth, but Giacomo shook his head behind

Marco's back. "If we don't have money, we could trade with beads instead, the way they do in Africa," he suggested.

Marco looked skeptical. "Why would anyone want beads on an island where there are already plenty?"

"Because they're well made, and beautiful." Giacomo picked up the rod from the annealing box with the new blue-and-white bead at the end, tapped the ash from it, and held it up to Marco. Marco rolled his eyes, but professional interest overtook skepticism, and he examined it with a critical eye. It was impossible to know what colors it would be yet, as it was cooling from orange to gray. But he could gauge its symmetry and the pattern drawn on it. Orsola waited, fidgeting. She'd had direct compliments from Antonio and Giacomo, and indirectly from Klingenberg. Would Marco follow suit?

"How much is it worth for barter?" he demanded at last. Acknowledging that the bead had worth was the closest he would get to complimenting his sister's work.

"Half a soldo per bead," Orsola said. "Normally it would be a whole soldo, but given our circumstances, people take advantage."

Marco narrowed his eyes. "Normally? What do you know about the price of beads?"

She shifted in her seat. "I sell a few here and there. I've been making them for a while now. You know that. You didn't think I would make them just for myself?"

Clearly Marco had given no thought at all to her beadmaking. Nor did he now, beyond saying, "Make enough to keep us fed." He didn't thank her or praise her, but it was enough that he had agreed.

✧

ORSOLA MADE AS MANY BEADS as she could for Antonio to use for trade, but she quickly ran out of cane. There was glass in the workshop, but it had been made for use in the hot furnace in great lumps, and her weak lamp had little effect on it. One evening she sent the last of the beads down in the basket to Antonio. "That's all," she said. "There's no more unless I get more cane. But I have nothing to buy it with. The cane makers won't sell any to us on credit."

Antonio was squatting by the basket, counting out the beads. "There's no one else you could ask?"

Orsola paused. "Elena Barovier. She might help."

Antonio nodded.

The next day there was a whistle outside, and she hurried to the window, keen to see Antonio. But it was Stefano, the Barovier servente, carrying a bundle of cane in various colors. As Orsola lowered the basket, Stefano looked around, as if to gauge who might be watching—though no one was, for the neighbors had grown bored of keeping watch over a quarantine family. They had stopped throwing rocks at the house, stopped reciting dirty couplets about the Rossos, stopped peeing against the door.

When he had secured the glass with rope, she hauled it up. The canes were of a palette that must have been chosen by Elena Barovier—mainly blues and greens and white, but a blood red as well, for Rosso. She had added a bit of her own taste too: a few canes of various diameters in yellow, a color Orsola rarely used.

"Thank Elena for me," she called down. "Tell her I'll pay her back as soon as I can."

Stefano nodded. Now that his deed was done, he seemed disinclined to leave. He stared up at her, his black eyes concerned, though he said nothing.

"How are things out there?" she asked. "Are the Baroviers safe?"

"Sì."

"Have others fallen ill? Or been quarantined?" Orsola felt as if she were on a boat floating away and throwing out a rope for him to catch and pull her toward shore.

But Stefano did not catch the rope. He simply nodded goodbye and loped off.

It was Antonio who told her that evening that five other houses had been quarantined, mainly glassworkers on the other side of the Rio dei Vetrai. One house was not far from Laura Rosso's family.

"What about my grandmother and aunt? And the children?" she demanded.

"They're all right."

"Have you seen Domenego? If only he could get word to Klingenberg somehow to send my money!"

Antonio shook his head. "But I have an idea. People like your beads. The color, the shape, the pattern. When someone picks them up, they want to hold them, keep them rather than sell them on. I handed over your beads to the old woman selling wine, and she held one between her finger and thumb and kept rubbing it. The next time I saw her she was still rubbing it."

"Like a rosary."

"*Sì, così.* Then I saw another woman doing the same thing. The baker's wife. When I asked her, she said she was holding on to it to keep the plague at bay. You haven't fallen ill. She thinks she won't either if she holds your bead."

Orsola had worried about the opposite: that no one would take her beads because they'd been made in a quarantined house. Now, however, they were being assigned magical properties. *She* was being assigned magical properties.

"You could make them," Antonio continued. "Beads specially to ward off the plague. With a unique design, to sell."

"But—I'm not sure that's how the plague works. Venetian Treacle is one thing—it has ingredients in it that might help. Dried viper and cinnamon and honey. But glass is glass. It's beautiful, but it's not a cure."

"Isn't comfort a kind of cure?"

Orsola still hesitated. "It is taking advantage of fear."

"But you need the money to keep your family going. Your aunt and grandmother have nothing left. They've asked me to tell you they need help from you to feed the children."

Orsola was pragmatic about her beads. It was one thing to wear them with pride around one's neck at a feast in a palazzo, or to sew them onto a mask for Carnevale. That was not magic, it was preening. But to carry one for protection was more like witchcraft. She wished her beads did save people, but she knew they wouldn't. However, comfort in the face of fear was something. She thought of her mother, caring for Nicoletta on that terrible island boatmen avoided because of the groans and the stench. If Laura Rosso had a bead to clutch, would that help?

"All right," she said. "I'll have something ready in two days."

✧

SHE THOUGHT ABOUT THE DESIGN for much of the night, as it was too hot to sleep. She knew what the shape would be: ulivetta spoletta, round in the middle and tapered at the ends, like a large pistachio or an olive. It felt natural rolling such a shape between the fingers—symmetrical but with an unpredictable element too. The surface would be completely smooth, as that was more comforting to the touch.

Deciding on the color was harder. She preferred red, the color of life itself. But the color of blood might remind people too much of illness—coughing it up, shitting it out. Blue and green were the colors of water—a part of daily Muranese life. Orsola did not want that to

be affected by association. She could use white—the color of purifica-
tion. But she was drawn to the yellow Elena Barovier had included.
The color of heat, of the fires that burned everywhere now to chase
away the miasma.

Early the next morning she began to work, making a few plain
opaque yellow beads for practice, but she sensed another color was
needed as well. A little bit of black, for the plague that was to be
driven out. Elena Barovier had not sent any, but she found a thin cane
of it in a corner of the workshop. She tried adding black dots all over
the yellow, but they looked too much like buboes. She tried stripes,
but it reminded her of bumblebees. The black needed to be present
but not so insistent.

She made a small black bead, then gave it an outer layer of translucent yellow, but the black was too visible. A layer of opaque yellow
rendered it invisible.

Frustrated, Orsola sat back and stretched her aching arms. She
needed another's eye.

Paolo was the first of the men to get up. Quiet and steady, he was
the silent muscle of the workshop, hefting punties with molten glass
on the ends back and forth between furnace and workbench, blowing
into the tubes while Marco or Giacomo shaped the glass, ferrying
pieces to the annealer. He wasn't particularly creative, but he was
practical. Orsola would not normally have asked his advice, but when
he glanced over her shoulder at her work, she found herself explaining her struggle.

Paolo was silent for so long that she began tidying the table around
her, gathering up cane and sweeping the excess bits into a pile. "The
bead needs to be hopeful, beautiful," he said at last.

"Shouldn't it refer to the plague in some way?"

He just looked at her, and his silence forced her to think. What
would people want in their pocket to ward off the plague? Not

something to remind them of it, but something simple and life-affirming. She had overcomplicated the design by adding black.

She started again, and made an ulivetta spoletta bead larger and fatter than the first ones, because it was about the comfort of holding it, so it needed heft. She used translucent yellow cane, for people couldn't see far ahead or know what would happen during the epidemic, but they needed to sense a hint of light shining through the glass. That was the beauty of translucence—the clarity and mystery at the same time. She added inside the bead a swirl of opaque yellow that looked like the smoke people were creating to chase away the plague. Orsola was so pleased with the result that the next day when it had cooled she gave the first one to Paolo in thanks. He smiled and took it over to Giacomo to admire.

Antonio was surprised by the yellow plague beads, perhaps expecting something more elaborate. But he began selling them for five soldi—the price of a chicken—and for several days they were popular, enough to provide Orsola and her brothers and the children with plenty of chickens.

But then the plague really took hold, sweeping across Murano so that most houses were placed under quarantine and many families sent to the Lazzaretti islands, and the community's brief belief in the magic of the beads waned.

Orsola already knew there was no magic in them, for five days after she gave Paolo the first yellow bead, Giacomo found him dead in his bed, the illness having crept in and taken him in the night. Orsola never forgot the wail that erupted from her kind, quiet brother, so loud it must have razed his throat. She and Marco ran to Paolo's room and found Giacomo clinging to his teacher's body and weeping. "No, Giacomo, no," she murmured, trying to pull his hands away. "You mustn't, it will make you ill."

"I want to get it!" her brother cried. "I want to die too!"

"No, you don't, of course you don't."

"I do!"

Marco pulled his brother back. "*Basta!* We must stick together, or the family will fall apart." Giacomo kept his eyes squeezed tight, sobbing, but Orsola nodded at her older brother. For the first time she found Marco's firmness a strength rather than a weakness.

✧

THEN THE DAYS became even harder. With Paolo's death, they had to open up the house to deliver his body to the authorities. The butcher as health magistrate visited again. This time he didn't demand more money to let them remain at home: there were now so many people on Lazzaretto Nuovo that there wasn't space for more. But he insisted the Rossos could no longer use the courtyard, no matter how much money Marco offered—money they didn't have anyway.

He had the door leading from the house into the courtyard nailed shut with the Rossos inside, first requiring that all the clothing they were wearing and the bedding Antonio had found for them be burned. Now Orsola had only one dress left—the reddish-brown one from the material Maria Barovier had given her. She had nothing to change into while washing it, and now that they were shut into the hot, dark house, she began to stink from sweat and cooking and beadmaking. Nor could they use the privy, but had to dump pots of shit and piss out the one open window onto the street below. The whole house was rank with the smell of sewage and fear.

Now it was not just individual houses that were under quarantine: whole calles and quarters were shut down. Markets were reduced to the most basic offerings. Boats were completely banned from travel; only fishermen could go out. Masses were stopped at churches, although processions were allowed. Orsola and her brothers watched as one passed under their open window, a priest at the head carrying a cross, another behind swinging incense that now doubled as a shield against the plague. Those Muranese who were not shut in followed, chanting prayers. Some glanced up at the Rossos in the window and crossed themselves.

The health magistrates and the plague doctor were often seen walking along the calle, though the personnel changed as the plague reached them too. With each appearance the plague doctor became less sinister and more ridiculous to Orsola with his beak and his glass eyes.

She and Marco and Giacomo spent most of their time in the room with the open window. It was the only place where there was natural light and any sort of air—even the stifling summer heat. Their quarantine had been reset from Paolo's death, and Marco scratched marks into the wall to keep track. Two days, five days, ten days, twenty days. Time played its tricks, moving like a silted-up canal. Sometimes Orsola felt she was a year older when only a day had passed. She stopped caring. Even to measure it seemed absurd.

Orsola's brothers did little but sit, waiting out the days. They stopped playing cards. They stopped discussing the future or the present. Giacomo was completely silent, Paolo's death etching deep lines around his eyes and mouth.

Orsola was a little busier, keeping track of their food supplies and cooking once a day. Other than that, she made beads down in the kitchen, where it was dark except for the candles she lit. Now that she was no longer making plague beads, she could make whatever she wanted, perhaps design something new to try to cut through her dread of wondering who would be next and if the death would be quick and merciful or drawn out and agonizing. She sat for a long time, looking at the cane she had to work with, but she couldn't find inspiration in the stifling darkness, where she couldn't see the colors clearly and her mind was preoccupied with every twinge in her gut and ache in her arms and legs. The heat made it harder to think. She was used to the heat of the lamp she worked with, and of the furnace that burned your face in winter even as your back froze. But the heat of a boarded-up house—even the keyholes were sealed with rags— was overwhelming. It was so hot inside that it was hard to tell where the heat ended and her own body heat began. It was like living inside a fever, even if she didn't actually have one.

Mainly, though, she simply didn't have any inspiration. Inspiration required the stimulation of the new: new people, new places, new stories, new food. New glass. Eventually she went back to the designs she knew and could make almost with her eyes shut. There was a comfort in the familiar colors and shapes where the mechanics of lampwork kept her mind occupied enough that she didn't have to think about anything else. Orsola turned out bead after bead—plain or decorated spheres and barrels and ellipsoids. She wasn't sure what she would do with them, whether Antonio could use them for trade when so many people were under quarantine now, or if Klingenberg would even be alive to sell them for her. But it was better than simply sitting.

Now that her brothers were in the room with her, Orsola could no longer linger and talk to Antonio alone when he came with supplies a few days into the new quarantine. When she spied him, she stood in the window as before and he smiled up at her. "Wearing that dress specially for me?" he tried to joke, before Marco joined her and fired down his own questions. Antonio brought grim news: many sick, many dead, many under quarantine. It was harder to get food, as the market offerings were sparse, the shops shut.

All the while Marco was hauling up the bedding and food Antonio had brought. Orsola unpacked the basket, then pushed back in next to her brother. "Are you all right, Orsola?" Antonio asked.

She wanted to cry. She wanted to jump down from the window to the street. She wanted to say that only his visits were keeping her going—although that was not entirely true. Her beads were too. "*Sto bene,*" she confirmed. "*Grazie di tutto.*" She gestured behind her at the bedding and the bread and cheese and lentils, then held up a tiny sack. "I have beads. Will people take them?"

Antonio hesitated. "Send them down," he said. "I'll try. Tell me what you need."

She wanted to ask for something fresh and sweet, something that didn't remind her of being shut in but of the gardens and fields in the north of the island. She wanted to say, Bring flowers. Instead she remained pragmatic. "Pancetta and flour. More oil."

"Peaches," Giacomo added, peering out from the other side of Marco. It was the first word he'd said in days. Paolo had loved peaches.

Antonio brightened at the request, and Orsola wished she had thought to ask for them. It was strange to think of peaches still growing and ripening when they were stuck inside, fearing death.

"How are Marcolin and Stella?" she asked.

"Fed up. Stella ran away. I had to search for her. She'd got all the way over the Ponte Longo and was running along the fondamenta."

Orsola smiled at her mischief, but Marco grumbled, "What's the matter with Zia Giovanna that she can't look after the children?"

Antonio frowned. "She's doing the best she can. It's not easy out here."

Orsola caught her breath. A garzone was chiding his maestro. She could feel Marco bristling next to her.

Antonio did not prolong the moment, but simply said, "I'll bring what I can in a day or two," nodded at her, then turned and strode up the calle. The Rossos watched his relative freedom with envy.

"*Muso da mona,*" Marco muttered.

"Don't," Giacomo countered. "We need him."

Two days later Antonio brought them peaches and fish. He had managed to go out in a boat with Muranese fishermen and catch enough to feed the Rossos and the rest of the family. The rest he was using as currency. "I'm afraid no one wants your beads now," he added apologetically. "I'll hold on to them and see if that changes, but no need to send down more."

Reddening, Orsola tucked away the beads she had been intending to give him. It had briefly been a heady feeling, having her beads be valuable enough to feed them.

She continued to make them, though, out of habit and for something to do. Giacomo too had begun making things, whittling bits of wood into toys he sent to the children via Antonio. Only Marco could not occupy himself but pestered them, even demanding that Orsola teach him lampwork, but not lasting long at it. "What are these little pellets of glass, they're *escrementi di coniglio*," he snarled, throwing one of her iron rods across the room with a misshapen bead attached. "Rabbit turds! I want to work with enough glass that my muscles ache. I want the heat of the furnace burning my face. I want to turn a lump of glass into the finest goblet, not make little turds!"

She understood. Marco wanted the dramatic scale of the workshop, with fire and glass and men all working to the rhythm he set, with him in the center. The glass dance rather than the solo effort. Given the chance, Orsola supposed she too would like to wield a punty, to blow and shape glass into a vase or a filigreed wineglass or a chandelier. But lampwork would have to suffice. In her beads, she would make miniature worlds, which had their own satisfaction. But their value was always less, and they would never gain Marco's admiration. Orsola would never become like Maria Barovier, a respected woman glassmaker. That door remained firmly shut.

✧

ONE DAY WAS MUCH LIKE the day before and the day after. Cook, eat, clean, make beads, sweat, wait for Antonio, exchange a few words or a look with him if he came, then sleep and wait for the next day.

Only one unusual visit broke the monotony: Stefano arrived with more glass cane from Elena Barovier. Orsola thanked him as she hauled it up. While she looked through the bundle, Marco leaned out and quizzed him on the latest news. Unlike Antonio, Stefano knew more about the comings and goings of the various workshops, and though he was usually a silent man, Marco pried information from him with endless questions: not just who had died and who was quarantined, but who was selling and what they were making and whom they were copying or stealing from with their designs. It was dull fare to Orsola—she would rather know if there were more peaches to be had in the market, or if the boats had started up again between Murano and Venice, or if anyone had heard anything of the people sent to Lazzaretto Vecchio, if anyone had heard of the fates of Nicoletta and Laura Rosso.

Later that night when it was a little cooler, Marco fell asleep first and Giacomo and Orsola sat by the open window, taking in the fresh air against the backdrop of their brother's steady snoring. It was rare they could talk without Marco hearing. "Why hasn't Marco said anything about Nicoletta?" she asked. "Or Madre? Or asked Antonio about Marcolin? Doesn't he care about his own son?"

"He cares," Giacomo replied. "Marco deals with bad things by ignoring them. It's easier. He's always felt the weight of being the eldest. It's a heavy burden, made worse by Padre dying when he did, before Marco was ready. You are as harsh a judge as he is."

"I am not!"

Giacomo didn't reply, and she had to tamp down her indignation.

They were silent then, listening to their brother's snores.

"What will you do without Paolo?" Orsola found it hard to say his name.

Giacomo shook his head. There was a long pause, then he swallowed, as if pushing down grief. "I learned most of what I know from him. Especially during the night shifts when Marco wasn't there. It was easier then, less tense. Paolo was very skilled but quiet with it. And he wasn't so quiet when it was just the two of us." Giacomo paused, and looked as if he was going to say something more, but then turned away, tears running down his face.

✧

ONE DAY THE HEALTH MAGISTRATE came past, and it was a rope maker, not the butcher. That evening Antonio told them the butcher had caught the plague and been taken to Lazzaretto Vecchio. Orsola didn't ask about the butcher's daughter.

Something about the way Antonio was standing in the street, looking up at them, made her pause. "You have something more to tell us."

He nodded, then looked down at his feet so that Orsola could only see the top of his head. Finally he looked up again. "Your nonna."

A few weeks before she would have sat down, wailed, fainted. But the plague had dug deep into them all, beaten them down so that they no longer felt anything. Marco and Giacomo were silent. Orsola swallowed, then simply nodded. "What about the children? Our aunt?"

"No one is sick. But they've been quarantined, so I can't stay there now."

"Where will you go?"

"The Riva di San Matteo. I'm sleeping in the boat there."

"Where you watch the mountains."

"Where I watch the mountains."

✧

Antonio came to see them most evenings, and when he didn't, Orsola worried he was ill, that he had gone to Lazzaretto Vecchio or Lazzaretto Nuovo, or was shut up, or dead in the Rosso sandolo, or buried in one of the plague pits with dozens of others. Then she carried around a tense dread until she saw him again. She didn't tell him she was worried. It was hard enough for him to get around the island, for many streets and bridges were completely shut, and movement was discouraged. Antonio risked a fine or even banishment if he wasn't careful. He didn't complain; he seemed glad of things to do, something to help not just the Rossos but others he ran errands for. She knew the feeling, the relief at being active rather than simply waiting for something to happen.

Every time Antonio left, the three Rossos watched him walk away down the passage, envying his freedom, waiting for the day when they too could walk freely along the Fondamenta dei Vetrai, stop to eat oysters in Campo Santo Stefano, have a drink at l'Omo Salvadego, step in to Santi Maria e Donato to say a prayer or admire the floor mosaics, stroll through the gardens in the north and pick cherries or sniff at lilies of the valley, stand in Campo San Bernardo and catch up on who was fighting and who was getting married, who was having a baby and who was struggling with too many children, which workshop was pulling ahead of the others and which might go out of business, whose wine had gone sour and who had a surplus of cheese, whom the Rosso apprentice was seeing and whom he really cared for. The small, important things in life.

Marco's marks on the wall accumulated, the one concrete measurement of time passing in a floating world. No one fell sick, and suddenly it was the fortieth day of the quarantine. Orsola was low on cane, and so made just a few beads, and a fish stew with lentils Antonio had brought the night before, then sat in the window with her brothers, watching the sparse activity in the street. It was hard to imagine rejoining it, free to go out, free for Marco to start up the furnace and work again, free for the children to return, for life to resume, for time to start up again, fast or slow.

Toward the end of the afternoon the health magistrate appeared with two men to remove the boards from the windows and doors while he told them of the restrictions they must abide by: which parts of Murano were shut, the prohibition on using boats or going to Venice or the other islands or terraferma. When he finished and they left, the windows open and the door thrown wide, none of the Rossos stepped through it right away, but stood on the threshold much as they had sat in the upstairs window and looked out. Up and down the calle there were doors with red crosses on them, windows boarded up as the Rossos' had been. Orsola felt as if she had recovered from a long fever and was having to learn how to walk again after weeks in bed, and how to talk to people, and how to live.

Only when Antonio appeared at the end of the calle did she move. Then she ran, her legs weak from lack of use, but running nonetheless, dodging cats and sewage and drying ropes, carts and beggars, all the signs of life continuing that she had missed so much, running and running until she was in his arms, sobbing, not caring that Marco and Giacomo and everyone in the street could see them. All she cared about was the sure solidity of him and his arms around her.

Over Antonio's shoulder she spied a woman creeping along the calle, dressed in filthy rags, hair matted, face sunken so the bones shone through her skin. It took Orsola a moment to realize it was her mother. Laura Rosso was clutching a bundle to her chest. It opened its lungs to loudly inform Orsola that she had once again become an aunt.

3

YOU HAVE SKIMMED THAT flat stone well and true across the lagoon's surface. Another skip and it touches down in 1631. Time *alla Veneziana* in action once more.

The plague has run its course, as plagues do, killing almost a third of the population of Venice. This will happen again and again. Luckily other things are also happening in the world. Shakespeare, for instance. The Bard even sets two plays in Venice; did he ever visit and buy a glass bauble? Galileo tells people they aren't the center of the universe. (This does not go down well.) Caravaggio masters chiaroscuro and kills someone. In Europe the complicated Thirty Years' War begins. Across the Atlantic lands are starting to be colonized. A myth grows that the Dutch have bought the island of Manhattan from the Lenape tribe for some trinkets and a handful of—yes—beads. It is so tempting to imagine they are Orsola Rosso's. But no. And the Lenape have a different sense of ownership; to them no one owns the land for it to be bought and sold.

Closer to home, Venice's reign as the center of trade is truly over. The City of Water is gently coming down to earth with a bump, but that bump will never wholly dislodge its Renaissance glory. And the

Island of Glass artisans are still acknowledged as the best glassmakers in the world.

At the kitchen table, Orsola is absorbed in turning back and forth in the flame a translucent yellow bead cloaking a swirl of opaque yellow. She looks up. Fifty-six years have passed in the outside world, and another plague has just begun to subside, but she and those who matter to her are no older . . .

✧

NICOLETTA, MADDALENA, NONNA, PAOLO. Four holes in the Rosso family to be filled.

The most urgent replacement was for Nicoletta: her baby needed feeding. Orsola took Raffaele—as his grandmother had named him—from Laura Rosso's skeletal arms and, despite having been quarantined inside for almost two months, walked him straight over to Campo San Bernardo to find the wet nurse they had used for Stella. Orsola had no idea whether the woman was still alive, or had a baby and milk to spare, but it was all she could think of to do.

Monica Vianello *was* alive, *did* have a baby—Rosella—and took Raffaele to her breast without hesitation. Monica was a fisherman's daughter, with a weathered face from working outside repairing nets and scarred hands from gutting fish. Her eyes were shaped like narrow almonds and colored a startling crystal blue, and she always wore an old blue dress that matched them. You would expect a wet nurse to have big breasts, but hers were small and hard, though she produced a prodigious amount of milk. Soon she came to live with the Rossos, for the plague had killed her husband and older child, and it was easier to keep her close by rather than bring Raffaele back and forth.

Monica fed Nicoletta's son, but what Orsola hadn't reckoned on was the wet nurse replacing Nicoletta in Marco's bed as well. When

Monica came out of his room one morning just a week after moving in, Orsola nearly dropped the pile of sheets she was carrying. The wet nurse glanced at her, then headed to her own room, where she attached both crying babies to her breasts and sat in the window looking out over the courtyard while they sucked. There was something so fierce about her that Orsola didn't dare question what she had been doing with Marco. They married as soon as they found a priest still alive.

Antonio laughed when Orsola told him about Monica and Marco. "I'm not getting drawn into the maestro's affairs," he said. "I'll stay out of his, and I hope he stays out of mine."

Giacomo shrugged when she told him. "It's a convenient solution. Marco needs a wife and a mother for the children, and she is there and she has the milk."

Orsola said nothing to her mother, knowing she would be horrified when she found out Nicoletta had been that easily replaced. Laura Rosso had returned so depleted from Lazzaretto Vecchio that she was almost unrecognizable. Orsola and Monica did what they could to try and fatten her up, but she had little interest in food. Her eyes were haunted by what she had witnessed there, and nothing could chase away those memories. Laura did not talk about her ordeal; all she would say was that it had been a blessing when Nicoletta died because it ended her suffering. The only thing that relieved her momentarily of the horror was Raffaele, who would always be her favorite grandchild.

The next hole in the family that needed plugging was poor Maddalena. This took longer, for many were fearful of stepping into a family affected by the plague. For a time, the Rosso women had to manage between them—Laura weak and low, Monica with her arms full of babies, Orsola run off her feet. Once again, there was no time for beads. It was just as well that it took months before business returned to normal and Klingenberg began placing orders again.

Eventually Monica convinced a cousin from her extended family to step in and help the Rossos. Isabella Vianello was another fisherman's daughter, quiet and hardworking, with a sideways glance that could kill if you were its target. She and Monica were nothing like Maddalena, who had been as soft as bread, crying easily and involving herself in every family drama. The Vianello cousins were more like fishhooks, sharp and glittery—productive when on your side, deadly when not.

Within a few weeks of moving in, Isabella too had secured herself a Rosso brother. After following her out of his room one morning, Giacomo looked dazed and a little confused, as if the sun glistening on the water were blinding him. This time Orsola didn't say anything to anyone, for these fisherwomen were no longer surprising her. And they were needed. Once Monica and Isabella took over, they ran the household far more efficiently than Maddalena ever had, though Isabella's cooking was less refined. Although she came from a fishing family, her sardines were never as tasty as Maddalena's had been.

Although Nonna was irreplaceable, she seemed to have climbed out of her own body and entered her younger daughter. Zia Giovanna had aged considerably during the quarantine, the lines on her face deeper, her hair grayer than Laura Rosso's even though she was the younger sister. When Giovanna brought Marcolin and Stella home after their quarantine ended, Stella ran from her without a word, and she handed over the boy, turned and hurried away without staying to eat or talk, not even to her sister. The next day Laura went to see her, bringing food, and came back sooner than expected, saying Giovanna would not talk except to announce that she was tired and wanted to sleep. It was like that for some: coming out of quarantine was almost harder than being in it. When locked in, there were few decisions to make: all you could do was to wait and keep yourself alive in the meantime. Once out, suddenly there was freedom, and with it, choices.

Both children came back changed. They had witnessed at close hand the death of Orsola's grandmother, and their subsequent quarantine with her aunt had marked them, though in different ways. Marcolin had become so accustomed to being inside that he now found open spaces frightening, preferring to remain in the kitchen or the glass storeroom or just inside the workshop. He screamed whenever Orsola took him to the market, or out on the water, or into a campo to play with other children. He was nervous of public spaces, of crowds, shying away from anyone standing too close to him, his dark eyes as fearful as his mother Nicoletta's had been.

Stella was the opposite: the confinement had made her even more determined to be outside, preferably with no one knowing where she was. The family had to keep the door to the calle locked or she would get out and run off. She still did, waiting for someone to go in or out and darting past them. Once Giacomo found her in the boat moored out back, struggling with her tiny fingers to unpick the knots in the rope so that she could float away. Eventually the Rossos gave up and let Stella have the run of the island, young as she was; it was easier. Orsola suspected her sister would always be the runner in the family—the messenger, the one to fetch someone or something. The one to run off, to Venice, or worse—to terraferma.

✧

ORSOLA SPENT HER DAYS searching for food, doing laundry, looking after Marcolin and Stella, reviving the Rosso garden—growing what little she could during the autumn—tending to her recovering mother, plowing through all the work so that when everything was done and cleaned and put away and the children and Laura Rosso were asleep and the Vianellos had taken her brothers to bed to entertain them—then she could slip away with Antonio. Sometimes they went to the

Riva di San Matteo, where it was quiet and far enough from home that all the strings of obligation that pulled at them began to loosen. Other times Antonio took her out on the lagoon in the sandolo, rowing around Sant'Erasmo and Burano and Torcello—always avoiding Lazzaretto Nuovo. Only the night fishermen were out, who knew what they were doing and did not disturb them.

Two months of being shut away during the quarantine—and the long time before that of keeping a respectful distance from each other—made them explode once they were together. Orsola had not thought it possible that someone's touch could affect her so much, or that her touching someone could excite them both. They couldn't keep their hands off each other. She stroked every part of him, exploring his broad shoulders, the rolling hills and valleys along his arms, his muscly calves and taut backside she could finally cup, feeling the dense, satisfying weight of him. Antonio ran his hands all over her, into her, every surface, every crevice; in doing so he gave her new knowledge of herself. Orsola had never paid much attention to her body, but now that someone else was, she became more aware of herself—her full breasts, her smooth back and soft inner thighs that he ran up and down with his fingers and tongue.

The first time Antonio entered her she was so shocked by the close pain and the rising pitch of sensation—so joyful after such months of hardship—that she laughed and cried at the same time. When they recovered, she wanted it again and again—as often as they could get away. Sometimes they ground against each other in the boat, rocking on the water, sliding in and out. Other times they stopped at the tiny uninhabited islands that dotted the lagoon, when they needed the hard ground to push against and steady their energetic bodies.

Orsola loved everything they did together—every touch, every thrust, every tease and laugh. But what she loved most of all was lying in the boat with Antonio afterward, gazing up at the night sky with its changing patterns of moon and stars and clouds. That was when she felt most content, cut adrift from time and the family and the workshop and the babies and their soiled clothes and her lampwork gathering dust.

They talked about many things as they drifted: getting Laura Rosso back on her feet, Zia Giovanna's withdrawal from the family, Stella's roaming, the direction the workshop was taking, the Vianello cousins' takeover of the household and of the Rosso brothers. Orsola was particularly suspicious of Isabella Vianello, as she couldn't fathom her and Giacomo fitting together in the way that she and Antonio so naturally did. Unlike Marco, Giacomo had always been shy with Muranese girls. His new wife was not shy, but sharp and impatient with her husband. It pained Orsola to witness it.

Antonio defended the cousins against her skepticism. "Fishing families don't make the sort of living a glass family does," he explained as they floated along one night, tired after their exertions. "They will always have plenty of fish to eat, of course, but they'll never have houses as big, or servants, or fine linen. Monica and Isabella saw an opportunity to better themselves. Can you blame them?"

Orsola was lying with her head on his shoulder and looked up at the outline of his cheek against the night sky, illuminated by a lantern they had brought with them. "Is that what you did too when you met us Rossos? Saw an opportunity and took it?"

"Of course. With an added bonus." He squeezed her thigh.

"That's what I am—a bonus?"

"*Sì, bella.* I am a lucky fisherman."

She bit his shoulder.

"*Ahia!* Maybe I'm not so lucky." Antonio rubbed the bite. "*Ecco,* don't worry about the girls. Your brothers are in good hands. Monica and Isabella never had any money, so they don't know how to spend it. They do know how to do things cheaply. They're quick about it too. No disrespect to Maddalena and Nicoletta"—he paused while she crossed herself—"but isn't the house better run with the Vianellos?"

"I suppose." Orsola knew it was but didn't want to concede the point that easily, for it annoyed her that Antonio so readily allied himself with the fishing family. He was now working with glass rather than fish; his allegiance should be with the Rossos. But he had had an easy relationship with Monica and Isabella from the start, as if they all spoke a language the rest did not.

What they did not talk about: marriage for themselves, though what they were doing in the boat and on the islands was its preamble.

✧

ONE DAY MONICA was feeding the babies and called out for a glass of water. When Orsola brought it to her, she set it down without drinking and nodded at her to sit. Orsola was surprised; she and her sister-in-law were not yet in the habit of sitting together to chat. But out of politeness she perched on the bed. It still amazed her to watch Monica feed two babies at once, tucking them under her arms like packages.

"Do you know how to be careful with Antonio?" Monica asked.

Orsola raised her eyebrows. "What do you mean?"

"All this fucking every night. You do that when you want a baby. Is that what you want?"

Orsola opened her mouth to protest, but Monica's direct, crystal gaze required honesty. "I don't want a baby yet," she said in a low voice.

"Then you know to make him pull out so his seed doesn't get inside you?"

Orsola shook her head, and tried not to look shocked when Monica explained in detail what to do.

"Is that what you do with Marco?" she asked at last, though she was appalled at having to think of her brother in that way.

"Of course not. I want a baby with him, though it's unlikely while I'm feeding these two. The body knows when the time is right. You didn't know? You don't know much, do you?"

Orsola felt the need to defend herself from this fishhook. "I know about glass. About beads."

"Beads?"

"I make them."

"For money?"

Orsola nodded, and explained about Klingenberg. "Don't tell Marco," she added, instinctively sensing that her sister-in-law was not the sort to tell her husband everything. "He doesn't know about the money. I need to get so good at making beads that he can't complain I'm wasting time and glass."

"Sensible. You'll teach Rosella when she's old enough?" Monica nodded at her daughter, now lolling asleep in one arm while Raffaele continued to feed from the other.

This surprised Orsola, for she had not given Monica's baby much thought. At that moment she was just another infant adding to the mountain of laundry.

"She needs to be able to look after herself, in case she's not accepted."

"What do you mean, accepted? Accepted by who?"

"The Rossos."

"Of course she'll be accepted by us!"

Monica's mouth twisted into a skeptical smile. "Will she, though? Be a Rosso? Marry a glassmaker? Wear the fur of a maestro's wife?"

"*D'accordo*," Orsola said after a moment. "I will teach Rosella lampwork when she's old enough. But I'll only continue if she is good at it."

Monica nodded, satisfied.

✧

THE PULLING-OUT METHOD Monica had described might have been helpful, if messy and slightly dissatisfying, but it was already too late. Orsola's *mar rosso* didn't come when it should have, she began to feel sick at strange times and her breasts grew sensitive. It was Monica she went to, not Laura Rosso. Monica's direct, practical advice delivered without judgment was what Orsola needed, not her mother's disapproval.

Orsola told her while she was once again nursing the babies with no one else around to hear. "You said before that you don't want a baby yet," Monica said, watching her carefully, her hands cupping Raffaele's and Rosella's heads as they sucked. "Is that still true with this one?"

"I don't have a choice, do I?"

"Of course you do. There are things you can take, a woman you can go to, over near the bleaching fields."

Orsola hesitated. She had heard rumors of such things and such women, but was never sure if they really existed. It was a sin that would get her barred from Mass, and worse, if anyone found out. And she could have a baby with Antonio; it would officially lock them into each other's lives. But another baby in a house already full of children and the number likely to increase—it was taking her further from her beads. "I'll think about it," she said.

In the end she didn't have to make a decision; her body made it for her. One morning she woke with her belly cramping and blood between her legs, and that was the first of many babies she would lose. Monica put her to bed, telling Laura Rosso her daughter had bad cramps from her *mar rosso*. No one questioned this, not even Antonio, though Orsola had to confess to him in the end, for Monica forbade her from going out in the boat with him for a few weeks, to give her body time to recover.

✧

THE FINAL REPLACEMENT in the family, of Paolo, the maestro's ser-vente, took longer, for the workshop couldn't get back to normal until Klingenberg began placing orders again. Marco managed to send word to the merchant at the Fondaco dei Tedeschi to find out what the Rosso workshop should produce, and got a terse message back: wait. But he and Giacomo and Antonio couldn't wait. Having no or-ders to fill meant they had the time to experiment and produce work that Klingenberg might eventually decide to sell. They had lost some of the younger workers—the garzoni and garzonetti—so they couldn't make anything that required more people. They could have restarted making the candlesticks with the dolphins entwined around the base that Klingenberg had been keen on, and which had sold well. But Marco said he wanted to create something new.

"He never liked those candlesticks," Antonio told Orsola as they sat together one evening at the Riva di San Matteo, leaning against the wall of a warehouse, legs entwined. They had managed to slip away while it was still light, and were watching the setting sun reach across to color the snow-covered mountains pink.

"Why not? They looked good, they did well, Klingenberg was happy."

"Marco doesn't like the dolphins. He says fish have no place in glass. That fire and water don't mix."

Orsola snorted. "Ridiculous. Plenty of glassmakers use fish in their work. One maestro made a chandelier almost entirely hung with fish pendants for a palazzo on the Grand Canal."

"The dolphins were mine, and he didn't like Klingenberg praising them." He paused. "He doesn't like me."

"That's—" Orsola stopped. She couldn't deny it. She had begun to sense that Marco now regretted his weakness in taking on Antonio as an apprentice, even when he turned out to be a lucky find. Antonio was open and cheerful, whereas Marco was closed and calculating and full of unpredictable shadows. After that first impetuous embrace in the calle when the Rossos came out of quarantine, Antonio and Orsola were careful not to display their attraction in front of others, in part because she knew Marco would try to wreck it if he could.

"He's working on platters now," Antonio said. "He had me and Giacomo make fruit to decorate them—but that's mostly Giacomo. Marco's making me tend the fire and sweep the floor as if I were a garzonetto rather than a garzone! I don't think I can put up with it for four more years until my prova." At the prova he would be tested on everything he knew about glass; if he passed he would become a servente. Most remained servente all their lives; only a few, like Marco, would become maestros. Everyone assumed Antonio would eventually fill the final gap in the family that Paolo had left as Marco's servente alongside Giacomo.

"I made something for you," Antonio continued. Digging in his pocket, he pulled out a tiny glass figure and dropped it in her hand. It was a blue-green dolphin about half the length of her thumb, with a long, slim shape and sharp fins like those on the candlesticks. Its snout and tail were curled into tiny hooks so that you could hang it on a chain or cord. "I chose the color similar to the beads you've made, like the color of the lagoon."

"*Bellissimo!* It looks so real. Have you seen dolphins yourself?"

"When I was fishing they sometimes came into the lagoon over by Giudecca. You can wear it if you like."

"*Grazie.*" Orsola kissed him. "I won't wear it, not yet. I don't want

Marco seeing it. But I'll keep it in my pocket." She did, alongside Maria Barovier's rosetta.

✧

A FEW DAYS LATER Stella came rushing into the kitchen to shout, "*Moro! Moro!*" Monica and Isabella looked puzzled, but Orsola ran through the workshop to the dock at the back. She and Antonio had heard nothing from Domenego and didn't know if he was still alive. She was smiling as she spotted him talking to Marco, and kept the smile bright even as she took in his drawn face, his skinny arms and legs, and the haunted expression she recognized from her mother. He had clearly been very ill but had somehow survived. Antonio stood next to him, as if to prop him up if he needed it.

Klingenberg was at last ready to see what the workshop was producing. Domenego brought word for Marco to take over a few pieces in a day or two. Orsola's brother grew excited by this request. "*Ecco*, all this work on new pieces was the right thing to do!" he argued, as if someone had challenged him. But she was glad for him and for the workshop. The Rossos were so dependent on the merchant that if he died or decided not to continue to represent the family, they could easily go out of business.

Domenego glanced at her as he turned to go, and Antonio, following his friend, tilted his head slightly. Orsola nodded, then slipped out and hurried alongside the Rio dei Vetrai to the riva, where the traghetti were once again running, and where she had first spoken to Klingenberg about her beads.

They weren't long, Antonio taking a second oar and rowing with Domenego—not as elegantly, but with more muscle. When they pulled up alongside, he held out his hand to help her on board. "Come with us, for fun," he said.

They rowed a little way apart from the stream of boats going back and forth between Murano and Venice—the surest sign that the plague was over—then both men sat and let the gondola drift along the Muranese shoreline up toward the Serenella Canal, which cut through the western part of the island. If they wanted to, they could have rowed all the way around Murano. But Domenego was content to sit. He looked exhausted. It must have tired him even to row from Venice.

"You've been ill," Orsola said.

Domenego shrugged.

"Did you go to Lazzaretto Vecchio?"

He shook his head. "They do not let mori go there. Just as well. That is probably how I remained alive."

"Where did you stay, then? Did they let you live at the Fondaco dei Tedeschi?"

He shook his head again. "The servants threw me out once I was sick. So I hid in an abandoned house, over past the Arsenale. The family had all died."

"With no one to look after you?" Orsola was horrified, remembering how much Nicoletta had depended on her and her mother, and wondering how anyone could be so cruel as to make him leave. On the other hand, no one wanted the plague in their house. Though she would never tell anyone, she had been secretly relieved when Nicoletta had been taken away.

"I am all right now," Domenego insisted. "I don't want to think about it."

"*Attenzione, bella*, you'll drown." Antonio flicked some water at her, clearly attempting to change the subject. Orsola flicked some back, then they were wrestling with each other as Domenego tried to keep the gondola from rocking.

"I see this has been progressing," he said, gesturing at them. They still had their hands on each other, though they were no longer wrestling. "It took you long enough."

Orsola tried to pull away, embarrassed at being so blatant in front of Domenego, who likely had no woman to wrestle with. He seemed so very alone. She managed to free her hands and set them primly in her lap.

"Klingenberg wants another order of beads," the gondolier said, delivering the second message he had come to Murano for. "Same as before, though if you have any new designs, he wants to see them too."

She thought back to the time in quarantine when she was making beads. Apart from the yellow plague beads, which she had no desire ever to make again, she had kept to the designs she knew. Since the end of the quarantine months before, she hadn't made any beads. The plague had thrown her off, thrown everyone off. The daily events that had measured their lives—shopping at the market, the passeggiata in the evening, Mass, visiting family—had been so disrupted that Orsola forgot how long it had been since she had done things, or even how old she was. In the middle of it, time seemed to stop. But afterward the whole episode felt very short. What she held on to now were the concrete moments: Antonio's touch. A laugh with Monica. A rare hug from Stella. Raffaele's grin when his teeth came in. Maybe now she also needed the concrete feel of glass between her fingers to anchor her.

✧

KLINGENBERG'S REQUEST THREW Marco into a spin. Although he had long been waiting to hear from the merchant, now that he had, he was suddenly unsure of what to show him. Old goblets, pitchers and candlesticks that he knew Klingenberg had sold before and could probably sell again? Or completely new wares—platters, carafes, wall sconces—that would display the workshop's creativity and flexibility? Or a bit of both? For two days he raced around the workshop, unable to concentrate, insisting on making new pieces when he had stacks of work in the storeroom. The Rosso women heard the sound of shattering glass in the workshop often during those days.

At last, after yet another crash and string of curses, Laura Rosso looked up from her mending as she sat in the courtyard. "Monica!" she barked.

Monica appeared from the kitchen, wiping her hands on her apron. It was rare for her mother-in-law to call her, and she stood before her, respectfully awaiting orders.

Laura jerked her head toward the workshop. "*Per favore*, sort out your husband, for all our sakes."

They held each other's gaze for a moment, then Monica nodded. She removed her apron, handed it to Orsola, straightened her blue dress and headed to the workshop, which she rarely entered; like his father, Marco was not keen on women being there. A minute later she was leading her husband out by the hand, into the house and upstairs to their room. They remained there for the rest of the day, except when Monica came out to give the babies their evening feed. Raffaele and Rosella were on solid food by then but still took Monica's milk before sleep. Isabella brought her cousin and brother-in-law up a tray of wine and food. "Like newlyweds," she said, chuckling. But a day and night in bed worked, for Marco emerged the next morning much calmer, and clear about what he would show Klingenberg. "Only the new," he declared. "He has a memory, he knows what we already make." He gave the garzonetti the day off, then he and Giacomo carefully wrapped up the pieces he chose and hired Bruno to take the two of them over to the Fondaco dei Tedeschi.

It was rare for the workshop to be completely empty, and Orsola and Antonio took advantage of that. Unlike his maestro, Antonio wasn't bothered about a woman touching glass in the workshop. He heated a piece of glass on the end of a punty, then had her kneel and blow through it while he twirled the rod, a glass bulb growing at the end. She sat at the bench and under his instruction ran the glass over the marver, using pressure and tongs to maneuver and shape it. It was very different from making beads—so much bigger, requiring different muscles, different movements, different timing. The furnace scalded her face but left her back cold, so that she sweated and shivered at the same time.

She broke several pieces, much to Antonio's amusement, but at last succeeded in shaping a simple green goto to drink from, bulbous at the bottom, tapered to a narrower lip, only slightly lopsided. They put it in the annealer to cool slowly over a day or two, hiding it behind other pieces so that Marco wouldn't notice, as it was far too crude for any of the men to have made.

"I can show you how to make beads if you like," Orsola offered as they swept up all the glass she had broken to make that one flawed goto.

"I'd like that." Antonio wasn't just being polite: he seemed curious about every process, taking in each technique, mastering many of them, and equally at home with both the large gesture and the small detail. He was turning into a fine glassman.

When they were done, the workshop cleared of her failures, they sat together on the dock at the back of the workshop, feet dangling above the water, thighs pressed together. "What do you think Klingenberg will choose from all the wares Marco is showing him?" Orsola asked.

"The platters," Antonio replied. "He'll like the fruit around the edges. Did you notice, though, that Marco only took over to Venice platters with fruit Giacomo made? He didn't take anything I had worked on. None of the wall sconces." Antonio had fashioned sconces with the holders made of fish. They were beautiful and playful; Orsola knew Klingenberg would have found it easy to sell them.

"It must have been an accident," she stated, though feeling less sure than her words implied. "It doesn't mean anything."

Antonio gave her a small smile. "You know your brother, Orsola. He doesn't do things by accident. For months he's been giving me stupid tasks—work a garzonetto could do. I feel I'm no longer part of the team. It makes me think . . ." He paused.

"What?"

"He wants to drive me away."

"But you're meant to take Paolo's place!"

"Am I, though?"

"*Da bon!*"

He didn't say more, but that conversation set off a low hum of anxiety that pulsed under everything Orsola did—when she was hanging out laundry or hoeing weeds in the garden or feeding the chickens or running after Stella or moving under Antonio in the boat at night. If he were to leave, where would he go? And where would she go?

⟡

MARCO AND GIACOMO RETURNED from Klingenberg jubilant. The merchant was pleased with the new pieces and had ordered fruit platters and carafes. "He said my work is better than ever!" Marco exulted over celebratory wine in the courtyard. "We'll be busy now. I have such ideas! They keep me up at night. That, and other things." He smiled at Monica, who was refilling his glass.

"What about Paolo's position?" Laura Rosso asked. She and Giacomo and Orsola crossed themselves. "Who will be the other servente along with Giacomo?"

"I'll get to that soon."

Orsola glanced across at Antonio, who was leaning in the work-shop doorway. When he turned and disappeared inside, she felt a pang, looking at the empty entrance.

One afternoon she returned home from gathering dried sheets from the bleaching field, a little late, for she had run into Zia Giovanna and, finding her unusually talkative, stayed to listen. When she got back the family was eating dinner at the table in the courtyard. "Guess what Zia Giovanna has decided," she announced as she hurried to her place. "She's going to enter the convent at Santa Maria degli Angeli!" Looking around, she stopped, for a guest sat with them: Stefano from the Barovier workshop. Stefano of the black-eyed stare, who had seen her when she was a girl creeping up to the Barovier furnace to dry herself, who had brought cane for her during the quarantine. He was staring at her now, sitting between Antonio and Giacomo. Giacomo looked miserable. Antonio looked as if he wanted to hit someone.

"Orsola, you know Stefano," Marco said, ignoring her news about their aunt. "He's joining the workshop as my servente."

"What, taking Paolo's place? But—" A small shake of Antonio's head stopped her. He was right: here and now was not the time.

Her lack of enthusiasm seemed to goad Marco into justifying him-self. "Stefano knows how to make mirrors! Already he has an idea to coat the fruit platters with a mirror surface so that fruit displayed on them will be doubled. And he can engrave a bit too. His skills will fill in the gaps in our workshop and allow us to expand what we make."

Orsola kept her temper. Stefano did have more experience than Antonio and was from a prestigious workshop. It was surprising the Baroviers had let him go, or indeed that he wanted to join the Rossos. She caught him still staring across the table at her and went bright red with embarrassment: she suddenly sensed what she doubted Marco consciously understood. Nor did Antonio, for though he was angry, he didn't have any reason to link her to this new assistant. She would say nothing. It was better that way; perhaps then it wouldn't happen.

She stood and began collecting plates, though they had barely finished. Laura Rosso frowned at her but didn't tell her to stop; behind the frown there was pity. She too was clearly sensing what the men hadn't.

That evening Antonio took her out in the sandolo but didn't stop in a quiet part of the lagoon or moor at a deserted island so they could lie together. He was too enraged, and needed to row and row until he had rowed out his anger. He could row all the way to terraferma and back, she thought, and he would still be angry.

"Why did he choose Stefano over me?" he repeated over and over. Each time she tried to answer in a way that wouldn't make him angrier. Because you're Venetian. Because you're a fisherman. Because you're handsomer than he is. Because Stefano brings Barovier knowledge. What she didn't say was the truth: that Stefano was more experienced and so a more skillful glassmaker than Antonio. One day Antonio might be, but Stefano had many years on him, starting as a garzonetto aged ten, and passing his prova to become a servente, which Antonio was still working toward. Purely from a business point of view, Marco wasn't wrong to choose Stefano over Antonio. It might not have been a loyal move, but it was a decision any ambitious maestro might make.

At last Antonio stopped rowing and sat down next to her. They were almost at Mazzorbo, the island next to Burano. It was a small place, made up mostly of vineyards, with a few houses scattered about. A boy was playing with a small black dog on the riva, throwing it a stick to fetch. He paused briefly to watch them, but the dog was more interesting than a pair of lovers, and after a cursory wave he went back to throwing the stick.

"Honestly, *mia amata*," Antonio said as he put an arm around her, "if it weren't for you I would . . ."

"Would what?"

He shook his head. "What's my future with the Rossos? Sweeping floors and making goti?"

"Of course not. Marco has you do more than that."

"But I'll always have to do what he says. And I hate working for him."

There was a splash and a cry. They looked over and saw the boy shouting and pointing at a small, dark form in the water. He must have thrown the stick into the lagoon and the dog had followed.

"*Maledizione!*" Antonio cried, jumping up and grabbing his oar.

"Don't dogs swim?"

"Not all of them." He was rowing furiously. "Be ready to pull him out."

Orsola didn't like dogs much—she didn't trust their bark or their teeth—but she didn't want to watch one drown. So she knelt in the sandolo, and when they came up alongside the little thing in the water, she caught it by the scruff of its neck and heaved it into the bottom of the boat. It seemed it was too late. Limp and waterlogged, it lay unmoving.

"*Maledizione*," Antonio muttered again, and Orsola began to cry because this was a terrible way to end a terrible day.

But then the small, wet body coughed and spat, and after expelling a stomach's worth of water, it began to bark. All this time the boy had been shouting. When the dog heard him it scrambled to its feet to jump out of the boat, ready to drown again to get back to its master. Orsola only just managed to catch it, and held on to it as Antonio rowed them to the riva. There they handed up the dog and it ran off, stopping once to turn and bark at them as if they were enemies. The boy followed the dog without thanking them, though without them his pet would have died.

"That's the people from Mazzorbo for you," Orsola said. "That dog probably almost drowns every day."

Antonio burst out laughing. "I can always count on you to come up with a sharp comment, *bella*."

He rowed them back in a slightly better mood, and they didn't talk about Marco or Stefano. But afterward she noted that it was the first time they'd gone out in the boat and come back without lying together. That night in bed she thought about the little dog, drowning but not drowning, dead then not dead, all in a moment.

✧

IT WAS A RELIEF to make beads again. When Orsola set up her lamp on the table in the corner of the kitchen, the Vianello cousins didn't question it or complain about the smell, but made sure no demands were made of her while she was working. Occasionally when she was soothing one of the babies, Monica even watched over Orsola's shoulder. Sometimes little Stella slipped in too to watch, though when her sister asked her if she would like to make beads someday, she always vigorously shook her head, curls whipping her cheeks.

Orsola went back easily enough to the lampworked beads Klingenberg already knew: plain blue or green or red paternostri with a clear glaze over the top, white oval ulivette spolette with the blue thread spiraling around it, clear canelle with green flowers. It was harder to think of new designs. She wasn't feeling creative, her head too caught up with Antonio, and with Stefano lurking in the background. The two were tense around each other, Stefano clearly aware that he had taken the place Antonio expected, the other trying to ignore him. Antonio began skipping meals so that he wouldn't have to sit with his rival, instead taking the boat out to fish, even though afternoons were not the best time for it. He and Orsola didn't go out so much at night together, as she was making beads and he was no longer in the mood. Stefano's presence brought out the worst in him: instead of his usual ease and charm, he was silent, sullen, abrupt.

One afternoon Giacomo appeared in the storeroom, where Orsola was packing platters. She looked up at her brother. He seemed tired; more than tired—sad. He had not been the same since the plague. Even marriage hadn't helped. Indeed, sometimes it seemed to have made things worse. There was little affection between husband and wife; Giacomo refused to argue with Isabella whenever she sharpened her words. Only Monica was able to silence her cousin with a look.

"What is it?" Orsola asked as mildly as she could.

Giacomo took a deep breath. "Can you say something to Antonio?"

"About what?"

"The workshop—we're no longer making such good work."

"Why not?"

"The combination of Marco, Antonio and Stefano—it's not smooth. Things were better before."

"With Paolo?"

Giacomo winced. "There's nothing wrong with Stefano. He's skilled, he can fit in. But Antonio is unhappy."

"What should I say to him?" Orsola asked, winding a long piece of linen round and round an opaque white oval platter, glass cherries and apricots and figs ringing the outer edge.

"Try to get along with Stefano."

"Why should he? Stefano has taken his place."

"If we can't work well together, the glass suffers. Marco may end up letting Antonio go if he thinks it will be better for the workshop. I understand why Antonio's angry, but if he continues like this he may be out of work altogether. You should warn him."

"Why don't *you* tell him? You work with him."

"You have more influence with Antonio than anyone else." Giacomo had eyes; he clearly saw what had grown between Orsola and the apprentice.

She sighed. "I'll try, when I find the right moment."

But there was no time for the right moment. That evening Orsola was too busy finishing the order of beads for Klingenberg to speak to Antonio. The next morning he went to Venice to see his surviving brother; he wouldn't be back until late the following day, for it was August and the men had shut down the furnace for the summer break.

Early in the evening Marco called Orsola out to the courtyard, where he and their mother were sitting, while Stefano stood awkwardly next to them. *Mio Dio, no*, Orsola thought. No. Not already. She had hoped to get pregnant again, and that this might stop what was about to happen. But Antonio's anger had overcome his lust, and they hadn't lain together so often. Her *mar rosso* had arrived that morning.

Marco was pouring out four glasses of wine. "Come, Orsola, we're celebrating." He handed her a glass.

"Celebrating what?" She looked at her mother, who would not meet her eye but was brushing the table free of imaginary crumbs.

"Stefano has asked my permission to marry you, and I've said yes. *Me ralegro*, sorella." He picked up a glass and saluted Stefano. "Welcome to the Rosso family!"

"No."

Marco raised his eyebrows and Laura Rosso sent Orsola a warning look. Stefano appeared embarrassed.

"I'm marrying Antonio," she declared.

"Orsola, you are not marrying a Venetian fisherman." It was not Marco saying this, but Laura. She was much harder to disagree with.

Orsola tried. "He's not a fisherman," she argued. "He's learned to work with glass, and he's good at it. Besides, Marco and Giacomo are married to fishermen's daughters."

"That's not the same. Your marriage will benefit the Rosso workshop by keeping Stefano in it." Her mother looked uncomfortable saying this; clearly it would have been better to make such a business-like argument without Stefano having to hear it, when he clearly wanted the marriage for reasons that had nothing to do with business.

"What about Antonio?" Orsola demanded. "Don't you need his skills too? How can you do this to him after everything he's done for us? He kept us alive during the quarantine!"

"We're not doing anything to him. It's you who has done it, leading him on when you had no idea if a marriage between you could take place. Shame on you, putting yourself before the family."

Orsola closed her eyes, tamping down her rising rage.

"Orsola, I will do everything I can to make you happy."

She opened her eyes to Stefano's dark stare. She was the reason he had joined the Rosso workshop, it was very clear now. Her mother was right: marrying Orsola would keep Stefano here. Their marriage would benefit everyone but her and Antonio.

Orsola was proud of her restraint. She didn't shout or snarl at her brother, her mother, Stefano. She set down her glass, turned and walked out through the door into the calle. No one called out or followed her and tried to bring her back. They would wait for her to walk out her anger.

She strode furiously around the island, avoiding people so she didn't have to talk, as she didn't trust what she might say. Later she slipped back into the house and went straight to her room. She slept badly that night, and the next day went out early to work in the family garden in the north of the island, lingering for as long as there were weeds to pull so she wouldn't have to be at home. Then she visited Zia Giovanna in her convent, bringing her some of the vegetables she'd picked. Her aunt was delighted that Orsola didn't seem to be in a hurry and was willing to listen to her dull gossip about the other nuns and complaints about the food.

When Zia Giovanna was called to prayers, Orsola at last went home. It was midafternoon and she wasn't expecting Antonio back yet, but she peeked in the workshop anyway. Stefano was showing Marco and Giacomo an engraving technique. They didn't see her, and she backed out.

Laura Rosso was sitting in the courtyard, the babies playing around her feet, except for Stella, who was tossing pebbles down the well. When she saw her big sister, she ran over and threw her arms around her legs. "Hot," Stella murmured, leaning her flushed face against Orsola's thigh. "Don't like the others. Just you."

Orsola placed a hand on her sister's curly hair, and they stood like that for a moment. Their mother started to say something, but Orsola shook her head. She was not ready to listen.

When she had disentangled Stella from her legs she went inside, where Monica and Isabella were clearing up after the midday meal. They pointed to a covered dish they had saved for her. "Later," Orsola said. "It's too hot to eat."

She looked around. For once there was nothing she had to do. The laundry pile was low, the children occupied, the meal made, the gardening done. She could make beads, though burning tallow in this heat made her feel sick even thinking of it. She could sleep. She chose sleep, though the bedroom she shared with Stella was like a furnace.

When Monica came in, Orsola was staring at the ceiling. The

shutters were closed to keep the heat out, but a thin shaft of light lit her sister-in-law as she sat on the edge of the bed. "Antonio was here," she said.

Orsola sat up. "When?"

"While you were out. He came back early."

"Does he know about Stefano?"

"I told him. Someone had to."

"Where is he?" She began to get up.

Monica touched her arm. "*Un momento.* He's leaving later."

"*Leaving?*"

"The *moro* is taking him to terraferma."

"Terraferma?" Orsola shuddered. "He can't do that! What will happen to him there?"

"Shhh!"

"I thought he would go back to Venice." I thought I was going to become a fisherman's wife, she almost added. Wasn't that why he had gone to see his brother—to ask to fish with him again?

"He couldn't get his things while the men are in the workshop. He asked me to fetch them and bring them and some food to him before he goes." Monica set a bundle on the bed.

Orsola snatched it. "Where?"

"San Matteo, in an hour." Monica paused. "He's expecting me, but I thought you should see him."

"He was going to leave without seeing me?" Orsola's voice began to rise again.

Monica looked at her with a sharp blue gaze meant to steady her. "Men are unreliable. It's best not to get too attached."

She was trying to help, but her words undid Orsola, and she began to sob. Monica was not a soft presence, but she put her arms around her sister-in-law and held her hard until Orsola had squeezed out every tear.

When Monica left to go back down to the kitchen, Orsola sat and thought. Antonio must have known he was going, even before Stefano asked to marry her. Otherwise he couldn't have so quickly organized for Domenego to take him to the mainland. He had already had a plan. Orsola opened his bundle. Apart from bread and cheese and sausage, there was a shirt, a tunic, some fishhooks, rope, a knife and some papers. She riffled through them. There were drawings of some of the pieces he had made, including of the tiny dolphin he had made her. Then there were sheets of writing she could not read, cursing herself for never learning how. But she suspected she knew what they were. Finally, wrapped in the shirt, was the lopsided green goto Orsola had made with him in the workshop. She looked at it for a long moment, then rewrapped it in the shirt and brought her fist down on it to hear the muffled crack.

She stuffed the papers in her pocket and retied the bundle. When she went downstairs and through the kitchen, she stopped only to squeeze Monica's shoulder. Then she was off, hurrying across the courtyard to the door, Laura Rosso and Stella both calling, "Orsola! Orsola!" She slammed the door shut and raced up the calle toward the Ponte di Mezzo. Soon she heard Stella pattering behind her, still calling her name, and she had to run faster to lose her. Her sister began to cry, but though it broke Orsola's heart, she didn't turn back.

Over one bridge, two bridges, three bridges. Passing the market at Santo Stefano, Campo San Bernardo, the Basilica of Santi Maria e Donato. Along the way she seemed to meet the entire island, all calling out to her. She refused to stop and explain where she was going, probably offending many. The drinkers outside l'Omo Salvadego shouted at her this time, but she didn't bother to throw curses over her shoulder. Maybe Antonio was in there, making a final toast to his future. She rounded the last building and stopped. He was not at their spot yet. She sat against the wall in a suspended state, exhausted now, hot and thirsty and unable to think.

He did not come from Murano the way a glassman would. He came from the water, like a fisherman, in Domenego's gondola—not from the canals, but from the lagoon. They had rowed together up the channel running to the east of the island, where few would see them, and were rounding the point to her. The wood felze was missing; it would have been taken off to lighten the load, for it was a long way to terraferma.

Antonio looked both relieved and ashamed when he saw her waiting for him. Even when Orsola hit him across the face. Even when she said, "I hate you so much, I'm glad you're going!" Even when she said, "You've always been an arrogant Venetian. Think you're better than me. Than us. No loyalty to Murano, to your furnace. I could kill you! I should stab you straight through your treacherous heart. Give me a knife and I'll do it now!" She cast about wildly as if looking for that knife.

He listened with the shame and the relief fighting in his face, and then he placed his hand on her cheek and said, "Orsola," and she stopped and stood still, leaning her forehead against his chest. She felt like Stella being coaxed out of a tantrum.

Domenego sat on the stern, eyes cast down, making his presence as small as possible.

"I've been offered a position that I'll never get with Marco," he spoke into her hair. "I'm guaranteed to become the servente when I've taken the prova, and I may become a maestro one day. But I have to go far away for that. Outside the Veneto." He paused. "There's nothing for me here."

Orsola raised her head. "*I* am here. Did you forget that? You were going to leave without even seeing me. *Bastardo.*"

Antonio took a deep breath. "Come with me."

170

She reared back. "To terraferma? Never." The thought made her stomach pitch as if she were in a boat on a rough sea. If she went with him, they would become unhooked from Murano and Venice and her family and enter a different world with its own pace. It felt impossible to choose that. Orsola couldn't quite believe Antonio was willing to take that risk. "Stay," she said. "Marry me. My mother will accept you. Marco . . . Forget about him. We can live in Venice if we must. You can go back to fishing. I'm not permitted to make beads there, but I will give up lampwork. For you."

"Orsola, my future is there." Antonio pointed at the mountains waiting for him to cross them.

"What future is that?" she cried. "In a place where you'll wake up without me? Where you won't know if I'm young or old, alive or dead?" Where *I* won't know, she thought.

"I will have to take that chance."

"Aren't you scared?"

"Maybe. But I'm excited too, for the change, the newness of it all."

Orsola was suddenly furious. Antonio seemed already to have taken a step out of the world they knew. "Go, then," she declared. "But you won't be taking Rosso secrets with you to sell to the northerners!" She pulled the papers from her pocket and threw them in the water before he could stop her.

Antonio made a move to go after them but stopped when he saw the ink swirl and dissolve in an instant. "I suppose I deserved that."

"And more. They'll come after you and kill you for taking Murano skills north—if time doesn't kill you first. And I'll laugh when they do." Even as she said it, she knew he didn't believe her.

But the fire was draining from her; it was too much to keep up. Orsola wanted to slump to the ground and lay her head on her knees. Instead she stood still and pleaded with her eyes with the man who was deserting her.

"It shatters me to leave you," Antonio said, his own eyes full and then spilling over. Orsola had only ever seen one man cry—Giacomo, over Paolo's death. Murano men didn't. It must be the Venetian leaking out of him, she thought.

She reached up then and threaded her fingers through his hair. Antonio responded by winding his fingers through hers. They stood there like that, hands in each other's hair, and it was the most painful and pleasurable moment of her life. Orsola had not understood before then that those two feelings could be so intertwined.

Behind them Domenego coughed. "We must go now. They will be quick to come after you when they realize you are gone. You need a day between you and them."

Later Orsola felt the brief moment on the Riva di San Matteo when they had their hands entangled in each other's hair was the point that everything in her life had led up to and then moved away from, like the tide rising and falling. Except that the tide always returned, and he was not going to return, for he had turned traitor to Murano glass and to her and was going to Berlin or Munich or Amsterdam, and she might never be able to forgive him.

Orsola stood on the riva and watched the boat pull out, Antonio not rowing yet but turned toward her in the dusk. His face was the size of a plate, then a saucer, then a dot as he moved farther and farther away until at last he and Domenego and the gondola winked out of sight. She watched the empty water for a long time, aching for one last glimpse. She could do nothing to stop that moment and that man from flowing out of her life.

She walked home from San Matteo and went straight to her room, avoiding her family. Lying in the darkness, she let tears cut hot grooves down the sides of her face. She couldn't sleep but turned over and over in her mind the decisions she and Antonio had made: he not to stay here with her, she not to follow him to terraferma. Both of them stubborn, neither giving in. Fueled by anger and a hurt sense of betrayal, her decision had seemed to make sense at the time, but now just a few hours later Orsola would have given anything to be in that boat with him, heading to a new, uncertain life.

✧

THE NEXT AFTERNOON Marco stormed into the storeroom, where she was listlessly sweeping, a task Monica had given her out of pity for the state she was in. Orsola was grateful—she could be alone there with the broom and her thoughts rather than in the crowded courtyard, where the children were playing and Laura Rosso and Isabella were shelling peas.

"Where is he?" Marco demanded. "His things are gone. You were out most of yesterday. Someone said he saw you over at San Matteo. Where is he?"

Orsola stopped sweeping and faced him with dull eyes. Of course, someone at l'Omo Salvadego must have seen her and reported this news to others. She and Antonio had not been discreet.

What did Domenego say? Antonio needed a day's start. *Amor mio,* she thought, you've had almost that. Run fast.

"He's gone to terraferma," she said, because Marco would work it out soon enough.

"And you let him? Why didn't you tell me right away?"

"You never listen to me. And it's your own fault he's gone."

"What do you mean by that?"

"If he and I could marry he would still be here, safe."

Marco snorted. "You would never have married that Venetian. *Comunque,* he's not that good. We don't need him. I just don't want him stealing Rosso recipes and peddling them in the north."

Orsola pictured the bits of paper in the lagoon, those recipes in Antonio's hand swirling away, and for a moment wished she had let him take them with him. He would probably remember much of it anyway; the skill was in his eyes and hands, not in writing.

"I'll tell the authorities he's gone," Marco said, heading for the door to the calle. "They'll send men to go after him." It was in the Venetian Council of Ten's interest to keep Muranese skills and secrets confined to the island. Taken north, they would aid competitors and steal customers. Few of the glassmakers who went to terraferma had ever come back. Rumors about their being killed were spread to scare people into remaining on Murano.

✧

AT FIRST THE MEMORY OF Antonio and that moment on the Riva di San Matteo was so fresh and strong that Orsola thought she could never possibly forget it; the feeling would always be burning in her like a fever. She went over the scene of his leaving, recalling every detail, unable to think about anything else while she was sweeping or scrubbing sheets or making pasta or taking the children out or sitting at Mass.

Men were not like women, she began to understand in those first days of her feverish state. They felt things differently, perhaps because they were usually the ones leaving rather than being left alone on the riva. Antonio would have new things to look at, new people to meet, a new pace to get used to. Distractions. No time to feed a fever. Whereas Orsola was playing the part of the woman left behind, walking along the canals she knew so well she could navigate them in the dark without falling in. Every building familiar, every person she passed someone to greet. Nothing was new for her.

Very slowly the details of that farewell faded, steadily shifting from a rich midnight blue to a pale morning sky. One day she realized she had spent only half of every minute thinking of Antonio and of that moment and what he had said and how he had touched her face. Another day it was every third minute, then every quarter hour, then every hour when the bells of Santi Maria e Donato rang. The measuring of time like this made her wonder if the bells wherever he was rang in the same way. The thought of its being different hurt.

She must have been awful to live with: somber, brooding, lost in a haze of thoughts. Tracking Antonio in her mind as he crossed the mountains and followed paths and saw things she could barely imagine, all so new and strange to someone who had grown up on water. Thinking back on all the time they had spent together in the boat and on deserted islands, sliding in and out of each other, pressed together, bringing each other pleasure. Remembering most of all and in vivid detail the moment she first walked into his arms after the quarantine and the moment he walked out of hers at San Matteo.

Orsola ate less because she no longer cared about food, her lack of appetite contrasting with the Vianello cousins, who were both in the blooming stages of pregnancy. They kept her out of the kitchen because her indifference made anything she cooked taste bland. She sat at Mass and said no prayers. She stopped gossiping in the market. She remained by herself in Campo San Bernardo rather than walking about during the passeggiata. She bored the children by not playing with them or even smiling at them. She could only bear Stella, who sometimes sat with her and patted her leg with her small hands and asked nothing of her.

At times the memory of Antonio's departure roared back as if it had just happened. But eventually the feverish state broke. With great effort—pinching herself hard when her mind strayed—Orsola managed to limit her thoughts of him to when she was in bed, her sister's steady breath beside her, blinking back tears in the dark; and also when she went to San Matteo, where he had left her.

She sometimes brought with her the yellow beads she had made to ward off the plague, which were reappearing around the island—people still carrying them, bartering with them in the market, children using them for their games. Orsola hated them for their false power, and for reminding her of Antonio. Whenever she could, she traded them for another of her beads, then took them to San Matteo and threw them in the lagoon off the riva. Eventually, she thought, they will all be there, gathered in one place, their magic gone.

During those feverish weeks, her family said nothing about the glassman who had run off—not even Marco, who kept news of the search to himself, though it must have been tempting to torment his sister with such information. Orsola suspected Monica's hand in keeping him quiet. Nor did he or Laura Rosso say more about her marrying Stefano. They were being patient with her, letting her stew in her grief, to recover and eventually reach her own decision. Again, Orsola suspected that in her pragmatic way, her sister-in-law steered them.

After a time, the memory of Antonio was smoothed into a story in her head, like a bead with its rough edges rubbed down so it can be worn. Doing so deadened the feeling, but it made it bearable. Orsola could now wear the story of her and Antonio without being cut by it.

✧

ONE EVENING MONICA stopped her as Orsola was scrubbing pans. "I'll do that," she said. "It will give you more time for your beads." She nodded at the corner of the room where the lamp and glass cane and tools sat on the little table. Orsola had not touched them since Antonio left.

She didn't answer but kept swirling sand around the pan.

"Don't you have an order to fill for the merchant?"

Orsola poured out the water and sand and rinsed the pan with more. "I'm not going to bother with beads."

"Why not?"

Orsola didn't answer.

Monica's eyes were on her. "Are you going to let that Venetian fisherman take away your beads too?"

Orsola turned red. "He's not—" She stopped. Monica was probably right.

"I want Rosella to learn one day," her sister-in-law continued. "You promised. You mustn't lose your own skills before you teach her."

Orsola closed her eyes for a moment. Then she opened them and stepped away from the pan, Monica seamlessly taking her place. She found some tallow and melted it in the tin lamp, then lit the wick. Passing through, Laura Rosso wrinkled her nose but said nothing.

She began pumping the bellows with her foot. When she picked up a cane at random and thrust it into the brightening flame, she felt something click inside her: the familiar flow of melting, turning, shaping. Whatever else was going wrong in her life, this process of creation was still in her hands and her eyes, still satisfying, still comforting.

✧

SLOWLY ORSOLA GOT BACK TO WORK. She was somber, but she was making beads again.

Only once did she allow the memory of Antonio into her lampwork, designing a bead for the two of them: perfect, translucent spheres of red glass—red for Rosso—with flecks of gold leaf inside to remind her of his hair. When she judged they were ready, she took a dozen of them with her when she delivered an order in person to Klingenberg. By that time she had been making beads again for a few months but had always sent them by messenger—Bruno when she could find him, for she felt bad that he had lost his mother to the plague and fought to survive on Lazzaretto Nuovo. He still flirted with her and made bawdy jokes, but his heart wasn't quite in it.

"You need to marry, Bruno," Orsola said once when she was handing over the latest order of beads. "That will cheer you."

"I could say the same of you," he retorted. "Shall we?"

This time she took a traghetto over to Campo San Canciano and walked the rest of the way to the Fondaco dei Tedeschi. Orsola was not so in awe of Venice now. Antonio had taken her over a few times, and maneuvering through the canals with a native who knew them well had made the city less mysterious. She had also lived long enough not to be so intimidated by the sophisticated Venetians putting on their show for all to see. Orsola wore her Barovier dress and a string of the red and gold beads she had made, so she didn't feel too shabby as she wove through the passages to the Fondaco dei Tedeschi. She didn't wear a mask, however. It was the end of December—the season of masks in the run-up to Carnevale—but the Rossos never wore them. Masks were for frivolity and secrets among the nobility; glassmakers didn't have the time.

Klingenberg was not expecting her, but he showed no surprise when she walked straight through the antechamber, ignoring Jonas writing in the corner, and appeared in the doorway of the merchant's chamber. He stood and bowed as his clerk spluttered behind her. "Ah, Orsola, you have come with more beads, I expect. I am always pleased to receive your order. Take a seat." He gestured to the same mahogany chairs with their lion-head carvings and kilim cushions that she and Giacomo had sat on to ask about Marco's whereabouts, the day she met Antonio. Everything seemed to point at Antonio these days. "Jonas," he called, "bring Signorina Orsola a glass of wine. I'll have one too."

Jonas disappeared and returned with two glasses and a carafe; Orsola recognized them as made by the Baroviers.

"*Allora*," Klingenberg said, "tell me why you've come." He was eyeing the beads around her neck.

Unnerved by his close attention—though she had worn the beads for that reason—Orsola took a sip of the wine. Deep and rich, it tasted far more expensive than the everyday table wine the Rossos drank at home.

"I've brought the most recent order." She waved at the package she'd laid on his desk.

"*Bene. Grazie.*"

"I noticed you haven't increased the order since I began making beads again. Usually you do."

Klingenberg sat back. There were gray glints in his hair now. "I am pleased with your work, Orsola. It is solid and reliable."

Orsola wasn't sure if those words were meant as a compliment.

"But you know that there are many others making beads now, in Venice as well as on Murano."

She did know, had been astonished to find that more beads were being made on Murano, mostly by women. She hadn't expected to have competition. And lampwork was now permitted in Venice as well as on Murano. For over three hundred years glasswork had been confined to Murano by law, but that seemed to be changing. If lampwork got a foothold on La Serenissima, could glass workshops move there too? Venice already had its painters, its boatmaking, its printers, its books, its papermaking, its perfumes. Let Murano keep its glass.

"Are you selling others' beads as well as mine?" She tried to seem merely curious rather than jealous.

"A few." Klingenberg sounded dismissive. "There is not quite as much demand for beads—and indeed for Murano glass—as there was before. You and your brothers must be aware that there are now glassmakers in Prague, in Germany, in Amsterdam. And their work is good. Some of them have glassmen from Murano who teach them." He paused, a silent indication that he knew about Antonio's flight. He had probably heard about it as Muranese gossip filtered through to

Venice. His departure had certainly been discussed on Murano. Orsola had had to endure months of sideways looks and whispers behind her back at the market or the passeggiata, as if in some way she were to blame for Antonio's leaving, when she was the one reason why he might have stayed.

"It is Amsterdam that troubles me the most," Klingenberg continued. "The Dutch are ambitious. They are building their trade routes and making Venice less relevant. You must have noticed there are fewer ships sailing in and out, though I suppose you do not see merchant ships from Murano. When you are out in Venice today, take a closer look. It is not quite the bustling city it was years ago."

Orsola must have looked dismayed. "Oh, trade is robust enough," Klingenberg tried to reassure her. "But I have lost customers here and there and found them harder to replace than I used to. Some of the Dutch customers are switching to Amsterdam glass. Why wait for shipments from Murano when you can buy almost as good on your doorstep, without all the shipping costs and tariffs?"

He hadn't reassured her. "Does Marco know this?"

"It has not affected his orders yet. Of course, his glassware has changed over the past few months with the . . . change in the workers."

"Has the work got worse?" Orsola was remembering his praise of Antonio.

"Not worse. But I can spot a different hand at work. The use of mirroring, for instance. That mirrored fruit platter is inspired. I even bought one for my daughter. It is the new servente, Stefano, isn't it? He has brought new skills to the Rossos."

Orsola was silent. She didn't want him to talk about Stefano.

"Do you know where Antonio Scaramal went?"

His direct question caught her off guard. Klingenberg too would want to protect Murano glass skills from being exported. "I don't know," she replied. "He didn't tell me. I didn't even know he was going until he left."

She swallowed the lump in her throat, determined not to cry in front of this suave German merchant who was watching her so closely and seemed to know about her life.

"He has loyal friends," he said at last.

From the antechamber she could hear Jonas grunt. He was probably taking note of everything she said.

"*Allora*, your beads. I would like to see those you are wearing."

This was what she'd hoped Klingenberg would say. Orsola unhooked the strand and handed them to him, warm from her neck. He rolled a few between finger and thumb to gauge their evenness, then held them up to the light. "Is that flecks of gold leaf?"

"*Sì.* The bead is not so hard to make," she added, then regretted her modesty.

Klingenberg smiled. "Never say that or the price will drop. Let us believe you struggled. Signorina Orsola, I am going to order twenty-four of these, enough for just two necklaces. The fewer you make, the rarer they are. We don't want to flood Europe with them."

"If they are to be scarce, then they're worth more. Also, they have gold in them. So you must pay me more. I need to pay for the gold leaf."

He nodded. "You're learning, Orsola. *Brava.* What do you suggest is a fair price?"

She named a price twice what she expected to get. Klingenberg leaned forward, and they haggled their way to a figure she wasn't entirely happy with. Nor was he. "You see," he said when they were done, "the true value of something is the price which neither side is quite content with, where each thinks he—or she—should get more."

Orsola smiled wryly. "That sounds like a lesson for life."

As she was leaving, she paused in the doorway. "You say you recognize the hand of the maker in the glass?"

"Usually."

"If you ever—" Orsola stopped to swallow another lump in her throat. "If you ever see Antonio's hand, will you tell me?"

Klingenberg frowned. "Signorina Orsola, I am not going to send my best beadmaker into the arms of a traitor." It was both a compliment and a warning.

She managed to get past Jonas and out of the Fondaco dei Tedeschi before beginning to cry.

✧

ORSOLA HUDDLED IN A CORNER where two buildings met, drying her eyes, no one paying attention. Did women weep in Venice every day for her to be so ignored? When she was done she ventured back out to see for herself what Klingenberg meant about Venice changing. She headed first along the Grand Canal. As she passed the Rialto Bridge, it seemed as crowded as ever, despite the city losing so many to the plague. The canal too was busy with boats.

In the midst of them all was the one gondola she recognized. Domenego was skillfully steering his passengers—Klingenberg's daughter and her maid, both masked for the season—through the other gondolas. Orsola was trying not to watch as she walked; trying not to draw attention to herself. Just as the fondamenta ended, Domenego spotted her. "Orsola!" he called. Klara Klingenberg whipped her head around, her mask glittering as she scanned the fondamenta.

Orsola turned into a passage and hurried away from the gondolier and the Grand Canal, Domenego still calling her name. The last time she'd seen him was six months before at San Matteo when he was about to take Antonio to terraferma. It wasn't his fault that Antonio

182

wanted to go, but she couldn't help linking him with her abandonment and had no desire to see him.

She ran into a campo, then along another calle, then into another campo, and on like that, the campos like beads spaced along the string of the passages. Orsola had no idea where she was, but slowed down and let herself be pulled along. Perhaps that was the best way to navigate Venice: let the city unroll itself around you and guide you rather than trying to master it with a map in your head. When she and Antonio had gone to Venice, she'd found that it was far easier to get around by boat than on foot. The main entrances to most of the buildings were on the water, and the noble families and many of the merchants' families moved around by gondola. She doubted Klingenberg's daughter walked these passages.

She reached Campo Santo Stefano, a large brick church at one end, and people busy crisscrossing it, and followed the stream along passages that eventually led to Piazza San Marco. Crossing it, she then passed through the piazzetta next to the Doge's Palace and beyond it to the riva where ships were moored in the lagoon. As Orsola drew near, it grew louder, with boys and men running past. The riva was a chaotic scene around the docked ships: ropes strung back and forth, men shouting, crates being handed onto smaller boats or carried toward the customs house, officials accompanying them so that goods couldn't be hidden away to avoid tariffs. There were no women in sight. No Carnevale masks either. This was a place for work, not play. Orsola kept well back so she wouldn't be noticed.

So this is where my beads begin their journey, she thought. She wished she could see them being taken on board and the ship sail out to sea.

Beyond the ships the Giudecca Canal—so wide it was more like a lagoon—was choppy with the motion of all the vessels. Across it was the island of San Giorgio Maggiore, and farther west the shoreline of the island of Giudecca, so calm by comparison, with its neat rectangles of colored houses and its bridges humped over canal entrances and its miniature figures strolling along the riva. She spotted the Redentore, an imposing church built after the plague that took Orsola's nonna and Nicoletta and Paolo and Maddalena. Every July a spectacular bridge made of boats lashed together was created all the way across the Giudecca Canal from San Marco to the Redentore, with pilgrims crossing it to give thanks to God for bringing Venice through the plague. Orsola had never been, for she didn't want to be reminded of that time, though she crossed herself four times for those she had lost.

It was fascinating to watch all the movement on the riva, and she did so for a long time until at last a whistle drew the sailors' attention to her, and she had to escape from the jeers back toward Piazzetta San Marco, where the people who benefited from all the commerce were strolling, ignoring the hard work being done so close by.

There Orsola ran straight into Domenego coming toward her with long, loping strides.

"Oh!" she cried, casting around for a passage to escape down before stopping herself from doing something so childish. She couldn't avoid him forever. "*Buongiorno*, Domenego," she said, pulling herself together. "How did you find me?"

"I asked. Everyone notices everyone in Venice. Why did you run from me?"

Orsola ignored his question. "Isn't Klingenberg's daughter waiting for you?"

"Signorina Klara is in no hurry. She is watching acrobats." He nodded across the piazzetta, where bare-chested men in tight breeches were balanced in a human pyramid, the acrobat at the top juggling lit torches.

Orsola had rarely seen Domenego on land; it was strange to witness him off his boat in his gondolier clothes—his red tunic and black-and-white diamond hose and red cap with its nodding ostrich plume. Away from his gondola he looked as if he were dressed up for Carnevale rather than for everyday life.

"I have something for you," he said. He pulled a packet from the pocket of his tunic and handed it to her.

Orsola stared at the packet, her hands shaking. She may have thought she didn't want to see Domenego, but he was her one tenuous link to Antonio. She opened the bit of linen tied with a string, grimy from the many hands that had passed it along the hundreds of miles. Inside was a tiny glass dolphin, white this time, as beautifully proportioned as the blue-green one in her pocket, and exactly the same size. Antonio had managed to replicate the first one without having it or the drawing he'd made to work from.

He is still alive, she thought, relieved. And he is thinking of me. What a fool Marco was to drive away so much skill. To drive him away from me.

"Do you know where he is?" she demanded.

Domenego winced. "I was asked that question many times. I do not know."

"How did you get this?" Orsola held up the dolphin and its linen wrapping.

"It came for me at Klingenberg's living quarters. Luckily Signorina Klara was there to receive it and she gave it to me. If it had been Signor Klingenberg or Jonas or anyone else, they might have taken it away, and questioned me again."

"Who questioned you?"

"Guild men." Again the wince, this time accompanied by him clenching his right hand. When he saw her looking, he hid his fist behind his back. Orsola's chest went tight.

"Domenego."

He looked over her shoulder toward the piazzetta. "I must get back to Signorina Klara."

"Menego." She deliberately used Antonio's nickname for him. "Look at me."

He reluctantly turned toward her.

"Show me your hand."

Domenego held it out. The middle finger was missing, cut off at the base, where it would have joined the hand.

Orsola drew in a sharp breath. "Who?"

"Guild men. Klingenberg stopped them from taking my thumb, or I could not hold an oar. As it is I do not row so smoothly now." He paused. "They threw my finger in the canal—to feed the fish, they said." His voice grew tight.

"But you couldn't tell them where Antonio is because you don't know!"

"That is true. He was sensible enough not to tell me."

"Didn't you tell them that?"

"That is not how torture works, Orsola."

"If Antonio had told you, you could have told them and saved your finger."

Domenego shook his head. "Even if I had known, I would never have told them. Torture does not deserve an answer."

He began walking toward the crowd where he had left his mistress. Orsola followed, clutching the dolphin and running her thumb over its smooth, curved back and the point at the tip of its fin. Many others might have handled it en route from Antonio to her, but she knew that some part of him was there—his fingerprints, his sweat. It touched her at the base of her gut, but also made her furious that this piece of glass was as close as she could get to him.

✧

It was hard to miss Klara Klingenberg. Even among the masked crowd watching the acrobats tumbling and turning flips, she stood out. She was taller than most girls and wore a silk dress the color of the pale-blue sky. Her blond hair was braided and coiled atop her head in a way that could only be done by someone else, unlike the messy bun Orsola had twisted and pinned herself. She was wearing a pearl necklace rather than beads. Everything about her—the dress, the pearls, the hair, the jeweled mask she wore that covered the upper half of her face, the maid hovering nearby to assist—was paid for by Rosso glass, among other things her father traded. She could wear those pearls because Orsola made beads.

A sudden rage—at Antonio's leaving her, at Domenego's mutilated hand, at a middleman making more money than the makers so that his daughter could wear silk and pearls with nothing to do but watch acrobats contort themselves—propelled her through the crowd to the girl's side before Domenego could hold her back. "Signorina Kling-enberg?"

Klara turned and pulled up her mask. Her eyes were very wide, and the same deep brown as her father's—which surprised Orsola, as she had expected her eyes would match her dress. Her skin was smooth and pale, her cheekbones sculpted, and her eyebrows arched like the stone bridges over canals. Now that Orsola could see her face, she realized that despite her height she was younger than expected. Her *mar rosso* might have started but her chest was not a woman's, and she was not yet at a marrying age. She didn't seem afraid of Or-sola, just puzzled.

Her maid—a pert little thing even shorter than Orsola—stepped between them. "*Vattene*, peasant."

Orsola bristled, but the crowd was turning toward them, sensing live entertainment better even than the acrobats, and she didn't want that sort of attention. "A word, please." Orsola turned and pushed her way through the people till she found a quieter spot at the edge of the piazzetta. There she stood with her back to the crowd, staring into the window of a glove maker displaying fine leather gloves dyed many colors.

Klara followed, her maid trailing behind. "How do you know who I am?" she asked. Unlike her father, she spoke Venetian like a Venetian.

"Your father sells the beads I make."

"Like those you're wearing?" Her eyes were fastened on Orsola's neck.

"Like those, and others."

"*Bellissime.*"

"*Grazie*, signorina. Your pearls are more beautiful." They were: they had a natural luminescence that even the best glassmakers couldn't imitate. Their white mirrored the whites of Klara's eyes and teeth—for she was smiling now.

Orsola took advantage of her good mood. "Send your maid away for a moment," she said in a low voice.

"*Che?*"

"Send her away." Orsola glanced at the maid.

"Benedetta, go and get me some sugared almonds, *per favore.*" Klara handed her a coin and pointed across the piazzetta to a vendor in the far corner. "I'll wait here."

Benedetta glowered, clearly suspicious.

"Don't worry," Klara added. "Domenego is close by."

The maid hurried off. Orsola wouldn't have much time. "You received a packet for your gondolier recently," she began.

"Yes, that was a surprise! He never gets packets, for why would he? I wondered what it was but he wouldn't tell me."

"It was for me."

"You?" Klara Klingenberg raised her already arched eyebrows. "You know Domenego? What was in the package?"

Orsola could have lied, or kept the dolphin hidden. But she needed her. She pulled out the glass figure and dropped it in Klara's palm.

"*Un delfino, che bello,*" the German girl murmured, examining it.

After a moment Orsola brought out the first dolphin as well. Klara took it and held the two up together. "Exquisite." She studied them. "Wait, I think . . ." She placed the hook of one's nose against the hooked tail of the other, twisted, and as if by magic the dolphins were linked together. "Isn't that clever!"

It was. She was quicker than Orsola, who wasn't sure she would ever have worked that out.

"Who sent them to you?"

Orsola hesitated. But she might not get another chance. "A man. He may send more."

Klara's eyes lit up. "Your one true love?"

It could have sounded silly, these words parroted from a ballad or a love poem, but she was so earnest that Orsola couldn't respond with cynicism.

"*Sì.*"

"Why has he sent it to Domenego rather than to you?"

"My family don't like him. He probably thought it would never reach me if he sent it to my family."

"Ah, *Romeo e Giulietta!*"

"Who?"

"'Star-crossed lovers.' It's an English play."

"He may send more," Orsola repeated, "and if your father or his clerk intercepts it, Domenego could get into trouble. More trouble." She tapped her finger where the gondolier had lost his.

Klara was as clever as her father, but in a different way. She pulled every string together and came up with the answer. "Your true love is the glassman who fled some months ago. I heard Padre talking about him."

Orsola nodded.

"You know he's in Prague?"

"Prague? How do you know?"

"I asked the messenger with your packet where he came from. He was delivering a consignment from Prague."

"Does your father know this?"

"No, just me." She looked pleased with her secret.

"Don't ever tell him, or Domenego."

"Why not?"

"If they think he knows, they will cut off another finger to find out."

Klara Klingenberg winced, much as Domenego had. "And my father?"

"He'll tell the guild and they'll send men to Prague to find him."

"But then you'll have him back."

"No. Then they'll kill him."

Klara sighed. "That is awful. But . . . Padre is trying to protect his business. And yours."

Of course she will defend Klingenberg, Orsola thought. Because he is her father. Over Klara's shoulder she could see Benedetta threading her way through the crowds back across the piazzetta. "He may send more dolphins if he can," she explained. "*Per favore*, signorina, intercept them and give them to Domenego for me without anyone knowing. Then both he and Domenego are safe."

"I'll do better than that. Next time one arrives I'll send a message back saying to send them addressed to me rather than to Domenego. What is your true love's name?"

Orsola reddened, not wanting to give that knowledge to this girl.

But she had no choice if she wanted to protect him from the danger of his own romantic gesture. "Antonio Scaramal."

"*Va bene.* I'll watch out for the next dolphin." Klara handed the glass dolphins back to her as Benedetta reached her side, carrying a cone of paper filled with sugared almonds. "No, I don't want to buy any of your beads," she said in a loud voice. "I have enough jewels." It was surprising how quickly she could sound haughty. But for her it was all a game.

"Of course, signorina." Orsola bowed her head. "I'm sorry to have bothered you."

Benedetta gave them both a look, and Orsola wondered if they'd managed to fool her.

✧

FOR MONTHS ORSOLA and Stefano avoided each other. At meals she sat as far from him as she could, and he was careful to keep his eyes down or to pin them to her shoulder. He seemed as embarrassed as she was about what had happened. She didn't doubt that he had asked Marco's permission to marry her, but he couldn't have expected it to result in the scandal of Antonio's disappearance, or that Orsola would have reacted so negatively.

She avoided Marco too, and he her. Monica kept him in line, and then she and Isabella gave birth in rapid succession to two boys—Andrea and Sebastiano—and the family shifted its attention to them and left Orsola alone. Andrea was born with a twisted foot and would need more attention to help him learn to walk. He was always going to be slightly behind the others. Six children under the age of four made it a demanding household. Once again there were more cloths for Orsola to wash, more babies to soothe; more work, especially for an unmarried member of the family.

One day as Orsola was running after Raffaele, who had grabbed a glass cane from her lampwork corner and dragged it out to the courtyard, she caught Stefano watching them from the glass yard. As she wrestled the cane away from her nephew, Stefano smiled and turned away. Another time after a meal she was clearing plates and caught his eyes on her. Again he looked away.

One afternoon she was walking back from the bleaching fields and ran into him on the Ponte di Mezzo. Without a word he took the heaped basket of clean sheets from her and carried them home. Orsola followed, too tired to be annoyed. When she thanked him, he ducked his head and hurried to the workshop.

He really was nothing like Antonio. Maybe it was easier that way. Lean, with a narrow face and dark eyes and hair, Stefano said little, and moved with a nervous energy, darting rather than strolling with casual intention as Antonio had.

On the name day of Saint Orsola in October—over a year since Marco first announced Stefano would marry his sister, and since Antonio had left—when Orsola was briefly alone in the kitchen, Stefano appeared and set on the table a small mirror he had made. It was round and had a narrow frame of wood carved into a garland and painted gold; simple and beautiful. Stepping back, he gestured at it. "Oh," she said. "I—I—*grazie*, Stefano." It was the first time she'd said his name in months. Immediately it felt like a betrayal. But Antonio isn't here, she reminded herself. He will never be here.

"You can hang it in your bedroom," Stefano said, then hurried off, as if saying even those words was too much.

That night there was a knock on her door. When Orsola opened it, Stefano was standing there, nervously rubbing his hands up and down his thighs. He did not look at her. "I've come to see how the mirror looks. Have you hung it?"

She nodded. She had, earlier that evening. It was the nicest thing in her room, though she was not particularly keen to look at herself.

"Can I come in?"

Recently Laura Rosso had moved Stella to a room to share with Rosella. "You need your own room," she had explained. Now Orsola knew why.

She looked at Stefano for a long moment. He raised his eyes to her. Then she stepped aside and let him in.

Part II

THREE
NECKLACES

4

STONE SKIMMING AGAIN. A long jump via time *alla Veneziana*, from 1633 to 1755. The stone lands in the middle of the Age of Enlightenment, when thoughts are loosening and the mind is expanding out of the long darkness of the past, led by Rousseau, Locke, Voltaire. Skipped over are an English civil war and plenty of other wars. In America, a different kind of war: natives of the land are being relentlessly pushed off, with guns and disease.

Art: Rembrandt and Vermeer and other Dutch painters steal the crown from the Italians, though in Venice Tiepolo is at his height.

Literature: the modern novel has been born. Celebrations!

In her studio Orsola Rosso is turning back and forth in the flame a translucent red bead with flecks of gold leaf suspended in it. She looks up. It is 122 years later. She and those who matter to her are eight years older. She is now twenty-nine, but she has no idea how old the one who matters most to her is.

The City of Water has changed. No longer a center of trade, it is now known for its parties, its gambling, its Carnevale season, when wearing a mask allows everyone to take liberties. It is the climax—in more ways than one—of the Grand Tour undertaken by young European men, and a few young women.

Less trade means less glass to be traded. Less work. More precarious times for glassmakers and other artisans.

Do the Rossos benefit from any of this freedom of thought and body? Is Orsola enlightened, or is she swamped by the more quotidian aspects of a household full of children?

✧

"BASTA!" Orsola was sounding more and more like her mother.

There was a brief silence while the ball stopped being kicked. It didn't last long: children have such short memories. Soon they had resumed banging it again and again into the wall of Orsola's studio, just the other side from the table where she was working, shouting out the number of kicks: "*Uno! Due! Tre!*"

Normally she didn't yell at them, for they couldn't help being noisy. But when they played right outside of where she was working, she couldn't concentrate, and her beads kept dropping from the metal rod she twirled back and forth. She had an order due for Klingenberg, he had asked to see her, and she couldn't afford to waste precious time. The children knew they weren't meant to come into the glass yard, which was probably why they were there. Marco had set that rule, reinforced by Monica, Laura Rosso and Orsola. But once children outnumbered adults, it was impossible to control them.

There were now eight children in the Rosso household, ranging in age from twelve years (Stella) to eighteen months (Angela). Marco had kept Monica busy in bed, and she had another girl—Francesca—as well as two others she had lost early. Giacomo and Isabella had just one more after Sebastiano: a baby girl with blond hair who looked nothing like Giacomo. Three months after the baby was born, Isabella ran away with her to terraferma, where a blond fisherman was waiting. Only Orsola spotted the relief cross Giacomo's face when he heard his wife had left. No matter how much his mother nagged him, he showed no interest in seeking another wife. It seemed even one had been too many.

The last of the eight children was Orsola's with Stefano: Angela, the blessing she had thought would never happen. She was pregnant four times before managing to give birth to their daughter. Stefano adored Angela; she crowed and ran to him whenever he appeared. It was a bond Orsola tried not to be jealous of. Stefano was a good man and deserved pure, unconditional love from someone.

The children were kicking the ball against the wall again and chanting each child's name, in order of age from oldest to youngest. "Stella! Marcolin! Rosella! Raffaele! Andrea! Sebastiano! Francesca! Angela!"

"*Per l'amor di Dio, basta!*" Orsola cried again as the rhythm of the bouncing ball began to grate. She set down the rod she had been turning and went to the door. "All of you, *andatevene!*"

The children obeyed, running to the courtyard to bother someone else. This drama they repeated most days. Often Orsola gritted her teeth and worked through the noise, sometimes she gave up and stopped making beads, and sometimes she shouted. She sat down again to concentrate on her lampwork, but couldn't help smiling: the children kept better track of themselves than she did. Though she loved them all, she had her favorites:

Angela, of course, because she was Orsola's daughter.

Stella, because she was Orsola's sister and the eldest, though she was rarely part of the crowd, always disappearing to her secret places on the island, but occasionally coming to sit and watch her sister make beads.

Marcolin, because he was Orsola's first nephew and Nicoletta's son, and so afraid of the world that his aunts often had to shield and comfort him from all those dangers he thought awaited him outside the Rosso house.

Rosella, because she sometimes joined Stella to watch the bead-making. She was too young to make beads herself, but soon she could play with honey between sticks, as Elena Barovier had taught Orsola to do. Elena was gone, having survived the plague only to succumb to tumors in her breast.

Finally, Raffaele, the golden boy of all the children. He was Laura Rosso's favorite and looked very much like his mother, Nicoletta, with wide brown eyes pinched at the corners and a delicate mouth you don't often see on a boy. Of Marco's sons, he was the preferred; Marco was embarrassed by Andrea's lameness and Marcolin's fear of the world. Raffaele was the natural leader of the gang of children. Unlike many leaders, though—and unlike his father—Raffaele was easygoing and kind to everyone.

The more children there were, the more mouths to feed, the more space was needed in the kitchen for the extra help: the girl brought in to wash the pots, the nurse to look after the babies, the old woman who helped with laundry. They were a big table at meals. Eventually there was no place in the kitchen corner for Orsola's table with her lamp and bellows. One afternoon after dinner the girl carrying the dishes in from the courtyard set some of them down on the table and knocked over a bundle of glass cane. Orsola swore at her as the glass rolled everywhere, and the girl burst into tears.

Monica went out to the courtyard, where Marco, Giacomo and Stefano were finishing their wine before heading back to work. "Orsola needs a place for her beadwork," she announced to her husband. "There's no room in the kitchen. I suggest dividing the storeroom and giving her part of it."

Marco stared at her, a hard look she sent straight back at him. "No women in the workshop."

"Orsola wouldn't be in the workshop. She would have her own space in the storeroom. There's plenty of room there"—she held up her hand as Marco tried to interrupt—"it just needs reorganizing, a few more shelves built. It won't be hard."

The storeroom was a chaotic misuse of space, with materials and finished glassware spread everywhere, for Marco had not inherited his father's organizational skills. Brought back to the way Lorenzo Rosso had kept it, there could be room for Orsola. It had taken Monica to see that.

"We need her bead business," she added. "She puts food in the mouths of the children and clothes on their backs." Monica gestured at the children swirling around the courtyard in their post-dinner daze: from Stella to baby Angela tottering after her cousins.

Orsola's beads were now a small but steady part of the Rosso income. A few years ago she had even got back from Klingenberg the money he had saved for her from lampwork sales and handed it over to an astonished Marco. It was a good amount. She made sure Laura Rosso and Monica knew about it, so that he wouldn't spend it on something stupid—gamble it away in one of the casinos that had opened on Murano, or buy a share in l'Omo Salvadego. Instead he was able to refurbish the furnace so that it burned more efficiently— not that he thanked her for it, or even acknowledged it was the *escrementi di coniglio*—the rabbit turds—that paid for it. Now her beads bought shoes for the children and better wine for the adults.

Marco scowled, but Monica stood firm, waiting for the assent he would have to give. At last he nodded. "But the storeroom farthest from the furnace," he said. "Don't want that stink anywhere near us."

Orsola was thrilled to have her own studio of sorts—so unusual for a woman—with the space to leave her tools out without having to put them away every time she had finished. On the other hand, sometimes she missed being in the heart of the house. In the kitchen she had known who was sick, who was tired, who was angry, where and when people were going. She had seen Isabella roll her eyes behind Giacomo's back long before she ran off. She had seen Laura Rosso feed Raffaele extra biscotti. She had seen Monica looking with pity at her son Andrea as he limped after the others with his lame foot.

Orsola was making things other than beads now, to sell in the little shop attached to the workshop. The idea had come from Stella. One day Orsola was sitting on the Riva di San Matteo with a pile of tiny glass dolphins in her lap. She never knew when one would arrive: sometimes they were just months apart, other times years would pass. She kept the first one Antonio had given her in her pocket alongside the Barovier rosetta; they were her constant companions. The others she kept among her beadwork at home, where Stefano or Marco would never look. Sometimes, though, she took them to San Matteo to get them out and spend time with them, feeling their weight, linking and unhooking them, letting them click against each other. The dolphins were precious to her, for they were the concrete indication that Antonio was still connected to Murano and to her. Perhaps the slow flow of glass remained in his blood, even on terraferma. She was willing to believe this.

"What are those?" she heard, and turned to find Stella looking over her shoulder. Her sister was adept at creeping all over without anyone noticing.

"Dolphins," Orsola replied. "Made by a friend. Do you want to see?"

Stella squatted beside her. She had sun-streaked brown curls that were starting to go dark as she moved toward adolescence, and a heavy brow almost permanently furrowed into a frown—not from anger, but from concentrating hard so that she could understand the world around her.

"No one else knows about them," Orsola added. "Just you and me. Our secret, *d'accordo?*" She didn't threaten her, for threats didn't work with her sister. Punishments too had no effect. But a shared secret would. Of all the children, Stella was the one who could best keep a secret.

She nodded. At that time Orsola had six dolphins, linked together, and she placed the chain of them in her sister's cupped hands. Stella didn't coo over them as other girls might, or say she wanted them for herself. She studied them with the attention of a scholar over his books. Immediately she worked out how they hooked together and unhooked them all, then laid them out from white to darkest blue. As the sisters surveyed them together, Orsola noted small changes between dolphins: longer fins, shorter snout, fatter body. One even had a few bubbles suspended in it. He must have been in a hurry with that one, she thought.

"Who is the friend?" Stella asked. "These weren't made on Murano or I would see them in the shops. But they're familiar."

There were now more shops selling glassware on Murano. The Rossos had more visitors these days—no longer just Venetians coming over to their palazzos and gardens, but foreigners too. French, German, British, all came to tour Venice for its churches and its art and its festivals—Carnevale and the Festa della Sensa and the Regata and the Redentore—as well as to gamble and visit the neighboring islands, buying lace from Burano and glass trinkets from Murano to take home: glass figurines of horses and fish and shepherdesses, also wineglasses, candlesticks and small mirrors. Even a few beads. The family accommodated this new market, though it meant Stefano made smaller, cheaper mirrors, Giacomo made quick horses and Marco made basic candlesticks. Their shop was bigger, their wares smaller. Stella was right: these dolphins could be sold in a shop here, and probably do well—though they were far better made than most of the pieces the Rossos sold to the touring types, whose glass would probably break on the long road home. But Marco would recognize the dolphin design and explode.

"They weren't made on Murano, but elsewhere," Orsola said.

Stella sat back, nodding. "I know. This is the design of the dolphins on the candlesticks Marco used to make but won't now. So these must be made by *il Giuda* Antonio."

Every family has its stories it retells around the dinner table over glasses of wine. The Rossos had Lorenzo Rosso with the shard of hot glass piercing his neck. Laura Rosso surviving Lazzaretto Vecchio and bringing Raffaele back alive. Orsola bewitching Maria and Elena Barovier into teaching her to make beads. Antonio too was a Rosso story: Antonio the Judas, stealing the family's glass secrets and taking them north to create competition. Even Stella knew about him. Orsola had been left out of the official tale, but whenever that story came up, she busied herself clearing the table or fussing over the children so she didn't have to listen to what they said. Stefano too didn't want to hear about the man his wife preferred to him, but slid his daughter from his lap and made an excuse to go to the workshop.

"Why are they being sent to you?" Stella asked.

Orsola thought about what lie she could tell. In the end, she didn't. "So that I won't forget him."

"It's working, then."

"*Sì.*"

"You could make these with your lamp," Stella suggested as she studied the latest addition, a bright-green dolphin like the algae that sometimes grew in the backwaters of the lagoon. "Then you could sell them in the shop."

"Not dolphins," Orsola countered. "But I suppose I could make other things."

"Seahorses, then. You can use the same fastening, on its nose and its tail." She began to hook the glass dolphins back together.

Stella's suggestion made Orsola's mind race as to a design: something she would sell not through Klingenberg, but in the Rosso shop. She spent long hours experimenting to get the seahorse right, asking fishermen to show her those they had caught in their nets and sketching the miniature, delicate horse heads with fringed manes, lithe bodies and tails curled in a tight spiral. That spiral could be hooked around a small loop at the top of its head. It was tricky to make, and not quite as clever as Antonio's twisting method of linking the dolphins, but a month after Stella's demand, the Rosso cavalluccio marino was born. To Marco's irritation and Orsola's secret pride, it sold better than anything else in the shop. Visitors bought them for their wives, their daughters, their mistresses. Orsola made other figures to sell: snakes and octopuses and starfish and cats and dogs. Always small and simple. But she never made dolphins.

✧

DESPITE THE GROWTH in glass figurines, Orsola's beadwork stagnated. Over the years Klingenberg had gradually increased his bead order as he consolidated regular customers who preferred the quality of Murano glass to the cheaper, brasher glass from other continental workshops. However, at a certain point he maintained the order but didn't increase it. Orsola had plateaued, her work predictable and less exciting. It felt to her like that moment in a story where it seems nothing is happening, awaiting the arrival of the dark stranger to enliven things.

One day she went to see Klingenberg to bring him her latest order, and with an idea. After congratulating him on his daughter Klara's recent marriage, and the merchant asking after Angela—professionally remembering her daughter's name—they got down to business. Orsola handed over her beads to Jonas, who took them away without even inspecting them, for they trusted her work now.

"I wanted to make a suggestion, Signor Klingenberg," she said. "About my beads. I wondered if I might do something a little different. Perhaps make necklaces with my beads rather than sell them singly?" Orsola sometimes made necklaces, for the women in her family and others on Murano, but the merchant had never asked her to do so.

"The buyers prefer individual beads," Klingenberg replied, batting away her idea without seeming to consider it. Seeing her face fall, he added, "However, we have had a request for a new bead, from a new market for me. Perhaps that will interest you."

Orsola had once asked where her beads went, and he had listed many cities. Some she could have guessed: Amsterdam, Paris, London. Others were farther afield: Damascus, Aleppo, Constantinople. Some she had never heard of: Baku, Boston, Lima. She had not even been to terraferma, but her beads had traveled far.

And now: "West Africa. Tribal chiefs wear them," he explained. "Glass is rare there. It sets them apart from other beads made from clay or seeds. Scarcity is what makes commerce work—it sets the price. The Africans do not know how to make glass, at least not yet, so they pay dearly for the privilege of wearing glass beads. And now they want millefiori beads."

Millefiori flowers were made from different colors of cane bundled into a pattern, usually with one color in the center and another color for its petals. They were then melted together, and when cool the new cane was chopped crossways to create tiny flower discs. These were then pressed in rows into an opaque bead. The result was a bit gaudy for Orsola, who preferred simpler patterns.

"How much are millefiori beads worth?" she asked.

"Five soldi a bead, though of course they pay with goods, there being no soldi in Africa."

"What goods?" She was curious what came from Africa.

"Skins of exotic animals. Gold. Slaves."

Orsola stared at him. "They trade their own people?"

"Sometimes. It brings wealth to the tribe."

As much as there were neighbors who annoyed her, other glass workshops that stole Rosso ideas, beadmakers she would be happy to see go out of business, Orsola would never betray them in that way. Muranese often feuded and hated one another, but they stuck together.

And there was Domenego, a friend who was also a slave.

She opened her mouth, then shut it. Klingenberg had been good to her: bought her beads when she was a novice, backed her after the plague, accepted the times when she was less productive—after Antonio left, after miscarriages, during her difficult pregnancy and the first days of motherhood. He at least valued her skill in a way Marco never did. Orsola owed him a great deal and didn't want to criticize and question. But the thought that her beads in some way played a part in enslaving someone like Domenego shocked her.

Though she said nothing, she clearly didn't hide her thoughts well enough. Klingenberg sat back. "Signora Orsola, you have spent your whole life on Murano, is that right? You and your family have never been to terraferma, where things work differently."

She shrugged. He made it sound like a fault that she needed to fix.

"You know very little about the way business works, then. I am sorry to tell you that the world of commerce turns because of human sweat, much of it unpaid. The American colonies we hear so much about, so successful with their manufacturing of textiles and sugar? They are successful because the raw materials—the cotton and the sugarcane—are produced by Africans there. Britain is rich from the slave trade. So are the Netherlands, Spain, France, Portugal. Your beads too are caught up in it. Slavery runs the world."

"As it runs your gondola in Venice."

Orsola had finally said it, the words popping out unfiltered.

From the antechamber, Jonas's pen stopped scratching. For the first time since she'd seen him seasick years before, Klingenberg looked less than smugly in control. Although he didn't move in his chair, his face subtly shifted into a defensive mode. "Domenego has a good life with us," he declared. "He is treated well."

"Is it his choice to work for you?"

"He can buy his freedom whenever he likes."

"What will that cost?"

"That is between him and me, Signora Orsola. Now, no necklaces. But I would like you to start making millefiori, please. I've had several requests, and want to give you the opportunity before I find another lampworker to fill the order. Send me a sample by the end of the month and we'll see how you get on." Klingenberg stood, looking weary; he had not managed to switch topics as smoothly as he normally would. He called to his clerk. "Jonas, will you see Signora Orsola out? My compliments to your mother and brothers," he finished, making clear any conversation about slavery or even beads was over.

Orsola felt the brief satisfaction of having made this powerful merchant uncomfortable.

Jonas escorted her out, although she had now been to the Fondaco dei Tedeschi many times and knew her way around. As they descended the wide marble staircase, the steps dipping in the center from centuries of merchants' shoes wearing them down, Klingenberg's clerk said in a low voice, "You have not helped your family with your little outburst. Herr Klingenberg will not forget. He gets fewer and fewer orders for Muranese glass since people like your old lover took the trade north."

"Don't mention him!" Orsola's cry echoed up and down the staircase. A passing clerk glanced at her with disapproval. Eight years on and with a husband, a child, her own workshop: most of the time these things protected her from Antonio's desertion. Yet it took only a casual remark from someone unexpected and unsympathetic to inflame a wound she thought was long scarred over.

"Venice was once the center of the world of trade," Jonas continued, ignoring her outburst. "Now, look." They had reached the bottom of the stairs, and he pointed at the open courtyard before them. "Think back to when you first saw this, how much busier it was."

He was right. That first time Orsola and Giacomo had come looking for Marco, the courtyard was so crowded with clerks running back and forth, with unusual goods being carried and inspected, that they were constantly jostled and had to step out of the way. Now the Fondaco dei Tedeschi was much quieter, not a busy Grand Canal with boats of all sizes skimming about, more a side rio with a few gondolas sedately gliding past.

"If you want what market there still is for Muranese glass, it is best not to criticize Herr Klingenberg by taking the African's side."

Before she could respond, he added, "Do you think, signora, that being paid for work makes such a difference? Sometimes you can feel like a slave even with coins in your pocket."

Orsola stared at him. Jonas was gazing across the courtyard so she could only see his profile, with its jutting cheekbones and straight nose; his bearded jaw was tight, and a vein was throbbing at his temple below the line of his black cap.

"But you have a choice," she said at last.

"A choice between starving and not starving is hardly a choice."

"Tell that to Domenego. I expect he would like that choice."

"The *moro* has the better life, out on the water all day in this beautiful city, while I sit inside copying figures."

"But he has no family."

"Nor do I."

"What happened to them?" she asked, though she wasn't keen to know his story, because it might force her to be sympathetic.

"Taken in plagues, all of them. My parents, my brothers and sister."

"*Che Dio li tegna.*" Orsola crossed herself. "Do you have a wife? Children?" Why was she allowing herself to be drawn in?

He shook his head.

"If you would rather be a gondolier, why aren't you?"

"It's not as simple as that, signora. Why are your brothers working in glass? It's what the family does."

This was true. Orsola couldn't imagine Marco or Giacomo doing anything other than glassmaking, but they had never been given a choice.

"My father was a merchant like Herr Klingenberg," he continued, "but he brought my older brothers into the business and so I had to find work elsewhere. Herr Klingenberg had no sons, so he took me on."

"Although you wanted to be on the water." Orsola was amused by the thought of this pale clerk rowing a gondola through the canals, singing and swearing.

Jonas did not reply.

"How much would Domenego's freedom cost?"

"One hundred zecchini."

Orsola drew in a breath. When he was not busy ferrying Klingen-bergs around, Domenego sometimes picked up fares around the tra-ghetto stations, taking passengers on short trips for a soldo. He would have to make over forty thousand such trips to raise the money. She would have to make over twenty thousand beads.

✧

WHEN SHE LEFT the Fondaco dei Tedeschi, Orsola made her way to the Rialto traghetto to see if Domenego was there. It had become a habit to see her friend after she met with Klingenberg. Sometimes when he wasn't busy with the family or other fares, he took her out on the Grand Canal. Even after years of this treat, Orsola still found it a thrill to dodge between other gondolas and admire the luxurious palazzos lining the water and watch the other passengers examining one another. Some of them even examined her, curious about this simple woman in a boat grander than she was, rowed by an African. Domenego seemed to enjoy it too, able to show off his skill at maneuvering the gondola without bumping into others or having to shout or swear, simply calling, "*A premando*" or "*A stagando*" to warn others he was turning left or right. If he did make a mistake, she wasn't going to judge as Klara or her father might. By now he had managed to accommodate the loss of a finger so that he was as smooth as ever.

Often they went toward San Marco, passing the Grimani and Ca' Rezzonico and Venier palazzos, Domenego naming them as they floated by. Usually they didn't get as far as San Marco, but only to Santa Maria della Salute, the enormous domed church that had been built after the plague of 1630. Adorned with statues and beautiful, unnecessary curlicues, la Salute was to Orsola the real landmark of Venice, rather than the church at San Marco or the Doge's Palace. It sat in an imposing and picturesque position at the entrance to the Grand Canal, and its generous curves were a balm to the eye after the narrow verticality of many of the houses and campaniles.

Every November a short wooden bridge was built across the Grand Canal, and Venetians made a pilgrimage over it to la Salute to give thanks to God for ending that plague, as they did in July to the Redentore. Orsola had not been to either festival. She had witnessed the

annual regatta, though, and one Festa della Sensa—Ascension Day—
Antonio had taken her out to watch the Doge marry the sea by throwing a ring into it from the *Bucintoro,* an astonishing boat in its size
and elaborate ornamentation, with its twenty-one red-and-gold oars
on each side being rowed in perfect unison.

Stop raking over memories, she thought now. Of course, that was
one of the reasons why she was looking for Domenego: he was her one
connection to Antonio. She never asked him, but at some point when
they were together, the gondolier would either hand her a packet or,
more often, shake his head. Klara Klingenberg had kept her word and
managed to get the dolphins to Domenego without her father knowing. But Orsola was worried what would happen now that Klara was
married and had moved into her husband's house in San Polo. She
wanted—needed—to speak to them both.

Orsola guessed Domenego would be rowing her to wherever it
was that married Venetian women spent their time. Going to Mass.
Visiting other women. Buying jewels. Going to the theater. Orsola
had no idea. Klara's world of sky-blue silk dresses was very different
from hers. Of course she was jealous of that dress, even though she
knew it wouldn't suit her. She was still wearing Maria Barovier's
tawny dress, though it was worn and patched in places and she'd had
to let it out in the bust and hips as a baby and age changed her. She
would have liked to wear blue silk and pearls for just one evening.

It was a foggy day, and at the traghetto she could spot only a few
boats. The other gondoliers were used to Orsola now, and being a
married woman and not quite so young and fresh, she didn't get the
attention she had done in the past. They knew she only ever took lifts
from Domenego. One of the gondoliers caught sight of her and called
out, "The *moro* has taken the German signora to Mass at Santa Maria
dei Miracoli. I can take you there, signora. Only four soldi."

Another gondolier cried, "*Ladro!* For you, only two soldi."

"One soldo," a voice from the fog called. "It's not far, signora. These thieves would charge you the Doge's gold to visit your madre!"

Orsola hesitated. If she was going to give away soldi to gondoliers, she would rather they go to Domenego—though he wouldn't take money from her. But with the fog and the cold—the kind of cold that makes stones ring and feet go numb—she didn't want to get lost wandering about in search of the church. So she called back, "*Sì!*" and when he appeared out of the fog she stepped into his gondola, to the jeers of the other boatmen. "You'll see he's the real thief!" the first gondolier shouted. "You'll see very soon!"

He was right—it took all of three minutes for the gondolier to deliver Orsola to the shallow steps by Santa Maria dei Miracoli. Of course, canals were always the direct route; walking via calles would have taken longer, especially in the disorienting fog. But it was still a high price for such a short trip, and Orsola told him so, trying to argue him down to six denari, though it was poor form to do so when a price had already been agreed to. He knew this, simply looked at her with pity for her gaucheness while waiting for his soldo. In the end she paid the fare, muttering "*Ladro fiol d'un can*" under her breath. The gondolier heard her and grinned. "*Complimenti*, signora, you are so gracious!" He rowed away, whistling.

Domenego wasn't moored by the steps as she'd expected, so she climbed up to the tiny campo around the entrance to the church. Santa Maria dei Miracoli loomed out of the fog. A small church by Venetian standards, it was a rectangle clad in yellowish marble, with a barrel roof and a dome at one end. The rio ran directly alongside it. The building was hemmed in on all sides by houses and water; indeed, it seemed a miracle it was there at all, as if God had dropped it from above into this cramped space. Nonetheless, its proportions and marble gave it a surprising elegance.

She peered along the canal, but the fog kept her from seeing anything beyond a gondola length. "Domenego," she called softly into the fog, but there was no response. It hadn't occurred to her that he might not be there. She shivered. It was cold and the fog was isolating. Venice had that sinister effect sometimes, when it closed in on you and you longed for light and water. Then you looked for the Grand Canal or the lagoon or Piazza San Marco to open up the city again.

She crossed the campo and found a narrow calle that ran along the other side of Santa Maria dei Miracoli. A few passersby emerged from the fog, hurrying past as if they had no problem making their way. Some were masked for Carnevale, but most were working people like Orsola with no time to be frivolous. She envied these confident Venetians. She would have to live here to move about so easily without getting lost.

Orsola reached the end of the building and another miniature campo with a bridge at one corner crossing the canal. There she saw Domenego's gondola tied up. Normally when he was waiting he sat on the stern, but today it was vacant. She looked around but could see so little that he might have been in the campo and she wouldn't have known.

The felze panels had all been lowered, the black cloth covering it completely. Perhaps he was inside, sleeping. She was about to call his name when one of the panels was pushed up and a woman emerged and clambered out of the gondola—the sort of woman whose dress was too bright and neckline too low. For a moment Orsola wondered how she and Domenego did their business without the boat careering all over the canal. It took some skill, and reminded her of being with Antonio in the Rosso sandolo in the lagoon.

The woman didn't look at her as she passed, but hurried over the bridge to head to Cannaregio. Soon after, Domenego climbed out of the felze. He froze when he saw Orsola, clearly mortified. After a moment he scrambled up to his usual perch on the stern.

"*Buongiorno*, Domenego," she greeted him, feeling her cheeks heat up.

He nodded but said nothing, busying himself with retying a red sash around his waist. The fashion had changed for gondoliers, and he no longer wore the patterned hose, red tunic and white plume in his cap. Instead he had on simple tan breeches and a white shirt under a brown jacket, the red sash matching his red cap.

There were thousands of whores in Venice, and many men used them. Why should she be surprised that Domenego did too? As an African slave, he was unlikely ever to marry. He had to satisfy his need somehow.

She wouldn't embarrass him more but would ignore what she had seen. "No package for me?" she asked, breaking her rule not to inquire directly about the dolphins.

Domenego shook his head. Orsola held back a sigh. It had been two years since she'd received any. Had one got lost somewhere along the way? Or—her heart sank—had Antonio died somewhere on terraferma? She swallowed. "Is Signora Klara at Mass? I need to speak to her."

He nodded.

Orsola could faintly hear the priest, giving the invitation to take communion. They had a few minutes before Klara Klingenberg would appear. "Domenego, do you have time to make a trip to terraferma?"

"Who wants to go?"

"I do." She only realized at that moment that she did. Klingenberg's casual remark about her lack of knowledge of the world had hurt. A brief trip there should be safe enough to make.

"You?" Domenego looked amused.

"Why do you laugh? Am I not allowed to go to terraferma?"

"Of course. Do you have business there?"

"No, I—I've never been, that's all. I should see it. I want to see it."

"I cannot take you, *mi dispiace.*"

"Why not?" Orsola didn't want to spend six hours in a gondola alone with someone she didn't know, or a gondolier like Bruno, who would flirt all the way there and back.

"I cannot afford to take that kind of time off and not be paid."

"Of course I'll pay you! That's what I meant! How much do you charge?"

He hesitated. "Fifteen soldi."

Fifteen simple beads, or eight fancier beads, or three millefiori. Or three chickens, or seven loaves of bread, or fifteen mackerel. It seemed reasonable. "All right."

As they were discussing when they could meet, Orsola heard voices inside the church. "Mass is over."

Domenego leaped up and untied the rope. "I must pick up Signora Klara at the other end. I'll see you there—she probably wouldn't like to see you getting a lift in her gondola." He paused. "You won't mention—" He waved across the bridge, the closest he would come to referring to the whore.

"Of course not. That's your business."

He nodded. "I am a man, after all," he said as he took up his oar and began to row.

"*De certo.*" Orsola turned and hurried across the campo and down the calle. When she reached the first campo, worshippers were spilling out from the entrance to Santa Maria dei Miracoli, coughing as they breathed in the cold fog after the relative warmth and dryness of the church. Eventually Klara Klingenberg appeared, instantly recognizable by her height. Her maid, Benedetta, was attached to her side, as she had been years before when they met by the acrobats. As the women hesitated in the fog, Orsola stepped up. "Signora Klingenberg, I am Orsola Rosso the beadmaker. I sell beads to your father. We met once before." She did not use Stefano's surname; no one recognized it as they would Rosso.

Klara turned to Orsola, her face a startled, pale oval with two brown marble eyes shining from it. Orsola had seen her from a distance a few times, in Domenego's gondola or walking through San Marco. When they'd met by the acrobats years before she had been an unformed girl. Now, up close, Orsola could see that she had grown up. Her face was thinner, with more experience etched into her eyes.

Klara was staring at her. "Ah, the dolphin woman," she said. "The glassmaker."

"*Sì*, signora."

"You have aged."

Orsola winced at her words, even though they echoed her own thoughts. No one wants to hear that they look older; they expect others to confirm they're as fresh-faced as they want to think they are. "It's been some time since we last met," she replied mildly. "And you are not long married? *Me ralegro!*"

"Yes, well . . . Benedetta, go and tell Domenego to pick me up at the other campo," Klara ordered. "I want to have a look at the back of Santa Maria dei Miracoli. Isn't it a jewel of a church? Sometimes I think that's why I married Federico, because he has always attended Mass here."

"But signora, you'll get lost in the fog!" Benedetta exclaimed.

"Nonsense, I'm not stupid. And Signora Rosso will accompany me. Go now."

Her maid frowned, but Klara had already turned from her, taken Orsola's arm and walked down the steps and around the corner into the calle. She seemed less concerned about the fog than Orsola was, strolling slowly but with confidence. "She will report this to my husband, of course," she said in a low voice. "She does everything else."

Today Klara was wearing a light-gray woolen dress and a black silk zendale draped over her head, crossed over her chest and tied at the back. From what Orsola could see, her hair was no longer in coiled braids, but falling in blond ringlets around her face. She was striking, almost beautiful, but her eyes were marked by the tension of a recently wed woman discovering what marriage was.

"*Ecco*, I have something for you," she said. "It just arrived. I hadn't given it to Domenego yet." Klara reached under her black scarf and pulled out the linen packet Orsola so longed to see. She handed it to the beadmaker, who made to tuck it in her pocket. "Oh, open it!" Klara cried. "I love to see them. I especially liked the bright-green one the last time."

Orsola picked open the knotted twine, unwrapped the packet and dropped the dolphin in her palm. It was clear glass, with a white filigree twist running through it.

"*Bellissimo*," Klara breathed. "What a clever maker!"

Orsola tried not to grimace. It was as if the German woman were in love with Antonio herself. She hurriedly wrapped up the dolphin again, preferring to study it more closely later, on her own. "Did it arrive at your father's quarters? Signor Klingenberg or someone else might have opened it."

"I thought of this when I moved to my husband's household, and wrote to say where to send the packages."

Orsola nodded. "*Grazie*, signora." It made her feel strange to think of Klara Klingenberg writing to Prague.

It seemed that whenever she was beginning to forget Antonio, or the idea of him—when that idea was losing its potency and fading like an old piece of cloth—a dolphin would arrive to brighten the color and strengthen the fabric once more. She was amazed and confused that they arrived, but also pleased. The dolphins were more than an amusement, they were a reminder: oh yes, there you are.

"You are married, *vero?*" Klara nodded at Orsola's wedding ring. "And with children?"

"One daughter."

"That must change how you feel about these dolphins, does it not?"

"I didn't marry for love, signora, but for business."

"As did I."

They had reached the other campo; Benedetta stood on its edge, peering toward them. The two women held each other's gaze for a moment, then Klara Klingenberg squeezed Orsola's arm. "*Arrivederci*, Maestra," she said, and floated off into the fog.

✧

To take a whole day away with a large family around, children to look after and work waiting for her was not easy. Orsola could say she needed to see Klingenberg and no one would question her, but that would take only a few hours. She could add a visit to cousins for another hour or two, but her mother would want details of family news. She could be honest and say she was going to terraferma, but Marco and Laura Rosso would forbid her from wasting all that time and money for no good reason. They were likely to find out anyway, but it was easier to cope with their complaining afterward than to fight with them beforehand.

Finally she made up a story about seeing Klingenberg and a client, a woman who might want to order a fancy necklace. Choosing a moment when her mother was scolding Sebastiano for stealing an extra fritola di Carnevale she had set aside for Raffaele, Orsola told her the client was very particular and it might take some time. As hoped, Laura Rosso nodded absently, more intent on punishing her grandson.

She left the house early so that no one would know how long she had been gone. Domenego picked her up by the traghetto at the southern tip of Murano, now called Colonna after the column there, which supported a statue of a former doge. The gondolier had taken off the felze to lighten the load when going such a long way, so Orsola sat exposed on the seat and wrapped herself in her shawl. Once she was settled he began the three hours of rowing to Mestre on the mainland.

For a long time they didn't speak. It was cold, with the sun not long up, the water calm, reflecting a wide palette of colors. There were fishermen out but no one else. The other gondoliers heading to or from terraferma would start an hour or two later when it was warmer, leaving from the western part of Cannaregio. It was blessedly quiet apart from Domenego's oar plashing and the occasional quacking duck. With eight children about, Orsola rarely got to hear such silence.

For once it was Domenego who broke it. When she passed him one of the hard-boiled eggs she had peeled for them he said, "*Grazie*," and popped it whole into his mouth. That one word seemed to warm up his tongue, for after he had chewed and swallowed the egg he said, "This is not the route I took him."

They never talked about Antonio, not even when he sent her a dolphin. Orsola swallowed her own last mouthful of egg with difficulty. It took a long time to clear her throat. "I know," she mumbled at last. The egg seemed to be sticking on the way down.

"That way is longer, to go north. Do you want to go that way?"

"No."

"I thought you were going to join him."

"What? No! No. Antonio left eight years ago, Domenego. If I were going to follow him I would have left with you two. I don't even know if he's—" She stopped.

"Then why do you want to go to terraferma?"

To stand on ground that connected in some way—through millions of footsteps and rocks and fields and snow and mountains—to where he was, or had been, making dolphins in a workshop up north. But she wouldn't say that to Domenego, because it was ridiculous.

She threw the eggshells in the water and a fish rose up to inspect them. "My beads have gone everywhere—even to Africa. But I have gone nowhere. I want to go somewhere."

Domenego smiled. "You think Mestre is somewhere?"

"It's better than here!"

He didn't answer, but soon enough she found out for herself.

✧

"*Mio Dio!*" she cried when Domenego set her down on Mestre's riva. "What's that smell?"

He laughed. It seemed he would be amused by her all day. "Horse piss and shit. That is how they get around on land. You get used to it." He wouldn't come with her, preferring to sleep in his gondola, to guard it and recover his energy for the trip back. "Don't trust the Mestrini," he warned her before closing his eyes.

The town was a tight mass of buildings and streets, with no canals to break it up, nor the movement of boats and glistening water to keep it fresh. Its equivalent was horses, moving goods and people about, but they were huge and unpredictable to Orsola. And they stank. She was constantly watching out for the piles of dung they left, and dodging their hooves as they clattered through the stone streets. It was hard to pay attention to anything else. Finally she reached a campo, where she could stand to one side and watch, looking for what would give her the experience of the world Klingenberg had said she lacked. His condescension still stung.

She didn't like what she saw and heard and felt. The Mestrini seemed to be staring at her, and laughing, and using words she didn't understand. Orsola had heard many languages in Venice, seen many foreigners, even dealt with them in the Rosso shop. It wasn't that she couldn't cope with strangeness. But these were her own—people from the Veneto region—and they were treating her as if she were a stranger. She supposed she was, to them. It was a feeling she wasn't used to, and she didn't like it.

She was also uneasy about what would happen on terraferma, where things worked differently. It rattled her. Orsola didn't stay long in the campo, but went back to the lagoon, drawn to the element she knew best, and to Venice in the distance, and to the safety of Domenego's gondola, reassuring herself he was still there, asleep on the stern, and had not abandoned her. Then she made brief forays back into the town. Eventually she returned and sat on the riva beside the boat, watching the activity around her. Fishermen were bringing in their overnight catches. A ferry had arrived from Padua along a canal, with the passengers disembarking and making their way onto gondolas heading to Venice and the various islands. This was the sort of scene she was more comfortable with: water and boats. No one stared at her or laughed at her or said things she didn't understand. There were many Venetians, and a variety of travelers from elsewhere: pale English, tall Germans, elegant French, some already masked and ready for Carnevale revelries and a different pace.

Eventually Domenego woke and sat up, yawning, then started when he found her beside the gondola. "Orsola, you have paid good money to have me bring you all the way to Mestre," he said, getting out his knife to pare an apple she had brought for him. "Why aren't you exploring it?"

"I did."

"Not for long. You did not like the horse shit?"

She gazed out across the water, where the many campaniles of Venice were just visible. "There's nothing so special here on terraferma."

Domenego studied her face. "You do not like being a stranger."

It was true. Orsola hated being stared at. She was treated like a bit of a stranger in Venice, though there wasn't so much separating Muranese from Venetians. One might make fun of the other, and the other might call them snobs, but given another rival such as the Mestrini, they banded together.

"I want to go back," she said.

"Already? You are sure?"

Orsola nodded. Domenego shrugged, clearly thinking her a fool.

As he was helping her into the gondola, they heard behind them, "What fare to Cannaregio?"

They turned. For a brief, irrational moment Orsola thought it might be Antonio. That was how confused terraferma was making her.

Of course it wasn't him. This man was tall, his curled white wig tied back with a dark-blue ribbon; he was wearing a triangular cocked hat and, under his cloak, a waistcoat embroidered with flowers. He had clear, bulging eyes with hooded lids, a generous mouth, and he smiled at her with small white teeth like a mouse's. "Signora," he said, "it is such a long, cold journey to Venice, especially with no felze to shelter in. Shall we not spend the time better together, warming and entertaining each other?" He spoke with a theatrical Venetian accent.

Before she could reply, Domenego took up his oar. "I can only take one passenger," he said to the man. "It is too far with two." With that he shifted them rapidly away from the shore.

"Ah, what a pity, signora!" the man called after them. "Perhaps we'll run into each other another time!" He bowed and turned toward the other gondoliers awaiting his fare.

"That was rude," Orsola said once they were out of earshot. She was tingling from the attention.

Domenego twisted his mouth. "So many men like that in Venice."

"I can handle men."

"*Mi dispiace*, Orsola, but you cannot. Not these men. Murano men all know you and your husband. They would never touch you. Venetians like him, though"—he jerked his head back toward shore—"they have no limits."

Orsola sat back. She wasn't going to argue with Domenego about the nature of men, especially men wearing embroidered waistcoats, for he undoubtedly had more experience of that sort than she did. Very occasionally such gentlemen came into the shop, but they tended to look straight through her as if she were a servant—which in a way she was.

They sat in silence for a time, with only Domenego's oar making its rhythmic splash. Then he glanced behind him and swore softly. Orsola looked around: a gondola was coming up fast behind them, rowed by two men. As they pulled alongside, the gondoliers called out a greeting, which Domenego returned with little expression. The waistcoated gentleman with the plump lips was their passenger; he was lounging back in his seat, smiling at her. "*Buongiorno, mia bella signora*, we meet again. I hope you're enjoying your trip so far. Are you going to Cannaregio as well?"

"Murano," she replied. Domenego clicked his tongue in disapproval; Orsola knew he was trying to signal that she should lie or say nothing. But she didn't feel like lying. She felt like courting danger, for terraferma had not given her whatever it was she had been looking for.

"Ah, you are Muranese. Of course, I should have known."

"How could you have known, signore?" Orsola was drawn in despite herself.

"Muranese women have a special quality."

"Have you met many Muranese women?"

He dipped his head. "A few. I go to the casino on the Grand Canal from time to time. And then the convent at Santa Maria degli Angeli has some very fine nuns." He said this as if he were talking about mirrors or chandeliers for sale. He must have seen her start. "You know it?"

"My aunt is there."

"I am sure your aunt is a most pious and honorable woman," he responded smoothly.

"My aunt would eat you like an olive that accompanies her wine."

Domenego snorted.

The gentleman took it well—he laughed. "I have no doubt she would. Perhaps I will seek her out and tell her just how *piccante* her niece is." He poured a glass of wine, then leaned across and handed it to Orsola without asking if she wanted it. She obediently took it and drank. She had never thought of herself as spicy.

"Orsola," Domenego warned in a low voice.

She ignored him and gulped more wine.

"Are your family glassmakers?" the gentleman asked.

Orsola nodded.

"What name?"

Domenego was trying to row faster but the two gondoliers easily kept pace with him.

"Rosso," she said after hesitating. If she lied he would probably catch her out.

"I will visit the Rosso workshop," he proclaimed. "What shall I buy?"

"A mirror," she answered promptly, "for it would get much use."

The man's gondoliers guffawed.

"A Rosso mirror," he said with satisfaction. "I will gladly buy one if it flatters me. And if *you* will sell it to me."

"I make beads," she blurted out, and turned red.

"Do you, now? I would like to see your beads—very much. Perhaps I will have you make a necklace for me. But who shall I give it to?"

"Your wife?"

"Now, signora, you're just fishing. You'll have to work much harder to discover if I have any wives. Meet me at the casino and maybe you'll find out!"

Abruptly Orsola's gondola veered away. "*Perdonatemi*, signore, but we head to Murano now," Domenego announced.

"Nonsense," the man said. "You can go almost all the way to Cannaregio before you need to turn toward Murano."

Domenego ignored him, with each stroke taking them farther from the other gondola.

"Would you like us to follow, signore?" one of his gondoliers asked.

The man sat back. "Let them go," he said, smiling at Orsola. "Signora Rosso clearly has important things to do back on Murano if she is in such a hurry."

"Your glass!" she cried, holding it out, though they were too far away to exchange it. It was poorly made and worth little, she noted.

The man waved his hand. "Keep it. Another reason for me to visit your shop to collect it." He donned a mask that had been dangling all the while from his fingers. "*Addio, bella signora!*"

The gondoliers had been holding back to remain with Domenego's gondola, but now they put their muscle into their rowing and pulled far ahead. They were in sight for a long while, though, and Orsola could hear the men's laughter across the water for even longer.

She finished the wine, not looking at Domenego, though she could feel his silent disapproval. The drink made her drowsy, and she curled up on the seat to sleep away the long hours back.

✧

ORSOLA SHOULD HAVE BEEN relieved that no one had noticed she'd been gone. Leaving early and staying for so little time in Mestre meant that she was back on Murano by midafternoon. No one was in the courtyard—it was too cold—and the men were all in the workshop. As she entered, Monica was working in the kitchen and Laura Rosso was coming downstairs with a cross, sleepy Angela in her arms. Orsola's daughter was never good at waking up from naps. When she saw her mother she reached out her arms and insisted Orsola hold her, burying her face in her neck. She and the fire warmed Orsola after the chilly hours spent out on the lagoon.

"Did the lady like your beads?" Laura demanded. "Has she ordered a necklace?"

Orsola thought of the gentleman on the lagoon. "Perhaps," she replied. "But perhaps not." Her mother was putting away some of the dishes from the midday meal and only half paying attention. But Monica looked up from scaling a fish and gazed suspiciously at her sister-in-law.

Later Orsola was in the storeroom, hiding the gentleman's wineglass behind Rosso glasses, when she heard from behind her, "Where did you go earlier?" Monica was leaning against the doorway, arms crossed.

Orsola went back to arranging glasses. "I told you: Klingenberg introduced me to a lady about a necklace." It was always hard to lie to Monica.

"I'll ask him next time he visits, shall I? I expect he'll tell me no. Where did you go?"

When Orsola still hesitated, her sister-in-law added, "You'd better not have a lover." Monica liked Stefano, appreciating his simplicity and his silence more than her sister-in-law did.

"How am I going to have a lover with the whole of Murano watching?"

"There are plenty of empty passages in Venice," Monica countered. "Isabella managed it." She rarely mentioned her cousin; Isabella's desertion was an embarrassment to the Vianello family. A dusty glass candlestick caught her eye, and she picked it up and polished it with her apron before replacing it in its row. "Things are working well here. The business, the children, the household. We're making money; everyone is well fed. We're happy. We don't need you to ruin it by running around behind our backs."

Orsola frowned. Monica seemed to be ignoring the tensions within the family. Giacomo might not miss Isabella but he was not happy. Laura Rosso favored Raffaele and it was annoying the other children. Marco didn't like her success at beadmaking and used every opportunity to put her down. Stella spent more and more time away from home, while Marcolin wouldn't go out farther than their calle. None of this fitted into Monica's picture of a happy family. But Orsola was not going to point out these things to her now.

"I don't have a lover," she said. "I—I went to terraferma. I have never been, and I wanted to."

"Terraferma? Why would you do that?"

"I was curious. I know it's different, and I wanted to see what it was like with that much land around me."

"And what *was* it like?"

Orsola shook her head. "Horrible. So many horses! So many strangers making me feel out of place. Solid ground is not as reassuring as people say it is. I felt nervous the whole time I was on land."

"Who took you there?"

"Domenego."

Monica's mouth twisted. "Ah. So the *moro* is your lover. I wondered."

"No! No. I trusted him to get me there without cheating me. That's all, *te lo giuro*."

"Then why did you go secretly?"

"Because—because Marco and Madre would tell me I couldn't. Because Stefano wouldn't understand. Because I don't really know why I went myself."

"You were not meeting a lover there?"

Orsola shook her head.

"Then why are you hiding that?" Monica reached around Orsola and pulled out the gentleman's wineglass.

"A man followed our gondola for a time, and he gave me a glass of wine. Domenego sent him off," she added, though she knew in truth that the man would have continued to follow them if he'd wanted to.

"Was he handsome, at least?"

"In a way. There was something about him, I can't explain. You can see for yourself if he comes here to pick up his glass."

"He knows where to come?"

"He knows our name."

Monica inspected the wineglass. "He'll be coming to see you rather than retrieve this old thing." Although brought up to distinguish between fresh and old fish, she had lived with the Rossos long enough now to gauge that the base was wobbly and bubbles were caught in the glass.

He did not come the following day, or the day after that. Orsola was trying not to notice, not to hang about the shop hoping to intercept him, not to care one way or the other. But she was worried. So far no one except Monica had discovered her trip to terraferma, but the man was likely to give away how they had met, and then she would have to explain herself to Marco, to her mother, to Stefano. Yet she wanted him to come too.

On the third day she was at her lamp, struggling to make millefiori beads that would satisfy Klingenberg and the African chiefs who wanted to wear them. She had mastered the design when she was using only a few flower discs dotted around a barrel of glass and pressed into place, then rolled on a marver. Their delicacy might please Parisian ladies, but the Africans preferred many more millefiori pressed close together in diagonal patterns all around the barrel. Pressed too hard, the flowers lost their shape and looked melted, or the rows lost their pattern like unruly soldiers fallen out of line.

"Do I have the pleasure of making the acquaintance of Signora Rosso?" she heard from the glass yard. Orsola recognized the mellifluous voice at once, but couldn't jump up, as she had just painstakingly placed red and yellow millefiori into even diagonal rows on a barrel of white opaque glass. If she applied steady pressure as she rolled them, she might at last produce a bead she was happy with.

"*Buongiorno*, signore," she heard Laura Rosso reply. "Would you care to step in and see what we have? Only the finest wares for a gentleman such as yourself."

"You are so kind, signora. I know of the Rosso reputation and have come to admire."

"Let me show you the latest candlesticks my son has made. Goblets as well. And perhaps a mirror?"

Thus far, no danger. Her mother was businesslike, not falling for his syrup.

"Oh, *bellissimo*. And there are beads as well? I have heard that a Signora Rosso makes the finest beads on Murano. That must be you, signora?"

Stunned by his words, Orsola held the millefiori bead a second too long in the lamp flame, and it melted off.

"My daughter makes them, not me."

"I am astonished. Surely you don't have a daughter old enough to make beads!"

Laura harrumphed. Orsola's mother had once been beautiful, but her face was pocked and worn from her time on Lazzaretto Vecchio. To remind her of that by flagrantly lying about how youthful she looked was clearly a misstep.

He seemed immediately to understand that he had made a mistake, for he dropped his honeyed tone. "These candlesticks: Do you make them only in clear glass?"

"We can make them any color you like. How many would you like to order, and what color?" If her mother was offended, she didn't let it stop her from selling. Indeed, she could take advantage of his discomfort. A sale was a sale.

Orsola listened as they continued discussing candlesticks, and once Laura Rosso had decided he was a serious buyer, she excused herself to fetch Marco. The moment she left, Orsola popped out of her studio and into the shop. The gentleman raised his eyebrows. "Ah, signora, what a pleasure." He was wearing another embroidered waistcoat under his black cloak.

"We have not met before," she stated in a low voice.

"Of course not," he agreed, smiling at the intrigue. "You must be the signora who makes the beads. Will you show me?" He glanced at the table where bowls holding different colored beads were displayed. It was an arrangement that always seemed to please visitors, but seen through his eyes, she now noted their gaudy simplicity, like something a child would wear.

"Come to my workshop next door," she offered. "I'm making something new."

He followed her, lips curling, wide eyes amused and then sharpening as he took in her lamp and bellows, the stacks of cane, the box of ash with rods sticking out. Orsola pulled out one she'd made the day before that was now cool and wiped it on the apron she wore to protect her from molten glass, then held it up before him. "Millefiori. I made this one yesterday." The bead was royal blue with yellow and white flowers delicately dotted around it.

He took the rod from her and studied the bead with the eye of a connoisseur of beauty. "These millefiori are exquisite," he said. "So delicate, and the colors are perfection." He paused. "Have you considered flattening them into rectangles or lozenges? Then they will lie securely on a woman's chest."

She hadn't thought of that. Normally when anyone other than Klingenberg made a suggestion about her work, Orsola became defensive. But this man wasn't being critical to get at her or elevate himself at her expense. He seemed genuinely to want to make even better something he had taken a fancy to.

"I could try flattening them, I suppose," she replied.

"If you do, I will buy enough to have a necklace strung."

This was the commission Orsola had been waiting for. She tried to remain calm and businesslike. "I can string it for you. Twelve large beads, with small beads in between to space them out. Are these the colors you prefer?"

He smiled. "Signora, I will leave the choices and the details to your superior taste."

They held each other's gaze for a moment longer than was polite, until Marco entered. "Signore, an honor to make your acquaintance," he purred, for he could be charming when he chose to. "*Prego*, come to the workshop, where I can show you some of our work rather than these trifles. It's warmer by the furnace and it doesn't smell."

Orsola was so used to the tallow stench that she hardly noticed it now. At least he had not called the beads rabbit turds in front of the stranger.

"Oh, I'm attracted to strong scents," the gentleman replied. "Especially animal and body scents. They are irresistible." He winked as he followed her brother.

Orsola didn't go with them to the workshop. Laura Rosso would put out a table with a cloth trimmed with Burano lace, some of Marco's best glasses and a bottle of good wine they saved for such customers. They would sit and Marco would talk to him about glass, with Giacomo and Stefano and the garzoni demonstrating techniques, blowing and pulling and pinching the glass into various shapes, adding theatrical twirls of the punties and stoking the furnace so that it roared. Giacomo would make a rearing glass horse, Marco a drinking glass with the flourish of lions for handles. All the while, Laura would refill the glasses again and again. This display would go on for as long as it took to make a decent sale, well into the night if necessary. Monica and Orsola would bring in more wine, platters of fried sardines and oysters, bowls of olives, plates of cheese, aniseed biscotti. Normally Orsola served quickly and left, for she hated seeing Marco get drunker and more insistent. Only Laura could give him a look that warned him he was going too far. Then he would pull back, and let his mother move in soberly to negotiate. Her age and experience made it harder to take advantage of her.

This time, however, Orsola was tempted to remain and watch. As she and Monica crossed the courtyard carrying platters of dried fruit and bowls of biscotti, Monica whispered, "Is it him? The man in the gondola?"

"Shh. Yes."

"Wait!" Monica ran back to the kitchen and came out wearing a fresh apron and carrying bowls of pistachios and olives. "In case he wants something salty," she explained. She had smoothed her hair, and though with her rough skin and beak-like nose she would never be beautiful, her crystal-blue eyes sparkled and she appeared bright and fresh. The two women looked at each other and began to laugh.

The men all looked up as they came in, Monica and Orsola still giggling like young girls. That was the effect the visitor seemed to have on women, even those like Monica who had only heard about him. He leaned back in his chair and smiled as they set the platters and bowls before him, while Marco and Laura Rosso tried to hide their annoyance. If a customer wanted to flirt with the wives of the family, they had to allow it if they wanted a sale.

"Ah, pistachios, my favorite," he said to Monica, who looked him up and down and, for the first time since Orsola had known her, blushed.

He had the sense, though, not to give them too much attention and alienate their husbands. He turned back to Giacomo and Stefano, who were making a goblet, Giacomo leading, Stefano assisting. "Why are you turning the rod like that?" he asked. "What are those called?" He pointed at the tongs Giacomo was using to shape the glass. "Do you ever burn yourself? Does the furnace ever go out? Do all the colors go the same orange when hot? How long does that have to cool?" He fired question after question at them. He was not asking just to fill the room with the sound of his own voice, though; he was curious, perhaps the most curious man Orsola had ever met. Antonio would hate him, she thought as she and Monica watched from the back of the workshop. He would sense a rival.

As Giacomo and Stefano put the last touches on the goblet, Marco began to brag about all the designs the Rosso workshop could make.

The man cut through his ramble like a hot knife through butter. "I would like to see what other glasses you have." He glanced at Orsola, and added with a smirk, "And mirrors. You can imagine how much I like mirrors. I hear yours are the best on the island." He stood, leaving most of his wine and taking charge of the tempo of the negotiation.

Marco jumped up after him. "Stefano can show you the mirrors. This way, into the storeroom."

Orsola and Monica didn't witness that negotiation, for they had no reason to follow. Marco and Laura Rosso—and latterly Stefano, to talk about mirrors—spent another hour with the visitor. Orsola and Monica crept to the entrance several times, in between chores, and were finally rewarded with a smile and a deep bow as the man was leaving. "Signore, it has been my ultimate pleasure to meet you." He let his eyes linger on Orsola, before turning to Laura and kissing her hand. "I will return soon to discuss the chandelier."

"Of course, signore," she replied. "We await your return with impatience."

Orsola had never heard her mother speak like that. His manner was rubbing off on her.

"Chandelier?" she cried when he had gone. "You're going to make him a chandelier?"

"And four dozen glasses, and a mirror," Marco replied. "Maybe even more than that!" He lunged at Monica and kissed her, a rare display of affection.

"There's plenty of juice left to squeeze in that plum," Laura Rosso added. She too was almost drunk from the man's presence.

"We don't make chandeliers!" Orsola protested. "That's work for bigger workshops, not Rossos."

They were too busy celebrating to listen. Even Monica was allowing herself to be caught up in Marco's excitement, laughing when he wouldn't put her down but held her in his arms as if she were a new bride. "I'm going to get you that fur I promised," he said. "A maestro's wife should wear a fur. And we'll hire more servants, give your little hands a break." He kissed them, with all their scars left over from gutting fish in her previous life. Monica looked embarrassed, but let her husband have his moment, as it was rare for Marco to be so happy and affectionate.

"I'm making him a necklace," Orsola announced, feeling the need to insert herself into the glee.

Marco glanced at her, his nose still in Monica's neck. "Don't ruin the moment, sorella."

Orsola turned red, deflated. Suddenly it was painful to watch as Marco cavorted with his wife while Laura Rosso called to Giacomo and the garzoni to join them for wine in celebration of all the fine work the Rosso workshop would be making. Only Stefano seemed subdued. Orsola sidled over and stood with her husband. She did not link her arm through his, and he did not put his around her waist. They had always had a formal relationship rather than a playful one. She never sat in his lap as Monica sometimes did with Marco. Only Angela sat in her father's lap, for Stefano and his daughter were much closer than he and Orsola were. She often felt guilty about that. "So you're making a mirror," she said.

Stefano nodded. "For the entrance to his patron's palazzo, so that he can adjust his hat before he goes out." He was clearly repeating the customer's words; it would never occur to him to check his own appearance before going out into Murano. "He seemed very familiar with you," he continued. "He knew all about your beads."

"Only because I showed him for a moment."

"He said he ordered a necklace from you. When was that?"

"Just before he began drinking with Madre and Marco." Orsola tried to steer the subject away from the gentleman. "As usual Marco drank too much."

Stefano grunted. "Fast work."

He could have been referring to her brother, but she knew better. It was a surprise to see jealousy bubbling up in Stefano. Orsola took a deep breath. If she didn't say something, this would fester and cause problems later. She needed her husband on her side. "Stefano," she began, putting her hand on his arm, "I'm making a necklace for him because he ordered it, the same way he's asked you to make him a mirror. That's all. It's business. Good for us. For the Rossos."

After a moment Stefano nodded. "I'll be helping with the chandelier as well. We'll all be working on it."

Orsola grimaced. The chandelier would require many weeks of planning and carrying out. They would have to stop making other pieces, putting them behind with Klingenberg, and buy the materials for huge quantities of glass. Of course it would be worth it if they made something spectacular, and if the gentleman actually paid for it. But his mention of casinos, as well as his extravagant nature, made her wonder if he had debts—and could drag them into debt too.

⟡

AFTER THE GENTLEMAN'S visit Orsola began experimenting, for she wanted more than ever to make a truly elegant piece that would impress everyone, not just the gentleman. With a glass necklace it came down to shape, color and proportion: choosing tones that worked together, and making the different elements the right shapes and sizes. Too big and the necklace would be heavy and hang badly. Too small and you couldn't see it. Colors could cancel each other when they needed to resonate and shine. Orsola was playing with flattening the beads, as the man had suggested, trying out different shapes and thicknesses, placing the millefiori carefully. She would only start making multiple beads once she was satisfied. If she got this necklace right, the gentleman and his friends might order more. It was an opportunity at last to increase her beadwork and begin making necklaces.

The gentleman had shaken everyone awake. Marco spent hours drawing different goblets, conferring with Giacomo about what shape the bowl should be, how each part of the stem should look, what embellishments should be added. Giacomo sculpted glass snakes, fish, mermaids, ivy and ropes before they settled on grapevines growing up the stems, carrying tiny clusters of purple and green grapes. They made model after model before sending one to the gentleman for his approval. Meanwhile Stefano was designing a mirror that was slightly curved, though no one would notice; it flattered viewers by making them look thinner. This was one of the tricks that made his mirrors so popular. The men had not even begun on the chandelier.

The Rossos were spending all their time on this man they barely knew. Even Laura Rosso, usually so down-to-earth, had fallen under his spell. It worried Orsola enough that she went to the one person she knew on Murano who might be able to tell her more about him.

Orsola visited her aunt at the convent every month or so; work and the children made it difficult to go more often. She never looked forward to the visit, for Zia Giovanna was not an easy woman. Since entering the convent after the plague, she had dropped the niceties of speech that made conversation flow. She never asked questions, and because her life as a nun was so unvaried, Orsola soon ran out of things to ask her and would begin to babble about whatever she could think of while the nun sat silent, watching her niece, never nodding or agreeing with her or saying, "I'm listening." Sometimes Orsola brought Angela with her as a distraction, though Giovanna's experience of being quarantined with Stella and Marcolin had put her off children, and she either ignored her great-niece or shouted at her, either of which made Angela cry. Their meetings were dissatisfying for aunt and niece, yet she complained if Orsola let too much time pass between visits. "You're forgetting me," she would grumble. "I'll just rot away here and no one will notice."

It was cold the day she visited, but crisply sunny, so they sat in the herb garden, which was laid out in a circle with two small, uncomfortable stone benches in the center. Orsola had sat there many times before. In summer she would inspect the plants, squeeze the mint and verbena and sage and oregano between her fingers to sniff until Zia Giovanna shouted at her to stop ruining the herbs. Now all the plants had died back to nubs in the bare soil except for the rosemary and lavender, which kept their leaves during the winter.

Orsola asked her aunt the requisite questions: Was she eating well, were there any new novitiates, had the leak in the chapel roof been fixed? She updated her on the family: Angela was speaking in full sentences, and her father doted on her; Andrea and Sebastiano had learned to read; Raffaele could now row the sandolo. She was careful not to mention Stella or Marcolin. She filled her in on glass business, and on neighbors who had married or given birth or died. She tried to remember the content of the priest's homilies at Santi Maria e Donato.

She did not fool Zia Giovanna. Perhaps she was a little too eager to talk, to flatter, to create a bond between them. She was in the middle of telling a story about how Sebastiano refused to go to bed because he was sure bats roosted in his room when her aunt interrupted. "What do you want?"

"What do you mean, Zia Giovanna? I don't want anything."

"Of course you do." Giovanna picked her teeth and examined what she had found before flicking it away. "Don't lie to me, Orsola. It's undignified."

Orsola tore off a sprig of leathery rosemary and broke it over and over between her fingers, releasing its sharp, woody scent.

"Don't do that. There'll be no rosemary left to cook with if you wreck it."

Orsola threw away the rosemary. "I wanted to ask you about a man who has visited the convent before."

For the first time in many visits, Giovanna looked interested. "Who?"

"His name is Giacomo Casanova."

Zia Giovanna recoiled as if a snake had crawled out from the non-existent herbs. Then she began to laugh, an uneven, rusty sound like a frog. Orsola hadn't heard her laugh since before the plague. Some laughter makes you want to join in, even if you don't know what's funny. This was not like that. It felt more like laughter as an attack: on her, on the family and most of all on the signore.

Orsola had to sit, turning redder and redder as she waited for her aunt to finish. Finally Giovanna stopped and wiped her eyes with the sleeve of her heavy black robe. "What do you want to know about him?"

"Is he trustworthy?" Orsola felt a little silly asking, as the laughter seemed to be her answer.

Zia Giovanna snorted. "With women or money? He's not to be trusted with either."

"How do you know him?"

"He used to visit one of the novitiates here. Well, not one, but two. Sometimes at the same time!" She chuckled, and Orsola gasped as she realized what her aunt meant. "Oh, he gave us plenty of entertainment! Why do you want to know? He isn't visiting *you*, is he, you stupid girl?"

"No, no, of course not! He's ordered work from the Rosso workshop, that's all." She didn't add that she was making a necklace for him, or that she thought he would bring in more business. Zia Giovanna had shown no interest in her beadmaking, even though beads had fed her during the plague.

"*Mariavergine!*" Her aunt crossed herself. "Has he paid you in advance? No, of course he hasn't. That man drinks the most expensive wine, brought his nuns the fanciest silk stockings and gloves of soft leather—so many they passed them around to us!" To her niece's astonishment Giovanna lifted her robe to reveal delicate white stockings. Her shins were scrawny rather than plump, and the stockings gathered in a ring of wrinkles around her ankles. "They're good on cold days, though you wouldn't expect that from something so thin."

She dropped her robe. "He has many debts at the casinos, both here and in Venice," she continued. At the look on Orsola's face she snapped, "What did you expect, girl? One look at him and you know he's the type to live beyond his means. What does he want Marco to make?"

"Four dozen goblets, and a mirror, and . . ." Orsola trailed off as Giovanna crossed herself again. Saying it aloud made her understand how absurd it was of Marco to agree to make forty-eight goblets without being paid a soldo in advance. And this was not even considering the chandelier, which she couldn't bring herself to mention to her aunt.

Zia Giovanna shook her head and rearranged her robe to cover her legs. "Marco is an idiot. But he is also up against a man who is an expert at getting what he wants. My advice? Cut the order to a dozen goblets, and deliver them in person to his patron, who usually ends up paying off all his debts. You know he's not of noble birth? His mother was an actress!" She spat theatrically. "If the goblets are paid for, then you add in another dozen, and the mirror. But slowly, coaxing the money out of him or his patron." Orsola's aunt had always been as shrewd as her sister—shrewder, in a way, because unlike Laura she had no emotional ties to the Rossos to cloud her logic.

When Orsola told her mother what her sister had suggested, Laura Rosso scolded her for going to Zia Giovanna in the first place. "She'll be telling the other nuns, and soon the whole island will know!"

"They already do: Marco's been bragging at l'Omo Salvadego. Three people stopped me in the market to ask about the chandelier."

"He's just proud to get such an eminent order, from such a man."

"'Such a man'—you don't know anything about him! His mother is an actress!" Orsola was parroting Zia Giovanna.

Laura clicked her tongue.

Orsola pushed on. "If Marco and Giacomo and Stefano spend all their time making these things rather than working on the order for Klingenberg, and the signore doesn't pay, the Rosso workshop could go out of business." She knew her mother knew this, but felt she had to say it.

"If you think the signore won't pay, why are you still making a necklace for him?"

Orsola tried to think of a clever reply but couldn't, for Laura Rosso was right. She didn't want to stop making beads for him. There was something intoxicating about making a beautiful piece for such a man, a necklace that she might even see around a Venetian woman's neck as she strolled around the piazzetta by the Doge's Palace during the passeggiata. Something everyone would look at and say, "Who is the maker? She is skilled!" It might just bring more attention to all the Rosso glasswork. It was a fantasy, but she held on to it because it pushed her to work harder and create better.

"I will get my money for it; it's not so much," she said. "But four dozen goblets, a mirror, a necklace and a chandelier? *Mariavergine!*"

Laura Rosso pursed her lips. "The Rossos have never made a chandelier before," she began. "Most other glass families have. Do you remember what your father was making when he died? A chandelier. For the first time. Then a piece of it killed him. After that, no one wanted a Rosso chandelier. Marco wants to break that curse."

Orsola stared at her. That was a day she tried never to think about. Now, though, an image of her father flashed before her: sitting frozen, tongs in his hands, a shard of glass sticking out of his neck. Then, when he'd pulled it out, a red river cascading down him and pooling at his feet until he fell into it. But before that, what he had been working on that killed him: the half-made arm of a chandelier in filigreed, translucent glass. Only now in her mind's eye did she recognize what it was.

"So I'm not going to tell him not to make one," Laura continued. "This is an opportunity we cannot turn down."

Orsola didn't argue further except to repeat Zia Giovanna's suggestion that Marco make a dozen goblets and take them to the signore to extract payment before beginning on more. She was ignored. All she could do was look after her own business with him. When she'd finished the millefiori necklace to her satisfaction, she would take it over to Venice and refuse to leave until she was paid.

Orsola worked hard, melting down bead after bead until she was satisfied. When it was at last done, the beads strung on a silk cord, she took it to the kitchen to show Monica and Rosella. She had used various shades of blue, with white dots in the centers of the millefiori to resemble pearls, as did the small white beads separating the larger ones. The flowers were not squeezed together as Africans preferred them, but spaced around dark-blue barrel-shaped beads, slightly flattened as the gentleman had suggested. The effect was of flowers spangled like stars around the neck. Monica and Rosella exclaimed when they saw it. Monica wouldn't try it on, but Rosella was eager to wear it, though it hung low around her neck, as she was not yet old enough to have the chest for it.

Orsola was explaining that she would go over to deliver the necklace in person when Stefano appeared in the doorway. He smiled at Rosella and the necklace. "*Sei bellissima*," he said to the girl. "Would you like to see yourself?"

Rosella nodded.

"Wait there." He disappeared, returning with a half-length mirror he set on the table and propped against the wall. The mirror itself was long and narrow. The frame was not the usual gold-painted wood, but a curling garland of glass, decorated with flowers along it, with a glass bouquet spraying out at the top. Two sconces curved out from the bottom to hold candles so that you could see yourself before you went out for the evening. Most surprising of all was the woman engraved in the center of the mirror, standing naked on a cloud, with long, flowing hair, her breasts round as oranges, a cloth barely covering her lower body. It was not at all his usual style, and far more elaborate than anything he had made before, but Stefano had understood that he needed to cater for a taste different from his own. Orsola wondered where he had got the inspiration for the woman; she certainly looked nothing like his wife.

Rosella stood in front of it, entranced first by her own reflection, then by the necklace, finally by the naked woman, which she ran a finger over.

"*Magnifico*, Stefano," Monica declared. "Is that for the signore?"

He nodded. "Just finished. I can take it over with your necklace," he said to Orsola. She gave him a look. "That is, we can go together," he corrected himself. "Wait for payment. We may have more success if there are two of us."

Orsola opened her mouth to protest, for she cherished the trips she made alone to Venice. They gave her freedom for a few hours, to wander and look and admire. She also suspected she was more likely to be paid if she was alone, given the kind of man she was working for. She had been looking forward to a bit of wine and flirtation. Nothing more, but enough to encourage him to open his purse. That was unlikely to happen with Stefano there as well. Perhaps that was why he wanted to come.

But he was her husband, and he asked so little of her that she could only nod and try to hide her disappointment.

The next morning Bruno rowed them across the lagoon and through back canals to the palazzo in Castello where the signore's patron, Senator Bragadin, lived. Bruno had at last married and had three children, but that didn't stop him from whistling rude ditties and calling out sweary greetings to the other gondoliers. He was amused that Orsola and Stefano were going to Venice together, and to a senator's house. Of course he knew whom they were going to see; all of Murano knew. "Gondoliers have made up a song about your signore," he said. "Want to hear it?" Before they could stop him Bruno began to sing:

> La Serenissima, lock up your daughters
> Your mothers, your aunts
> Even your grandmothers are not safe!
> Casanova is back, and he will conduct them all
> With his lively baton—

"*Basta!*" Stefano cried. "You embarrass us and yourself."

Bruno sniggered, for little embarrassed him. He continued to hum as he brought them gliding up to the portico steps of Ca' Bragadin. It was a pale-pink four-story building, with rows of windows framed by pointed arches on two of the levels. Less grand than the palazzos on the Grand Canal, and in a quieter, less ostentatious location, it was nonetheless elegant and well maintained, its gleaming stone render freshly applied. On the balcony of the first floor, two women sat drinking coffee and looking out over the canal, wearing loose gowns that indicated they were not long out of bed. They took no notice of their visitors. Orsola glanced at Stefano: he had shaved and she had brushed her hair, and they were wearing the clean new clothes they would wear to Mass, but compared to the Venetians they were poorly turned out. While respected on Murano for their glass, here they were simply workers to be ignored.

Stefano stood up in the gondola but hesitated stepping onto solid ground, clearly intimidated by his surroundings. The women on the balcony tittered, and though it was probably about something that had nothing to do with them, it made Orsola ashamed of her husband's timidity. Antonio would have stepped into the palazzo with confidence, she thought, then shook off the idea. She tried never to compare the two.

She jumped up, rocking the boat and sending Stefano toppling back into his seat as she clambered up the portico steps. "*Oe, signora!*" Bruno called. "Is that how you feel about your husband, that you want him to fall into the canal? No wonder you only have one child!"

Orsola gasped as if the boatman had punched her in the stomach. She had miscarried again only the month before.

This time the women on the balcony *were* laughing at them. Bruno joined in; he must have been delighted to be entertaining two noblewomen.

Stefano grabbed his mirror—wrapped in linen and tied with twine—and handed the heavy package to Orsola before climbing onto the steps. He turned to Bruno, whose grin dimmed as he began to realize he had gone too far. "*Vattene!* We won't be coming back with you. Nor will we pay you. You've insulted my wife. *Canagia!*" Orsola had never heard him so angry.

As Bruno began to splutter, "It was a joke! Can't you take a joke?" Stefano picked up the mirror, took her arm and led her into the dark androne, its stone floor still damp from a recent high tide. From the dimness she turned to look back at the bright rectangle of sunlight, where Bruno stood in his sandolo, shouting that they were ladri who could not be trusted.

"Are you all right?" Stefano asked, squeezing her arm. Orsola laid a hand on his and squeezed back, suddenly grateful he was with her.

"I will never hire him again," she said. "And I pray to the Madonna that neither of those women up there ever wears this necklace." Orsola clutched the packet holding her millefiori.

They glanced around the androne. This was where business trans-actions often took place in palazzos. Crates of wine lined one wall, with a basket of early cherries and another of sardines sitting on top. A wide marble staircase at the far end led up to the main, dry part of the palazzo.

Orsola and Stefano looked at each other. They had not talked about what they would do once they got there. She had never been inside a palazzo, not even the more modest ones on Murano. She had assumed someone would be there to greet them. "Should we go up?" She nodded at the staircase.

Just then a man came running down it—a servant of some sort, though he was better dressed than they were, in a new white linen shirt and gold thread stitched down the side of his breeches. He grabbed the baskets and was about to run back up when Stefano called out, "Signore!"

At this he jumped, then squinted at them in the dim light. "What are you doing here? Out!"

"We've come to see Signor Casanova."

At the name, the servant looked Orsola up and down, then glanced at Stefano, as if puzzled that he was with her.

"We come from Murano and have some things he ordered from us," Orsola explained. "A necklace, a mirror. They are ready."

"Leave them here." The man gestured at the crates of wine. "I'll take them up later."

"They're far too precious to be left here," Stefano said. "We want to hand them directly to the signore."

"He's still asleep."

"We can wait," Orsola said.

"Then you'll be waiting all day. The signore keeps late hours. Leave them there; they'll be safe enough."

"We've come to be paid," she added.

The man laughed. It reminded her of the women's laughter upstairs, and of Zia Giovanna's laughter when Orsola first mentioned the gentleman to her.

Just then there was a shout out on the canal, someone telling Bruno to get out of the way. At the top of the staircase a group was beginning to descend, headed by an older man in a red cloak, a three-cornered hat perched atop his ample wig. His authoritative bearing—straight back, steady trot down the stairs a few steps ahead of everyone else, eyes fastened on the bright world outside—made his status clear. This must be the patron, Orsola thought. As the servant they'd been dealing with took a step back, she stepped forward and opened her mouth, hoping to save the Rosso family from the ruin a chandelier, a mirror, a necklace and four dozen goblets could bring on them. And maybe she would have. If Senator Bragadin had even glanced to his right and noticed them, she might have been able to unstick her tongue from the roof of her mouth and tell him they had made good work for his ward and that they were poised to make more, to make a chandelier that would be the talk of Venice, that she was depending on this necklace to establish her reputation and drive more business her way—if only he would pay them. But he did not look at her and Stefano, and Orsola's tongue remained glued as they watched him step out into the sunlight and onto the gondola awaiting him, doubtless taking him to a very important meeting with another very important person—perhaps the Doge himself. The women on the balcony above called to him, and he removed his hat and waved it over his head at his admirers before sitting down inside the felze.

When Senator Bragadin was gone, the servant seemed to become aware of Orsola and her husband again, and jerked his head toward the door onto the canal without even bothering to say *"Andate."* Go.

They set the necklace and the mirror on top of the wine crates. "We'll leave by the calle," Orsola said, not wanting to face Bruno out on the canal. They could make their way on foot to the northern riva and hire a traghetto back to Murano.

The servant led the way to a door opposite, which opened onto a familiar courtyard scene: a square wellhead in the middle adorned with lions, benches in the sun occupied by old women sewing, a woman stirring sheets in a cauldron, children crisscrossing the space in a chasing game.

Orsola stopped, remembering Domenego's long-ago lesson. "We need a receipt for our goods," she declared, folding her arms and planting her feet, as if bracing herself.

The servant rolled his eyes, but he had clearly had this demand made before, and didn't seem surprised. "*Un momento,*" he said, and hurried back inside. As they waited, they watched the children and the women, none of whom showed any curiosity about these mere tradespeople. They could have been gondola oars leaning in the corner for all they were noticed.

"Do you think we'll ever be paid?" Stefano murmured.

Orsola shook her head. "I don't know. But you must tell Marco about this, about how we were treated. Maybe he could get Klingenberg to negotiate payment for the chandelier." Klingenberg didn't normally get involved in local sales; his trade was with other countries. But he might know how to deal with their unreliable customer.

"Your brother won't listen to me."

Orsola knew this. Marco may have had more respect for her husband's work than for hers, but he did not take advice from either of them.

A few minutes later the servant returned with a sheet of paper, a quill and a bottle of ink, and wrote out a brief description of the mirror and the necklace. Orsola had at last taught herself to read, but could only make out the name Casanova, which was written twice as large as any of the other words.

✧

No money arrived, of course. Instead Domenego did, two months later. One of the garzonetti came to fetch Orsola from her studio. As she passed through the workshop, Marco was carefully attaching one of the twelve flowered arms to a chandelier, held up by ropes and a pulley—a delicate operation, for any mistake could break off parts of it that would take days to fix. They had already attached most of the arms, and the bunches of grapes hanging from them swayed as Marco pushed the hot glass against the central globe.

Orsola had not seen the chandelier whole before, but only glimpsed individual pieces being made before they were assembled: an arm or a flower adornment or a long, curled leaf. Now she stopped to take it in. The body of the chandelier consisted of a stack of blown shapes in different lengths and widths, the main one a sphere from which the arms emerged. Above it was a smaller tier, with masses of flowers and leaves growing out from it. Grapes dangled from every arm and curled leaf. It was all made of a combination of clear and translucent glass with accents of turquoise on the edges of some of the pieces and on the grapes. It shouldn't work—blue flowers and long leaves and grapes? But it did. When he put his mind to it, Marco had a clever eye.

"*Meraviglioso*," she said in a low voice, careful not to disturb the men at this crucial moment. The work required intense concentration from Marco and Giacomo and Stefano. They had been working for almost a month on the chandelier, pushing aside all other work, including orders from Klingenberg, which were normally sacrosanct. Everyone was dripping with sweat from the heat and from nerves. Orsola wanted to stay and watch, to admire her husband and brothers working so intently. But Domenego was waiting at the back of the workshop, so she pulled herself away and slipped out to the dock.

The gondolier was looking particularly somber, and her heart skipped a beat. Antonio, she thought, hugging herself. Even after all these years, that was her first thought.

It was not Antonio, however. "I thought you should hear this from me, Orsola, rather than in the market," he said. "Your Signor Casanova has been arrested. He is being kept in the Piombi in the Doge's Palace."

A cry went up from the workshop. For a moment Orsola thought they had heard Domenego's news. Instead they were celebrating the final arm being successfully attached and completing the chandelier no one would now pay for.

5

THE SKIMMED STONE SKIPS forty-two years now, touching down in 1797. Two major revolutions have taken place during those years. First, the American, which Muranese glassmakers and Venetian nobility can overlook. Second, the French. Being closer to home, this revolution is harder to ignore. It spawns Napoleon Bonaparte, and he is not about to let any European ignore him. His army marches across the continent, conquering territory, and when it reaches the Veneto region it seizes Venice, the prize jewel. The Venetian Senate votes itself out of existence, senators shedding their velvet as they flee the Doge's Palace, and the City of Water is a republic no more.

Elsewhere, the arts have become neoclassical—all longing gazes back to ancient Greece and Rome. Goethe and Schiller are leaders of Weimar Classicism in Germany. But the disruptive Romantics are brewing. Wordsworth and Coleridge have met in England. William Blake has written *Songs of Innocence and of Experience*. Inimitably, Jane Austen has begun her witty novels *Pride and Prejudice* and *Sense and Sensibility*.

On the Island of Glass, Orsola Rosso is turning back and forth in the flame a blue millefiori bead dotted with yellow and white flowers. She looks up; she is now thirty-seven. She and those who matter to her are another eight years older. Their fate is linked to that of their nearby city. And Venice is suffering. We are going to skim through that suffering, expanding and contracting our way within those years so we don't linger on them . . .

⟡

WHEN ORSOLA RECEIVED WORD that Klingenberg wanted to see her immediately, she did not jump up and head across the lagoon, though Domenego brought the message, even leaving his gondola and coming into the Rossos' kitchen to deliver it, and was waiting to take her over to the Fondaco dei Tedeschi. "Is it that urgent?" she demanded. "I'm busy here." She was indeed busy, though not with beads. Orsola, Monica, Rosella and Stella had picked all the aubergines and zucchini, the tomatoes and garlic and peppers, the plums and pears and apples, and were preserving and pickling them for the winter. Since the Murano glass business had declined so much, they were even more reliant on the produce they grew to keep them fed. Now was not the time to be traveling over to Venice.

"He did not tell me why," Domenego replied. "But he rarely asks anyone to come quickly." The gondolier seemed tired, and the hair at his temples was graying. The long tan tunic he had on didn't fit him as well as the short, tight red tunic and diamond-patterned hose he'd worn when Orsola first met him, which had suited his tall, lean figure. Now he looked drab and weary—as did everyone. A few months before, the French had taken over the Venetian Republic and proclaimed it dead, and the Rossos and Murano and Venice were all waiting to see what would happen to the city. Klingenberg's orders for glassware and beads had reduced to a trickle again. The merchant had not been pleased with the long delay Casanova's chandelier and goblets had caused years before, and cut back his orders from the Rossos as a punishment. It took several years for Marco to regain the merchant's confidence, and by that time Napoleon was on the horizon.

But Domenego was right. Klingenberg wouldn't send for her unless it was important. A commission, perhaps. The Rossos needed one. Orsola wiped her hands of tomato juice, removed her spattered apron, apologized to the others and went to Venice.

The Fondaco dei Tedeschi was tomb-like, the German merchants much reduced in number, and those left were waiting like the rest of the city for Napoleon's decision on their fate. Jonas was sitting in the antechamber, writing as always in a ledger, though there must be much less to record with trade so low during Napoleon's campaign to take control of the Italian states. Perhaps he was pretending to look busy and if Orsola glanced over his shoulder, she would see simply scribbles. They nodded to each other, their courteous détente holding now that there were bigger enemies to face, like the French. Jonas led her in, calling out, "Orsola Rosso here to see you, Herr Klingenberg."

"Ah, Signora Orsola, thank you for coming." Klingenberg stood and waited for her to sit. His chamber was still comfortable, but it felt less luxurious than it had once been. His Persian carpets were thread-bare; in earlier times he would have replaced them. His desk was battered, and his fur-trimmed robe hanging in the corner looked moth-eaten. In the past Klingenberg had prided himself on maintaining plush comfort in a timeless manner, but now it felt old and almost shabby. Klingenberg too had aged: his hair and beard were now entirely silver, and he sat down carefully, as if afraid to jolt his bones. But he was as hospitable as ever. "Jonas, Malvasia and bussolai for our guest!" he called. After a moment Jonas brought in a decanter and two glasses on a lacquered tray, as well as a red glass dish full of the popular Venetian biscuits. Orsola found them too dry, even when dunked in wine. But she gamely took one and nibbled at it. He is courting me, she thought. What does he want?

He asked after her mother and daughter and brothers, but his interest was perfunctory. He set down his wineglass hard, making Orsola start. Klingenberg never crashed glasses.

"You will know, of course, that we are waiting for General Bonaparte to act, one way or the other. It is not at all clear who will be put in charge of Venice."

"The French, no? They took over in May."

The merchant waggled his head. "Some hope the city will remain independent. Myself, I do not share that hope. There is speculation Napoleon will use Venice and the Veneto as a bargaining chip with the Austrians when he ends the war with them."

Orsola knew little about the French, except that they had been occupying Venice all summer. She knew nothing about the Austrians except that they spoke German. "Wouldn't you prefer Austrian rule, because of the language?" she suggested. "They are more like you."

Klingenberg smiled the diplomatic smile he had perfected over the years. "I have always been welcome here. I like the Venetian way of life. My daughter has married a Venetian; my grandsons are Venetian, though I speak to them in German so they will be comfortable in that language." He paused. "I do not think Austrians and Venetians make a good match. They are temperamentally very different. If Venetians are water, Austrians are earth."

"What is Bonaparte?"

"Fire. He conquers, he leaves. That is why I wanted to see you."

"He's coming?" It felt as if the city had been waiting for him for months.

"His wife, Josephine, is coming."

"She is?"

"It is imperative that she gains a good impression of Venice. There will be balls laid on for her, an opera, a regatta. She will stay in Palazzo Pisani Moretta, one of the finest. She will be showered with gifts—the best the city can provide. Fabrics, spices, paintings, a gondola to be transported to Paris. Jewelry." He fixed her with a look. "She has a passion for jewelry. A group of merchants at the Fondaco dei Tedeschi has joined together to present the General's wife with a gift. We want you to make her a necklace, one that she would never see elsewhere and that will always remind her of Venice and its master glassmakers."

Another necklace, Orsola thought, remembering the Casanova necklace she had never been paid for. She had not said anything to Klingenberg about it or the mirror, though of course he knew of the chandelier: after unsuccessfully trying to sell it himself, Marco had reluctantly asked the merchant for his help. But Klingenberg had not been able to find a buyer either, and the chandelier now gathered dust on a shelf in the storeroom, its grapes and flowers losing their luster. Many of the four dozen goblets they had not managed to sell also sat in dusty rows like soldiers, a reminder of the debacle the Rossos had never fully recovered from.

"We will pay you, Orsola, of course," Klingenberg assured her. "But this is about more than money. If Josephine samples the beauty and spirit of the place, she will be more inclined to encourage her husband to allow us our independence. Your necklace would play a part in that."

"This is not my city," she said. "Murano is my home."

Klingenberg's jaw tightened; he was clearly irritated by the distinction. "Of course," he replied. "But what affects Venice affects Murano."

She considered the request. A necklace for Josephine Bonaparte: another chance to boost her business, or another failure?

"When do you need it?" she asked.

"In two days."

"*Mariavergine*, I can't make it in two days! Not if it's to be good.

The beads need at least twenty-four hours to cool. And I need time to experiment."

"Three days, then. Josephine arrives tomorrow."

"You couldn't give me more notice?"

"It was only at the last minute that she announced she was coming. Everyone is scrambling."

"How much will you pay?"

"Don't focus on the time or the money, Signora Orsola. Ask yourself what you can make in three days that the wife of the most prominent man in Europe would wear."

"What does she look like?"

"They say she is graceful rather than beautiful. Holds herself well, with a good figure. Dresses with taste."

"That could describe most of the rich women in Europe. I need more specifics. What color are her hair and eyes? What complexion? Is her neck short or long? What shape is her bosom?"

Klingenberg looked so taken aback by this last question that Orsola had to suppress a laugh. "If I am to make an exceptional necklace, I need to know what bed it will rest on," she explained.

There was a discreet cough from the antechamber.

"What is it, Jonas?" Klingenberg called.

His clerk appeared in the doorway. "Herr Klingenberg, your daughter may know. Women pay attention to such details."

"Go and fetch her, then."

While they waited, they spoke of glass, of the shortages, of the French soldiers who had taken over Piazza San Marco, of the paintings and sculptures Napoleon had his eye on to take away and display in Paris.

"They've left Murano alone, so far," Orsola said.

Klingenberg leaned forward. "If you have anything you value, hide it. They will strip the churches, then shut them." He poured her more

Malvasia. As Orsola sipped the sweet wine, she wondered if Klara Klingenberg might slip her that bit of glass wrapped in cloth that would tell her Antonio was thinking of her. Klara had kept her word all this time and gave them to Domenego to deliver to Orsola.

It had been seventeen years since she had watched Antonio row away from her at San Matteo. His face was now so far away that she couldn't remember his specific features, only generalizations: dark-gold hair, eyes like the lagoon. She couldn't even remember how he had made her feel. He was like the faded scars on her arms from accidents when glass dropped or exploded: they hurt at the time, but after a while she couldn't recall either the incident or the pain.

Whenever a dolphin arrived, however—whether six months or six years after the last—Orsola felt a jolt of satisfaction. Time might race and freeze, expand and contract, but the continuity of Antonio's dolphins, the knowledge that she was still remembered after so long, was the solid foundation upon which her life was built, like one of the millions of trees pounded into the bed of the lagoon to create the base that held up Venice. She didn't understand it, but she was not sure she could remain standing and steady without it.

It had been a long time since Orsola had seen Klara Klingenberg. With two children now, her waist was a little thicker and her hair had darkened, though still dressed in the fashion of the day, high off her neck, with ringlets around her forehead. Her dress was silver, not new, but still flattering.

She lit up when she spied Orsola. "Signora Rosso, what a pleasure!"

Her father looked puzzled. "You know each other?"

"We've met."

"Venice is not so big," Orsola added, not wanting the merchant to probe more and find out about the glass dolphins.

Klara turned to her father. "What is this mysterious request of yours that made Jonas rush across the Rialto to fetch me? He is out of breath from running!"

Jonas turned red and began to protest, but Klingenberg waved him down. "Signora Orsola would like to know what Josephine Bonaparte looks like," he explained.

Klara looked puzzled. "Why?"

Orsola glanced at the merchant, who nodded. "Your father wants me to make a necklace for her," she said. "To help Venice seduce her so that she lets us go free."

"Ah!" Klara clapped her hands in delight, reminding Orsola of when she first saw her as a gawky girl. Now that she knew what was expected of her, she sat, draping her silk skirt about her so it wouldn't crease. Jonas handed her a glass of Malvasia and she took a dainty sip but did not touch the bussolai. "*Allora.* Josephine is the talk of the coffeehouses. She is tall and slim, with a long neck and a well-rounded bust. Her décolletage is pale—probably powdered—and she shows a fair bit of it. She favors a round neckline. She has dark-brown hair she wears up and in ringlets about her forehead—very like mine, but darker. Her eyes are also dark brown and sit like plump raisins in her face. Her mouth is small and pinched, for her teeth are black and she smiles and laughs without showing them. Her cheeks are full, her nose indifferent. Her complexion is quite dark, but she wears powder to whiten, and then rouges, rather more than she ought, I am told. They say she is intelligent, and looks about her with curiosity, though her expression can be a little sad. She often wears white, and in flimsy fabrics. She likes pearls—but what woman doesn't? She knows how to dress well, and how to carry herself." Klara paused. "I think she is the kind of woman who wears her clothes and her jewels, rather than letting them wear her."

Orsola nodded. "Thank you, signora, that is very helpful."

"If she is to wear glass beads, I would not make them in white, trying to imitate pearls, since she already has so many," Klara added. "Better something completely different."

"Millefiori?" Klingenberg suggested.

"Too busy, I think, from what I have seen of them. Too gaudy for Josephine. They are not quite refined enough."

"Cornaline d'Aleppo?" Orsola proposed. "The red beads with the green or white centers."

Klara turned her head to one side, considering. "I think perhaps too plain."

Jonas coughed. "We have sample cards of Signora Orsola's work. Shall I bring them out? Then you can see her range."

Klingenberg nodded, and Jonas moved to a large oak cupboard in the corner. When he unlocked it and opened the doors, the scent of cinnamon and nutmeg wafted out. Orsola smiled to think of her beads being considered precious enough to be kept under lock and key with exotic spices.

Jonas brought over tan cards on which examples of Orsola's beads had been strung with numbers written next to them. Included there was the range of everything she had learned to make over the years: plain beads in a variety of colors and shapes, the millefiori Klara had described as busy, the red cornaline d'Aleppo, round beads decorated with swirls of vines and flowers, the red beads with gold leaf flashing inside the glass that she had made after Antonio left. She had never seen her own work organized for the eyes of buyers. It was a strange, distancing feeling, as if it were not Orsola Rosso who had made those beads, but some other lampworker on Murano.

Klara studied the sample cards as carefully as if she were choosing lace to trim a gown. As Orsola stood beside her, she was even more conscious of the physical differences between them: Klara so tall and fair and pale, Orsola short and round and dark. Klara no longer wore her sky-blue dress, and Orsola no longer wore the brown dress with its hint of red, but they were not far off: Klara in silver satin, Orsola in brown linen. Older now, they had knocked the bright tones from their clothes but kept the underlying base note, like the musk and cedar of a perfume or the core color of one of Orsola's beads.

"I think," Klara began, taking her time with her opinion, "a strong color to contrast with Josephine's white gowns. Red, blue or green. Red is perhaps too garish, but a variety of blues or greens, like your dolphins—" She stopped, confusion then horror crossing her face before she masked them.

Her father was quick to notice. "Dolphins?"

"Seahorses," Orsola broke in, hoping Klara would recover and follow. "I make them for visitors to Murano. Signora has seen them."

"Yes, of course, cavallucci marini, not delfini, how silly of me. But those colors," Klara added, eager to get back on track. "Colors of water, to remind her of Venice. Not murky canal, but sparkling sea."

"There should be gold as well," Jonas added. "She is the wife of a powerful general. She wears pearls and diamonds and other precious stones. The glass needs to look like more than just glass if it is to compete."

They all stared at him, and the clerk ducked his head, embarrassed. Orsola had never even glanced at what he wore, but saw now that his shoes were highly polished, their simple silver buckles winking, and his short cloak was a deep-burgundy velvet with black stripes on the sleeves. His close beard was evenly trimmed, and he held himself very straight.

"I don't want to make beads that look like sapphires or emeralds," Orsola said. "Otherwise you might as well simply give Josephine sapphires and emeralds. The point is to show her the unique beauty of Muranese—Venetian—glass."

"Agreed," Klingenberg declared. "I think we should let Signora

Orsola get on with what she does best. Domenego will take you back to Murano now, and will pick up the necklace in three days."

Orsola gulped down the rest of her wine, hoping it would give her the courage she needed for this commission.

Klara left at the same time, with Jonas trailing them to escort her home. As they descended the wide staircase together, Klara leaned in. For a moment Orsola wondered if she would hand her a glass dolphin. Instead she said, "I have one more suggestion. Make her earrings to match. She will like that. It is the style."

✧

Back on Murano, Orsola told as few people as possible what she was doing. There would be jealousy, or requests for loans or for work, but mainly criticism of her pandering to the French. She told her family only that she was making a necklace for an important person, but not who it was.

She decided not to follow Klara's advice about colors, but to make a dark-red necklace and earrings, in part because she thought it would go better with Josephine's natural coloring, but mainly because she associated the mix of blues and greens with Antonio and his dolphins and did not want them hanging all together around the neck and in the ears of a French general's wife.

First Orsola experimented with the many shapes she could make in glass: round paternostro, cylindrical canella, olive-shaped ulivetta spoletta. She made large, small, graduated sizes. The next day when they had cooled, she tried stringing them together, using many beads, few beads, only one bead. Nothing seemed to work; there was never that moment she normally experienced when a piece came together in her hands and felt just right. The pressure of having so little time was getting in the way, and she began to panic that she would come up with nothing suitable at all to send to Klingenberg.

During the afternoon Stella came in to watch Orsola work. She was now a young woman, with a wide face, serious, deep-set eyes and brown hair sticking out like a mop. Despite now being twenty, she still had the nonchalance of a child, unbothered by the adult world with its worries and woes. Chin propped in her hands, she studied the myriad beads Orsola had made the night before, spread out on a white cloth. Then she disappeared, returning a few minutes later with Rosella. Monica's daughter had grown up to look very little like her mother, her face delicate and cat-shaped, with a sharp, pointed chin and a small nose. Her brown eyes were fringed with lashes so long they got tangled up in themselves and she had to comb them out with her fingers. Orsola had begun teaching her to make beads several years before, but with so few orders, it seemed a futile effort. Still, Rosella had a natural ability and a good eye.

"There." Stella gestured at the table. "What do you think?"

Orsola sat back, amused at the thought of handing over the design of such an important necklace to these two young women. But sometimes an outside opinion was what was needed. She thought back to Paolo suggesting that her yellow plague beads should be beautiful. So much time had passed, yet sometimes it felt as if she had experienced those confined quarantine days only the week before.

Rosella studied the beads, serious in her role. "Who is this for?" she asked. "What kind of woman?"

"Pale, dark hair," Orsola answered.

"What kind of character?" Stella interjected. "Flashy or quiet? Does she think much of herself? Does she want everyone to look at her? Would you like her if you met her?"

Orsola paused. Stella was such a definite presence. She almost wanted to make the necklace for her—but her sister would never wear a necklace. She cleared her throat. "It's for Napoleon's wife."

Rosella's eyes widened, while Stella's narrowed. "The General's wife? *Maledizione!*" She picked up one of Orsola's small iron rods and, before her sister or niece could stop her, pricked one of her fingers with a pointed end.

"Stella, what are you doing?" Orsola cried.

Her sister held out her finger, a drop of blood hanging from it. "It would look good around a woman's neck," she said as the droplet fell to the floor. "Especially on a general's wife. The blood dripping down her chest."

"*Sì,*" Rosella agreed. "That shape and that color, they go together."

Orsola opened her mouth to disagree, but had a sudden vision of Josephine at a ball at Palazzo Pisani Moretta, dancing under Muranese chandeliers, her white silk gown and powdered décolletage setting off a double strand of graduated blood-red drops, picked apart by tiny gold-leaf beads, complemented by droplets cascading from her earlobes.

She nodded. "*Grazie, bellissime ragazze.*" She leaned over and kissed her sister and niece. Stella flinched; she never liked hugs or kisses. "Now go," Orsola added. "I have work to do."

✧

LATER ORSOLA LAUGHED at herself for some of the fantasies she'd had while working on this magical necklace, imagining she might see Josephine wearing it while floating down the Grand Canal, or entering La Fenice to see an opera, or strolling around Piazza San Marco while being entertained by musicians and acrobats. The red blood drops with their tiny gold beads glittering in between would be admired by everyone around her, and the world would discover that it was the beadmaker Orsola Rosso who had made it. Soon she would have so many orders from wealthy Venetian families that the Rossos could survive on her work alone rather than on the workshop glassware.

Domenego picked up the jewelry from Orsola, but she couldn't resist going over to Venice herself the next day to visit all the places where Josephine might be. She spent hours tramping back and forth between likely spots, but she got no glimpse of a red necklace on a white décolletage. For all the excitement in the city about Napoleon's wife, Orsola couldn't find her. Later Jonas admitted to her that when Klingenberg and the other German merchants presented the necklace and earrings to Napoleon's wife on her visit to the Fondaco dei Tedeschi, she didn't even glance into the cedar box Klingenberg opened for her so that she might view the gift. Orsola wasn't sure Josephine ever wore them.

Only Domenego spent any time with Napoleon's wife, for Josephine spied him moored by the Fondaco dei Tedeschi and requested that it be the *moro* gondolier who rowed her up and down the Grand Canal to her suppers and balls and operas and picnics. Klingenberg gladly lent his gondolier, hoping this would also help the Venetian cause. Domenego was not so pleased. Such favoritism did not go down well with other gondoliers, given he had a tricky relationship with them at the best of times. They waited until Josephine had left Venice to reward him with a black eye and his gondola a broken forcola.

The necklace did not save Venice. Afterward—when Josephine didn't convince her husband of the value of an independent Venice, and Napoleon handed over the city to Austria—Orsola wondered if there might have been a different outcome if she had followed Klara Klingenberg's advice. Could Josephine have been seduced by jewels the colors of Venetian water rather than of blood? Perhaps it was too much to ask of a mere necklace, but on witnessing Venice subsiding into ruins during the long Austrian reign, she sometimes felt guilty.

Klingenberg and the other German merchants felt the slight even more keenly. Not only were they out of pocket for the necklace, but when the Austrians took over, among the changes they made to the city was to move the merchants from the Fondaco dei Tedeschi and turn it into a customs house. The Germans could no longer work or live there. "There is absolutely no reason for them to do this," the merchant raged when Orsola visited him for the last time in his chambers to be paid a final installment for the necklace. "There is a perfectly good customs house by la Salute! The Austrians are doing this out of spite. They haven't moved the Greeks or Turks or Armenians. Why only us?"

Orsola hadn't seen Klingenberg's genial mask slip like this since she'd spoken to him about Domenego years before. "Perhaps they like the building more," she replied. "The Fondaco dei Turchi has not been looked after as well." This was true of many buildings in Venice, which had begun to crumble as trade stagnated.

Klingenberg shook his head as if dislodging water from his ear. Behind him Jonas shook his head likewise, and Orsola fell silent. When a man wanted to rage, it was best not to reason with him, but let him burn himself out. She was there to be paid, not to console.

He muttered for a few minutes more, squaring his papers, lining up his pens, shifting from one side of his desk to the other a glass paperweight full of suspended millefiori that Giacomo had made him.

"I'm sorry, Signor Klingenberg," she said at last. "Where will you go?"

"Somewhere—not far." He paused. "Though perhaps I should return to Augsburg."

Jonas started. Clearly he hadn't heard of this possibility before. "Herr Kling—" He stopped when the merchant held up his hand.

Orsola waited as Klingenberg took from his desk drawer some coins, which was the balance of the zecchino she was being paid for the necklace. He may have been disappointed that his plan to influence Napoleon through his wife didn't work, but he was an honorable man and would pay what he had agreed.

"Thank you, Signora Orsola," he said, handing the coins to her. "The necklace may not have had the desired effect with Josephine, but you should be proud nonetheless. It was your finest work, certainly the finest glass necklace I have seen in Venice. Maestra."

✧

THE PAYMENT FOR Josephine's necklace kept the Rossos fed through the winter and spring, before the truly hard times began when the city and surrounding countryside were batted back and forth between the French and the Austrians. They took away Venice's free-port status and charged high tariffs for any exports going to terraferma—effectively wrecking its already precarious trade and undermining its manufacturing.

By the time Napoleon was definitively defeated at Waterloo and the Austrians truly took charge, Venice and its citizens were on their knees from poverty, and a necklace of blood-red drops for a future empress and all the commissions that might result from it felt like a dream that had never happened.

So began the lowest period for Venice, for Murano and for the Rosso family, their fates linked—for when Venice went into decline, Murano glass did too. It was a time that lasted much longer than the plague, though not so many died. It was grimmer, in a way, because it came to seem this grinding poverty would always exist, rather than burn out rapidly as the disease had. It was a constant throb rather than a sharp pain, a low-grade fever rather than a spike overnight where the sheets are soaked with sweat. The long, dull ache of missing a lover over the years rather than the shock of seeing him row away from you across the lagoon.

It was a time to be skipped over, condensed as much as possible.

It might have been tolerable if it were just the Rossos who had fallen on hard times. Orsola might even have accepted that it stemmed from Marco's mismanagement of the business. But all around them there were similar stories of glass workshops going out of business, garzoni abandoning Murano and taking their skills to terraferma as there were no longer authorities to go after them, glassmen being forced to take up other work—gathering wood, gardening, fishing, selling goods. Faces became haggard, houses grew shabby, boats began to peel. There were fewer festivals, fewer feasts, fewer celebrations. When Orsola walked past l'Omo Salvadego, it was never as busy as in the old days but had solitary drinkers sitting over glasses of wine they nursed for hours because they couldn't afford another.

And it wasn't just Murano. Orsola used to love crossing over to Venice, cruising up and down its canals, walking its labyrinth of calles, admiring its piazzas and churches and palazzos. As she grew older it had become more familiar and less intimidating, though she still sometimes got lost and had to ask for directions.

Now, though, she found the city depressing. If a campo wasn't full of drunk Austrian soldiers in white tunics, it was full of beggars. There were fewer residents than before, many having headed to terraferma to look for work or to rent land they could farm to feed themselves. When the Doge handed over the city to the French, there had been an exodus of nobility, who in a moment had lost all status in Venice and had to seek it elsewhere, or a place to lick their wounds. Their palazzos stood empty, for few could afford to buy them. No longer lived in or maintained, they began to look unkempt: moss growing, stone render crumbling, paint peeling from the salt breeze off the sea. A building with no air circulating through it soon lost its life, as did a glass workshop.

Not all palazzos fell into ruin. Some were turned into inns; others were rented out to the travelers who continued to flow into Venice, seduced by its reduced state. Orsola was not a fan of these visitors: she resented people coming to gawk at Venice's melancholic ruin, which they seemed to find romantic. To her there was nothing romantic about living among rotting shutters and flaking masonry and piles of rubble, with your stomach never entirely full. The visitors could admire it all and then travel back to their comfortable homes without having to survive amid the destitution. However, she understood their necessity: the visitors brought the lifeblood of demand that gave Venetians a reason to open their tavernas and produce their plays and look after their gondolas and make their marbled paper and their masks and their glass baubles—someone might pay them for it.

The orders Klingenberg sent Orsola for markets abroad shrank to almost nothing, and her work was now primarily in shop trinkets. But she hadn't realized quite how bad things were until one day she stepped out of her studio into the courtyard to fetch water from the well and discovered Marco sitting on the bench, drunk, an empty bottle on the table. It was ten in the morning; her brother never drank this early.

"What are you doing?" she demanded.

Marco waved a hand at her but didn't answer.

Stella was leaning over the laundry cauldron in the corner, pushing a paddle through sheets. She glanced at her older sister, then jerked her head toward the workshop.

The moment she stepped inside, Orsola knew. It was not just that the workshop was quiet, without the whistling and singing and shouting that normally went on. The dull roar of the furnace was missing, and its heat. The furnace was a hungry mouth that must be fed for eleven months of the year. Now it was cold, and the studio dead, as if its blood had stopped circulating. The Rosso boys who had begun helping their fathers were gone: Andrea and Sebastiano were not fetching wood and feeding the furnace and sweeping the floor; Marcolin and Raffaele were not swinging punties and running with pieces to the annealer and laying out ground glass in various colors to use for decorating goblets. She looked around and found Stefano and Giacomo in the back, silent at the benches where cold work was done: filing the bottoms of bowls and vases so they sat straight, painting decorations on goblets, carving frames for mirrors. They had worked together for years now and were companionable, though not close in the way Paolo and Giacomo had been. They glanced up, then went back to their work. Orsola could see the dejection in her husband's hunched back, and her heart ached for him.

"Where are the boys?" she asked.

Stefano kept carving, but Giacomo paused, his brush daubed with white paint. "Out in the boat."

"Why is the furnace out?"

"There is no more work."

"What are you making, then?" Orsola nodded at the goblet Giacomo held—he was painting a ring of flowers around its rim.

"For the shop. But we have so much stock we couldn't sell it all even if boatloads of visitors came every day."

"There are no orders from Klingenberg? None at all?"

"Klingenberg is going back to Augsburg."

"What?!"

"He told Marco yesterday. He said there isn't the business there once was. With these high tariffs, people are buying their glassware from Prague instead."

She flinched at the name of Antonio's city.

Stefano was watching her. Could he read her mind? She shook her head to clear it. "What about my beads?"

"You'll have to find another merchant to sell them for you."

Orsola had been receiving orders from Klingenberg for half her life, taking for granted his role as the link to the world beyond Venice. How would her beads get to Paris, to Africa, to America, without him? Once he left for terraferma, he was gone from her world.

She went back to the courtyard to confront Marco, but he was asleep and she knew waking him when he was drunk would make things worse. Instead she went to find her mother.

Laura Rosso was standing at the range, stirring polenta, which could not be left long or it would burn. They had begun to eat polenta more often, as had many Murano families, not just the poor ones, who had long been called Yellow Face to tease them about their poverty. No one was teasing them now.

Orsola leaned against the table and folded her arms. "Madre," she said, "Marco has let the furnace go out."

"So he has." Laura kept stirring. Her hair was now entirely gray.

"What are we going to do about it?"

"Do other things."

The answer reminded Orsola of Maria Barovier long ago telling her to make beads.

"What else can we make?" she said. "We've already expanded to beads and mirrors and little figures for the shop. And chandeliers," she couldn't resist adding.

"I didn't say make other things. I said *do* other things."

Orsola stared at her mother's profile. "What do you mean?"

"Things other than glass."

"But . . . we're a glass family."

Laura Rosso did not respond. Taking the pot off the range, she spooned the polenta onto a wood slab, using the ladle to shape it into a long rectangle.

"What kinds of things? Pulling cane for other studios? Grinding glass?" Orsola stretched further. "Making ash to mix for glass? Delivering wood?" She wasn't sure about the last suggestion, for it required a large boat they didn't have, and trips to terraferma.

"All you suggest are things to do with glass. If we were going to support glass, we might as well be making it."

"Then you mean . . ."

"Murano glass is dead, Orsola. No one is buying it because of the tariffs the Austrians are charging to export it. And it's not essential to Venetians. We must think of the things that are needed every day. Fish. Vegetables. Laundry. Boats."

"You want Marco and Giacomo and the boys to become fishermen?" Orsola said it sarcastically and was stunned when her mother replied with a shrug.

"And I will *not* do other families' laundry," she added.

Laura smoothed the polenta with the back of the ladle and sprinkled sprigs of rosemary across the surface. "You may have no choice."

✧

THERE HAD TO BE A CHOICE. Orsola took a traghetto over to see Klingenberg. He had moved to a house near his daughter on Campo San Polo—the largest open space in the city after Piazza San Marco—which she and Giacomo had once crossed while searching for Marco. His house was not a grand palazzo, but its salmon-colored front was still impressive, broken up by rows of windows framed with Gothic arches.

A servant showed her through the androne and upstairs to the merchant's chambers. They were much like they had been at the Fondaco dei Tedeschi, complete with Jonas at a desk in the antechamber. Even with the packing chaos in other parts of the house, Klingenberg had not yet had his Persian carpets and books packed, as if clinging to his old life until the very last moment. "Signora Orsola, *buongiorno,*" he said, rising from his desk and bowing. Orsola detected a hint of embarrassment in his tone, perhaps because the merchant hadn't spoken to her before telling Marco of his departure. "It is early for wine, but coffee? Or chocolate? Jonas?"

"Neither, *grazie,*" she replied as Jonas appeared. "I've come to ask if it's true that you're leaving. But I can see for myself that it is." She indicated the rest of the house, where swathed furniture and crates waited to be taken by boat to terraferma and the long haul by cart through the Alps to Augsburg.

"Please," Klingenberg replied, waving at the mahogany chair across from him. It seemed incredible to her that this was the last time she would sit in that chair. He was as steady a part of her life as her mother, her brothers, Monica, Angela, Stella, Domenego.

"Domenego!" she cried. Would he be lost to terraferma as well?

"*Perdonatemi?*"

"What will happen to your gondolier?"

Klingenberg frowned. "You have come to ask me about my gondolier?"

"I just— He's not going with you to Augsburg, is he?"

"His skills would not be of much use in Augsburg. Domenego will work for my daughter and her family. He already does much of the time anyway. *Allora,* to what do I owe the pleasure of this visit?"

"I've come to thank you for your kindness to me over the years. For supporting me with my beads. I'm very grateful."

Klingenberg nodded. "It is thoughtful of you to say so. But I would not have taken you on if your lampwork was not good. You are a skilled beadmaker, Signora Orsola. One of the best in Venice—or Murano. It has been a pleasure to sell your work."

Orsola bowed her head. "*Grazie,* signore. But what am I to do now? My mother says we may have to become fishermen!"

Klingenberg sighed. "These are hard times, certainly. The Austrians have not treated Venice kindly. Not out of spite, but being rule-minded and land-bound, they don't understand how a port works, and the importance of free status to keep the city's lifeblood flowing. I am not sure Venice will ever recover its trading position. Mind you, we can't entirely blame the French and the Austrians. Though most of us have ignored it, the city has been in a long, slow decline ever since ocean trade routes were established and the Mediterranean Sea became less important. La Serenissima has been relying on its beauty and charm for many years now. That, and the magnificent work done by its skilled artisans."

"Is Madre right, though? Will we have to leave glass and take up fish?"

"That may be extreme. I have faith that the Austrians will eventually come to their senses and abolish tariffs, and trade will recommence. Not soon enough for me, I'm afraid, but you will recover."

"How? We need your good sense to tell us what to do."

"Until things change, focus on the local market."

"What local market? There are fewer residents than ever, and they have little to spend. Don't you see all the beggars in Campo San Polo?"

"Not Venetians. I refer to what are now being called 'tourists'—a most annoying word. Many thousands of visitors come to Venice every year to marvel at our unique beauty, their pockets full of money to spend. The Rossos should focus on serving them. Then there is no worry about tariffs or a merchant like me as middleman. You can sell direct to them. You already do so in your Murano shop. My advice to your family? Set up a shop in Venice near Piazza San Marco, where every visitor goes, and stock it with small, sensible glassware they can easily take home with them. Simple glasses for the English for their sherry, the French their brandy, the Germans their schnapps. Also figurines of dogs, horses, shepherdesses. Perfume bottles. And of course bead necklaces and earrings."

Orsola wished she had agreed to a coffee so she could hide her scornful mouth behind the cup. Klingenberg spoke sense, but it was difficult to bear. The Muranese had always prided themselves on remaining separate from Venice and able to look after themselves. It was painful to admit they needed the city to survive.

She didn't say this to Klingenberg, whose allegiance was to Venice, even though he was German. "Why sell a hundred small glasses when you can make the same selling one large vase?" she countered. "Otherwise it becomes more about selling than making. Quantity rather than quality." Marco had said much the same to her about her beads compared to his larger pieces. They had less value. "We're not salespeople. We're makers."

"That is true," Klingenberg agreed. "But it may be that this is what you have to do if you want to continue working with glass."

They spoke a bit more, delaying their goodbye. When it came time to leave, Orsola pulled out a small leather pouch and handed it to the merchant. "For you, Signor Klingenberg, with thanks for all that you have done for my family for so long."

Klingenberg raised his eyebrows. "Really, there is no need, signora . . . Ah," he breathed as he shook out a rosary into his palm. Orsola had spent a day and a night making fifty small round beads, each set of ten separated by a larger bead, with a beaded cross hanging at the end. They were the same dark red as the Josephine necklace, to remind him of what she considered their joint triumph, even if it didn't achieve what they had intended. Klingenberg gazed at the rosary, then began to rub the beads between his finger and thumb as he would if he were saying prayers. "*Bellissimo*," he murmured. "It is exquisite, Orsola. The perfect size, the feel, the color. Your judgment is sound, as always. *Grazie*." He bowed low.

As Orsola left, she thought she saw him wipe his eyes.

Jonas accompanied her to the door. His beard was still cut close to his jaw, his hair still smooth and tied back, his clothes still plain and well looked after. He had never taken on the dandified appearance other Venetian men succumbed to. Despite his distance and his irritating precision, Orsola suspected she would miss him.

"Where are you going now, Signora Orsola?" he asked.

"Back to Murano, I suppose. Though I'm tempted to go over to San Marco and look around for a place for a shop, as Signor Klingenberg suggested. But I am not sure the Rossos want to become shopkeepers."

"His idea is a good one, but if you want to remain working with glass, I have another suggestion. May I show you?"

Orsola nodded, surprised, and followed as he led the way across Campo San Polo to a nearby canal, where Domenego was moored. The gondolier was sitting in the sun on the stern, arms around knees, head on arms, asleep.

"Domenego, take us to the Ghetto Nuovo, *per favore*," Jonas commanded sharply.

Domenego raised his head and took in his passengers without comment. He stood and handed Orsola into the boat, but Jonas helped himself, sitting down across from her so he was facing backward. It felt odd to her to ride in this gondola with someone else, and she sat stiff and upright. Domenego also treated her formally, saying nothing and keeping his eyes on the middle distance.

Orsola looked around as they glided through the narrow rios of San Polo and Santa Croce. There were fewer now, for the Austrians didn't like water, and had filled in canals, widened calles and built bridges so that they could get around the city more easily on foot. Venetians bitterly complained: Why rule a city built on water if you didn't know how to get around on it?

The Austrians might have changed some things, but the underlying fabric of the city remained. Houses colored ocher and tan and pink and yellow towered over them, blocking out the light, elegant with their filigreed arches, balconies and sculptures of lions adorning the facades. Laundry hung high above them, catching the sun and wind to dry. All around was the constant lapping and the damp, salty, smelly tang, and the shifting ripples of light from the water around and under them, providing the reassuring backdrop to Venetian life.

Orsola expected Jonas to tell her of his idea, but he sat and said nothing. "Are you looking forward to living in Augsburg?" she began, in an awkward attempt to make conversation.

Jonas shook his head. "I am not going to Augsburg with Herr Klingenberg. I will remain here." His Venetian was still clipped by his German manner and pronunciation.

Orsola widened her eyes. "Will you work for another merchant?"

"I am going to set up on my own."

"*Davvero?*"

She hadn't meant to sound so incredulous, but disappointment at her surprise flitted across his face before he masked it with a tight smile. "I have learned a great deal from Herr Klingenberg. I have contacts on both sides, buyers and sellers. Herr Klingenberg had a broad business, encompassing Venetian wares but also serving as a middleman for trade from the East." Jonas paused. "Perhaps he spread himself a bit thin." He pressed his lips together, as if to keep himself from voicing more criticism of his master. "My intention is to concentrate on finding markets for local artists and artisans. Including the Rossos, if you'll allow me."

Orsola studied him, trying to picture Marco and Jonas doing business together. The clerk's stolid, fastidious manner would annoy her brother, she was sure. He lacked the elegance of Klingenberg that had kept Marco in check. "Have you asked my brother?"

"Not yet."

"He's let the furnace go out. It will be hard to get him going again."

"That may be true. But it should not stop you from doing your own work. You use a lamp rather than the furnace, correct?"

She nodded.

"Then you can decide separately if you wish to continue. Your decision does not have to be connected to your brother's. After all, your business with Herr Klingenberg was separate from the family. Nonetheless, my suggestion is for all the Rossos."

"What are you taking me to see?"

"Beads." From his pocket Jonas pulled out a small, semicircular rawhide bag decorated with tiny brown, cream and red beads forming geometric patterns.

"This must have ruined someone's eyes," Orsola remarked, squinting at the exquisitely even beadwork.

"The bag was made by Indians in America," Jonas explained, "using seed beads made in Venice."

For some time now Venetians as well as Muranese glassmakers had been producing seed beads: beads the size of sesame seeds or even smaller, made from pulled glass cane that had been cut into fragments, and used to fashion necklaces and earrings and brooches, or to decorate everything from handbags and belts to dresses and shoes. Though technically they were beads, the process was so different from Orsola's lampwork that she never gave seed beads much thought. "What do these beads have to do with us?" she asked.

"I am looking for beadmakers to sell into North America," Jonas replied. "That could be you."

✧

JUST OUTSIDE THE WALLS of the Ghetto Nuovo, where for hundreds of years Jewish Venetians had been required to live, there was a cluster of small passages lined with houses less prosperous than those Orsola and Jonas had passed in San Polo and Santa Croce. Among them were a few glass factories as well—Orsola could smell glass in the air and hear the furnaces. In the calles they passed groups of women seated together in low chairs in front of doorways. Laid across their laps were sessole—shallow wooden pans—full of seed beads that needed to be strung. Each woman held a fan of long, thin wires that she thrust into the heap of color, pushing with her other hand so that the minuscule beads were caught up. Once the wires were full, the stringer pushed the beads down onto the long linen threads that were hooked through the ends of the wires. When those had all been strung, they were twisted into a heavy hank of beads, ready to be shipped abroad.

The bead stringers were chatting and singing as they worked. They ignored Orsola, but paid more attention to Jonas, perceiving his merchant status from his clothes, pale skin and soft hands. As they passed there was whistling and jeering, and a few called out, "Come and feel my *perle*, signore! Don't you want to see my *conterie?*"

Klingenberg's clerk reddened but doggedly continued along the calles, Orsola following. They reached a small campo, where women were gathered in one corner and he and Orsola could stand far enough away to watch them without being heard. Orsola could not connect herself with these impiraresse, for she was a maker rather than a stringer, a creator rather than a packager.

Jonas nodded at them. "You see all these women and girls? There are hundreds of them stringing beads, in Castello and here in Cannaregio near the factories that make them, and also working for Murano factories. You see, there *is* still a successful glass industry of sorts. It is possible to make a living from making beads on a large scale. Perhaps not fancy lampwork beads, but glasswork nonetheless."

A young impiraressa wearing a tan apron dotted with black spots raised her head from her pan of yellow beads and stared at Orsola. She sat very straight, hands poised with a fistful of wires. Turning her head, she spat before returning her defiant, hawklike gaze. Orsola felt her cheeks blaze.

If Jonas noticed this exchange, he didn't comment. "There is no market at the moment for the lampwork beads you have been making for Herr Klingenberg," he said. "Nor is there for the work your brother does, as fine as it is. The Austrians—and the Czechs with their burgeoning glasswork—have undercut Murano. But there *is* a market for seed beads. When I set up as a trade merchant, I will be looking to take on a factory to supply seed beads. That could be you. The Rosso workshop could make the beads, and your daughter, your nieces, your mother could string them."

"Seed beads?" Orsola snorted. "*Mio Dio.*" Their making was not artistry, but mechanics. And the Rossos were not a factory, but a small business; they had always referred to themselves as a workshop. "It's a completely different process making seed beads from making lamp-work beads," she said. "It needs a furnace, a lot of space, and several men, not one woman bent over a lamp at a table."

"Your brothers can do that."

"Marco, pull cane? You clearly don't know my brother!"

Jonas waited a moment, then continued in his persistent manner. "Your brother has little choice. And it is not such a bad life, doing this." He gestured at the group.

Orsola looked over again at the women stringing beads. The hawkish girl was now ignoring her. Sitting in the sun, laughing over something one of them had said, united against the wealthier world around them, the women appeared happy enough. But the merchant knew nothing about the kind of manual work they were doing twelve hours a day, with aching backs, tired eyes and hands cut from the wires, paid just enough for a chicken for the pot now and then.

However, she pictured Angela, Francesca, Rosella and Stella, over-seen by Laura Rosso, sitting in the courtyard or in the calle outside the house, stringing beads, and found she could imagine it, for the sake of the family business. Except for her sister: Stella sat still for no one.

"Signora Orsola, the offer is there," Jonas said. "Go back and speak to your mother. She is a sensible woman. Win her over and she will convince your brother."

✧

LAURA ROSSO WAS NO LONGER the active adviser she had been just after her husband died. Marco was consulting her less and less as she grew older and he gained more experience. She had been relegated to looking after her grandchildren and tending the garden while Monica and Orsola and Rosella and Stella handled the harder physical work of cooking, cleaning, laundry and hauling back provisions from the markets. Though she spoke less often, when she did give her opinion, Marco still listened.

Orsola took Monica to see Laura in their garden behind the convent at Santa Maria degli Angeli, where Zia Giovanna had lived out her days; Orsola's aunt was now buried in the Murano cemetery. Gray and stooped, Laura was kneeling in a row of early lettuces, picking off the snails. She sat back on her heels as Orsola and Monica approached. "Don't know why I bother to do this," she grumbled. "No one likes lettuce anyway."

"I do," Orsola lied. "After fish, with a bit of oil and lemon and salt."

Laura Rosso grunted. "Doesn't fill you up, though. I may replace them with more substantial vegetables. Zucchini and aubergine, or carrots and cabbage in winter."

"We already have plenty of those," Monica remarked, setting down a bottle of water. "*Ecco*, we've brought you some bussolai."

"You two want something," Laura said. "Why would you come all the way here to bring me biscuits otherwise?" She picked off a snail and threw it toward the hedge bordering the garden. That was the polite way to dispatch them. Orsola had seen her toss them into others' gardens when she was annoyed with her neighbors.

She chuckled. It was impossible to hide anything from her mother, who could always detect the existence of an underlying motive. "We need to talk to you about the future."

Her mother was looking for more snails to dispatch. "What future?"

"The Rosso future."

"Why?"

"Why? The furnace is out, the garzoni and garzonetti gone, there are no orders, Klingenberg is leaving, Marco is drunk at ten in the morning, and you're asking why?"

"We've always managed before. Something will turn up."

"Something has turned up, but it won't happen unless we make it."

Laura sat back again and waited for her daughter to explain.

Orsola set out the idea: the men pulling cane and making it into seed beads, the women stringing them into hanks for shipping, Jonas selling them—and Orsola overseeing it all.

"It's a good plan," Monica added. "Sensible."

Laura was silent for a time. "Marco won't allow his sister to rule over him," she said at last. "He must remain in charge."

"But he knows nothing about beads!"

"He knows about business. And these are not your sort of beads."

"I agree with your mother," Monica said. "You have to let my husband retain his dignity."

Her sister-in-law's words, usually so sparing, stung. Orsola did not want to give her brother back his dignity; she wanted to punish him for running the family business into the ground, and for always dismissing her work as trivial. "He won't want to make seed beads," she grumbled, aware that she was backtracking. "Not after goblets and vases and chandeliers. Beads are women's work to him."

"The children need to eat," Laura Rosso said. "I'll talk to him. Monica will talk to him. The important thing is that there is an order to fill, not what the order is for."

"I'll tell him what Jonas has suggested, then."

Monica and Laura chuckled. "You will not," her mother replied. "You'll keep your mouth shut."

"I can be diplomatic!"

"You and Marco, it's impossible for you two to agree on anything. Whatever you say, he'll do the opposite. And you as well! You're more alike than you realize. Leave this to Monica and me. Give us time to soften him. Then we'll discuss."

And so for a week Monica and Laura waged a campaign to prepare Marco for the idea of making seed beads. They started by feeding him his favorite dishes and wines, though it cost money they didn't have. They humored him when he was drunk, soothed him when he was hungover. Monica took him to bed more often, and there whispered to him the idea of making beads to save the family. Orsola had to stand by and watch this charade.

When the Rossos met at the end of the week to discuss the possibility of making the complicated switch from glasswork to beadmaking, three factors swung the decision. First, they met in the evening, when Marco had been drinking and was merry but not yet vicious or hungover.

Second, the workshop had expertise they'd forgotten about. While Marco and Giacomo were struggling to work out the logistics of pulling cane to make seed beads, Stefano sat silent. Finally, as they argued about how long the length of glass should be pulled, he spoke up. "One hundred yards. Longer than for normal cane."

Orsola stared at her husband.

"First you heat glass and marver it into a pastone—a uniform cylinder the right size and shape. That is what the maestro does." Stefano nodded at Marco. "Then you take tweezers and pierce a hole through it. Then attach the glass at both ends to punties and we tiradori"—he pointed at Giacomo and himself—"we run in opposite directions, pulling it between us and laying it out on wood planks spaced so the cane doesn't touch the ground. If you have shaped it well and we have pulled it well, it will be a perfect round cane with a hole running through it."

"How do you know this?" Marco demanded.

"I pulled cane for the Baroviers when I was a garzone."

Orsola had forgotten that Stefano had had a life before her and the Rosso workshop. "And seed beads," she said. "How do you make those?"

"We didn't make them—just the cane. But I have cousins who know."

"I don't want to make *escrementi di topo*. Mouse shit. Women's work!" Marco gulped down his wine. He was entering the dangerous stage of his drinking. Stella moved the carafe of wine away from her brother.

At that moment, almost on cue, the third factor—Francesca—came running in from the calle, where she had been playing with the neighborhood children. "I'm hungry, Mamma. I want some bread!"

"No bread," Monica replied. "Only polenta."

Francesca made a face. "But I'm hungry. Always hungry!"

"You're not going to give my daughter more polenta and turn her into a Yellow Face!" Marco roared, banging down his glass. He began searching his pockets. "Here's a soldo; go and buy some bread." But he couldn't find even a denaro, and Francesca began to cry—more out of frustration than actual hunger, Orsola suspected, for she had seen her niece eat plenty at dinner. She also knew there *was* bread in the kitchen; Monica would give her some later.

His wife faced him calmly. "I wouldn't have to fill her up with polenta if we were selling beads."

"*Va bene!*" Marco shouted, jumping up. "We'll make the *escrementi di topo.*" And he stomped off to l'Omo Salvadego.

With those words the Rosso workshop became a bead factory.

✧

MARCO WAS WRONG: making seed beads *was* man's work. First they had to clear enough space in the workshop and outlying buildings to pull one hundred yards of cane. Marco had to practice forming a uniform, proportional pastone that would then be heated and pierced, and Stefano taught Giacomo, Marcolin and Raffaele how to pull it into a long cane. A cousin of his showed them how to chop the cane into tiny cylinders, sieve out the fragments and fill the holes with a paste that kept them open when heated. Then the beads were turned and stirred in a hot drum filled with sand to smooth the edges, and polished in sacks of wheat chaff. Only once they were sorted by size did the women get involved.

When enough beads were ready to be strung, Orsola and her mother and daughter and nieces sat down together in a circle in the courtyard, sessole on their laps and wires in their fists, and scooped at the beads. What had seemed a simple process when watching the women in Cannaregio proved to be much more difficult. They filled the wires with beads, but slowly, with nothing like the efficiency of the Venetian impiraresse.

Humiliated, Orsola took a traghetto over to Venice and made her way back to the small campo where the experts were at work. As she approached, the girl in the spotted apron turned her head and stared at Orsola. Orsola drew in a deep, angry breath. How could a girl less than half her age make her so nervous? She cleared her throat. "May I speak with you, signora?" she said, addressing one of the older women in the group, who seemed to be the leader. She had the same straight back and direct gaze as the girl. "I have a proposal."

The woman gave Orsola a sharp look. *"Allora?"*

"I am Orsola Rosso from Murano. I am a beadmaker. Lampwork. My family—the Rossos—have begun making seed beads. We need one of you to come and teach us how to string them."

"Bring the beads to us and we'll string them here for you."

"My family will string them. I'll pay one lira a day for someone to teach them."

"Two," the woman countered without a pause.

"One lira is what you get paid for your work here. I'll pay that."

"Why would any of us want to go over to Murano when we can sit here and get our one lira? We want one lira ten soldi."

"Va bene, I'll find a girl elsewhere who needs the work and is not so greedy." Orsola turned away.

"One lira five soldi, and you pay for the boat and give her dinner."

She turned back. "All right. Who will do it?"

"My daughter Luciana. She's quick." The woman nodded at the girl in the spotted apron. The other girls grumbled, wanting the five extra soldi.

"Come over to Colonna at eight tomorrow morning and I'll meet you," Orsola said.

Luciana scowled, making her brow even heavier. "Why do I have to go to Murano? You come here instead."

"You don't think we're all going to traipse over here with our beads, do you?"

"You're here now."

"There are five of us to teach. It has to be on Murano."

Luciana hesitated, glancing at her mother. "I've never been there."

"It's not far. No different from going to any island." Orsola observed Luciana's continuing discomfort and suddenly understood. "You've never been on the lagoon at all, have you?"

"*E allora?*" Luciana flared up.

Orsola noticed now that the girl was barefoot, the collar of her dress frayed. So poor she had no shoes, and no money to go out on the water. She felt a pang of pity. "*A domani,*" she said, and turned away before Luciana could say more.

She had no idea if the girl would show up. But just after eight the next day, Luciana stepped onto the riva from a traghetto, pale among the other passengers, clutching a sessola under one arm and dangling a small sack. She was wearing her spotted apron and her scowl, and had shoes on this time: old boots with busted toes that were too big for her and must be a brother's. Her first steps back on land were wobbly, confirming that she never used boats, and she had none of the cocksure confidence she had displayed in Cannaregio. She looked around warily, her face relaxing just a little when she saw her employer.

Orsola turned to lead the girl to the Rosso workshop; to her surprise Luciana grabbed her elbow, tucking her hand through it so that they were walking side by side, as if they were cousins. Was this how Cannaregioti behaved? Orsola wanted to pull her arm away and reestablish her superiority. But Luciana was clearly nervous about being in strange territory, and so Orsola let her hand remain as they walked together up the Fondamenta dei Vetrai. A few glassmakers were opening their shops along the calle, hopeful that they might sell enough trinkets to tourists to pay for the day's fish or bread. Luciana slowed down in front of each display, drawn to the gaudy figurines of gondoliers and leaping fish and rearing horses rather than the more sophisticated and expensive drinking glasses and candlesticks. She stopped dead in front of a green mermaid holding an orange parasol.

Orsola pulled at the girl's arm. "*Andiamo*, we have work to do. There's no time to gape at trash." Trash that you could never afford, she added to herself.

Luciana stared hard at everyone they passed, and they stared equally hard back at her. "What's wrong with everyone?" she complained. "Looking at me like I'm the devil!"

"You looked at me like that too when I walked through your campo."

"No, I didn't."

"You did."

"I didn't! I'm not so rude."

Orsola didn't continue to argue, for she was remembering how she felt when she visited Mestre and thought everyone was staring at her.

Laura Rosso and the girls were sitting in the courtyard, sessole on their laps, trying to string beads. Luciana took in the scene and began to laugh, her nervousness vanishing now that she was faced with something familiar. Orsola wasn't even able to introduce her before she was striding over to Angela. "No, no, no, *sempia!* Sit with your feet up on the chair rung; otherwise the basket is unstable and will do this." She nudged Angela's sessola and it tipped over, spilling white beads everywhere. Angela shrieked and burst into tears, to Orsola's shame—she'd thought her daughter was tougher than that.

"Once you've had to pick them all up and wash them, you'll never spill them again." Luciana turned to Francesca, who immediately moved her feet up so that the sessola sat more stably on her lap. "*Ben cussi*," Luciana crooned, changing her tone.

"Madre, how could she do that?" Angela was still crying.

Orsola shook her head. "Pick up the beads and wash them," she ordered, embarrassed by her daughter's tears. She gestured Luciana to a chair. "Teach us how to do it properly."

Luciana filled her sessola with small red beads the size of caviar and picked up a handful of wires. Fanning them out between her thumb and first two fingers, she showed the group how to dip the wires into the beads with short, rapid scoops, like scraping a carrot. With three dips she'd strung all the wires she held, then pushed the beads down them and to the ends of the threads. Once she had demonstrated the technique, Luciana watched each bead stringer and changed the fan of the wires or their angle in the beads or how they held up the threads—all apart from Laura Rosso, whom she left alone, out of respect for her age. When they had filled their threads, Luciana taught them how to twist them together into a heavy hank and fasten them with a red thread, ready for shipping.

She didn't look around, go into the kitchen, peek into the workshop or the storerooms or Orsola's studio. Though the privy was pointed out to her, Luciana didn't use it, or help herself to water from the well, only drinking some when Rosella proffered it. She didn't seem curious, or she was nervous, and so remained within the safe circle of chairs. There, she dominated, whether teaching or correcting, or humming or singing. The Rosso clan usually chatted rather than sang, but the presence of a stranger made them all a little shy, even Laura Rosso, who normally led the conversation. Luciana strung to a rhythm that she set with song, tapping her toe and scooping the beads in time. After a while the girls joined her in the songs they knew—even Angela, who had recovered from her tears and was now eagerly copying everything Luciana did, from sitting very straight with her feet up to holding her hands up to push the beads onto the threads to tapping her foot and singing softly.

When Stella passed through the courtyard with food from the market, Luciana raised her head and stared at her, much as she had first done with Orsola in Cannaregio. Stella stopped and glared back, and the two young women locked eyes until finally Luciana lowered hers.

Around noon Monica called Rosella and together they laid the table in the courtyard and began bringing out platters of fish, stewed aubergine, bread, cheese, dressed lettuce and jugs of wine and water. Luciana watched this procession with keen eyes, then tugged at the sack she had brought.

Orsola understood. "What have you got there?"

Luciana pulled out a slice of cold polenta wrapped in a bit of rag; it was only big enough to make the eater hungry for more.

Orsola shook her head. "Put it away. I agreed with your mother. You eat with us." We may have little work, she silently added, but we still eat more than polenta.

Angela ran to call the men. Marcolin and Raffaele emerged first from the workshop. As they washed by the well, pouring pitchers of water over their heads and arms to cool themselves, Marcolin spotted the new girl and turned his face away, for he was not good with strangers. Raffaele was laughing as he poured water over himself and shook his wet hair like a dog. He was a tall, wiry eighteen-year-old, his features—big brown eyes, sharp cheekbones—as delicate as his mother Nicoletta's had been. Recently he had developed the arms and shoulders of a glassman. He glanced over at the circle of chairs, where Luciana was still sitting, watching the family mill about, her brow furrowed now that there were more new people to contend with, for Marco, Giacomo and Stefano had appeared as well, Angela holding her father's hand. Raffaele froze, water still dripping from his hair, and stared at the new girl.

She must have felt his attention, for she looked at him, and then— unlike her usual direct stare—she looked away, the one indication that she'd noticed him.

Orsola saw it and recognized the moment from what she had experienced on first meeting Antonio, her stomach tightening at the memory. Monica saw it and smiled. Stella saw it and frowned. Laura Rosso saw it and looked alarmed. "Raffaele, go and help bring out the food," she commanded, clearly trying to break the wire that was being pulled taut between her grandson and the new girl.

Raffaele turned to his grandmother with a puzzled look. The boys never helped in the kitchen, and the food was already on the table.

Orsola called Luciana to come and sit next to her; otherwise the girl would have remained frozen in place. Raffaele seated himself at the other end of the table, and Orsola could feel his eyes constantly on the new girl. Luciana sensibly paid all her attention to her food, eating steadily and taking seconds before it was polite to do so.

"Who's this, then?" Marco demanded, when he'd cleaned his plate and sat back, only now bothering to notice Luciana.

"She's from Cannaregio," Orsola replied. "Helping us with stringing. Already we're faster."

"You'd better earn your keep, girl. We don't take charity cases, or Venetian thieves."

Luciana lifted her chin. "*Va' al diavolo, bastardo.*"

Marco leaned forward. "*Che cosa?*"

"*Madonna mia!*" Laura Rosso cried. "Hot as a furnace, this one!"

"Luciana, come with me." Orsola grabbed the girl and pulled her from her chair. "I need to find you some better shoes." As she hurried her toward the house she hissed, "Don't ever speak to the maestro like that or you'll have no work here!" Though Marco often made her angry, she could not have a girl like Luciana being insubordinate.

"Who was that across the table?" Luciana seemed unperturbed by the ruckus she'd caused.

"Who, the maestro you insulted? That was my brother Marco."

"Not him. The boy with the yellow hair."

"That's Raffaele. Marco's son. The man you just insulted."

Anyone else would have cried, apologized, worked to right the wrong. Luciana just laughed.

✧

IT TOOK ONLY SIX MONTHS for the impiraressa to pry Raffaele from his family. Orsola suspected she could have done so sooner if she'd wanted, but Luciana took her time to get whatever she could from the Rossos. The way she ate at dinner—with a full plate and seconds—as well as asking Monica for leftovers to take home at night indicated how poor her family was. Slowly she lost her boniness, cheeks and arms and bust filling out. Orsola had found her an old pair of Stella's shoes that fit, and when one day the skirt of her dress got snagged on a nail and ripped, she reluctantly passed on to her the old Maria Barovier reddish-brown dress, which no longer fit her, Stella was too tall for, Rosella too small, and Francesca and Angela too young. She hesitated before handing over something that had been important to her, but it was what was available, it fitted Luciana perfectly and it suited her coloring, even with her old spotted apron over it. When she wore it, Raffaele stared at her even more.

Luciana scavenged all sorts of things from the Rossos that they would have thrown out. From the storage rooms she found lopsided goti that old apprentices had made and left behind, a chipped candlestick, lampworked beads Orsola was not satisfied with but hadn't bothered to melt down. She took home tops of beetroots for soups, fish heads for stock, peapods to dress with vinegar, bread crusts, rancid oil.

Though Orsola and Laura Rosso sometimes chided her, they didn't stop her from taking what she needed. These were hard times under Austrian rule, and families had to get by on whatever they could find. Luciana's resourcefulness at winkling out treasure from trash was a reminder to them all that they were lucky to have enough to throw away for others to take. She was also valuable to the Rossos. While only meant to stay long enough to teach the Rosso women how to string beads, she made herself indispensable, and oversaw the impiraresse so that Orsola could go back to lampwork, with Rosella helping her aunt, making beads and glass figures for the Rosso shop.

Giacomo and Marcolin and Raffaele took to making seed beads easily enough, with Sebastiano and Andrea assisting. It required muscle and precision but was less pressured than the elaborate creations the workshop had previously turned out. The boys seemed happy, and Stefano and Giacomo worked willingly, but Orsola caught them gazing over at their old workspaces and knew they would rather be making mirrors and goblets and even figurines for the shop.

Marco was more vocal about his disgust at seed beads, for he had quickly lost enthusiasm once he actually had to make them. He was only willing to form the pastone, the cylinder of glass that started the process; he refused to pull cane, chop beads, polish or sort them, regarding this as assistants' work rather than a maestro's.

Rather than helping the others, Marco drank in the courtyard. Even Monica could not stop him. Once when she told him off for being drunk in the middle of the day, he made to hit her, but stopped when she stood her ground and stared him down, not even glancing at his fist. Then he took his drinking to l'Omo Salvadego.

There was no one Orsola could complain to about Marco: not her mother or her sister or her sister-in-law. Each had her own way of dealing with him. As his mother, Laura Rosso was always going to love and support him. Stella ignored her brother, as she ignored most people. Monica was in the trickiest position, wanting to stay on her husband's good side but also most able to influence him. She chose her battles with care. Orsola often wondered how she remained with him, but understood her pragmatism. Until Austrian rule the Rossos had lived well, and Monica had had few worries about her children having prosperous futures. It had been a step up from a fishing family.

Every day Orsola was thankful for her own husband, who quietly stepped into the leading role with the seed beads, without complaining or boasting. Stefano oversaw the others, he discussed quantities and timings with Orsola, he stood back when his maestro was sober and took over his work when Marco was drunk.

Jonas had maintained a few of Klingenberg's customers, carefully feeding the tiny fires to keep them burning, and expanding into the seed bead market as the Rossos found their working rhythm. He wasn't charming like Klingenberg, but Orsola found she preferred his straightforwardness. She could deal with him more easily; when he said something, she didn't have to dig beneath the words to find a separate meaning. With his help Rosso glass was slowly coming back to life.

What they all knew to be true, but no one said aloud, not even Marco when he was drunk: the Rossos were shifting from workshop to factory, from quality to quantity, from art to commerce. It kept them fed, but they paid a price. Sometimes Orsola thought about the Josephine necklace and Klingenberg's praise of it, and wondered what might have happened if only Napoleon's wife had looked down into the cedar box and fallen in love with what the beadmaker had made. She might now be designing necklaces for empresses instead of counting hanks of tiny beads to be shipped to other creators.

As the Rossos began to build their business back up, heading down this new path, Venice too was being rebuilt. The Austrians had finally come to their senses and made Venice a free port again, abolishing tariffs on exports so that makers could start making without being punished. It was about to change in another way too.

At dinner one afternoon, Luciana made a surprising announcement; usually she never spoke. "The Austrians are going to build a bridge."

Everyone looked at her. She swallowed a defiant mouthful of risotto and loaded her fork with another.

"*Allora?* Austrians have built many bridges," Stella countered, "so that they don't have to ride in boats. They prefer their horses. Bridges over canals, even one over the Grand Canal." Stella hated Luciana; the feeling was mutual, for they were two strong characters.

Luciana gave her classic stare across the table. "A bridge to terraferma." She ate another forkful of risotto.

"To terraferma?" Laura Rosso exclaimed. "Why would they do that?"

They had to wait for Luciana to swallow her food. She took her time, clearly enjoying the attention. "For the trains," she said at last. "My brothers are going to work on the bridge. Good money there." She looked across the table at Raffaele.

"That's nothing to do with us," Laura declared, as if her words could build a barricade between her grandson and this bold girl. "Trains will never come here."

"They might," Marcolin broke in. "The English have many trains now, and the French and Germans are beginning to build railways."

"Nothing wrong with a boat. You know where you are with a boat."

"If the bridge connects Venice to terraferma, does that mean it's no longer an island?" Sebastiano asked.

Stella rolled her eyes. "No, it means it's an island with a bridge to it, that's all."

But Orsola knew what her nephew meant. Venice would no longer be so cut off from the mainland, with such an effort needed to reach it. A train along its own metal path would bring far more people to and from Venice than gondolas from Mestre could. How would that change the city? Would it lose its uniqueness?

And then: Prague would not take so long to get to, she thought, if I were willing to take the risk. Stop that, Orsola, she chided herself. When she looked up, Stefano was watching her. She tried to smile at him, but her face seemed to be stuck.

The next day Orsola was in their bedroom gathering clothes to wash when her husband appeared—he had singed a sleeve in the furnace and needed a new shirt. As Orsola dropped the bundle of clothing to fetch him one, there was a clink on the floor. They both looked down, and Orsola froze. It was the first dolphin Antonio had made for her and which she carried still; it had fallen from the pocket of a dress in the pile.

Stefano leaned over and picked it up. As he studied the blue-green figure, Orsola saw his face shift from puzzlement to recognition. She waited for him to get angry, to shout, even to hit. He did not. He looked at her with his black eyes, and all she could see was sorrow.

"Is this from him?" he asked quietly. He would know, of course, because Antonio's dolphins had wound around candlesticks Stefano had once helped to make. A glassman did not forget his wares.

"He gave it to me long ago," Orsola replied. "Before he left. It means nothing."

"Nothing but you carry it always. I've heard the sound of it before in your pocket."

That's Maria Barovier's rosetta, she wanted to say, but knew that arguing would just make it worse. Above all, Orsola didn't want Stefano to know that there were handfuls of glass dolphins in her studio.

"Are you going to go to terraferma once that bridge is built?" he said.

Orsola made a noise that sounded as if she were exasperated with a child, though that was not what she intended. Stefano flinched. "Of course not," she replied as gently as she could. "*Comunque*, I'm married to you. Isn't that enough?"

Stefano dropped the dolphin on the bed and picked out a clean shirt from the cupboard. "I'm lucky to have a daughter who loves me as much as Angela does," he said. "That is enough."

"Stefano," she said, but he left without looking back. Orsola sat on the bed for a long time, dry-eyed but feeling as if inside she were crying. Her husband deserved better.

After that, every time Angela leaned against her father after a meal or held his hand as they walked to Mass, Orsola felt it like a flame burning her fingers.

✧

THE NEXT TIME she visited Jonas to discuss an order—in far more modest offices in Dorsoduro than Klingenberg's had been in the Fondaco dei Tedeschi, and without a clerk to assist him—she asked him when the Rossos could begin making and selling more luxurious glassware again. "Be patient, Signora Orsola," he replied. "These things take time."

"But you found a market for seed beads."

"That is because seed beads are popular among American Indians."

"Are you sure there isn't a demand for goblets somewhere? Just because Venice has been reduced to poverty doesn't mean rich people in other places don't want to drink from fine goblets. You only need to find them. Marco needs to make something other than beads."

Jonas sat back. "It is not as simple as that. For one thing, prices. Goblets from Prague cost less, partly because until recently tariffs were higher here. But the Bohemians have also developed a different style—heavier and not so elaborate as Muranese glass. It seems to be popular. And the English with their clear and simple glassware are also in demand. Murano has more competition these days. The world has caught up with you, even if you have not caught up with the world."

After seeing the merchant, Orsola walked over to Cannaregio to
pay Luciana's mother, the girl not wanting to handle her own money.
The impiraressa was sitting in the small campo with other women,
including a younger sister in Luciana's old place at her side. As she
approached they were singing:

> Oh, where is my lover, where could he be
> He must be on the sea, and here I am home alone
> He must be on the sea drawing in the nets
> And here I am at home threading needles
> He must be on the sea setting sail
> And here I am at home stringing beads

They stopped when they spotted Orsola. She handed over Luciana's pay to her mother, who glanced at the coins, thrust them in her
pocket and said, "Who's the boy with the yellow hair?"

Orsola shook her head, pretending not to know what she meant.

"Your nephew. What's his name?"

"Raffaele. Why do you ask?"

"Raffaele Rosso." Luciana's mother rolled the *R*s as if tasting them.
"Luciana doesn't tell us much about what goes on over on Murano,
but she does mention him."

"What does she say?" Orsola's shoulders tightened.

"She makes fun of him."

"That means she likes him," the younger sister added.

"Tell her to leave him alone." Orsola knew she sounded just like
her mother.

The group began to laugh. Only Luciana's mother didn't join in.
"Maybe if you pay her more, she will."

You wily fox, Orsola thought.

Instead she did the opposite. Orsola went back to Murano and
told Luciana she was no longer needed.

Luciana didn't react to being let go with anything more than a shrug. Perhaps she had been expecting it, for the Rosso women had got better at stringing beads and her help was no longer crucial. Angela and Francesca cried out, however, and protested on her behalf, swearing they would set down baskets and wires unless she was allowed to stay.

"You will not," Laura Rosso asserted.

Angela stamped her foot, then ran into the workshop and led out Raffaele, who stood nervously between his aunt and his grandmother. "Are you really letting Luciana go?" he said.

"This is not your business," Orsola replied. "It's women's work. Leave it to us and go back to yours."

"But I love—"

"Don't you dare say that," Laura interrupted. "Don't even think it. You know nothing about such things. No grandson of mine is going to take up with a rude, foolish girl from Cannaregio."

Luciana was smiling, as if she'd not heard the older woman's insults. She picked up her basket full of yellow beads and dumped them out onto the ground as if emptying a bucket of water, yellow splashing everywhere. Angela and Francesca screamed and began to cry. Tucking her sessola under her arm, the Venetian gathered her shawl and bag with her wire needles and strode across the courtyard, humming one of her songs.

Orsola dug into her pocket. "Here is today's pay," she called after the girl, determined not to leave any loose ends. Luciana paid no attention, but pulled open the door and disappeared into the calle, brushing past Stella as she came in with a basket of laundry. Orsola looked around at the crying girls, at stunned Raffaele, at frowning Laura Rosso. "Stella, run after her and give her this," she said, holding out a coin to her sister.

"No!" Raffaele cried, snatching the coin. "I'll go!"

"Don't you do that!" Laura stepped in front of her grandson. "Raffaele, *mio caro, di grazia*," she pleaded, grabbing his arm. "We have been through so much together, you and I. You made the worst time of my life, on Lazzaretto Vecchio, better when you arrived. You made me want to live again. Don't take that away from me."

Raffaele stared at her. "*Mi dispiace*, Nonna, but I was just a baby, I don't remember any of that. That is your life, not mine. *This* is my life." He wrenched his arm away, sending his grandmother reeling, and ran into the calle without seeing her fall and crack her head against the ground.

✧

WHILE ORSOLA AND MONICA settled Laura Rosso in bed, Stella went out to search for Raffaele. She came back looking grim. "Bruno took them both across to Venice," she told Orsola quietly. "He said Raffaele was talking about working on the railway bridge."

"Of course Bruno took them. *Cretino*." Although she and Stefano had made their peace with Bruno—unlike some Murano families, the Rossos didn't nurse feuds with others for generations—Orsola still avoided hiring him. "Don't tell Madre, or Marco. Raffaele will come to his senses. I'll go and bring him back tomorrow."

"I'll go," Stella insisted. "They won't want to see you, since it was you who sent Luciana away."

Orsola tried to imagine her sister with the impiraresse in the Cannaregio campo. In her way Stella was as tough as they were. Perhaps she might succeed in getting Raffaele to come back.

She went early. Laura Rosso asked for Raffaele the moment she woke, and Orsola had to lie, saying he had been sent to borrow sand from another glass workshop. His grandmother sat in the courtyard, mending a shirt, waiting.

Stella returned midmorning and found Orsola in her studio, Laura following her in like a dog that knows exactly where trouble lies. "He's staying in Venice," Stella explained. "He's already found work on the railway bridge. I had to go over and find him there, working with all those Austrians shouting at him. Orsola, he doesn't have the muscles for moving rocks and hammering logs into the lagoon bed. Glassmen have a different sort of strength."

Laura Rosso slumped against the doorway.

"Madre!" Orsola jumped up, dropping the bead she had been decorating, and she and her sister rushed to hold up their mother. They led her to the courtyard and sat her on the bench by her sewing, then gave her some water.

"Do you know," Laura began, gripping the glass so that her knuckles turned white, "Nicoletta was already dead when Raffaele was born? I didn't think that was possible. She was in labor but so weak from the plague that she couldn't push when it came time. She tried once, and it burst her heart and she died right then. They were going to take her away and dump her on the pile with the others, with the baby still inside her. I wouldn't let them."

Monica had come to stand in the kitchen doorway, and Marco, Giacomo and Stefano filled the workshop entrance, all listening.

"I quickly took my knife and cut her open," she continued. "I had seen a midwife do it once. It was a bit like skinning a rabbit, though I had to be careful—so careful not to cut Raffaele. I did it, and he came out alive. So you see," she finished, looking around at them all, "Raffaele is special to me, because I saved him. I couldn't save Lorenzo or Nicoletta, but I saved him. I don't want to lose him now. I must go over to Venice to speak to him."

It was the most Laura Rosso had ever said about her time on Lazzaretto Vecchio.

"What is this about Raffaele?" Marco demanded. "What's happened to my son?"

The night before, Orsola had made excuses for Raffaele's absence from supper. Now she explained, trying to keep her voice low so that her brother would remain calm. But she hadn't finished before he began to shout. "That Venetian *puttana* was bad news from the start! How could you let her in here to steal Raffaele away? *Bauca!* What a useless sister!"

"Stop it," Monica intervened. "It's not Orsola's fault. Whatever has happened, you need to fix it. Take your mother to Venice and find Raffaele. And take Orsola too. She knows Luciana's mother and can persuade from that direction."

That afternoon three angry Rossos went over to Venice, with Laura Rosso insisting they be rowed for free by Bruno, whom she blamed for taking Raffaele and Luciana from Murano. Orsola and her mother sat as far from him as possible, and he was subdued—for Bruno. He stayed away from personal topics that might implicate him, but he voiced strong opinions about the railway bridge—mainly anger laced with fear that the train would replace the gondoliers bringing tourists from the mainland. Not that Bruno made that run himself, but he was indignant on behalf of his fellow boatmen. Laura glared at him the whole time.

"*Basta!*" Orsola said finally. "We don't want to hear about the bridge; we just want to get Raffaele back."

"*Va bene,*" Bruno replied. "But the lad needs to think about us boatmen before he starts working for the enemy."

"*Sta' zitto!*" Laura Rosso barked. She was not about to let anyone outside of the family criticize her grandson.

Bruno subsided as instructed, and simply hummed as he rowed them across the lagoon and west around the tip of Cannaregio to the Church of Santa Maria delle Penitenti, close to where the bridge would be starting from. Peate were clustered in the water, heavy with building materials: wood, stone, bricks, lime, iron. Despite her worry about Raffaele, Orsola was curious to see how such a long bridge across the lagoon could be made, given it was over two miles to terraferma. She had seen bridges constructed or repaired over small canals and supposed the principle was the same: lower a wooden frame into the water to trap it, and empty out the water with buckets; then pound logs down into the lagoon bed to make a solid foundation and build stone piers on top.

So it was with the viaduct bridge. In the end it would be twelve feet above the water, thirty feet wide, and span the lagoon with 222 brick arches. At the moment, though, they were working on the first few piers. Men clambered all over the boats, heaving and lifting and shouting—most of them Venetian, with Austrian soldiers supervising, in their striking white tunics, blue trousers and high metal caps.

Laura Rosso eyed the soldiers and spat. "*Patate*," she muttered, for the Austrians loved their potatoes and so earned that nickname.

"They don't do much real work, do they?" Bruno remarked, trying to get back in Laura's favor. "Lazy *patate*."

"Never mind the Austrians," Marco interjected. "Where's my son?" He had been quiet up until now, watching the men working away at this seemingly impossible task of linking Venice to terraferma. But impatience took over, as it always did with Marco.

It was Bruno who spotted Raffaele, out on a peata, helping to unload logs brought from the mainland that would be driven vertically into the mud.

"Row us closer to him," Marco commanded.

Orsola had never thought of her nephew as slight, but compared to the men he was working with he seemed tiny, his arms and shoulders barely strong enough to lift his end of a log. As they drew close she could see the strain and exhaustion in his face. And this was only his first day.

"Raffaele, get over here!" Marco shouted. "*Adesso!*"

"Hush! That's not the way to do it," Orsola hissed.

"Don't tell me what to do! He's my son and he'll obey me."

Raffaele was concentrating on lugging a log with others from one end of the peata to the other, where they lifted it to the next boat, and onward to its place in the lagoon bed. He looked tense and nervous, trying to keep up with the bigger men. He didn't see his family until Bruno managed to row them close enough. When Marco called his name again, Raffaele glanced over and was so startled he let go of his end of the log. It tipped down, rocking the peata and unleashing a volley of curses from his fellow workers.

Marco stood at the prow of Bruno's gondola, trying to steady himself as it moved with the waves. "Come here, Raffaele! You're wanted back home."

Perhaps if he had left it at that, his son might have obeyed. But Marco couldn't resist sharpening his words. "Who do you think you are, turning your back on your family and thinking you can make your place in this *sestiere de merda* doing this *lavoro de merda?* Your life is glass, not shifting logs for Austrian *patate!*"

"You're calling this work *merda*, are you?" One of the men on Raffaele's peata reached over and grasped the gleaming metal ferro on the prow of Bruno's gondola to pull the boat closer.

"*Ehi*, don't touch that!" Bruno cried. "Nobody touches my ferro!"

"No? It looks like I am, though. Shall we go for a ride?" The workman began to push and pull at the ferro, rocking the gondola and making the women hold on to the sides.

Bruno rushed forward to join Marco at the prow and grabbed the workman. The three men grappled together, then suddenly Marco was in the water, Bruno trying to pull him out, and the Venetians were whistling and jeering. Amid the chaos, Raffaele stood still, his face pale. Then he bolted, leaping from one boat to the next, falling when they rocked, scrambling up again and jumping to the next, until he reached land. He glanced back, as if to check that no one had followed him, then ran. Orsola watched as the white shirt his grandmother had mended many times disappeared into Cannaregio.

Bruno had managed to haul Marco back into the gondola, where he spluttered and shook his head, spattering drops of water about. "*Càncaro!*" he shouted at the Venetian. "I'll cut off your dick and feed it to my dog, who will complain he's still hungry because it's so small. I'll fuck your mother, then make her eat the shit of our son. I'll—"

"Bruno, *basta! Basta!*" Orsola had heard him curse many times before but never with such vicious depth.

The Venetian would have gone for Bruno, but the men's fight had attracted the attention of Austrian soldiers overseeing the work, and they were now gliding toward them in a sandolo to restore order. One shouted something in German and, after one last exchange of curses with Bruno, the Venetians turned back to their logs.

Laura Rosso was sitting frozen in her seat, seemingly unaffected by the rocking. "Are you all right, Madre?" Orsola asked.

"Take me to her mother."

Orsola directed Bruno along the Rio de Cannaregio to the Ponte delle Guglie, named for the stone spires the Austrians had added when they'd rebuilt the brick-and-stone bridge some years before. Lining the arch were grimacing faces of men and lions, their moods reflecting her own. She had Bruno let them off by the bridge and instructed him to take Marco to cool down at a nearby taverna until they returned.

Luciana was back stringing beads in the little campo with the other women, looking much as she had done when Orsola first met her, though she was now wearing Maria Barovier's dress, Stella's shoes and a string of glass beads around her neck that she had scavenged from the Rossos' storerooms. She looked up as the Rosso women entered the campo and her jaw tightened, but she kept her face blank.

Laura Rosso marched up and stood next to her, expectant. Luciana tried to ignore the intruder.

"Get up, girl, and give your seat to your elder," Laura declared. "Who raised you to be so rude?" She looked around at the group of women. Luciana's mother puffed up in her seat. Laura eyed her. "Tell your daughter to show better manners. I want to talk to you and I'm not going to stand here to do it."

The two women stared at each other. At last the mother jerked her head at her daughter, and Luciana set down her sessola, stood and sauntered over to a shaded wall, leaning against it to witness the proceedings as if she were watching acrobats.

Luciana's mother was probably Orsola's age but appeared much older—closer to Laura Rosso's; it was a reflection of the family's poverty. The two women regarded each other. Then Laura surprised Orsola. "I want my grandson to be happy," she said, "and to see his family from time to time. That is all."

"*De certo*," Luciana's mother agreed.

"But I know he won't be happy working on that Austrian bridge. Have you seen what they must lift? Raffaele is strong for glass, not for lifting logs. Not as strong as your sons."

"This is true. I don't know what my daughter sees in him!"

Luciana made a face.

"So I ask of you: find him a job in one of the bead factories here. He pulls cane well. And keep him in Cannaregio. It is at least close to Murano. Don't let your daughter drag him all the way over to Castello. Keep him here and in glass, and I promise you we will leave you alone."

Luciana's mother pondered this. "And if I don't find him glass-work? What will you do then?"

"The men of Murano will come over and burn down these factories, and you'll have no more work, any of you." With that threat, and against the indignant murmurs of the group, Laura Rosso stood.

"Ho! Tough Muranese, eh?" Luciana's mother chuckled. "I like that spirit. Let's hope your grandson has some of it. He's lucky to have such a nonna to fight for him. *Va bene*, I'll find him work."

✧

ORSOLA LED THE WAY BACK to the Ponte delle Guglie, the two women silent. They were passing along the calle when a flash of white shirt met them from a doorway, and Raffaele fell into step beside them. He didn't say anything, but stopped when Laura Rosso did. She looked him up and down, then slapped him hard across the face. "You better make me proud. And your madre—she's watching from up there, you know." She pointed at the sky.

"I know. *Grazie*, Nonna." Raffaele threw his arms around her, squeezed her hard, then let her go. Nodding at his aunt, he disappeared back toward Luciana and his future.

Laura watched him go. "How many more will we lose to this terrible city?" she said, then turned and stumped along the calle.

6

THE STONE SKIMS ACROSS the water, landing in 1915, several months into the Great War. Orsola Rosso is turning back and forth in the flame a red bead in the shape of a drop of blood. She looks up, and seventy-one years have passed since the Austrians began that bridge. She and those who matter to her are four years older. Orsola is forty-four.

So much change in so little time. Austrians, kicked out of Venice. Italy, unified. Electricity, harnessed. Factory production line, perfected. Cars, invented. Motors, ubiquitous. Human flight, a spectacle at Kitty Hawk. In other words, planes, trains and automobiles. A civil war in America, freedom for enslaved people but hard lives still and Jim Crow laws and no sign of truth and reconciliation. Also, an archduke assassinated at Sarajevo, and its geopolitical consequences.

Let's not forget Dickens, Balzac, Flaubert, Eliot, Tolstoy. The novel has come of age. (Virginia Woolf is just getting started.) And art: the Pre-Raphaelites, the Impressionists, now the Cubists and a whiff of Modernism. The world is running faster, even in Venice. Except for glass and its makers . . .

✧

IT WAS ROSELLA who voiced best how Orsola felt about seed beads. One day she and her niece were waiting on the dock at the back of the workshop for the peata due to arrive and take the latest crates full of hanks over to Venice for Jonas to inspect. Rosella was counting the hanks of coral- and tan-colored beads laid end to end in crates like fish, while Orsola struggled through the paperwork. She had taught herself to read rather late, so it always took her longer, but she never revealed this to her nieces or daughter.

Rosella had grown into a thoughtful young woman who worked with the others to string beads when necessary, but was happier leaning over a flame and making lampworked beads. She had a good eye, a steady hand, and she handled glass so naturally that Orsola was surprised, for she had no Rosso blood in her. It had been the same with Antonio. It seemed the mastery of this most fickle substance had nothing to do with the blood in your veins or your mother's milk. Orsola would never say this aloud, however, for it would be like a bomb dropped in the middle of the unshakable Rosso belief in their innate superior skill with glass.

She and Rosella occasionally made beads and glass figurines together, sitting across from each other at the table Orsola had worked at since she first learned from Elena Barovier, and which had been adapted by Giacomo for two to sit at and use lamps. They sold their work in the Rosso shop, and a few beads via Jonas, but the seed bead business often pulled them away, and many other lampworkers were now competing for customers, some of them producing striking work. Orsola had to accept that though she was more experienced, she was no longer unique.

Now Rosella sighed.

"What's the matter?" Orsola demanded. "Are we short?"

"How many beads are in this crate? Hundreds of thousands?"

"Millions."

"Yes. We've made millions of beads. Millions and millions. But none is special. They're not even that good." Rosella picked up a hank and dangled it between them, the beads sparkling in the sun. "When you look at them individually they're lopsided, the holes are different sizes, they're chipped. Not like lampworked beads. Don't you wish we could spend all our time at our lamps rather than counting—what does Padre call them—*escrementi di topo?*" She dropped the hank back in the crate.

Orsola paused her tallying of the numbers. She often had to reassure herself that switching to seed beads had been the right thing to do. Jonas found buyers, and the Rossos scaled up the operation, hired more workers and were able to flourish again—as was Murano glass in general. Rosso beads meant food on the table—not just sardines and polenta, but veal and coffee and sugar, and wine that was not half vinegar. Faces filled out, the young ones had more spark, the adults were cheerful, mainly. Not Marco, of course. He hated the direction the Rosso business had taken. Beads were below his talents.

"They're made into beautiful things," Orsola suggested. "Bags, purses, cushions, lampshades, fringe on women's dresses."

"But it's the *thing* that is beautiful rather than the bead," Rosella said. "Don't you want your beads to be admired for their own beauty?"

"*De certo.*"

"We need a commission. Otherwise we'll spend our lives producing beads that others will use to make the beautiful things in the world. Like Luciana does, making wreaths out of seed beads."

When the Great War in Europe had begun months before, Luciana had astutely switched to fashioning wreaths and bouquets for graves. French families in particular seemed taken with these beads strung on wires and shaped into elaborate flowers, for they lasted through rain and snow and wind and harsh sun. Orsola could not deny Luciana's skill at re-creating flowers; her lilies of the valley, violets and pansies looked almost real. Luciana called her business I Fiori di Rosso—for she had married Raffaele and had the use of his name now. Orsola balked at this: I Fiori di Luciana sounded better, she thought, and using Rosso was taking advantage of the reputation of the Rosso glassmakers of Murano. There was nothing she could do about it, though. Luciana was now family.

Not only that: Raffaele adored her. They'd had three children in quick succession: Venetian Rossos. Raffaele worked at a bead factory in Cannaregio, pulling cane, and seemed happy. His factory had joined the newly formed Society for the Bead Industry, a cooperative established on Murano that consolidated workforces, equipment and finances. This meant the prodigal son might eventually work back on Murano. Orsola doubted he would visit home, though: as long as Luciana wasn't welcome at the Rossos', he would not come to see his father or grandmother. Laura Rosso refused to allow anyone to say Luciana's name in her presence.

Instead members of the family went to see him. Orsola visited the factory to say hello whenever she made a trip to Venice, and also looked in on her great-niece and great-nephews tumbling about in the tiny campo where Luciana and her family still sat, now making beaded flowers. Orsola was careful to be cordial; Luciana was not. "Orsola R-r-r-osso," she would say, rolling the R as if there were a marble in her mouth. "Checking on how the Rosso flowers are doing?"

"I've come to see how the little ones are." Orsola crouched and kissed the top of her great-niece's head, where her hair was pulled up into a bunch and tied with a white ribbon.

"Come to make sure they're getting enough to eat, are you?" Luciana smiled, then picked up her baby son from a cradle at her feet and pulled out a breast, not bothering to cover herself with her apron or shawl as other women did when they fed their babies in public.

That was how the visits always went.

Others' visits, though, were more consequential. Francesca liked to go over to see her little niece and nephews and stayed to learn how to make beaded flowers from her sister-in-law. One day she didn't come back, sending word via Bruno that the baby was sick and they needed her. After a day Monica became suspicious about her daughter; she didn't like going to Venice, so she sent Orsola over with a salve for the child's chest. There was no sick baby; he was asleep in the cradle while the other children played and Francesca sat with the women, making flowers and singing. She looked guilty when Orsola appeared. "I'm just helping Luciana with this order from France," she gabbled. "There's so much to do, and they need me more than you do. Besides, making flowers is much nicer than stringing beads."

Orsola didn't want to argue with her niece in front of Luciana and her family, all of whom had the same bold stare, which they were aiming at her now. It felt like being pelted with stones. "What should I tell your mother?" she said.

Francesca gulped, but a nudge from Luciana made her set her jaw, and Orsola caught a flash of Marco in his daughter.

Monica then reluctantly ventured to Venice herself to try to lure her daughter back, but returned alone. After supper Orsola caught her sister-in-law crying into the dishwater—the only time she'd ever seen her cry.

Three months later, Francesca married one of Luciana's brothers. Another Rosso lost to La Serenissima.

✧

ROSELLA'S COMMENT about a commission nagged at Orsola. Another necklace? Would the third time be the luck that would finally bring her the business she still secretly craved? Or had the Josephine necklace been her peak?

Her luck arrived in the form of a dressmaker sent to her by Domenego. The seamstress made clothes for the Marchesa Luisa Casati, a flamboyant woman known for her sumptuous parties and outrageous dress sense. Orsola knew of her; everyone did. Muranese glassmakers vied for her attention after one of her parties, where each of the hundreds of guests had been given a hand-blown glass lantern made specially for the occasion. That work had kept one glass workshop afloat for a year. The Marchesa also liked to make a scene at the passeggiata in Piazzetta San Marco, wearing a red-and-gold Fortuny cloak and parading on the arm of her African servant Garbi, who held in one hand a parasol made of peacock feathers and in the other a pair of drugged cheetahs on diamond-studded leashes. Sometimes at midnight the Marchesa took the same walk, but nude under a fur cloak.

When she wanted to raise the stakes, she hired Domenego to row her gondola, replacing her white gondolier. The abolition of slavery throughout Europe had finally released the gondolier from his obligation to the Klingenberg family, but he still worked for Klara and her husband, though his spare time was now his own. The Marchesa would lounge upon silk cushions while Garbi stood at the prow with the cheetahs. Orsola had come upon this sight on the Grand Canal and was startled that Domenego was playing a part in such a spectacle. He swore to her that he was paid well for his services and was not afraid of the big cats, though when Orsola watched the gondola pass, she noted her friend's tense jaw and stiff pose.

The dressmaker Domenego sent to her was in despair over the Marchesa Casati's demand for beaded fringe on a dress. The amount of beads she wanted sewn to the chest would be far too heavy and uncomfortable to wear, but the Marchesa wouldn't listen, believing herself to be an excellent designer. The dressmaker told Orsola she suspected that once she tried on the finished dress the Marchesa would be horrified by the weight and refuse to pay. This had

happened before, with a collar of amethysts. Orsola was asked to accompany the dressmaker to the palazzo with a bag of seed beads so
that the Marchesa could feel the weight herself.

The Palazzo Venier dei Leoni, where she lived, was not far from the
Ponte dell'Accademia—the second bridge to span the Grand Canal, and
one of the last contributions the Austrians made to Venice before they
left and Venice became part of a unified Italy. Only one story of the
unfinished palazzo had been built. As Orsola and the dressmaker
waited in a hired gondola at the portico gates, she was thankful that
Garbi came to let them in without the cheetahs in tow. "Wait," he said,
leaving them in the androne. The marble floor was covered with rotting
Persian rugs damp from a recent acqua alta, the moldy smell not quite
masked by enormous vases of lilies shedding petals and crimson pollen.
Scattered about were bits of old gondolas painted gold, marble table-
tops and wrecked mahogany chairs that they perched on as they waited.
In the distance they could hear the screeches of peacocks in the garden, the howling of monkeys and a parrot inside squawking, "*Merda!*"

"Who puts rugs in an androne knowing it will be flooded?" Orsola
whispered to the seamstress, who shrugged.

After half an hour, Orsola wanted to go. "No. We wait," the seamstress said, hands crossed patiently in her lap. "This is how she is. This
is why we charge her four times what we do others."

At last Garbi led them into the Marchesa's cluttered salon, buzzing
with newly installed electric lights. The Marchesa Casati was a tall,
cadaverously thin woman with a powdered face, bright-red lips and
enormous eyes—so large the whites were entirely visible around her
irises. She had outlined them in kohl and topped them with enormous false eyelashes. Her short hair was dyed orange and stood out
from her head like a halo. She wore a sumptuous kimono in clashing
reds and oranges and pinks.

The Marchesa gave no explanation or apology for keeping them waiting. When she offered them absinthe, Orsola didn't know what it was but instinctively declined. She watched with fascination while the Marchesa splashed green liquid into a glass, placed a slotted silver spoon over the lip with a sugar cube balanced on it and dripped water onto the melting sugar and into the glass, turning the green absinthe a cloudy yellow. She then wandered around the room, sipping her drink and cooing at the parrot, which switched its curse to *"Puttana!"*

Orsola and the seamstress glanced at each other and tried not to laugh. Over the years Orsola had encountered plenty of eccentrics in Venice—it was a city that seemed to attract them, encouraging theatricality and outlandishness. On Murano, glassmakers were sometimes commissioned to make far more outré pieces than simply hundreds of lanterns: jugs in the shape of a woman's torso where the wine poured from the nipples; candelabras with arms shaped like naked women; chandeliers with dangling priapic demons. Orsola had heard of a glassmaker who quietly specialized in glass dildos. But that was all business, made and handed on; none of it affected the behavior of the glass families, how they dressed or acted. Muranese women did not brighten their eyes with belladonna as it appeared this marchesa did. Maestros did not stroll the rivas with cheetahs on leads or keep peacocks in their courtyards. They ate sardines, not caviar. Very occasionally Orsola brightened her cheeks with rouge before going to Venice, but she would never wear powder and kohl and false lashes to make herself stand out from the crowd. The Marchesa Casati clearly didn't know any other way of being, even when she was home alone with no one to see her. It must have been exhausting to live like that.

The dressmaker cleared her throat. "We've come to see you about your dress, Marchesa—the one with all the beads. This is Orsola Rosso, Murano's finest beadmaker."

Orsola blushed at the praise from someone who hardly knew her and was saying it to impress. It wasn't accurate, either: she did not

make seed beads. She nodded at the Marchesa, who wasn't even looking at them, but plucking dead flowers from the floral displays dotted
around the room and dropping them on the marble floor, presumably
for someone else to pick up.

"We are concerned about the weight, Marchesa," Orsola explained, "and wanted to make sure you don't feel it's too heavy on
your chest." The dress itself was simple, a long black silk sheath, but
the collar would be made up of black-, silver- and gold-colored cylindrical seed beads, hanging halfway down her chest in a mighty, semicircular yoke, like shimmering armor. Orsola had worked out how
many thousands of beads would be needed and placed the equivalent
in pouches they now hung around the Marchesa's neck. She stood
still, clearly enjoying people fussing over her.

"I love the weight on my chest," she declared. "It makes me feel
safe, feel loved, it's like an embrace. *More* beads, if anything!"

"Are you sure you'll be comfortable enough wearing it at your
party, Marchesa?" Orsola queried.

The Marchesa waved her hand, spilling some of her absinthe and
just missing the black silk. "Oh, this isn't for a party. Parties are dead
now with the war on. No one is coming to Venice. I shall have to go
where the war is—to Paris, to Berlin—so I can see people. No, this is
for the passeggiata. And I want all the beads. All of them!"

"As you wish, Marchesa. I've prepared a bill and will be happy to
string the collar once I've been paid."

The dressmaker looked alarmed at this naked talk of payment,
and the Marchesa sighed. "Oh, money . . . Must we?"

Orsola stood firm, ignoring the seamstress's pleading eyes, the
dead flowers on the floor, the smell of spoiled fruit and unwashed
skin, the parrot now squawking "*Becco fotuo!*" "I will string the beads
once I've been paid. Not before. If I didn't demand this, I would
never stay in business."

The Marchesa gazed at Orsola with her enormous, melancholy eyes, then smiled, which did not dispel the sadness. "I like to see a woman so firm with her business." She leaned over and kissed Orsola hard on the mouth. "All right, glassmaker, you have my blessing. Go and give Garbi your bill and tell him you won't leave until you're paid."

Stunned by the kiss, Orsola didn't move. Over her kimono the Marchesa had flung two long strands of pearls, one white, one gray. Necklaces.

The beadmaker took a deep breath, as if to inhale some of the Marchesa's boldness. "Would you like me to make you a long necklace like that of glass beads?" she suggested. "Something more striking than pearls, in whatever colors you like."

"Black beads decorated with red and gold," the Marchesa Casati replied, decisive in her taste. "*Très à la mode.* Add it to the bill."

✧

SINCE THE UNIFICATION of the Italian states into one country, Venice had stabilized enough that tourists and exports had increased—at least until the Great War began—and artisans were back at work. Beads had already found a market, but fancier glasswork was resurrected almost singlehandedly by Antonio Salviati, a lawyer who sought out Murano glassmakers to produce glass tiles for new mosaics in the Basilica of San Marco. Eventually he had them resurrect the making of other things—vases, glasses, chandeliers. Of course, tastes had moved on from earlier times, and there was still all the competition from other parts of Europe to contend with. But slowly many of the workshops were reopening and beginning to make the luxurious pieces Murano had been famous for.

The Rossos, however, continued their seed bead work. They were set up for it now: the furnaces, the space to pull cane, the skills of the serventi and garzoni. Each had his specialty. Giacomo made the glass to Rosso recipes, altering them as needed for cane glass rather than glass for blowing. Marco made the pastone that Stefano and Sebastiano then pulled into cane between them, Andrea turned beads in a heated metal drum to smooth them and Marcolin sorted beads by size, weeding out those that were misshapen or lacked holes. Despite being maestro, Marco had no interest in overseeing the operation, and usually let Stefano, with his past knowledge, take over.

One morning her brother sat down across from Orsola at the table where she was finishing the last of the lampworked beads for the Marchesa's necklace. She nodded stiffly, always tense when he came near her as she was making beads. At least he smelled of coffee rather than of wine. He played with the nozzle in front of him where Rosella sometimes worked.

"Why are you making those?" he asked, picking up one of the black beads decorated with red and gold. "You don't often use black. It's all blues and greens and reds with you."

Orsola couldn't hide her surprise that Marco had even noticed the colors she favored. "It's for the Marchesa Casati—the one we made all those black and silver and gold seed beads for."

Marco turned the bead between his fingers. "She likes black, does she?"

"Yes. Other colors too, but black seems to be a favorite." Orsola restrained herself from snatching the bead from him. Instead she focused on the line of gold she was winding onto the barrel-shaped black bead, snaking it like a vine. She would then add red dots to indicate poppies. Though it was different from her usual style, she was pleased with the design, and confident that the Marchesa would feel it was contemporary enough to suit her tastes.

"She's the one with the leopards, isn't she?"

"Cheetahs."

"Tell her I'll make her black goblets with cheetahs entwined around the base."

Orsola opened her mouth to say no, but a vision of those goblets flashed before her, ones with such shallow bowls they could hold little wine—like the goblet Marco had made long ago when she met Antonio. The Marchesa would adore their impracticality. And it would mean Marco could get back to doing what he was best at.

She had stopped turning the bead; it melted in the flame and dropped to the table, ruined.

"I bet it feels good," Marco commented.

"What?"

He waved at her lamp. "Making something other than mouse shit."

She considered a sarcastic reply. But he seemed to be serious, and he wasn't drunk. "It's wonderful," she said.

"Glass is in our blood."

It was the first time Marco had ever acknowledged her ability, and that made her generous. "I'll ask the Marchesa about cheetah goblets."

"*Bene.*" Then, of course, he had to ruin the moment. Jumping to his feet, he added, "*Allora*, get back to your *escrementi di coniglio.*"

◇

MARCO DIDN'T WAIT for an answer from the Marchesa Casati. He immediately began designing, and asked Giacomo to make black glass and find him gold leaf for the cheetahs' spots. He even went to Piazzetta San Marco for a few evenings to watch for the Marchesa so that he could sketch the cheetahs, as he had never seen one. He was rewarded with a brief glimpse of her and the cats and was so inspired he convinced Orsola and the dressmaker to wait until he had finished the goblets so that he could accompany them when they delivered the dress and necklace.

To get to Venice they took a vaporetto—one of the new steam-driven water buses that were putting boatmen like Bruno out of business and turning gondolas into purely tourist attractions rather than daily transportation. But Marco insisted that they arrive at the palazzo itself by gondola on the Grand Canal, and Orsola was mortified to discover he had hired Domenego to row them there from the Rialto Bridge, even ordering the gondolier to don his old-fashioned red tunic and black-and-white hose rather than his usual uniform of white shirt and black trousers. Marco himself wore a modern black suit and a fedora he had borrowed from a wealthier cousin. He'd had his hair cut and hadn't shaved for a few days, so a shadowy beard sculpted his jaw. Orsola rarely thought of her brother as anything other than an irritation, but even she had to admit he looked handsome as he stood in the prow while she and the dressmaker sat, the seamstress staring at Marco as if he were Neptune himself gracing their boat.

They arrived at Palazzo Venier dei Leoni in midafternoon, and Marco must have paid a servant to make sure the Marchesa was up and standing at her window, looking out over the Grand Canal and drinking coffee as they pulled up. Marco removed his hat and bowed to her. This seemed to please the Marchesa, who blew him a kiss and waved them inside.

This time Garbi didn't make them wait in the androne but led them straight to his employer's salon. She was wearing a dark-green velvet robe and smoking a cigarillo in a long onyx holder. Today her hair was auburn rather than orange. Her makeup was less extreme—no powder this time, and her lipstick had rubbed off on her coffee cup—but her kohl and mascara looked slept in. She squealed when the dressmaker held up the dress, weighted with its bead armor. "I'll try it on now!" she cried, and stepped out of her robe to reveal her naked body. Before looking away, Orsola noted that her pubic hair was dyed the same auburn as her head.

Marco was gripping the wooden box containing the goblets, his knuckles white against the mahogany. He couldn't take his eyes from the Marchesa. Hers was not the sort of beauty or behavior he would be used to. Orsola was delighted to see her brother so out of his depth.

It seemed the Marchesa did have an eye for design: the dress looked stunning on her, making her into a vampiric Boudicca. And despite the heaviness of the beads and her bony frame, the Marchesa managed to wear them lightly. "Perfection," she breathed. "You have worked miracles." She said this to the whole room, as if all of them had made the dress.

"Marchesa." Orsola bowed, then stepped forward, unfolding a swatch of ivory-colored velvet. "Your necklace."

Perhaps she got the timing wrong. Or the necklace did not go with the dress—not that that seemed to have stopped the Marchesa Casati from wearing what she liked. Perhaps she needed more time to admire herself in her beaded armor. Or she was distracted by the man in the room. She picked up Orsola's necklace, stated, "Glorious," and handed it to her maid, who opened a cedar chest heaped with gold, silver, pearl and myriad other colors of necklaces, dropped it in and shut the lid. The black, red and gold necklace was going to disappear without a trace among all the other necklaces, never worn, and the commissions Orsola had imagined from the Marchesa's friends would disappear with it.

At least I've been paid, she thought. But no more fancy necklaces for rich people. I am done.

Marco looked at his sister with something like pity. Then he turned to the Marchesa. "Perhaps, Marchesa, you would like a drink to celebrate your new dress?"

"An excellent proposal!" The Marchesa seemed unsurprised that a strange man was in her room, offering her a drink.

"I have just the glasses for you. Allow me." Marco set the box on a table and indicated to the maid to move aside a jumble of clothes, cigarettes, vases of dried flowers, a plate of moldy oranges. When enough space had been cleared, he unfurled a piece of gold Indian silk and took his time smoothing it. Enchanted by his theatricality, the Marchesa moved closer. Marco pulled out the goblets from their nest of cotton and velvet, placed them on the silk and stepped back.

The Marchesa shrieked, making everyone jump. "Genius!" she cried, snatching up one of the goblets so greedily that Marco stepped forward as if to restrain her. "*Spettacolare*," she proclaimed as she turned the glass in her fingers, admiring the sinuous cheetahs, the string of baubles making up the stem, the rows of gold flowers Giacomo had painted around the rim of the glass. "*Magnifico*." The Marchesa looked down on Marco—for she was a good deal taller than he—her liquid eyes shining. "You and I must drink to your skill."

Her words made clear that Orsola and the dressmaker were not included in this celebration. Orsola looked at her brother. Now that his work was on show, he was more confident. But would he be confident enough to make sure he was paid?

"My brother's work is in high demand throughout Europe," she said. "But for you he will charge the special price of one thousand lire for the pair."

Marco stared at her. They had not discussed price and the special Marchesa inflation. "That is—" he spluttered.

The Marchesa interrupted him with a laugh and a wave of her hand, at once agreeing with Orsola and dismissing her. "Sort that with Garbi on your way out."

Orsola raised her eyebrows at Marco. "*In bocca al lupo*," she mouthed as she left.

✧

GARBI DIDN'T BLINK at the ridiculous price for the goblets; he was used to Venetians overcharging his employer. He handed her a roll of notes, which she stuffed in her pocket, then led her to the portico opening onto the Grand Canal. Domenego was leaning back on the curved stern of his gondola, reading a newspaper. Since few could continue to afford private gondolas with two boatmen, the boat's shape had been modified over the years to accommodate one gondolier rowing, with the felze gone and the curved stern making the boat asymmetrical but helping to keep it moving straight. He sat up when they appeared, nodded at Garbi, then handed Orsola in. "Aren't we waiting for your brother or the dressmaker?" he asked as Garbi shut the portico gates.

"She went out the back way. Marco will be some time. No need to wait. If you take me back to the Rialto I'll go from there."

"If you're not in a hurry, I'll take you to Fondamente Nove through the back canals. I have time."

Orsola nodded and settled back on the seat facing him. They chatted easily now that Marco wasn't there, about the new war, which, though far away, affected tourism, about the glass business, about the Rossos. Although Domenego was never garrulous, over the years he had grown more comfortable with Orsola, and occasionally offered opinions. He thought, for instance, that Italy would not remain neutral in the war, but join France and England so that they could fight against Austria. "Austrians will always be the true enemy here, not the Germans," he remarked, plying his way through a narrow canal by the Palazzo Contarini del Bovolo, with its elaborate spiral staircase like a tall wedding cake bolted onto the exterior. "Whatever the treaty they already have with the Germans and Austrians, Italians want to punish Austrians for what they did to the Veneto."

"How do you know all this?"

Domenego pointed at the paper on the seat next to her. "And I listen to my passengers. They don't all gossip about who is visiting whose bed."

"But—does this mean we'll have to muster an army?" Orsola was thinking of the young men in the Rosso family, trying to imagine Marcolin, Raffaele, Sebastiano, Andrea, as soldiers. Impossible. They were glassmen.

"Probably." Domenego then called out, "*Oe! A premando!*" before steering them left.

"You know Signora Klara's husband has lost money," he remarked after a moment.

"Now who's gossiping! Everyone knows he gambles."

"This time he lost a great deal."

It was unlike Domenego to talk about his employers. Orsola waited.

"They are letting me go and selling the gondola. They have to. Besides, they don't need me any longer. They can take vaporettos or motorboat taxis, or walk. Gondolas are—" He waved his hand and didn't finish.

Orsola stared at him. "What will you do?"

Domenego didn't answer—he was maneuvering past a gondola heading the opposite way. The two gondoliers nodded but didn't greet each other with a joke or a curse or a song the way the others did. So many years of rowing on Venetian canals made him a familiar sight, but not a friend.

Orsola could feel the wad of the Marchesa's notes in her pocket—enough to feed the family for months. Should she give it to Domenego? "Would you go back to Africa if you could?" she asked.

He rowed for a bit. "I am not the person I was there," he said at last. "It has been so long. You know my family will be long gone. I do not know if anyone there now would accept me."

"Of course they would!" Even as she said it, Orsola wasn't sure. She said no more, because the question had clearly caused Domenego pain, and she did not want to inflict more.

"It is not just me and the boat," he added. "Signora Klara and her husband will have to move from Campo San Polo to something smaller. He lost the house in a wager."

"*Mariavergine.*" Orsola crossed herself. Marco had done stupid things—he was doing one now—but he would never bet the Rosso house.

✧

HER BROTHER was gone for three days. Monica seemed unbothered. When Giacomo and Stefano offered to look for him, she refused. "I don't want to know what he's up to. He'll come back."

When he returned—minus his shirt and the fedora, his suit torn, circles under his eyes and still a little drunk or high—Monica duly slapped him, because it was expected of her, and he played the hangdog husband as expected of him. But they quickly got back to normal. Orsola found this hard to understand. If Stefano were to go off with a louche marchesa who had a tendency to drop her clothes, she would be furious.

"Marco is Marco," Monica explained, "and Venice is Venice. It's not Murano, *grazie a Dio*. I expect nothing of him when he's over there. Here"—she stamped the ground—"he behaves."

The Marchesa Casati was so taken with her black cheetah goblets that she ordered more from Marco and was specific about the colors and animals: white goblets embellished with swans, blue goblets with fish, yellow with parrots, red with snakes. They'd amused themselves trying to drink from the impossibly shallow bowls of the cheetah goblets, but even the Marchesa understood that they were too impractical, so Marco made the swan goblets with deeper bowls. When he went over to Palazzo Venier dei Leoni with them—this time displayed in an ivory box lined with black velvet—Orsola and Monica did not expect him back that day. However, Marco reappeared a few hours later, clothes intact, box in hand, sober. It turned out the Marchesa was gone. To Milan, to Berlin, to London—no one was sure where. A slap from Monica was unnecessary.

When it became clear the Marchesa wasn't returning anytime soon, or ever, Marco put the swan goblets in the window of the Rosso shop for the few tourists still coming to Venice who had not been scared off by the war. Two days later they sold, though for only a fraction of what the Marchesa had paid for hers. After that he made the pair of fish, then the snakes and parrots, and sold them almost as soon as they were displayed. He began to get orders for more. Marco had at last found his new signature piece, and grew more cheerful, whistling as he worked, grabbing Monica as she served supper, teasing his nieces.

Orsola thought of her necklace locked away in the Marchesa's treasure chest. She did not try to replicate it.

✦

DOMENEGO AND THE PEOPLE he listened to in his gondola were right: Italy resigned from the Triple Alliance it had made with Germany and Austria-Hungary and entered the war to fight the Austrians on its northern border. Orsola wasn't sure what that meant for Italy generally, and Venice, Murano and the Rossos specifically. But she did go and see Jonas. While Italy had remained neutral, Germans in Venice were allowed to continue to live and work there. Would that change now?

He was behind his desk as always, looking harassed. Gesturing Orsola to a seat, he asked after the family, including Raffaele—for though the merchant didn't represent his bead business, he took a professional interest in him. Apart from shipping seed beads, Jonas had also rekindled interest in Orsola's and Rosella's lampworked beads and had even been considering taking on Marco's animal goblets.

There was a pause after the polite chat, and Orsola found it hard to ask what she had come for, because she was worried about the answer.

"You are here to find out what I will do now that Italy is at war," Jonas said, sitting back much in the manner of his former employer, though without quite the smoothness. "Everyone is asking." He paused, hands resting on his desk, fingertips pressed together. "I had hoped," he continued, "that Venetians would be sensible enough to understand that I am not at war with anyone here. I am a business-man, not a politician or a soldier. My feelings about the war are neu-tral. I want to live peacefully and run my business. Venetian officials agree—they have not stipulated that Germans must leave the city or be detained in any way."

Orsola allowed herself to hope, until he spoke again. "However, in the few days since Italy entered the war, I have been abused in the campos and the calles, spat at, threatened. My house has been vandal-ized: every morning my servants—those who have not left—must wash off the rotten vegetables and worse that have been smeared on the door. This situation will not improve. So I am very sorry to tell you, Signora Orsola, that I will be closing my business by the end of the month and moving to Germany." Jonas sat very still when he fin-ished, but he could not stop his mouth from briefly trembling.

Orsola crossed herself. "I'm sorry too, signore. You would not have that kind of reception on Murano, I assure you. You and Signor Klingenberg have helped the Rossos for so many years, through all our hardships. It's because of you that we've been able to maintain our business. What will we do now?"

Jonas smiled. "Have some faith in yourself, Orsola. You do not need me. If I am honest, you have not needed me for some time. Trad-ing merchants are not what they once were, just as Venice is not what she once was. Back when trade was everything to this city, we were indispensable. We were the heart that kept the blood pumping. Now the Fondaco dei Tedeschi is a post office. That magnificent building, a post office! A trading system all its own. You should get to know it, Orsola—that may be how you and your brother will send your work to buyers." He got up and, unlocking a cupboard in the corner, brought out stacks of sample cards of Orsola's beads and set them on the desk in front of her. "These are yours. Your history. I thought you should have them. And this." He selected a black leather-bound ledger from the shelf behind him, identical to the many she had seen him write in over the years. "The Rosso ledger," he explained, handing it to her. "This will be even more useful to you. The entries extend all the way back to your father's father. Herr Klingenberg let me keep it when he left. At the back are the addresses of the many merchants your work has been sold to. I suggest you and Marco write to the recent ones and establish your own connection, without the middleman."

It felt as if Orsola were holding the original Gospels in her hands. "Are you sure?"

Jonas waved a hand, like a benefactor bestowing treasure. "They will be good for your lampworked beads and Marco's goblets," he said, "but not for the seed beads. That will be more complicated. Bigger, heavier shipping is involved that you know little about. For that I suggest you join the Society for the Bead Industry. May I give you one more piece of advice?"

"*Per favore.*"

"As a Muranese, you are very skeptical of Venice. I think you should allow yourself to value the city a little more. We are not all bad over here. And most of the tourists remain on La Serenissima rather than visit Murano. Years ago Herr Klingenberg suggested you open a little shop near San Marco. You did not take his advice then—instead you took mine to go into seed beads. If you had a shop now, however, I think you would find a ready market for your jewelry and Marco's work. Think about it, Orsola," he added when she pursed her lips. "Don't dismiss Venice because you think it looks down on you. Not at all—we admire you."

"Ah," she replied, "but you're not really Venetian. You're German." She paused. "Aren't you nervous about going to terraferma to live? It is so . . . different from here. From us."

Jonas gave a tight smile. "I am not so worried about that aspect. That will be an adventure."

✧

ORSOLA WAS WORKING OVER her flame in the studio when Angela came running. "Mamma, it's Nonna!"

In the courtyard Laura Rosso was sitting motionless, her wire needles lying in a sessola of yellow beads. In the years since losing Raffaele to Luciana she had spoken less and less, and recently had grown slower. Though she didn't tell her mother, Orsola had stopped counting her hanks of seed beads as part of the weekly quota. But she didn't ask her to stop; she did not want Laura to feel she was no longer useful.

Her mother's eyes were still open, though they seemed unfocused. Orsola knelt and squeezed her hands, veiny with age. "Madre, what is it?"

For a long moment it seemed Laura Rosso could not hear her daughter. Then at last she looked at her. "The war. The choice. He must be here."

Orsola sighed, her mother's cryptic words perfectly clear to her. This was the conversation about sons that must take place in every Italian family now that the country had joined the war. She glanced around at the family who had gathered: Marco and Giacomo and Stella standing uncertainly over their mother, Monica and Rosella with their arms around each other in the kitchen doorway, Angela clinging to Stefano. Marcolin and Sebastiano and Andrea stood in the workshop doorway, hands awkward at their sides, knowing that this was about them. There was just one young man missing.

"Stella, go and get him," Orsola ordered.

Her sister nodded and slipped out; she would get Bruno to take her across to Venice in the motorboat he had bought to replace his obsolete gondola.

When he arrived, Raffaele knelt by his grandmother and took her hands, much as Orsola had done.

"You are not going to war," Laura Rosso declared.

Raffaele flinched—a clear sign that he had been thinking of joining up. "*Ma no*, Nonna . . ." He didn't finish.

"Every family has to send one son," Laura continued, having redis-covered her voice, "but it must not be you. You have three children to feed. And did I keep you alive on Lazzaretto Vecchio only for you to become target practice for Austrian *patate?*"

The family was silent. This was a decision being made in house-holds all over Italy, and there was never a good answer. How did you choose a son to sacrifice to the Austrians?

With his damaged foot, Andrea clearly could not become a soldier. Marcolin could barely make it down the calle outside their door.

Sebastiano cleared his throat. "I'll go. *Va bene*, Nonna?"

Giacomo stifled a cry.

This outcome was as predictable as Marco getting drunk, Marco-lin cringing, Angela weeping. When compared to his cousin Raffa-ele, Sebastiano was less in every way: less strong, less handsome, less skillful with glass, less funny, less charming. He was simply himself, and that was not his fault. It shouldn't make him the family choice to fight in a war no one understood. But there was an inevitability about it that made him speak up, and no one argued against him, not even his father.

Laura Rosso gave her less favored grandson a long look, then nod-ded. *"Che Dio ti tegna."*

Sebastiano nodded back, then swallowed. Suddenly he looked young and fearful.

Marcolin, Andrea and their father were staring at the ground. Ev-eryone knew neither son was soldier material, but still, they hadn't volunteered, even to be turned down.

Laura Rosso looked around and smiled a rare smile. She touched Raffaele's cheek and stroked his hair. Then, leaning back in her chair, she closed her eyes for the last time.

✧

THE CEMETERY ON MURANO had long ago been moved from across San Matteo to a larger rectangular space behind Santa Maria degli Angeli, where Orsola used to peg out sheets to dry in the sun. Lo-renzo Rosso had been exhumed and placed in a new plot, where his wife now joined him.

After the funeral the family, neighbors and representatives from every glass family gathered back at the house to honor Laura Rosso with food and drink and memories. Orsola was busy setting out dried fruits and bussolai—her mother's favorite foods—when one of the neighborhood children tugged at her sleeve. They were all playing out in the calle—for even in sadness, children can't remain solemn for long, and the Mass had been long enough. "Someone wants you," he informed her.

"Who?"

He shrugged. "The Venetian. She's out in the calle." Before she could ask more he ran off.

It took Orsola some time to get out to the passage, for with every step she was stopped by a cousin crying, a neighbor laughing, a maestro remembering her father as well as her mother, a drunken Bruno declaring that Laura Rosso had been the best mother in the world.

Luciana was leaning against the wall in the calle. She had come across from Venice to accompany Raffaele to the Mass and funeral procession, but did not come back to the Rosso house for the reception, for she knew how she would be received. At Santi Maria e Donato she had held her head up and stared at any of the Rossos who glanced her way, but she knew behind closed doors it would be different. Older now, a wife, a mother of three, managing a business, Luciana was still a scowler, and still very sure of herself.

Orsola crossed her arms. "What do you want? Now is not a good time. *Ovviamente.*"

Luciana shifted from one hip to the other. "Good time for what?"

"For business. That can only be what you're here for, isn't it?"

Luciana nodded. "I have a proposition."

Orsola wanted to turn on her heel and go back inside, but for Raffaele's sake, for the sake of her great-niece and great-nephews, she stayed to listen. She might not like it, but Luciana was family.

"We combine forces. Raffaele brings his skills to you, you give me Rosella and Angela for the wreaths. We make beads together, and Marco trains Raffaele to become a maestro. He is making goblets again, isn't he?"

So Luciana was not content after all with her place in the world. She was ambitious, she wanted more. She wanted to wear the maestro wife's fur.

"Marcolin will be maestro," Orsola replied. "He's the oldest. He's training now."

Luciana gave her a sideways look, and Orsola wondered how she had got her information. For Marcolin was not really training to become a maestro. He was the most reluctant servente ever. He had no interest in making Marco's elaborate goblets, or in passing his prova. His strength lay in sorting beads rather than making them.

"Now that your mother is gone—"

Orsola crossed herself, and after a pause Luciana followed suit.

"Now that she's gone, there's no reason we can't merge. Rosso e Rosso. I know she didn't like me, but she would have wanted the family to reunite. Besides, with your German merchant gone, you'll need someone to sell your beads for you. We are already set up for that through the Society for the Bead Industry."

She certainly had all the information about the Rossos.

"You would move here?" Orsola couldn't keep the scorn from her voice.

"Why would we do that?"

"Because the business is here. Our home. The Rossos have lived here for hundreds of years. We're certainly not going to move to Venice."

"Raffaele and Francesca didn't mind moving. They like Venice. They prefer it. More action, more interest."

Orsola frowned, and Luciana changed tack. "We don't have to move. We can all stay where we are. Raffaele can come over each day, and Angela and Rosella can come to me."

Orsola looked so horrified that Luciana laughed. "*Ecco*, it's only fifteen minutes by vaporetto. It's not like going to terraferma. You need to think a little more openly about Venice." Though she put it differently, she sounded like Jonas.

Orsola pulled her shawl tight around her shoulders. "Show some respect, young lady. I don't need someone so much younger than me telling me what to think."

"Then I'll leave you to consider it." Luciana turned on her heel and walked away down the calle, skirts swishing at her ankles.

Orsola stood in the passage, missing her mother. Laura Rosso would have given strong advice.

"I want to slap her," she heard. Stella was leaning in the doorway, biting her thumbnail. "She's going to take over."

✧

Sebastiano died fighting in the mountains the Rossos could see on clear days from Murano. Orsola didn't know he was there when she sat at the Riva di San Matteo and looked at those mountains. He died as the Italians fought in the Isonzo valley north of Trieste. It took four months for the Rossos to hear of his death. There was no body to bury in the Murano cemetery.

✧

By then Rosso e Rosso beadmaking was doing a steady business, exporting as much as Jonas had ever got them, and without having to pay his middleman fee, but paying the Society for the Bead Industry's lower one instead. Angela and sometimes Rosella joined Luciana and Francesca in Cannaregio each day to make bead wreaths, and because of war casualties, demand for them continued to grow.

Luciana and Raffaele brought with them energy and knowledge, folding Giacomo and Marcolin and Andrea into their operation, and there were enough of Luciana's family to fill any other positions needed. They even bought a motorboat to ferry workers back and forth between Venice and Murano.

It all worked, Orsola had to admit. Everyone had their place in the bead business—except for her and Marco.

One evening she walked over to l'Omo Salvadego, where her brother was drinking, going early enough that he'd had a mellowing glass or two but wasn't yet drunk. He was sitting with two other glassmen, laughing at something one of them had said. He seemed comfortable, displaying a side she rarely witnessed. When he saw his sister, Marco stopped laughing, though he didn't frown as he often did around her. The glassmen nodded at her, offered their seats and backed off to give brother and sister space. It was rare for a woman to go into the osteria, but she was old enough and skilled enough to be treated with respect.

Marco indicated to the barman to bring her a glass of wine. "You never come here, sorella. What do you want?" He held up a finger. "Let me guess: Luciana."

Occasionally he could be astute. "*Sì*. She is . . ." Orsola wasn't sure how to describe her.

"Taking over. I know." Marco paused, knocking back his wine. "Let her."

Orsola stared at him. It didn't seem to bother him that Luciana had lured away two of his children.

"*Ecco*, she knows her beads, she's made a success of it," he continued. "Much better than we ever did. She has a big family"—there were now five, Luciana having given birth to twins a few months before—"and she wants a big business to go with it. And why not?"

"Why not? Because she's not a Rosso!"

"Madre wasn't a Rosso either, but she became one. The most Rosso of the Rossos! I have no problem if the Venetian scowler wants to take over making seed beads. It means you and I are completely free from the *escrementi di topo*."

She waited for him to add something about the *escrementi di coniglio*, but he was in a good mood.

The barman brought over her wine and Orsola focused on it, trying to catch up with her brother's thinking. She wasn't used to him convincing her of change; usually it was the other way around. It was true that she and Marco now had more time to make what they wanted: Orsola her lampworked beads, with Rosella joining when she could, Marco his animal goblets, with Raffaele assisting. As Luciana had demanded, Marcolin stepped back from training to become maestro and let his brother take his place. He seemed relieved to be only sorting beads.

Raffaele traveled back and forth between Venice and Murano, never complaining. But Orsola had found him in the house one day, studying Giacomo's bedroom.

"They want to move here," she said now to Marco. "I can feel it. They want to take over the house as well as the business!"

Marco did not seem surprised. "It makes sense. They're cramped where they are with the children in Cannaregio. There's more room here, fewer tourists. They wouldn't need the motorboat."

Orsola gave her brother a sideways look. "Why have you become so sensible all of a sudden? Has Raffaele been working on you? You've probably got this all sorted out between you, and you were only going to tell me the day they move in." She was working herself up into indignation, and slammed her glass down so hard the base broke.

He laughed. "Fiery Rosso! *Ecco*, Raffaele has said nothing, but I can see with my eyes, can't I?"

✧

WITHIN THREE MONTHS Raffaele and Luciana and their children had moved to the Rosso house on Murano, and suddenly there were babies and mountains of laundry and many more mouths to feed, with huge meals that kept Monica in the kitchen all day, for Luciana was no cook.

Raffaele asked his uncle to let him and Luciana use his bedroom, and of course Giacomo couldn't refuse. Stella was forced to share her room not only with Rosella but with a great-niece too. "Just until we build more rooms," Luciana informed her. It was the first Orsola had heard of the house being expanded.

Orsola didn't mind the children: it was a pleasure to have little ones around again, filling the gaps left by her daughter and nieces and nephews growing up. She didn't mind the noise and the chaos. A washing machine now took care of the laundry. She *did* mind that Luciana began running the household. But there was no Laura Rosso around to put a stop to it. Marco didn't care as long as he could make his glass. Monica rolled her eyes but wanted to keep the peace. Giacomo probably agreed with his sister but had so withdrawn into himself after the loss of his son that he no longer voiced what he thought.

Only Stella complained. "That Luciana has found her way into this house like a wasp in an apple," she said one day, marching into Orsola's studio and standing over her as she turned a bead in the flame. "She'll sting us all. But I refuse to do what she says. She's not our mother; she's not you. I'm older than she is!"

"What has she done this time?"

"She tried to tell me the best way to iron sheets. I can't stand it any longer."

Orsola smiled. Stella had never been good with an iron. And she had never really found her place in the household, even before Luciana's arrival. She wasn't interested in glass or the business behind it, she turned potential customers away in the shop with her brusque tone, she hated cooking and cleaning and laundering. At thirty, she was past the age of marrying; indeed, Orsola had never heard any gossip about her sister spending time with any man. She had few friends except for odd ones—an eighty-year-old nun, a mute rope maker, a priest who liked his wine. She did odd jobs, packing glass for shipments, running errands. Often she disappeared for a day, and the family stopped asking where she'd been. Now Orsola found out.

"I'm going to help out at the front," Stella announced. "I'm going to be a nurse."

"What?" Orsola dropped the rod holding her bead. "You've never even been to terraferma!"

"Of course I have."

337

"When?"

"Many times. I've been to Mestre, to Marghera. Once I went all the way to Padua on the canal ferry. No one even noticed I was gone!"

"But it's dangerous, and you know nothing about wars and fighting."

"Nurses don't fight, silly. I'll be behind the lines. I'll be perfectly safe."

Orsola sat back. "You don't care enough about people to nurse them." It was the harsh truth.

Stella shook her head. "You don't have to care about people to look after them. Indeed, some say emotions get in the way of looking after them."

"How do you know all this?"

"I met some nurses—Italians—home from the front. They told me about it, and what to do to join."

"But—"

"Don't argue with me, Orsola. I'm telling you what I'm going to do, not asking your permission." Stella paused. "I want to do something with my life, not wash baby clothes and pack glass and be bossed around by a wasp."

Orsola regarded her sister. Under her bravado, under her indifference to the family and glass and Murano, there was a woman who was hurting—had been hurting since she was a small child locked away from her mother and sister during the plague.

Thank God I have my beads, Orsola thought. And Angela. And Stefano. *Grazie a Dio*, I have things I care about.

"Have you told Marcolin?" she asked. The only person Stella showed any attachment to was her nephew who had been shut up with her during the quarantine.

Stella grimaced. "Not yet. I will. He'll understand. The bead sorting has steadied him."

She was right. Marcolin had never liked working under pressure from the demands of glass, as well as from his father to become a maestro. He didn't work well in a team, preferring the comforting repetition of sorting seed beads into different sizes and grades. He could rapidly pick out the irregular, narrow-holed, chipped, no-holed beads, and produce a clean tray for the impiraresse to string. Rosso e Rosso beads were praised for their uniformity and few irregularities, and some of this was down to Marcolin's skill.

He too had never married. Unlike Stella, though, he remained close to home, and rarely left Murano or even their calle. He had been to Venice only once, when he was fifteen and Marco insisted he come with the family to the Redentore—the annual festival celebrating the end of the plague. Halfway across the bridge of boats built over the lagoon between San Marco and the Church of the Redentore on Giudecca, Marcolin had panicked and sat down in a boat, blocking the pilgrims making their way across. Orsola had had to wave down a nearby sandolo and have it take him back to shore, with Stella accompanying him to calm him down.

For all their differences, Marcolin and Stella were close, bound together by their experience of the quarantine, though as far as Orsola knew they never talked about it. When he was upset over something—Marco shouting at him, his nieces and nephews teasing him, Luciana rolling her eyes at something he did or didn't do—it was Stella's arm thrown roughly around him that steadied him.

"What will he do without you?" Orsola said.

Stella blew out her cheeks. "I can't live my life based around what Marcolin needs. I should have left years ago."

Orsola rubbed her eyes, her way of warning tears not to arrive. "What has happened to this family? Padre, Madre, Nonna, Nicoletta, Sebastiano, all dead. Isabella run off, Francesca married into Venice.

Raffaele tied to the wasp. Now you. You'll go and you—" She couldn't finish her sentence. You'll go and you won't come back, she thought. You'll be lost on terraferma, where things are different, and you'll disappear from me. Like Antonio. "The Rosso family is falling apart."

"No, it's not, it's just changing. Families do that. And you still have Angela. She'll marry and stay close. She's completely devoted to Stefano, even if you aren't. And *ovviamente* there's Rosella. Her skills are wasted on stringing beads. When will you go into business with her? Rosso e Rosella."

Perhaps it needed someone else to say it aloud. Rosso e Rosella—the women's alternative to Rosso e Rosso.

"Her fiancé won't like it," Orsola said. Rosella had been picky about choosing a husband, but was at last due to marry a glassmaker from another family and move out in a few months.

Stella waved her hand and made a rude noise. "Rosella is as tough as her mother. She won't let a husband get in her way. And if it brings in money, why would he stop her?"

"Maybe." Orsola contemplated the glass canes in a line at her side. Rosella likened them to shiny candy pieces.

"I have two suggestions," Stella said. "First, open a Rosso e Rosella shop in Venice, not Murano. There are many more tourists there, especially around the Rialto and San Marco. You can sell your beads and your seahorses and all sorts of things besides. You can even sell Marco's goblets if you want."

"You sound just like Jonas, and Signor Klingenberg before him. And the other suggestion?"

"You and Stefano move out of the house."

When Orsola began to protest, her sister talked over her. "Do you really want to live with Luciana bossing everyone around? And her children so out of control? Things are changing, Orsola. Families don't always live together."

✧

ONCE STELLA HAD TOLD ORSOLA, she rapidly made plans to go, though she waited until the night before she was leaving to tell the rest of the family. At the end of the day she took Marcolin for a walk around the island, which he only ever did with her, and at dusk. When they returned, his face was red and he went straight to the back room where he sorted beads. He didn't appear for supper. "I'll write to him every week," Stella whispered to Orsola. "I promised." They both knew, though, that letters were inadequate, and might not even arrive.

When Stella told everyone else, their responses were typical of themselves. Marco shouted, forbidding her to go, though his anger was more for show, to try to reassert his authority, rather than because he actually cared what his sister did. Giacomo looked grave at another family member lost. Monica nodded. She had always been irritated by Stella disappearing and not pulling her weight at home. Stefano said nothing. Raffaele looked embarrassed that his aunt was joining the war effort when he hadn't. Luciana openly displayed relief at no longer having to deal with someone who didn't hide her dislike. Rosella went over and hugged Stella, and Stella let her. Angela cried, because Angela cried at all change. But no one except Marcolin was really that upset, for Stella had never sat easily within the family. Perhaps terraferma would suit her better.

She was planning to take the train from Venice to Trieste—the first Rosso to ride one. She refused to let Marco or Giacomo take her over to the train station in the motorboat they had recently acquired; she was simply intending to take a vaporetto. But Orsola couldn't bear to see her brave and foolhardy sister slip away without ceremony; at least she would make the first part of the journey memorable. She sent word, and the next morning Domenego appeared out of the thick fog that had developed overnight to ferry Orsola and Stella to the train station. A gondola seemed more dignified, as well as more Venetian.

As he and Orsola waited by the dock at the rear of the workshop while Stella said her last goodbyes to her family, Domenego leaned across and handed Orsola a new dolphin, this one made of pale-green opaque glass. She closed her hand around it and squeezed, feeling the sharp tail and fins dig into her palm. It was a little bigger than some of the others, but then the dolphins had varied quite a bit over the years—as had her own beads. Before she could thank the gondolier, Stella appeared, the family trailing behind her. She wore a green felt hat and a long gray wool coat that flared out from waist to calves, with a double row of large black buttons down the front. It was the first time she had ever looked stylish.

Stella handed Domenego her bag, then took his hand and stepped into the gondola. For thirty years of life lived, she did not have much with her. She wasn't crying—she left that to Angela, sobbing among the family gathered on the dock—but she looked grim. "*Andiamo, mio Dio,*" she muttered. "I can't bear long goodbyes." She raised a hand to the Rossos left behind as she and Orsola glided away into the February fog, and seemed to be looking for a last sighting of Marcolin, but he did not come out from his sorting room.

Partway across the lagoon she said, "What did Domenego give you?"

"Nothing. What are you talking about?"

Stella shook her head. "You need to lie better than that. He gave you something while I was saying goodbye. Show me."

Orsola withdrew the green dolphin from her pocket and handed it to her sister.

Stella held it up in the dim light. "You're still getting these after all these years?"

"*Sì.*"

"Strange. Where are they from?"

"Prague," Orsola answered without thinking, then regretted it, for Stella raised her eyebrows.

"Have you ever thought of going there?"

"Why? I don't even know what I would find. Besides, it wouldn't be fair to Stefano."

"Stefano, the world's most boring husband."

Orsola heard what sounded like a snort from the stern of the gondola, but when she glanced back, Domenego's face was neutral, his eyes fixed on the thick fog, watching out for other boats. The Venetian skyline wasn't far, but not yet visible.

"Don't say that about Stefano," Orsola countered. "He has been good to me. Steady. Better than I've ever been to him." To her mortification her eyes filled with tears.

"I think you should do what you want to do," Stella declared.

"*Ecco*, I'm not like you. None of us is."

"No, you're not. You're chained to the family and to Murano."

"I'm *loyal* to the family and to Murano. Most people are. And scared of what happens on terraferma. Aren't you?"

Stella shrugged and leaned back, regarding the tall buildings emerging from the fog along the Cannaregio riva, tan and ocher and pink, the arched windows, the balconies, the orientation toward the water—always the water. "I won't miss this at all," she said.

Oh, but you will, Orsola thought, remembering that distant day when she had stumbled around Mestre, trying to avoid horses, longing for a glimpse of water. Water ran in Muranese and Venetian veins, even in cold-blooded veins like her sister's. And though Orsola had not been to other cities, she had heard enough tourists remarking on the beauty of Venice to know that Stella would miss it—perhaps not right away, but eventually.

At the station she hugged her sister tight, next to the gigantic, hissing machine that was to take her away. She wasn't so worried about Stella dying in the war—her sister knew how to look after herself, and she would not be fighting as Sebastiano had. But she sensed that

Stella was moving away from Murano and Venice for good. Once on the mainland, her ties would be cut with this unique place. Orsola tried to take her cue from her sister: Stella remained dry-eyed and excited, impatient to get on the train and start her new life. Orsola watched it pull out, with an accelerating huff-huff-huff and a dramatic belch of steam, to start across the bridge Raffaele had briefly helped to build for the Austrians. Only then did she allow herself to cry.

✧

NOTHING COULD REALLY CHANGE until the war ended and the tourists returned. But it did, and they did.

One day, several months after the Armistice, Monica and Rosella presented themselves to Orsola, one nervous, the other excited. "We're taking you to Venice," Monica announced.

"It's a surprise," Rosella added.

Orsola stared at them. Monica never went to Venice. But she held back from asking why; she would allow them their intrigue.

They took a vaporetto across to Fondamente Nove and walked south, Rosella leading them past the Rialto, through Campo Sant'Angelo and Campo Santo Stefano. They then turned east, joining a stream of foreign tourists making their way toward Piazza San Marco. The women didn't go that far, stopping abruptly at a small shop wedged between a bakery and a mirror shop.

"Here is where we can set up Rosso e Rosella," Rosella explained.

"Ah," Orsola said. "Stella gave you that idea."

"*Sì*. She reminds me every time she writes. I've been keeping an eye out for a place ever since. And this came up. It's in an excellent location, with plenty of visitors walking past between the Accademia and San Marco."

Orsola peered in through the dirty window. The space was dark and empty but for a pile of broken crates.

"It was a paper shop," Rosella continued. "The owner died and his sons didn't want to continue. It's dry inside, no smells or anything."

"You've been in?"

"The landlord showed me. He's coming in a minute with the key so we can look around."

"It's dark. How will customers see anything?"

"Electricity."

I am getting too old for all this change, Orsola thought. Trains and electricity and motorboats and women going off on their own to other countries to find work. As expected, Stella had not come back after the war but headed to London. At least some changes were for the better. Orsola no longer used tallow for her lampwork, but gas. It burned hotter, was more reliable, and it didn't stink.

Rosella seemed to read her mind. "*Ecco*, we could sit in the window and work over the flame, so people can see what we're doing," she suggested. "That will draw them in."

"I'm not going to work here," Orsola snapped. Like a *puttana* on show, she thought. "I'm working at home."

She looked at Monica for support. Her sister-in-law was watching the stream of foreigners with suspicion; she clearly wanted to be back on Murano. But she would also want to support her daughter. "It's a good spot. Take it," she said.

"What will Marco say? It's he who would sign the lease."

"I'll deal with him," Monica said, as she had been ever since marrying him. Orsola had never understood how that relationship worked.

"Once we're set up, the shop will pay for itself," Rosella added. "Padre won't have to have anything to do with it. *Allora*, what do you think, Zia Orsola?"

"It's a big step," Orsola replied after a pause. "A big, big step. Every day you would have to come here and go back. Forty-five minutes each way is a lot of time spent traveling when you could be at home. What will your husband say?"

"He won't mind," Rosella insisted, a little impatiently.

"She's bored with home," Monica put in.

"Taking a lease on a shop in Venice is not entertainment," Orsola scolded. "It's serious. It could put us in debt again."

The owner of the mirror shop had come to lean in his doorway and was watching them. He had that calculating Venetian expression, hard and dark from dealing with tourists all day. Was that what she and Rosella would look like if they opened a shop here?

She lowered her voice so he couldn't continue to eavesdrop. "I need to walk about a bit and think. I'll see you later."

Orsola walked the passages around the spot, studying the shops and the people going in and out of them, lingering outside the few glass shops, making her way steadily toward Piazza San Marco. Around her in the narrow calles a variety of languages intermingled: French, English, Spanish, Dutch, even some German now that the war was over. It felt strange to be outnumbered by non-Italians. They were looking in the windows of the shops, and buying things Venetians made well: marbled paper, candles, carved statues, leather bags, silk handkerchiefs—and glass. Orsola watched as tourists chose glass candlesticks from a window display and inspected bowls and glass chess sets and figurines of animals. Rosella was undoubtedly right that a shop could be a success. Orsola wasn't so sure Marco would agree, however.

She reached Piazza San Marco and wandered across. Though she had been there many times before, she was surprised every time by the elegant proportions of the building facades lining the square, with their rows upon rows of columned arches; the basilica at the far end with its floating domes; and the campanile, the tallest tower in

Venice, rebuilt some years back after it collapsed. Orsola could see why visitors flocked to San Marco; it was irresistible.

Passing Caffè Florian—Venice's oldest coffeehouse and a venerable institution, though Orsola had never been—she spotted Klara Klingenberg sitting alone at a table under one of its arches. Orsola had not seen her since before the war and was shocked by how much she had aged. Though she was still elegant, her looks were ragged around the edges, like a well-cut suit with a worn collar and cuffs. Her hair was streaked with gray, her face lined, and her hat was no longer the latest fashion. She was gazing wistfully into her china coffee cup. Then she looked up, saw the beadmaker and waved. "Orsola Rosso! Over here!"

Orsola took a breath, then stepped over to the table. "*Buongiorno,* Signora Klara."

"How lovely to see you! Sit, take a coffee with me."

"No, *grazie*, signora, I couldn't." A coffee at Florian would cost her two beads, or a day of bead stringing. She still made such calculations.

"A chocolate, then. Their hot chocolate is divine!" Klara gazed at Orsola almost desperately. "*Per favore*, I want you to." She patted the chair next to her. "You would be doing me a favor. There is nothing so pathetic as sitting in a café alone. My treat, of course," she added, though she looked as if she could no longer afford such treats.

Orsola opened her mouth to protest, for she had no money for a chocolate at Florian, and she was not one to take handouts. However, just then a waiter passed by and the seductive scent of chocolate wafted toward her. She sat. "*Va bene, una cioccolata, grazie.*"

Klara Klingenberg smiled. "We haven't spoken in ages; it will be good to catch up." She waved a hand at the waiter. "Tell me your news," she said, leaning closer as if they were the best of friends. "*Dime*, how are things over on Murano? Do you know I've never been? No, wait, I went once, to a party at a palazzo on the Grand Canal. But I've never visited the glass shops. I must come, and you will show me around."

That will never happen, Orsola thought, then chided herself for her cynicism. "We're not too bad," she replied mildly. "I make lamp-worked beads, my brother Marco makes goblets decorated with animals that sell well. Perhaps you've seen them? And his son Raffaele is in charge of seed beads; they're also doing well."

"Seed beads? You make beads out of seeds? What happened to glass?"

Orsola tried not to roll her eyes. "They *are* made of glass. They're called seed beads because they're tiny the way seeds are. They are the beads you see sewn on your dresses," she added, then regretted her words, for it was doubtful Klara Klingenberg could now afford beaded dresses.

But Klara smiled. "I'm delighted to hear the Rossos are doing so well, even without my father or Jonas to look after you."

"Do you hear from Signor Jonas? I wondered if he might return now the war is over."

"He is not coming back. He wrote to say he prefers to remain in Germany, where he can be his true self."

"What does that mean?"

"Did you not know that his family was originally Jewish? He is— or was—a Marrano. He purported to be Christian so he wouldn't have to live in the Ghetto, but secretly practiced his original faith. It was something of an open secret."

"*Davvero?*" Orsola was shocked that she didn't know something so fundamental about the family merchant.

"*Sì.* It seems now he feels able to be more open in Germany with a larger, freer Jewish population. Safer there."

The waiter appeared then with the chocolate in a small porcelain cup decorated with the logo of a lion in gold and blue. He set it in front of Orsola with an elaborate flourish, and she wondered if he was making fun of her.

"Try it." Klara gestured at the cup. "I want to see your reaction."

Orsola put the cup to her mouth and took a sip. Startled, she set it down. "That," she pronounced, "is the most delicious thing I have ever tasted."

Klara laughed. "Oh, I'm so glad! Watching that has cheered me enormously. Have you really never tasted chocolate?"

"Never." Orsola took another sip. The second taste was as good as the first; even better, for the anticipation.

She sat marveling at the precious drink, then forced herself to focus on her companion. "But why do you need cheering?"

A look crossed Klara Klingenberg's face that Orsola had seen on the faces of many Italian mothers, and she had her answer. "I'm so sorry, signora, I didn't know," she said softly before Klara could tell her where and when one of her sons had died in the war. "We share your sorrow. My brother lost a son at Gorizia."

Klara gave a clipped nod, and they sat in silence over their cups. Orsola didn't dare take a sip in the face of such news, and watched as a milky scum formed across the top of her chocolate.

"What brings you to San Marco?" Klara asked at last.

"My niece wants to open a shop here to sell our work. We've just been looking at a place."

Klara brightened. "Where is it?"

Orsola described the location. "But we can't afford it," she finished. "My brother will never agree to a Venetian rent, no matter what his wife says. He'll think the shop won't work."

"What do *you* think?"

"I think my niece is right, as were Jonas and your father. There are far more visitors in Venice with the money to spend on glass. I'm not keen on working over here and having people watch me make beads the way my niece wants me to. But there would be more sales." She paused. "However, we need money to start, for rent and to set things up. Money to make money."

Klara Klingenberg was growing taller in her chair, like a young girl told to sit up straight. "I can help you. I'll loan you the money until you're established."

"*You?*"

Orsola's tone of disbelief made Klara pull her head back like a turtle in its shell.

"*Mi dispiace*, signora, I didn't mean to be rude," Orsola said, trying to placate her. "But—well . . ." She didn't want to make things worse.

"What?" Klara pressed her. "Go on, what were you going to say?"

"People know your husband has lost money." Orsola didn't add that it was due to his gambling habit. "You moved from Campo San Polo, you let Domenego go. I'm guessing you don't have the money to help me."

Klara Klingenberg sat back, smiling as slyly as her refined features would allow. "But I do."

Orsola stared at her companion.

"You know my father was a careful businessman," Klara began, turning the handle of her coffee cup back and forth. "Well, he was careful with his daughter as well. He did not like my husband, did not trust him. He only agreed to the marriage because it was advantageous for a German girl to marry into a good Venetian family. And he could see that I was crazy about my husband, at least at the beginning, as girls so often are. We talk ourselves into most things . . . But Padre set aside some money for me, should I ever need it, money my husband didn't—doesn't—know about. If he did he would have gambled it away. Jonas looked after it for me, and arranged for someone else to do so once he left, a money lender in the Ghetto, very honest.

Over the years I have spent it on little things, for the children, some-times for me. Never anything too expensive, or Federico would take it. He gambled away all my jewelry. Even my wedding ring." She held up her naked hand. "I don't dare use the money for something big that my husband would notice. But he will never notice a glass shop run by women." She smiled again, and for a moment resembled the spirited girl Orsola had met before life as a wife and mother drained it from her.

"That's a very generous offer from you, signora," she began. "Very generous, indeed." She smoothed her skirt, brushed nonexistent crumbs from the table. "But I'm not sure my family would approve."

"Orsola." Klara leaned forward. "Wasn't there a woman who invented a bead once and was given her own furnace? Baronia, Barosia . . . ?"

"Maria Barovier." Even saying her name made Orsola hold her head a little higher. "She told me to make beads, got her cousin to teach me."

"What would Maria Barovier say?"

Orsola took a breath, remembering Maria Barovier as she first met her the day she fell in the canal, standing solid by the furnace, looking as if nothing could knock her down. "She would accept your offer with thanks." Orsola paused. She picked up her cup and drained it of the chocolate. Setting it down with a decisive clink in the saucer, she added, "And I too accept with thanks."

Part III

REAL

DOLPHINS

7

T HAT STONE YOU HAVE SKIMMED over the lagoon touches the surface again, and it is 2019. In her studio Orsola Rosso is turning back and forth in the flame a black, red and gold bead. She looks up, and one hundred years have passed. She and those who matter to her are seventeen years older. Orsola is now sixty-five.

One who mattered to her a great deal is gone: Stella, who was working as a nurse in London during the Blitz when a bomb fell directly on her air raid shelter. Orsola's stubborn, outspoken, beloved sister's death is a reminder that you never recover from losing someone; you just learn to accommodate the hole it makes in you.

How to summarize one hundred years of the fastest, most extreme change ever? From Mussolini to Berlusconi, FDR to Obama, Hitler to Merkel, Gandhi to Martin Luther King Jr., Amelia Earhart to 747s. Typewriters to computers, encyclopedias to Wikipedia, telephones to smartphones, walks in the park to runs on treadmills. Penicillin. The Second World War. Hiroshima. Korea, Vietnam, Iraq, Afghanistan. The Cold War, an agreed end, another cold war brewing. Walls falling, walls built. New nations created out of old nations. Women wearing trousers and voting. Robots. Conspiracy theories.

Venice has 4.8 million visitors in 2019. Every day giant cruise ships pass through the Giudecca Canal like sideways skyscrapers, disgorging passengers who head to Piazza San Marco to take photos, buy key rings that dangle gondola charms, leave. Speaking of gondolas, it now costs eighty euros to ride in one for half an hour; forty of Orsola's beads. The Fondaco dei Tedeschi is now a luxury department store. Meanwhile, the population stands at just over fifty thousand, half of what it was back when Orsola was born. One thousand people are leaving each year.

Underneath all that change, the planet is heating up. The sea is rising, Venice is sinking—leading to one precise moment, 10:44 p.m. on November 12, 2019 . . .

✧

AT 10:44 THE WATER began bubbling up through the tiles in Orsola's studio. She and Stefano had spent the past hour moving everything they could to their apartment upstairs: her torches, the gas canisters, the annealers, the tools for pinching and rolling and shaping, the hundreds of glass canes in every imaginable color, the drawers and cases full of her work that was not yet on display at Rosso e Rosella in San Marco, or had not sold and was being stored to wait for fashions to change.

They couldn't move the table she worked on—big and heavy, it was never meant to be taken upstairs. The old table with the bellows Orsola had worked at when she was first making beads with a lamp and animal fat was up in the apartment, kept for nostalgic reasons. She and Stefano ate at it in their kitchen, maneuvering around the bellows below and the metal spouts above that still stuck out of the table.

An acqua alta had been predicted for that night, but no one expected it to arrive at the same time as a fierce storm with high winds. The combination of the two and the lack of warning meant that most Venetians and those on the outer islands were caught out.

"Stefano!" Orsola cried when the water lifted the floor tiles. He was up in their apartment rearranging what they had brought up.

He ran downstairs and watched with her as the water rose inexorably around the soles of their rubber boots. Everyone in Venice had boots for the acqua alta; cheap collapsible boots were even sold to tourists for the floods. Ramps were set up along fondamentas and rivas and across campos and even through Piazza San Marco to take pedestrians safely over high water. The city was used to it, but this one was going to be far worse. Orsola and Stefano had moved everything they could; there was nothing more they could do.

The lights went out then, the electrical system flooded. They switched on their torches and listened to the wind howling outside. A neighbor's shutter had come loose and was banging; eventually it would be blown off and found a hundred meters away.

"Let's go up," Stefano said, and pulled his wife toward the stairs.

In their apartment she glanced at her phone; at least the network was still working. There were missed calls from Marco and Angela and Rosella.

She rang Rosella first, revealing only to herself her priorities. Angela often accused her mother of caring more about her business than her daughter—something Orsola always denied, though there was probably a kernel of truth there. At any rate, she knew Angela was safe—Stefano had spoken to her earlier. She and her husband and three children lived on Giudecca, on the second floor of an apartment building, high above the water, with no business on the ground floor to worry about. Angela came to Venice to help in the shop, but that day would have left long before the storm. Later Orsola would see online footage of the moored vaporettos being tossed together by the waves like toy boats in a bathtub and be grateful her daughter had got home in time.

As for calling Marco, he had Raffaele and Luciana, Monica, Marcolin, Andrea and his wife to help, with Giacomo nearby. He didn't need her.

It took some time for Rosella to answer. "Orsola," she panted. "It's—" She started to cry.

"You're in the shop?"

"*Sì.*"

"How high is the water?"

"Up to my knees."

"*Mio Dio.* Are you alone?"

"There are others in the shops next door. We're all trying to—to—" Rosella stopped; she was crying too hard.

"Rosella, listen to me." Orsola made her voice steadier than she felt. "Stay with the others. Help them, and they'll help you. Look after one another. And go home as soon as you've secured what you can. You don't want to get caught with the calle so flooded you can't get home."

"All right." Rosella drew a shuddery breath. "I wish you were here." Rosella had always been calm and confident, like her mother. It was a surprise to hear her so shaken. She sounded like a girl rather than a forty-six-year-old woman.

"Have you moved everything up that you can, out of reach of the water?"

"Yes, but it happened so fast. I've never seen water like it. By the time I got here the water had knocked over some of the tables. The beads, the jewelry—"

"Don't worry about the beads; we can salvage most of it. Water doesn't hurt glass."

"Orsola, my phone battery is running out. *Merda*, why didn't I charge it earlier! And there's no electricity."

"Go to the others."

The line went dead. Orsola sighed. Rosella had been living for a long time on her own in a tiny apartment near the shop; she refused to move out despite the high cost of living in Venice. The first member of the Rosso family to get a divorce once it was legalized in Italy, she still shocked Orsola with her choices. The world was changing so fast.

She rang Marco, but there was no answer. He was probably in the workshop futilely trying to save the furnace. Although she no longer lived there, she was still concerned about the Rosso house and workshop, for they held her family's history.

Orsola and Stefano had moved across Murano a year after she opened the shop in San Marco, taking an apartment near Santi Maria e Donato, with a studio downstairs for Orsola. Stefano still went to the Rosso workshop every day, but Orsola visited less often, preferring to meet Monica at the market at Campo Santo Stefano, or at Mass, or at the café she liked by the Ponte Longo, where they watched the tourists browsing for cheap glass trinkets next door. Monica was a patient soul, pragmatic about most things in life, but even she said more than once, "I envy you, living on your own. I'm not used to being bossed about in my own kitchen. And the children are terrors. They never go to bed!"

Orsola suspected Monica of exaggerating the difficulty of living with Luciana so that her sister-in-law wouldn't regret moving out. Because she did, sometimes. Family was meant to be everything, and she wondered if she had abandoned hers—even though she was only a ten-minute walk from them. But perhaps Stella had been right when she'd advised that things were changing. Orsola's own daughter, Angela, hadn't hesitated to move to Giudecca when her husband got a job at the flour mill there—Angela, who cried every time there was change in the family.

When Orsola finally got hold of Marco after the worst of the flood had passed and the water was beginning to recede, he didn't even say "*Pronto*" when he answered. Her phone screen displayed a jumble of dark images as her brother rushed around, swearing and shouting orders.

"Has the water reached the furnace?" she asked.

"And the annealers." Marco turned his phone around so she could see the damage.

"Is Giacomo with you?" Like her and Stefano, Giacomo had moved to an apartment not far from the Rosso house.

"*Ovviamente.* Stefano should be over here helping as well!"

"He can't. We're flooded too. He's been moving my things upstairs."

"That's right, just think about yourselves, not the family. *Tipico.*"

"Don't be such a bastard! You have plenty of help. Here there's just us two."

"And who chose that?"

"Luciana did! You and Luciana. There was no room for us all, and you allowed them to move in and push us out. Do you call that thinking about the family?"

"*Bauca.*"

"*Cretino.*"

"*Stronza!*"

"*Bastardo!* You've always been one!"

"*Impestada!*"

Stefano was leaning against the kitchen counter, arms folded, listening to this escalation of curses. As the swearing continued, he reached over, took the phone from his wife and switched it off.

"*Ehi!*" she cried. "What are you doing?"

Stefano set the phone on the counter. "That wasn't helping either of you."

It was rare for her husband to take action.

"Marco has lost more than you," Stefano added. "Your torches weren't affected, your annealer was small enough to bring up here. You'll be up and running in a few days. It will take the Rosso workshop months to recover."

Orsola nodded, then did something rare: she walked into her husband's arms to be comforted.

✧

STEFANO WAS RIGHT. After the flood receded and they had pumped out the water and brought in fans and dehumidifiers to dry out the studio, and scrubbed and repainted, he and Orsola moved everything back down and she was able to restart work after a week. The Rosso e Rosella shop in San Marco reopened after two weeks, though it took some time to eliminate the damp feel and smell. However, it took three months to rebuild the Rosso workshop's furnace and annealers.

The flood also drove away tourists, who were not keen on experiencing the City of Water underwater, with the accompanying power outages, shutdowns and travel restrictions. Venetians usually complained about being inundated with millions of visitors a year. The flood reduced them temporarily to a trickle.

"Floods in Venice, fires in Australia, drought in California," Orsola's granddaughter Aurelia listed when they talked on their phones a few days after the acqua granda, as it was being called. "Look at what's happening, Nonna. And all because of the stupid choices people have made!"

"Actually, there have been worse floods than this one. The one in nineteen sixty-six, for example."

"And you're adding to it," Aurelia declared, ignoring her grand-mother's response. "All these furnaces on all day and night. Do you know how much fuel you're burning?"

"*I* don't run a furnace. I use a torch, and just turn it on when I need it. Remember when I showed you how to make beads?"

Aurelia shrugged.

It mystified Orsola how completely uninterested in glass her daugh-ter and grandchildren were. Angela helped out in the shop for the money and the people, not for any love of glass. None of the grand-children planned to go into glassmaking as a career. This was true of most glass families—those that remained. There were only a few dozen now, when once there had been over a hundred.

"The glass workshops can't keep burning fuel twenty-four hours a day," Aurelia argued, once again ignoring her grandmother. She seemed to be looking at another screen as they spoke, the way teen-agers often did. "They'll have to share furnaces, learn to cooperate, use them in shifts through the night."

Orsola chuckled. "You think maestros will cooperate? They each have their own way of using a furnace. Ask your great-uncle Marco. No one will trust one another to keep them clean. And no one wants to work at three in the morning."

"Nonna, those are excuses. You're not listening. Things have to change or there will be constant floods and Venice will become un-livable. Do you really want that for your descendants?"

Orsola found it hard to believe that a city such as Venice could disappear. We will just keep building upward, she thought, to keep the sea out. Sometimes, though, when she was working in the San Marco shop, when she fought her way through the tourists crowding the vaporettos and passages, when she watched the giant cruise ships moving through the lagoon, she wondered if Venice had already been obliterated. Murano too was not what it had been—an island full of maestros making and selling the finest, most inventive, most beautiful glasswork. She thought back to the huge, intricate chandeliers that graced many of the palazzos along the Grand Canal, and mourned their passing. They were now in museums or shipped abroad as curiosities. The chandelier Marco originally made for Casanova, for instance, had been bought by a junk trader for a pittance and now hung in a colorful Belgrade restaurant alongside other curiosities: mannequins wearing lampshades, giant jeweled insects, monkeys swinging from the rafters, papier-mâché air balloons, neon signs. One of Luciana and Raffaele's children had sent a picture of it, a novelty among novelties in a kitsch graveyard. They thought it was funny. Orsola hoped they hadn't shown the photo to Marco.

Tourists didn't want chandeliers and intricate goblets. They wanted glass figurines and glass sweets in glass wrappers and glass balloons and glass jigsaw pieces—much of it in badly chosen colors, poor designs and quick, shoddy work. Sometimes when she walked past the shops along the Fondamenta dei Vetrai, Orsola had to close her eyes so that she wouldn't see the ugliness that passed for glasswork being pushed at tourists.

Basta. "We have the flood barrier they're building out past the Lido," she said to her granddaughter. "When they finally finish it, it'll keep the water out." The project had begun thirty years before but been bogged down in politics and corruption. Still, it was hope.

"*If* it works," Aurelia countered, "and doesn't destroy the salt marshes and the whole ecosystem that keeps the lagoon alive!"

It was hard to swallow her granddaughter's pessimism. And Aurelia hadn't asked Orsola a thing about the flood and how it affected her and her business. She was sitting happily in a dry room at home, with no interest in her grandmother except to lecture her. Laura Rosso would never have put up with it.

Mercifully, Orsola was saved by a beep on her phone. "*Mia cara*, I have another call I have to take. I'll see you Sunday, yes? You'll be there for dinner?"

She switched to her other call, surprised by the name that flashed up on the screen. "Domenego, *buongiorno!* How are you?" It was rare for him to ring her.

"I am all right, *grazie.* I would like to see you." He was very formal on the phone.

"*Sì, sì.* When?"

"Now, if possible."

Domenego never asked her for anything, and so she couldn't say no. "Where are you?"

He told her where to meet him in Dorsoduro. So many of the vaporettos had been damaged in the storm that a reduced service was running; it would take her over an hour to get there. But she went.

He was standing on a fondamenta by a small canal across from Squero di San Trovaso, one of only two boatyards left in Venice that still built and repaired gondolas. Orsola smiled as she approached her old friend. Even in his sixties he was lean and fit, without the belly so many older gondoliers developed. His hair was gray, but because he kept it close-cropped, it wasn't dominant, especially when he wore the straw hat—along with the black trousers and blue- or red-striped shirt—of the current gondolier uniform. He wasn't wearing it today, though, but had on brown trousers, a button-down white shirt and a gray anorak that hung on him. At his feet was a small leather suitcase, the old-fashioned kind with straps around it and no wheels to make that irritating rolling sound so ubiquitous on Venetian calles now. Orsola stared at it, her stomach tightening. Domenego never went on trips.

He nodded at her as she came to stand next to him, then turned to look across at the boatyard. Squero di San Trovaso was a large open space next to the canal, bordered by buildings. Two gondolas were sitting on trestles, being varnished in their traditional black. There was little room for the men to work, for spilling into their space was a huge number of gondolas, not carefully lined up on their sides, but heaped together into a pyre that looked ready to be lit to make an enormous bonfire. They were all broken in some way: hull cracked, prow torn off, sides bashed in. All the work of the storm, and judged irreparable, their broken bodies to be scavenged for use in making new boats. "*Mio Dio!*" Orsola crossed herself.

"One of them is mine," Domenego said. "My hat is there too." He nodded toward a wooden building to one side of the boatyard; on the wall hung a cluster of the beribboned straw boaters. Orsola wasn't sure why the hats were there, but the tourists who congregated across the canal where she and Domenego stood to watch the men working liked to take pictures of them.

"Oh, Domenego, *mi dispiace*," she murmured. Her friend had spent many years saving up the money to buy his own gondola and had only managed to a year before. "Do you have insurance?" She already knew the answer. Domenego had always lived hand to mouth; insurance was a privilege in another kind of life. It would take a year and sixty thousand euros for a new gondola to be built—time and money he didn't have.

"I have sold my gondola license to buy a plane ticket."

Back when Domenego began rowing for the Klingenbergs, there had been ten thousand gondoliers in the city, but of course motors had changed that. Now there were only four hundred licensed gondoliers in Venice, a number strictly controlled. Licenses were mainly passed down from father to son, although an aspiring gondolier also had to complete four hundred hours of demanding apprenticeship. Gondolas had become purely an expensive treat for tourists, though an important one too as a symbol of the city. Venice without gondolas was unimaginable, to residents and tourists alike. Still traditional, the gondoliers had diversified a bit, with Domenego no longer the only oddity. A few years back the daughter of a gondolier had earned her license, and now there were five registered women gondoliers. Domenego was still unusual among the mostly white gondoliers, though, and she often spotted him patiently posing for selfies with his passengers, though he never smiled.

"You're going back to Africa," she said, a statement rather than a question. "That's why you've hung up your hat over there."

He nodded. "Ghana. I am from Ghana."

Orsola swallowed. She had been hoping for years that he would visit the place of his birth, but she hadn't really expected him actually to go.

"Have you found anyone—anything—online?"

"I have located the village, I think. I am just going to go there and see what it feels like."

Orsola glanced at his suitcase—all the contents of his life in that small space, or in the pyre of wrecked black boats across the canal. "You're going this minute? So suddenly?"

He nodded.

What if I hadn't been able to see you now? she thought. Would you have just left without saying goodbye? "But how will you— A passport?" Of course he had no formal papers, nothing to prove where and when he had been born.

"You can buy anything if you have the money."

"Will you—will you come back?"

"There is nothing here for me now."

"But . . ." Orsola had such a huge lump in her throat that she couldn't continue.

Domenego moved his gaze from the boatyard to look down at her. "I wanted to say goodbye. You have been a good friend."

"Menego . . ." Orsola wasn't sure she *had* been a good friend. For her the gondolier had primarily been a link to Antonio, someone who had known him well. Now she was losing that last link. It was over forty years since she had last seen Antonio. The bruising was long gone—just a light press on her heart, the ghostly trace of her desire.

But she was now also losing a friend. Orsola stepped up to Domenego and threw her arms around him. She sensed his hesitation; theirs had always been a formal relationship, with no physical contact apart from him handing her in and out of his gondola. After a moment, however, he wrapped his arms around her and squeezed her tight. His eyes were moist when at last they pulled apart.

"Text me when you get there?" she said.

He nodded, but she knew he never would. He picked up his suitcase and walked toward Zattere and the water-bus to the airport.

Orsola watched him, his straight back, the bunched muscles in his shoulders from thousands of hours of rowing. Then she ran after him. "Domenego!"

As he turned, she reached into the pocket of her dress—she had never taken to the fashion of wearing trousers—and pulled out Maria Barovier's rosetta, which she still carried with her. "A little bit of Murano to take with you," she said, handing the bead to him.

He smiled then, a smile he never showed to tourists. "*Grazie*, Orsola." He dropped it in his coat pocket and turned back toward the lagoon to begin his journey home.

✧

"DOMENEGO'S GONE," she said to Klara Klingenberg over her hot chocolate. They had been meeting regularly at Florian's for years now, at first so Orsola could update her investor on the progress of the shop; then—once she and Rosella had repaid Klara's loan—as friends, and occasionally for Klara to hand over a glass dolphin. Since their first meeting there, Orsola had become addicted to Florian's chocolate, but it had grown so expensive to sit at the café tables that they used the locals' trick of perching at the counter at the back, where the prices were cheaper.

"What?" Klara dropped her cup onto its saucer with a bang, a rare inelegant gesture. "Where?"

"To where he's from. Ghana."

"But why? He had his gondola. He was doing well!"

"He lost the gondola in the storm, and felt it was time."

"What will he do there?"

"Reconnect with his village and his family, if he can find any."

Klara waved a hand laden with silver rings. "Yes, but after that. What work will he do? There are no gondolas in Africa."

"He—" Orsola had not thought of this. Klara could be very pragmatic, which was what made her a good businesswoman. She and her husband had finally separated several years before, though he refused a divorce, and on the back of her success getting Rosso e Rosella off to a good start, she had begun making loans to new businesses to launch them. She seemed instinctively to know what tourists to Venice wanted: artisanal ice cream, upscale leather goods, handmade notebooks they would buy for their beauty but never use, and lots of decorated masks once Carnevale became popular again. She single-handedly set up a glass artist who made those multicolored glass balloons and jigsaw pieces that Orsola hated; now everyone had copied them and they were for sale everywhere. One chain of gelaterias that she had brought to success even named a flavor after her: Crema di Klara K, a caramel cream with a swirl of chocolate and cherry through it as a nod to her German black forest gâteau heritage. Klara had also had her hair cut short and let it go silver, wore black, white, gray and taupe designer clothes and had a string of lovers she described in detail to Orsola. She was, finally, happy.

"Domenego's at an age to retire," Orsola began again. "I expect he'll just rest."

"I doubt he had a pension or many savings. Did you ask?"

"No. But his family . . ."

"His family will be long gone. You know that. We may well see him back again soon."

"Why don't *you* give him a pension?" Orsola suggested. "You owe him one after all the years he worked for you and your father, for no pay. There's a word for that," she added.

The German shifted on her stool. "That was my father, not me. Times were different. My husband paid him when he worked for us. We were an honorable family. We treated our employees well. We helped them—when we could . . ." Her words faded. Orsola knew whom she was thinking of: Jonas. She had got her granddaughter to do the research, and Aurelia found his name on a list: Klingenberg's sober clerk had been murdered in one of the camps during the Second World War.

Klara looked down at her long fingers clutching her coffee cup. "Do you have Domenego's number?" she said after a silence. "If he's kept it? I'll call him and see what I can do."

◇

ORSOLA SPENT most of her time at her lamp on Murano. She couldn't bear to work in front of spectators as Rosella often did in the shop. These days tourists were expecting more demonstrations, and on Murano glassmakers had begun opening their workshops to visitors. Tourists were brought by boat from Venice to demonstration rooms where, between cigarette breaks, assistants made the rearing glass horses that had been a test during the prova exam—to make one in just a minute that stood evenly on two feet and the tip of a tail. It was a tricky figure to get right: it had to be done fast, and it was challenging to make a thick body and mane and thin legs and tail without one or the other shattering. It required pinching and pulling with tools to shape the horse's head and face. The proportions had to be exact so that the horse could balance on two legs and a tail. It was clever, and audiences appreciated their magicking a complicated figure out of a lump of glass in just a minute. The glassmakers had made so many as practice that most could do so literally with their eyes shut. If they didn't want to think about what to make, they reached for their muscle memory and made a rearing horse, as a final flourish lighting a cigarette from the hot glass.

Orsola had seen so many of these horses—between them, Marco and Giacomo and Raffaele and Andrea had made hundreds for practice before passing their provas—and the assistants looked so bored making them, that she had grown to hate them and the lack of creativity they represented. There were so many things they could make—for glass was wonderfully versatile. Why reach for the familiar? Because it was easier not to have to think, she suspected. Orsola herself was at times guilty of making the same beads again rather than creating something new. More and more this was the case as she grew older and more jaded.

After the horse demonstration, visitors were herded into elaborate showrooms where salespeople applied the techniques they'd learned in Milan or New York to persuade visitors to buy overpriced, often hideous glassware. Why glassmakers felt they had to apply pressure in this way was a mystery to Orsola. It embarrassed her to think of how more discerning visitors must view them.

Marco was also disgusted by the paid demonstrations, the sales techniques, the glass horses—he banned them from being made at the Rosso workshop, even though it probably cost them in sales. Chinese competition had recently knocked the Rossos out of the seed bead business, and they were back to making only glassware. Opening the workshop with reluctance to visitors who wandered in, Marco answered questions as he worked, but Luciana's daughters assisting in the Rosso shop were forbidden from following people around and pushing pieces on them. "Let them look," he insisted. "If the work is good enough, they will buy."

Murano glass was not all kitsch, designed for quick sales. Some glassmakers had begun to challenge that aesthetic and used glass for more artistic work. Raffaele—now Marco's servente and expected to take over as maestro when his father retired—was introducing a different style, nudging the workshop toward simple, clean lines and carefully chosen colors. For several years now their bestselling item had been a small, translucent blue bowl with a line of yellow around the rim that Raffaele had designed. It was just the right size to hold olives or pistachios, proportionally pleasing, and the ultramarine was sumptuous, the rim glowing like a halo. Visitors wearied by the island full of glass kitsch fell upon that simple bowl with relief.

A pride had grown about the history of the island and its glass; there was now a glass museum celebrating the achievements of workshops old and new. Orsola liked to go to the Museo del Vetro and nostalgically admire the old work on display, especially that of the Baroviers, which included Maria Barovier's rosette as well as an elaborate ultramarine-blue wedding cup painted with figures, made around the time Orsola was born. Other Murano glass families were represented as well—even the Rossos, with one of Marco's candlesticks with Antonio's dolphins wound around the base. Rosella was encouraging Orsola to donate the sample cards returned to her by Jonas. She would, one day, but she was not yet ready to let go of her history. At the moment they hung on a wall in the shop; most people ignored them, but occasionally Orsola would see a woman studying them closely and think: she is a maker.

Orsola and Rosella worked hard to make customers feel comfortable and not scrutinized or pressured in the small space of the Venice shop. Floods aside, Rosso e Rosella was doing well enough, but a year earlier a souvenir shop had opened across from them, selling the usual key rings, phone covers, T-shirts, plastic wallets and fridge magnets, all adorned with pictures of gondolas, Santa Maria della Salute, the Basilica of San Marco, the Doge's Palace or the Venetian lion. It also sold glass baubles and figurines, advertised with a handwritten MURANO GLASS sign but which Orsola knew were made in China. China had become Murano's main competitor. Muranese glassmakers had to protect their market by placing a special Murano stamp on their work—though Venetian vendors and tourists often ignored that. Orsola wanted to shout at her neighbors for selling such stuff across from a real Murano glass shop, but instead Rosella spoke to the manager in a softer, more placatory tone—with no results. It turned out the shop was owned by a Chinese investor.

Orsola had to sit and watch the stream of tourists glance in her window at the high-quality, more expensive work, then turn instead toward the cheaper offerings across the calle. It depressed her so much that she cut back on working there, leaving the sales to Rosella and Angela.

Now, however, she was back in the shop to help during Carnevale. Three months on from the flood, the women had got the shop almost back to normal, apart from a watermark thirty centimeters up the wall that customers seemed fascinated by. Floods were only fascinating to those who hadn't experienced them. For the first time since the acqua granda there were substantial numbers of tourists. It was a relief to have them back in Venice during the two weeks of Carnevale, even if it meant passages crowded with increasingly drunken revelers, many masked and in costume. Plenty still went into the souvenir shop to buy cheap masks, but some came into Rosso e Rosella looking for gifts, or for one of the beaded masks displayed in the window that Rosella made every February in a nod to the festival.

Orsola looked up as a German couple came in. She could usually tell which nationality someone was before they even said anything. She nodded at them and tried not to stare. They were not wearing Carnevale masks over their eyes, but white medical ones that covered their noses and mouths. The woman's eyes looked embarrassed, the man's defiant. They didn't stay long or buy anything.

"What was that about?" she asked Rosella, who was bent over a flame at her workstation.

Her niece didn't look up, but focused on the tiny red octopus she was shaping for a key ring—for they too had succumbed to including a few cheaper souvenirs alongside their pricier necklaces and earrings. Orsola still made her seahorses; they sold well. "Probably worried about that virus from China."

Orsola snorted. "How absurd! How could it come here?" But a knot tightened in her stomach as she recalled the disease that long ago sent Nonna and Maddalena and Paolo and Nicoletta to their graves and the Rossos into quarantine. That can't happen now, she thought. We have modern medicine, we're clean, we don't get such things. Not us, not now.

✧

Us. Now.

✧

ORSOLA WAS INCENSED THAT she could not see her family. Her and Stefano's apartment was more than two hundred meters away from the Rosso house, and under quarantine rules they were forbidden from walking that far without facing a fine of three thousand euros (fifteen hundred beads). Nor could she stroll through Campo San Bernardo for the passeggiata, or visit her parents' graves, or sit in the sun with Monica over an espresso at the café by Ponte Longo. Only brief shopping for essentials was allowed. Everything else was locked down.

Sometimes she coordinated with her sister-in-law to meet outside the supermarket and stand in the queue together. Monica would bring one of Orsola's great-great-nieces—Luciana was already a grandmother—and they chatted across the one-meter gulf. The first time the little girl saw her great-great-aunt, she didn't understand and ran to her for a hug, to gasps all round, and tuts at Orsola for daring to put her arms around the girl rather than push her away. She knew they were envious of the touch that was now forbidden.

The market was still running, in a reduced state, but there was less talk, and no one lingered. A few exchanges, asking after health, cataloging symptoms no one had ever noticed before: the tickly sore throat, the cough out of nowhere, the aching limbs, the headaches. Everything felt like a sign that could lead to the virus.

Orsola heard that Covid might have come to Italy from a Chinese man visiting a German car factory, and a part then being sent to northern Italy carrying the virus. It seemed far-fetched. Yet the world had been interconnected like this for centuries; any Venetian knew that. Rats had come off trade ships from Turkey or farther east, and the fleas they carried brought the plague. The fleas themselves may have come from marmots in Kyrgyzstan. Now, though, the transmission of this new virus was faster and more wide-ranging, because the world had become faster and more intertwined.

Orsola was lucky: she could still work in her studio downstairs, at least for as long as she had the glass and the gas to do so. But her work suffered, for she could not concentrate. She burned glass, causing bubbles to form. She dropped pieces, didn't leave beads long enough to cool properly, was sloppy with decoration, her normally steady hands shaky so that dots turned into blobs, flowers into squiggles.

She seemed to have lost her natural feel for symmetry, and her beads were off-center and lumpy. It was almost as bad as when Elena Barovier first taught her many years before; Orsola felt like an apprentice, back to moving honey between sticks. And she was uninspired, unable to create anything new, but the copies she made of previous designs weren't anywhere near as good. She often didn't have the right colors and thought wistfully of the rainbow of glass rods she would order if she could, the twenty different blues, the thirty different greens. Several years before, new environmental laws had been brought in to regulate the fumes from furnaces, making it harder for raw glass to be made on Murano. Currently there was only one Murano factory manufacturing cane, and it was shut.

Why make anything anyway? The shop was closed, and no one knew when tourists might return. Orders from abroad had dried up too. Gradually Orsola stopped going to the studio, but remained in the apartment with Stefano, obsessively reading the news or watching daytime television or videos of people doing silly things to try to cheer up the world.

Life was dull without the stimulus of variety—of places, sounds, people. Orsola was sick of herself and missed others. Seeing her family and friends on her phone wasn't the same as being in the room with them. Luciana would laugh at her for admitting it, but she missed Venice. She missed the presence of strangers, the tourists who wandered around the San Marco shop, picking up and setting down glass pieces, watching Rosella as she made a bead. She even missed the irritating ones, who handled glass offhandedly or complained about the prices or said rude things about the work without considering that she might be the maker.

One thing she was thankful for was Stefano's steady presence. He didn't talk much, but they were comfortable together in the silence, watching television or reading. Orsola was not a big reader, as she hadn't learned until she was an adult, but Stefano was making his way through a biography of Napoleon—"to understand what he did to us and why." Next he was going to read Casanova's memoirs, though he refused to agree to read the racy bits aloud. Orsola wondered if he had written about meeting a beadmaker on a gondola from Mestre.

Sometimes she leaned against Stefano as he read and was calmed by his quiet breathing.

✧

IT WAS IN THE SUPERMARKET queue that Orsola finally learned about Giacomo. "He's gone," Monica whispered when she asked after him.

"Gone? What do you mean, gone? Where?"

Monica looked around. It was hard to exchange family secrets when you were standing a meter apart and everyone was listening.

"He went to Mestre just before lockdown and didn't come back."

Alarm rose in Orsola. "He got stuck on terraferma?"

"He didn't get stuck." Monica said it in such a low voice that at first Orsola didn't hear, and when she worked it out, she didn't understand. During online family chats Giacomo had changed his background to waving palm trees and made jokes about it. Orsola had assumed he was in his Murano apartment.

"Who is he with, then?"

Monica looked around again, but there were too many gossip-starved neighbors around. She got out her phone and texted instead.

> **He's staying with a friend**
> **A "friend"? At last Giacomo has a girlfriend!!**
> **Not a woman**

Orsola gazed across at Monica, who shrugged.

"How long have you known?"

Monica went back to her phone.

> I suspected for a while. Things Isabella said
> I didn't want to say anything because maybe I was wrong
> I asked him finally and he told me

In a rush Orsola looked back over her brother's life, and pieces of it clicked into place. His grief at Paolo's death, which she had put down to upset over losing a teacher rather than a lover. The lack of passion or enthusiasm between him and Isabella, and his indifference to finding another wife once she left. The unease he displayed when Murano men were acting particularly macho. His lack of interest in drinking at l'Omo Salvadego. The way he never joined other men in discussing or whistling at passing women. The sideways glance she'd seen him give men, which Orsola never thought to question. The unspoken sense that he was never entirely comfortable in his skin, and a feeling that he was hiding something.

> What does Marco think
>> He ignores it. Thinks G got stuck in Mestre
>> Expects him back. Maybe better that way
> Maybe

Orsola wanted to ring Giacomo immediately, but she waited until she was alone in her studio. When he answered her video call, she simply said, "Why didn't you tell me?"

The fear and relief that crossed his face before he wiped the expression clean nearly broke her heart. Her gentle brother, who had always looked out for her, who had been through so much with her. She had never really known him. Now terraferma was holding him hostage to its own rules. Would he ever get back? Did he want to?

✧

IT STARTED WITH A HEADACHE. Then a cough. A metallic taste, then no taste. Fatigue. Fever. Tightness in the chest. Hard to breathe. Harder. Even harder. Ambulance. Hospital. Ventilator.

When the water ambulance came from Venice, the medics—dressed in white suits like astronauts—strapped an oxygen mask on Stefano and he couldn't say anything even if he had wanted to. As they carried him downstairs, Orsola followed and watched them secure him on a wheeled stretcher out in the calle. Neighbors were poking their heads out of windows, then quickly withdrawing them.

They began to roll Stefano toward the canal. Orsola wasn't allowed to accompany him or visit at the hospital. "Wait!" She ran after them with Stefano's phone. "Call me," she said, pressing it into his hand, then squeezing it. He looked at her, his dark eyes as intense as that first time she saw him when he was a garzone in the Barovier workshop and Maria Barovier was scolding him. Orsola had never been in love with Stefano, but she loved him. He had gone through their long marriage knowing from the start that she would have preferred to marry Antonio. It must have been deeply humiliating, but he'd never directly complained. She did not know how to put into words how grateful she was.

He raised a hand at her. Orsola raised hers back. Then they rolled him away.

The next day his photo flashed up on her screen; it was not him, but a weary nurse using his phone to tell her Stefano had died.

✧

FUNERAL SERVICES HAD BEEN BANNED, so there would be no Mass for Stefano at Santi Maria e Donato. Only immediate family could attend the burial at the cemetery. Stefano's parents were long dead, his brothers far away. And it was illegal for Angela to cross the lagoon from Giudecca to see her beloved father to his grave. She cried so much on the phone that Orsola was quietly relieved she wouldn't have to deal with her daughter in person.

The night before the burial the family met online to honor Stefano, but Orsola found it dissatisfying, for the technology didn't allow more than one person at a time to speak or for conversations to overlap. The men—Marco, Giacomo, Raffaele, Marcolin, Andrea—were somber, feeling keenly the loss of the silent man they had worked alongside for so long. The women—Monica, Angela, Rosella, Francesca, even Luciana—focused on Orsola's health, fearful that she might be sick too, though she had displayed no symptoms so far.

"You can't go to the burial alone," Monica declared.

"No, you can't," Rosella echoed.

Angela began to cry again. She had only just stopped.

Orsola tried to look braver than she felt. "There's no choice. It's illegal otherwise. And if I do have the virus you could catch it from me. Besides, the funeral won't last long. No priest, and not even flowers are allowed." As she spoke she began to dread it.

The next morning she walked the long way through the streets to the cemetery, since she had a valid reason to be out beyond two hundred meters from home. It was eerily empty, apart from the odd masked figure in the distance hurrying home with provisions. However, people were hanging in their windows above the calle, talking to neighbors across the way. They went silent as Orsola passed, knowing where she was going, for of course all of Murano knew there had been a death from the virus, and who it was and who she was. There were no secrets here. "*Mi dispiace*, Orsola," they called. "*Dio accolga* Stefano."

When she reached the walled cemetery, it was locked, and she had to ring the bell and wait until the keeper opened up for her. He nodded and let her pass, then locked the gate and led her along an avenue of cypress trees before veering off to the right and passing between rows of standing tombs. Gesturing ahead of him, he stepped aside to let her go on alone.

She saw the cart with the coffin on it in the distance—they would have wheeled it around from a boat on the nearby canal. Waiting were four undertakers in space suits like the ones the medics had worn, rather than their traditional black. With them stood a slight figure in a well-cut black suit. Orsola smiled despite herself.

He got out his Armani, she thought.

Marco was stupidly proud of that suit, which he'd bought for his sixtieth birthday. He looked handsome in it with his wiry physique and his silver hair. He had risked the hefty fine to come over to the cemetery, even when Stefano wasn't immediate family. As she approached, he had pulled off his mask and was arguing about the coffin that had been chosen for Stefano. "Those handles haven't been polished. And the wood's too knotty—look!"

"Marco." Orsola pulled off her mask. For the first time in her life she willingly walked into his arms and laid her head on his shoulder. She began to cry, at last.

✧

AFTER THE BRIEF BURIAL, Orsola and Marco went to their parents' grave. She led the way, for she visited more regularly than he. Many of the graves had photos at their bases or hung on a cross. At the Rosso grave there wasn't one of her father—there would never have been a photo of him. But there was of her mother, an elderly Laura Rosso looking serious as she held herself still and gazed directly at the camera. Orsola felt an empty pit in her stomach. "Madre," she whispered, touching the photo. "How I miss you!"

It had been a long time since she had been alone with her brother. They did not get on; they knew it, accepted it. Now as they stood by their parents' grave, Marco asked how business had been at the San Marco shop, before the pandemic and the flood. He had never asked such a thing before, but she couldn't detect sarcasm or condescension, so she answered honestly. "It was good. We were doing well. Not so well as the souvenir shops, but well enough."

"Padre would have been pleased."

"Really?"

"*De certo.* He always liked you more than me."

"No, he didn't."

"Yes, he did."

Orsola stared at her father's name chiseled on the tomb: LORENZO ROSSO, MAESTRO DEL VETRO. Then she nodded at Laura Rosso's level gaze. "Well, Madre thought I didn't do anything right, so it balanced out. Even when I was forty she was still criticizing how I did laundry. She never valued my beads. She preferred you."

"Yes, she did." Marco's acknowledgment felt factual rather than cruel.

Orsola brushed dead leaves from the grave. "I wish I could have brought flowers," she said.

"Ah, I forgot." Marco reached into his pocket and handed her a small beaded wreath, exquisitely fashioned from multicolored seed beads strung on stiff wire and twisted into flowers and vines. Orsola hadn't seen such a wreath since Luciana made them years ago when they were popular. She wanted to hate it, but she couldn't help admiring the work. Luciana rarely made them now. She had moved on from seed beads altogether once the Chinese began producing them cheaply; these days she rented out properties on Murano and Venice to tourists. "Luciana suggested we put it on Stefano's coffin," Marco said, "but the undertaker refused because of the virus. *Bastardo!* We could put it here." He patted their parents' grave.

Orsola was tempted to say no, but it seemed churlish to refuse.

"How is Luciana?" she asked, setting the wreath on the tomb, a tiny crown perched on a granite head.

"She's all right. You've always been hard on her."

"Because she took over!"

"That's how you see it. She's part of the family. She and Raffaele are still crazy about each other, you know. I hear them every night."

"*Basta!*" Orsola patted the grave. "I have to get back."

"To what? An empty apartment? More terrible television and phone calls with people who have nothing to say because there's nothing new to say? Me, I'm glad to get out of the house!"

She looked at him, at the fine lines around his eyes and the hands that trembled ever so slightly with age—though probably never when he held glass, for it was a steadying trade—and said a word she never used with her brother. "*Grazie*, Marco."

"What for?"

"For coming here when you could have been fined for it."

He made a noise. "No one's going to stop me coming to my brother-in-law's funeral. He was a good worker, Stefano. His mirrors, his engraving. He showed us how to pull cane."

"But you could get sick. I could have it and not know it."

He made the noise again. "Fuck Covid. You're my sister."

That was as good as him saying she was the best beadmaker on Murano. Better.

They smiled at each other. "*Cretino*," she said.

"*Bauca!*"

As they walked back to the gate, where the keeper waited with his keys, Marco cleared his throat. "*Ecco*, do you want to come and stay with us? Monica would love it."

For a moment Orsola was tempted to return to the family—to be cooked for, to gossip with Monica, to take sustenance from the children who managed to ignore the news and live in the moment. To speculate about whether Giacomo was happy, and if he would return to Murano when he could or take his chances on terraferma.

"*Grazie*, Marco," she replied after a moment, a second thanks in one conversation, after a lifetime of silence. "But no. I'm too used to living quietly, without the chaos. Without all the laundry."

He nodded. "I know. I would give anything to escape to l'Omo Salvadego for a drink. But if you change your mind, the offer's there."

Orsola nodded, then reached out and squeezed his arm, still strong from lifting glass. Tomorrow they would undoubtedly fight, but she would always remember that today they hadn't.

✧

SHE WALKED HOME the long way, along the canal near the apartment. Because no boats were allowed out, the water was transparent rather than translucent, so still that you could see the bottom and the fish that had always been there but were usually covered by the mud churned up by boats. Orsola peered down and spied orange coral growing that she had never known existed. Nature was continuing its march, indifferent to human suffering. Whatever was happening to people, the world would always be here, the tides flowing in and out, the flowers blooming, the birds singing. It was not an original idea, she knew, but she found it comforting. In a way, humans too continued their march, eating and sleeping and making and loving, whatever the circumstances.

She couldn't yet face going back to the empty apartment. Instead she slipped through the deserted calles to Campo San Donato and past the basilica, crossed the bridge and made her way toward the Riva di San Matteo. It was farther than two hundred meters from home, but she assumed no one would report her, given the circumstances.

She passed the closed Omo Salvadego and the remains of the church of San Matteo. Surrounding San Matteo were small glass artists' studios carved out of an old factory. Though it was a reminder that the era of dozens of family workshops producing the finest glass pieces for the world was long past, at least this old building was now full of individual glass creators rather than left derelict and falling to pieces as so many factories around the island were. Orsola suspected eventually they would be recognized as prime real estate and get replaced by hotels or luxury rentals for tourists—if Venice recovered from the double blows of the pandemic and the acqua granda.

It *would* recover, she expected, whatever pessimistic predictions she heard on the radio or in the shopping queue. It always had. Orsola had witnessed its recovery from many setbacks: the discovery of sailing routes to Asia and the New World that moved the center of trade from Venice so that eventually it became a travelers' playground instead. The various plagues. The invasion of Napoleon and the subsequent crumbling ruins created by the Austrians. The great floods. The cruise ships and hordes of tourists gutting the local population. The sea inching its way up. But Venice was nimble, it adapted, it relied on its uniqueness, on its timeless beauty, to attract admirers.

And the city was *real*, a feeling you didn't get with newer, cleaner places. Raffaele had been to Las Vegas for his and Luciana's fifteenth anniversary—at his wife's request, Orsola suspected—and afterward described to his aunt how each casino was built around a different theme, often a place: Paris, Rome, Egypt and, of course, Venice. He showed her pictures of a mock campanile, a Doge's Palace, a Rialto Bridge, and canals full of chlorinated water clear and blue like a swimming pool. There were even gondolas, though some of the gondoliers were rowing the wrong way—even the authentic gondoliers brought over from Venice. When Raffaele pointed this out to one of those Venetians, he swore authentically. "And people were loving it," Raffaele said of "Venice." "I heard an American say, 'Why bother to take that long flight to Italy when you've got all you want here at the Venetian in Las Vegas, plus gambling!'"

Venetians complained about their city becoming a theme park, but Orsola knew that as long as Venice's canals stank of sewage, its rooms were dark and damp, its people melancholy and sardonic, it would maintain its true nature, which was so seductive. A pearl needs grit to be beautiful; beauty comes from the scar on the lip, the gap in the teeth, the crooked eyebrow.

She reached the Riva di San Matteo, the scene of the tip of her life. For forty-five years—sometimes it felt like several hundred—Orsola had stood on this spot and paused for the loss she'd had there, for the path that she had not followed, instead choosing to watch Antonio row away from her. There had been the hurt, and then the memory of the hurt, and finally the memory of the memory, which was where she had been stuck for many years, looking back at that moment with Antonio as if through a telescope, inspecting the feelings with the objective curiosity of one who did not feel them any longer. Every now and then when she received a glass dolphin there was a flare-up, like a tooth irritated by a long-ago ache.

She gazed out over the water. There were no boats in sight, because it was illegal to go out, even to fish. The lagoon was a still glass sheet spreading all the way to the mountains, interrupted only by the airport in the distance, tranquil now without planes bringing tourists to and from Venice. Today the mountains were so clear the snow on the tips looked painted on as if by a child. Orsola had not thought about what lay beyond them in a long time.

Soon after the quarantine began, there had been reports of dolphins spotted swimming in the lagoon around Venice, now that there were no boats out. It had been many years since they'd been seen in the area. The story was picked up and spread all over the world. People repeated with wonder: Dolphins have returned to Venice! Look at what nature does when there are no people! It was soon exposed as fake news; the video of the dolphins had been shot off Sardinia. Orsola scoffed with other Venetians at the sentimental gullibility of the rest of the world when it came to Venice. They wanted to believe.

Nonetheless, as she gazed across the open water now, she too looked for a ripple, a fin, a knife cutting through the lagoon that indicated the return of the dolphins. Because Orsola too wanted to believe. If there weren't dolphins returning to the lagoon, what was the point of this plague? She'd heard some say God had sent the virus to force people to change their ways, that this was a giant reset button for humanity. If that was the case, Orsola doubted people would indeed change. As soon as they could, they would go back to consuming, to traveling, to using the world as a playground the way Venice had been used for centuries. And she was a part of that, making beads that did not need to be bought, pretty things enticing tourists to Murano who did not need to come. She should think about this, now that she had the time to. But it was a thought so slippery that she couldn't hold on to it, preferring instead to fret about a grandchild's stammer, or to worry that she was running out of flour, or to wonder if she should buy a new coat. Anything but the big questions.

When she did think about it, though, she tried to remind herself that beads brought color and beauty to many parts of the world, whether in the West Indies or the Americas or Africa or New York or even Venice itself. There was a pricelessness to these tiny, hard things. They endured, and retained the history of their owners, and of their makers.

⟡

IT TOOK SOME TIME to get back to normal. But eventually a vaccine combatting Covid was created, numbers subsided, travel restrictions were eased, and Orsola and Rosella could reopen their shop in San Marco. For all her complaints about tourists, Orsola was relieved to see them. She knew Venice and Murano needed tourists to survive. It had needed them for centuries.

She was slowly getting used to living alone in her apartment and working in her studio down below. Everyone—not just her family, but the whole Murano community—treated her gently, not knowing quite what to do with the knowledge that she had lost Stefano. Sometimes when she was at the supermarket, someone would be raging about how everyone had overreacted to the virus, that it was no worse than the flu. Then their companion would nudge them and gesture at Orsola, and the apologies would be profuse. She was sick of it.

There were two clear pieces of good news. The first was that the new flood barrier was raised for the first time during a storm that would have flooded Venice again, and it worked. The sea level might continue to rise, but at least for now there was some defense against the destructive flooding that had brought misery to Venetians and Muranese and all the islanders.

The second good news: dolphins really did return to Venice. A year after the first, false sighting, footage appeared during the second lockdown of two striped dolphins swimming in the Giudecca Canal close to the entrance of the Grand Canal. It was real this time—Santa Maria della Salute was clearly visible in the background of one of the videos. The dolphins had become disoriented, and a rescue team of boats herded them back out to sea.

After that, whenever Orsola walked out to San Matteo during her evening stroll, she looked again for signs of dolphins.

8

THE STONE HAS CROSSED most of the lagoon, because you have thrown it that hard, and has touched down at various points over five hundred years. It now makes one final small jump, lands and sinks off the waters of Murano into the present. Orsola Rosso is in her late sixties. She is once more turning in the flame a translucent red bead with flecks of gold leaf suspended in it. Her Antonio bead. She looks up and sees a man . . .

✧

HE IS STANDING at the intersection of two calles, where Orsola has her studio, looking around. A tourist, she guesses. But there is something about the way he stands, feet apart, like a Venetian fisherman riding on the choppy lagoon; and his curly hair a gray that was once gold; and the shape of his face with its wide cheeks and deep-set eyes. Her heart skips a beat, two beats. She remembers suddenly the little Mazzorbian dog long ago, lying between her and Antonio in the sandolo, seemingly drowned but then spluttering back to life.

If glass dolphins have come to me all these years, Orsola thinks, and real dolphins have come back to Venice, why not him, come back to me? It is what she wants to think, what she has needed to think all these years, though she knows it is irrational. She wants him to be that little dog, come back to life.

As she watches the man, she stops turning the red bead, and it drips off the iron rod. When his eyes reach the sign above her door, they light up. Orsola has no time to prepare herself before the door opens and he is in the studio with her. It is a small space, crammed with her worktable and gas canisters and many colors of cane, as well as a glass case full of work for sale for the odd visitor. Like this man.

Orsola turns off her flame and stands. She resists smoothing her wiry hair and pulling in her stomach. He must take her as she is.

"*Buongiorno*, signora." The man has the unplaceable accent of someone who is fluent in Italian but is from elsewhere. A bit like Klingenberg. Middle Europe.

"Antonio?" she says softly, because she wants to believe. The man smiles but does not respond to that name. And he clearly does not recognize her.

Orsola's heart sinks. "You are—?"

"Alessandro. Alessandro Scaramal."

"Ah." It's Antonio's son. Or—Orsola pauses. This man is about her age. Of course he is not Antonio's son; he's too old. She swallows.

"You are Orsola Rosso?" the man says.

Orsola nods. She is being forced at last to confront the reality she has tried to ignore all her life. Antonio joined terraferma long ago, where time runs differently. That means this Alessandro must be a great-great-great grandson. No, many more greats than that. A dozen greats. And it means—it means Antonio died long ago. Centuries ago. She has lived her life without him.

This is something Orsola has never really accepted. It is so hard to face the truth. She takes a wobbly breath.

"But the dolphins," she says. "He sends me dolphins."

Alessandro Scaramal looks surprised. "So it *is* for you. I wasn't really sure." He reaches into his pocket and pulls out a tiny gray-green dolphin similar to those Orsola has received over the years. It is also exactly the color of the real dolphins that appeared in Venice during the pandemic. "It's been a tradition in our family to make one of these now and then and send it to Venice. We've been doing that for hundreds of years."

Orsola stares at the dolphin. "Why?"

Alessandro shrugs. "No one knows. We've just been told to by our fathers, who were told to by their fathers, and so on. I'm visiting Venice on holiday and thought while I'm here I would try to track down where the Scaramal dolphins end up. I found a Signora Klingenberg connected to the address in Venice, and she sent me here. So you have others?"

"I have quite a collection of them." Orsola doesn't tell him they are in a drawer by his knee. Now she understands why they're not entirely uniform: various hands have been making them over the years. "Did you make this one?" She nods at the newest dolphin.

Alessandro looks sheepish. "No. My father was annoyed that I didn't follow him into glass."

Orsola sighs. "My child didn't either. Nor my grandchildren."

"But my sister did. She made this one. She's very good, a much better glassmaker than I would have been." Alessandro pauses. "It's funny, her middle name is Ursula. Like yours. Another family tradition. Scaramal daughters are always given that middle name."

For a moment Orsola thinks she may sob.

Alessandro gestures with the dolphin. "Please, take it." Orsola holds out her hand, and he drops it into her palm. She grips it hard, feeling the fins prick at her skin. At her heart.

"*Ecco*, I would like to see the other dolphins," Alessandro says, "if you are happy to show me." He looks around. "And your work—I would like to see that too. *Per favore.*" He seems genuinely interested.

Orsola pauses. These days she doesn't open the dolphin drawer very often. But: "*Sì*," she says. "Take a seat." For him, she will.

ACKNOWLEDGMENTS

The Rosso family and their friends and neighbors have emerged from my imagination. But a few people did exist. Maria Barovier indeed invented the prized rosetta bead; her descendants still make glass on Murano today. Casanova, of course, existed, as did Josephine Bonaparte, who visited Venice in 1797 but did not manage to save it from her husband's ravages. And the Marchesa Luisa Casati did live for a few years in the Palazzo Venier dei Leoni, which now houses the Peggy Guggenheim Collection. The Marchesa was every bit as outrageous as I've made her out to be. The cheetahs, the nudity, the hundreds of Murano lanterns – all true.

Domenego is based on the unknown, elegant gondolier depicted in Carpaccio's *Miracle of the Relic of the Cross at the Ponte di Rialto*. I had not known there were enslaved people in Venice until I saw this astounding painting. It is housed at the Gallerie dell'Accademia in Venice, and reveals a lot about fifteenth-century Venetian life.

Why glass? Many years ago a reader approached me after a book event in Milan and suggested I write about Venetian trade beads, as they were one of the few areas of glass that women became involved with over hundreds of years. He then handed me some booklets about beads, which I duly filed away on a bookshelf to gather dust. It seems Giorgio Teruzzi understood my interests better than I did myself, because I didn't forget about beads; years later I dusted off those booklets and began research. I even got to meet Giorgio again at a glass conference in Venice and was able to report on my progress and ply him with questions. I would like to thank him for inspiring me to travel down this esoteric route.

There are so many books and articles and online sources about every aspect of Venice that a researcher's problem becomes not what to read, but what *not* to read. I will only suggest two general books for readers who want a short dive: *Venice* by Jan Morris (1960) and *A Brief History of Venice* by Elizabeth Horodowich (2009). The deep dive is the definitive *A History of Venice* by John Julius Norwich (1982).

There are not so many books about Murano, but one on its earlier history that stands out is *The Revolt of Snowballs* by Claire Judde de Larivière (2018). Claire was also really helpful with sources and answers to detailed questions.

Of the many books about glass beads, Muranese and otherwise, the most helpful to me were *Trade Beads: From Venice to the Gold Coast*, edited by Giorgio Teruzzi and Anna Alessandrello (2007), *Perle d'Africa, da Venezia al Mondo* by Giorgio Teruzzi (2009), *Glass Beads from Europe* by Sibylle Jargstorf (1995), *Beads of the World* by Peter Francis Jr. (1999), *The Worldwide History of Beads* by Lois Sherr Dubin (2009), *Glass Beads: Selections from the Corning Museum of Glass* by Adrienne V. Gennett (2013) and *The Glory of Beads* by Nicole Anderson (2017).

More than books, it was people who helped me to understand and appreciate glass, including, on Murano, several glassmakers whose studios I haunted. Above all, I thank Maestro Davide Fuin and his serventi, who let me watch them make glass after glass and ask questions. I was lucky to be taught to make beads by Alessia Fuga, and back in

London by Samantha Sweet and Phil Vallentin. Thanks to Laura Sparling for an enlightening chat about translucence. I spent a happy and sometimes scary afternoon blowing glass at London Glassblowing; they know their stuff, and I have a wonky vase and a thick bowl to prove it (mistakes all mine!). Big thanks to glass Maestro Cesare Toffolo, who has an original lampwork table, complete with bellows, and showed me how it works. Thanks too to Marisa Convento, Venetian expert on seed beads. And to Mauro Stocco, who opened the archives at Murano's Museo del Vetro (Glass Museum) for me. It is a wonderful place to visit, stuffed full of glass from beginning to end. Another shrine to glass is the Corning Museum of Glass in upstate New York; I thank Kit Wright for introducing me to this remarkable place.

My highest thanks go to the glass artist Amy West, who opened her Murano studio, her home and her heart to me, introducing me to many people I would never have met otherwise, explaining both glass processes and what it's like to live as a Muranese. I could not have gone so deep without her, and am truly grateful for her knowledge, her patience and her generosity of spirit. I don't always make friends on my research travels, but with Amy I now have a glass friend for life.

For their deep and varied knowledge of Venice and their willingness to share it, I want to thank Michelle Lovric and Catherine Kovesi. And Nan McElroy of Row Venice, who took me out on the canals and didn't laugh at my rowing form.

Storytelling is a delicate balance between clarity and mystery. When you mess around with time as I have here, things can go a little wobbly. That is where editors are gold. Suzie Dooré and Andrea Schulz went platinum for this book, questioning, cajoling and gently pushing me into rewriting again and again until finally it worked. Andrea and Suzie, this novel would have been a disaster without you; thank you for your insistence. And thanks to their assistants, Nidhi Pugalia, Elizabeth Pham Janowski and Jabin Ali, for all their help.

ACKNOWLEDGMENTS

Enormous thanks to Sabine Schultz and Stella Boschetti at Neri Pozza publishers in Italy, who read and corrected my many Italian errors. And to Pieralvise Zorzi, Venetian historian, who fixed mistakes and added Venetian, and taught me some choice Venetian curses in the process! Also to copy editors Sarah Bance and Hilary Roberts, to proofreader Kate Griggs, and to my German translator Claudia Feldmann and my French translator Anouk Neuhoff for gently pointing out the errors. Any mistakes left are my own.

My agents Jonny Geller and Deborah Schneider, I bow down before your better judgment. You always have my back, and my back knows it.

Thank you too to Jonathan Drori and Susan Elderkin for reading and commenting on a draft when I was at my wit's end, certain that playing with time like this wouldn't work. You showed me that it could, and how to do it. And Susan reminded me that a close, tight edit is always a good thing.

Finally, thanks from the heart to my friend Ronna Bloom, to whom this book is dedicated. Ronna has been my partner in Venice exploration; together we have discovered its poetry and its prose.

ITALIAN AND VENETIAN GLOSSARY

Most words are Italian, but I have sometimes used Venetian (V) for moments of high emotion: curses, exclamations, blessings.

acqua alta—an exceptionally high tide that causes flooding
addio (V)—goodbye, adieu
adesso—now, right away
a domani—until tomorrow
ahia!—ouch!
alla Veneziana—in the Venetian style
allora; e allora—well, so; and so?
amore mio—my love
andate—go, leave
andatevene!—go away!
andiamo—let's go
androne—ground-level area in house, which could be flooded in high tides
a premando (V)—left, in gondoliers' slang
arrivederci—goodbye
a stagando (V)—right, in gondoliers' slang
avete capito bene?—do you understand?

basta—enough
bauca (V)—stupid

bea (V)—beauty

becco fotuo (V)—fucking cuckold

bella—beauty

bellissimo/a/e—beautiful

ben cussì (V)—well done, well said

bene—good, fine

bigoli al nero di seppia—pasta with squid ink

bufòn (V)—stupid person; buffoon

buonasera—good evening

buongiorno—good day

bussolai (V)—Venetian biscuits

buzaròn/i (V)—swindler

calcedonio—glass that looks like chalcedony stone

calle—passage, street

campo (V)—square

canagia (V)—rogue

càncaro (V)—cancer, used as an insult

canella/e—cylindrical bead

caorlina/e—long, narrow boat with bow and stern curved upward

Carnevale—Carnival festival celebrated from December 26 to Lent

caro/a—dear

cavalluccio/i marino/i—seahorse

cazzetto (V)—small dick

che bea cocheta (V)—what a beauty

che bella/o!—how beautiful!

che cosa?—what?

che Dio abia pietà della so anema, e de la nostra (V)—may God have mercy on
   his soul, and on ours

che Dio li/la/ti tegna (V)—may God bless them/her/you; also, good luck

che San Nicolò te tegna 'na man sul cao (V)—may Saint Nicholas keep a
   hand on your head

cicchetti—snacks

comunque—anyway

con complimenti—with compliments

conterie—beads, especially seed beads

così—like that

cretino—idiot

cristallo veneziano—Venetian crystal

da bon (V)—of course
d'accordo—all right
davvero—really
de certo—certainly, of course
delfino/i—dolphin
de longo (V)—straight, in gondoliers' slang
demoni—demons
denaro/i—small coin like a penny; 12 denari = 1 soldo
di grazia—by grace, please
dime (V)—tell me, talk to me
Dio—God
Dio accolga (V)—may God accept (you, your prayers, your soul, etc.)
ducato—ducat; 1 ducato = 124 soldi

ecco—listen, here
ehi!—hey!
escrementi di coniglio—rabbit turds
escrementi di topo—mouse turds

felze—cabin on gondola
ferro—decorative metal piece on prow of gondola
fondaco—warehouse
fondamenta (V)—street running parallel to canal
forcola—rowlock on gondola
fritola/e (V)—fritter

garzone/i—glassmaking apprentice
garzonetto/i—young boy working for glassmakers
il Giuda—Judas, traitor
goto/i (V)—everyday drinking glass
grazie—thank you

impestada (V)—tainted, infected (the root is *peste*: plague)
impiraressa/e—bead stringer
in bocca al lupo—good luck; literally: into the wolf's mouth
in mona a to mare (V)—go fuck your mother

ladro/i, ladronetto—thief, little thief
ladro fiol d'un can (V)—thief son of a bitch

lavoro—work

lira/e—coin used in Venice until 1797; Italian lira was official money in
  Italy from 1861 until 2002

madre—mother

maestro—master

magnamerda (V)—shit eater

maledizione—damn

mamaluco (V)—idiot

Mariavergine—Virgin Mary, used as an exclamation

mar rosso—menstrual period; literally, red sea

me ralegro (V)—congratulations

meravigliosa/o—marvelous

merda—shit

mi dispiace—I'm sorry

millefiori—bead imprinted with many flowers; literally: a thousand flowers

mimorti! (V)—good heavens!; literally: my deads!

mio Dio—my God

molto belle—very beautiful

mona (V)—cunt

moro/i (V)—Moor

Muranesei maganzese (V)—dour Muranese

muso da mona (V)—cunt face

naturàl (V)—of course

nonna—grandmother

nuovo/nove—new

ocio! (V)—watch out!

oe—ahoy

l'omo salvadego (V)—the wild man, a popular Carnival mask

ovviamente—obviously

padre—father

palazzo—grand residence

passeggiata—evening promenade

pastone—cylinder of glass

patate—potatoes

paternostro/i—round bead, as in a rosary

peata/e—large, barge-like boat
perdonate/mi—sorry, pardon me
per favore—please
perfetto—perfect
per l'amor di Dio—for the love of God
perle—beads
peste—the plague
piazza—public square
piazzetta—small public square
piccante—spicy
ponte—bridge
prego—please, after you, you're welcome
pronto—hello; literally: I'm ready (on telephone)
prova—exam to become glass servente or maestro
provveditori alla sanità—health authorities
puteletto de Muran (V)—little boy from Murano
puttana—whore

ragazze—girls
rio (V)—canal
riva (V)—embankment alongside a large body of water
rosetta/e—barrel-shaped bead in red, white and blue originally created by
    Maria Barovier
rosso—red

sandolo/i (V)—flat-bottomed boat
sarde in saor (V)—marinated sardines
scusème (V)—excuse me
sei bellissima—you're beautiful
sempia (V)—idiot
La Serenissima—the Most Serene; sobriquet of the Republic of Venice
    since 1462
servente/i—assistant to a glass maestro
sessola/e (V)—shallow wooden pan for bead stringing
sestiere/i (V)—district in Venice
sì—yes
signor/e—mister, sir/s
signora/e—missus, madam/s
signorina—miss, young lady

soldo/i—coin of small amount used for daily purchases in Venice until
    mid-nineteenth century
sorella—sister
spettacolare—spectacular
spia—spy
spigoli (V)—card game like poker
sprotìn (V)—little wise ass
sta' zitto—shut up
sto bene—I'm okay
stronzo/a (V)—turd, shithead

ta morti cani (V)—your dead relatives are dogs
te lo giuro—I swear
ti—you
tipico—typical
tiradori (V)—cane pullers
ti xe imatonìo? (V)—are you punch-drunk?; also: are you stupid as a brick?
traghetto/i—gondola used as a ferry; also, place where gondoliers wait for
    fares
tutto/i—all, everything

ulivetta/e spoletta/e—oval-shaped bead

va' al diavolo—go to hell
va bene—all right, okay
vattene!—go away!
vecchio—old
vero—truly, really
vetrai—glassmakers
vetro—glass
visdecasso (V)—dickface

zecchino/i (V)—coin of large amount; 1 zecchino = 440 soldi
zendale—black shawl
zia—aunt